PRAISE FOR *ALOSHA*

"A fast-paced combination of intrigue and fantasy. Readers are sure to be captivated . . . [an] entertaining plot complete with dwarves, elves, fairies, and trolls."

—*School Library Journal*

"Will undoubtedly entertain. The backstory is compelling, the action is fast-paced, the danger is real. Sure to be a blockbuster." —*Bulletin of the Center for Children's Books*

PRAISE FOR THE WORKS OF CHRISTOPHER PIKE

"A fine tale that hooks the reader . . . [an] exhilarating story."

—*Midwest Book Review* on *The Blind Mirror*

"Sparkling characters . . . a compelling and intellectually satisfying read. Highly creative."

—*Rapport* on *The Cold One*

"Highly recommended."

—*Rocky Mountain News* on *The Cold One*

"Like any good read, this is a hard book to put down. But more than that, it's hard to let this one come to an end. By the end . . . you can't stand the anticipation. That feeling in the pit of a reader's stomach must be one of the best compliments we can pay an author."

—*The Greeley, Colorado Tribune* on *The Cold One*

ALSO BY CHRISTOPHER PIKE
PUBLISHED BY TOR BOOKS

The Blind Mirror
The Cold One
The Listeners
Sati
The Season of Passage

ALOSHA

Christopher Pike

TOR

A TOM DOHERTY ASSOCIATES BOOK
NEW YORK

This is a work of fiction. All the characters and events portrayed in this book are either products of the author's imagination or are used fictitiously.

ALOSHA

A Tor Book
Published by Tom Doherty Associates, LLC
175 Fifth Avenue
New York, NY 10010

www.tor.com

ISBN 0-765-34960-4
EAN 978-0-765-34960-6

First Tor Teen edition: September 2005

Printed in the United States of America

0 9 8 7 6 5 4 3 2 1

For Jason

CHAPTER ONE

It was the beginning of summer, early morning, and Alison Warner had big plans for the day. A group of lumberjacks were planning to chop down a bunch of trees on the mountains that stretched behind her house, and she was hoping to stop them.

Of course, at thirteen, Ali was old enough to realize she was not going to save a single tree. Her intentions for going were more symbolic. She wanted to make the men who cut down the trees feel bad about what they were doing and, hopefully, force them to think twice about doing it next time. They all knew her. She had been to the site twice to call them barbarians. They had just laughed; they thought she was funny.

Ali hoped to bring her best friend, Cindy Franken, with her on the long road to the logging site. But the problem with Cindy, especially during summer vacation, was getting her out of bed before noon.

Ali braced herself for a struggle as she left her house.

It looked like it was going to rain, she thought, as she stood on her front porch. Gray clouds had blown in from far out at sea. They gathered overhead like a fog bank, filled with menace. Although it was mid June, there was still a chill in the air, a shadow even; it was as if nature herself brooded over what was about to happen to the forest.

Ali had on a sweater her mother had made for her two years ago, and carried an olive-colored waterproof poncho in her day-pack. Before she jumped on her bike, she slipped on a pair of black leather gloves. From experience, she knew how the cold air could sting her fingers once she built up speed.

Cindy Franken lived only six blocks away. Ali had known her since kindergarten. They had met over finger paints and sand castles. They told each other everything—well, almost—and always stood up for each other. However, they had completely different personalities. Cindy's mouth was directly tied to her brain. She usually said exactly what was on her mind, which annoyed people. Ali was forever getting her out of trouble. Ali herself seldom spoke without careful consideration. People her age—even two teachers at school—had told her she was more an adult than a kid. That might have been true, but she was still young enough to wonder if that was an insult or a compliment.

Ali did not bother knocking on Cindy's front door, but snuck around the side and poked her head in her friend's window. They had set their plan to ride into the mountains only the night before, but Cindy was fast asleep on her back with her mouth wide open. Watching, Ali saw her closed eyelids twitch, and wondered if her friend dreamed, and if she was there with her in the dreams.

"Wake up sleepyhead," Ali said.

Cindy opened her eyes. "I'm awake," she mumbled.

"Can I come in?"

Cindy rolled over. "You're not a vampire. I don't have to invite you in."

Cindy was shorter than Ali, with long blond hair and a hundred curls the size of gold coins. Her face was more *appealing* than *beautiful*, but she managed to stay tan even in the dead of winter, and she laughed so easily and often that she had more friends than Ali. Her eyes were a dark blue, quick and bright, and she was a lot smarter than she acted.

Ali climbed inside and sat beside Cindy on the bed. Her friend had closed her eyes again and was threatening to pass out. Ali shook her gently.

"You know the lumberjacks get up before dawn. They're probably already sawing down the pines and firs on Castle Ridge," Ali said.

Cindy kept her eyes shut. "We're not going to stop them by tying yellow ribbons around the trees."

"I brought red this time."

"Same difference."

Ali hesitated to explain that she had another reason for visiting the logging site. She wanted to say goodbye to some of her favorite trees. Many of the pines and firs that stood behind their town were the same age as she. They had grown up together; they were like old friends. Even her father did not realize how often she rode her bike into the forest. Since her mother had died in a car accident a year ago—on her twelfth birthday, no less—it had become more home to her than the city.

Being in nature did not allow her to completely escape her loss, yet she often felt at peace as she walked beneath the swaying trees. There she could sing, there she could cry. The trees did not judge, they did not speak back. They only listened.

"We have to try," Ali told Cindy.

Her friend opened her eyes and hugged her pillow. "Write a letter to a senator or something," she mumbled.

"I did that already, to both of them. They didn't write back."

"Write the president."

"I heard the guy can't read."

Cindy yawned. "Do you know what time I went to bed?"

"I don't want to know. You said you'd go with me. You promised."

"I was forced into promising." Cindy suddenly grinned mischievously. "Take Karl with you."

"Don't start that," Ali warned.

"You know you like him."

"I don't like him."

"You don't hate him," Cindy said, as if that were a huge plus.

"Why are you in such a hurry to set me up? We're not even in eighth grade yet."

"Because by high school every guy who is not a total nerd is taken."

"I like nerds. Why do you think you're my best friend?" Ali asked.

Cindy smiled. "Why is it so hard to admit you like him?"

"Okay, I like him! I just don't want to marry him is all."

"It could be romantic staring down the lumberjacks and their chain saws with the boy you love by your side."

Ali sighed. "You know what your problem is?"

"I watch too much TV?"

"Yes. Are you coming or not?"

"Will you go if I don't go?"

"Yes."

Cindy closed her eyes and smiled sleepily. "Have fun."

Ali left the house in disgust.

Breakfast was not a big deal to her—she usually skipped it—but she had a hard climb before her and knew she would be starving by the time she reached the logging site. Before heading out, she decided to stop by Sam's Subs, which had the best sandwiches in town.

Breakwater, the city where she lived, was small, population a measly three thousand, maybe twice that at the height of the tourist season. Its only landmark was a turn-of-the-century steeple church that had recently been painted a tacky green by the new mayor. An article in the local paper said the guy was color-blind.

It was the Interstate—and the cheap motels and all-night diners that lined it—that fed Breakwater. There weren't many jobs in town, and most of them were lousy. That was why her father had to leave the city in his truck to keep a roof over their heads.

Ali rode to the sandwich shop with her hair tied back; it was a good thing. Her maroon hair—her mother used to say it was fine as wine and exactly the same color—reached all the way to her butt. A favorite silver clasp kept it from her eyes. Later in the day, though, on the mad dash down the mountain, she would let it fly like a witch's cape over her shoulders.

Sam Carter—owner and manager of Sam's Subs—looked like one of his sandwiches. A six-foot-long ham and cheese, Cindy called him, although Ali thought he was more of a steak man. The guy was nice and everything—especially to kids—but he ate up all his profits. He weighed four hundred pounds.

Ali ordered a medium-sized turkey, with lettuce, tomato and cheese—and asked for a can of Coke. She would eat it when she was high up on the mountain, and could see up and down the coast, and far out over the ocean. Sam threw in a bag of chips free.

"You don't have to do that," Ali said.

Sam waved his hand. "Your mother always bought you chips."

Sam had gone to high school with her mom, had played football on the team when her mother was a cheerleader. He had cried at her funeral.

She smiled and stuffed the food in her daypack. "Thanks, Sam."

"Any time, Ali."

She had just left the store when she ran into a strange little man. He was hanging around the parking lot, looking either lost or up to no good. He was dressed in a green coat and a yellow bow tie, and wore a green wool cap over his head, covering his ears. He must be a midget, she thought, he couldn't have been three feet tall.

Yet his proportions were odd. His head was bigger than her father's and his hands were long and bony like a skeleton's; never mind his hook nose, which was shaped like a bent hanger and dotted with dozens of tiny bumps.

He appeared to be wearing women's makeup; the stuff was thick and poorly applied. It gave his skin a sickly yellow color, or else, she thought, that was his natural color and he was trying to cover it up.

Whatever, she didn't like the look of him and tried getting on her bike when she saw him staring at her. But he called and came running over, and she felt she had to stop. She did not like being rude to people.

Still, she glanced around for support, and was relieved to see Sam watching her from inside his sandwich shop. She preferred to trust people, but she was not careless. If the tiny man tried to harm her, she would shout out, and Sam would be there in a second.

"A second, Missy. Need to ask you a few questions," he said as he approached. Close up his eyes were as weird as the rest of him. Large and deep set, they were bright green but splintered with gold streaks that seemed to swim around black pupils. Peering at her from beneath brown eyebrows that were so bushy he could have combed them like mustaches, his big eyes seemed to glow. She wondered if he was nuts, if he had decided to dress up for Halloween a few months early. In his left hand he carried a white pillowcase that appeared loaded with goodies.

"Yes?" she said.

He glanced at her sandwich that stuck halfway out of the pack on her back. "What's that?" he asked, interested.

"Lunch. What can I do for you, sir?"

He offered his right hand. "Paddy O'Connell, a pleasure to meet you, Missy. It is I who would like to serve you."

She shook his hand quickly; it was hairy on top of everything else. "I'm sorry, I don't need any service today, thank you."

She turned to go. He blocked her path.

"A moment, Missy. I have here items I know you're going to like. Items I'd be willing to part with—for you—for less than a fair price."

He lifted his pillowcase, drew forth an elegant gold watch and held it out for her to inspect. "Note the fine workmanship, the gold band and the many diamonds set in the exquisite face. This watch must be worth a thousand dollars. But I'd be more than happy to give it to a young lady such as yourself for . . . oh, three hundred dollars." He stopped and grinned; his crooked teeth were as yellow as his weird skin. He added, "What do you say, Missy?"

"I don't have three hundred dollars," she said.

He stopped, scratched his big head. "How much do you have?"

"None of your business. If I had a thousand dollars, I wouldn't buy that watch. It's obviously stolen."

He drew back, shocked. "Stolen? How dare you say such a thing? Paddy may be new to these parts, but that gives you no reason to judge me so harshly."

Ali felt a pang of guilt. He might be telling the truth. It was possible he made his living selling stuff out of his bag. She couldn't see him working in a normal store.

"I'm sorry," she replied. "I shouldn't have said that. But I don't need a watch and I couldn't afford one even if I did." She turned to walk away, but once more he stopped her. He brought a Walkman out of his bag, held it out for her to study.

"I'm sure you could use one of these," he said. "I'd be willing to part with this for a much smaller amount."

Ali was curt. "I already have a Walkman."

"But this is a brand-new . . . Walkman." He added, "I wager it could help you walk your man much better than the one you own."

At first she thought he was joking. "Walk your man?" But then she realized the little guy had no idea what a CD player was. He continued to stare at her eagerly. Once again it made her think the items were stolen.

"Where are you from?" she asked.

He was cautious. "Why do you ask?"

"You said you were new to these parts. Where are you from?"

He slipped the Walkman in his bag and averted his eyes. "The old country. I only just arrived a few days ago. I mean you no harm." He paused and stared at her sandwich again, adding, "I haven't had lunch today."

"You're hungry?" she asked.

"Very hungry. I've not had breakfast yet, either. I'm sure a bite or two of your bread would satisfy me." He added hopefully, "If Missy wishes to share it?"

Ali handed him the sandwich. She could always buy another before she left town. "Take it, that's fine," she said.

He took a step forward and grabbed it, ripped off the wrapper in a second. His mouth, when he opened it all the way, was gigantic. He put an entire end of the sandwich in his mouth and chewed hungrily. Then he started to sniff her daypack.

"You have chips?" he asked.

"Yes."

He set down his own bag. "May I have some, please?" Before she could answer, he grabbed the bag of potato chips—and the Coke—and began to stuff himself. Ali had never seen anyone eat so fast. "What else do you have?" he asked between mouthfuls.

"I'm not giving you any more food."

He waved the sandwich. "Now, now, Missy, I meant no offense. Just a starving traveler, I am." He reached for his bag. "Could I interest you in a wallet or purse? I have a fine selection."

"No. Take that stuff to the pawnshop if you want to get rid of it."

He paused, interested. "A pawnshop? Where is that?"

"On Hadley. That's around the block from here."

"They buy things there? They pay go . . . cash?"

"Yes. Don't you know what a pawnshop is?"

"I do indeed," he said, putting the remainder of the sandwich in his pillowcase. "It's been a long day for me and I really must be on my way. Thanks for your time, Missy."

"No problem," Ali muttered as she watched him disappear in the direction of the pawnshop. Even the way he moved was odd; he was like a squirrel on two legs. What a strange fellow! He almost didn't look human.

Ali turned and walked back toward Sam's Subs, reaching in her pockets for her money. She had brought a twenty with her, and knew she had over fifteen in change.

But her pockets were empty.

It took her a moment to realize what had happened.

"That guy stole my money!" she exclaimed.

She fumed. Fifteen bucks—that was a lot of money to her. Paddy had probably swiped it when he had grabbed the sandwich. For sure, he must have stolen all the watches and wallets he had in his pillowcase. She wondered if she should call the police.

In the end, though, she did nothing. She didn't even bother asking Sam for a free lunch, although she knew he would have given it to her in a second. The day was wearing on, trees were dying. Suddenly, she was anxious to get up in the woods.

Turning her bike in the direction of the forest, Ali rode out of town.

CHAPTER TWO

Later, high on the mountain, she found herself surrounded by trees so green they seemed to breathe fresh air, and a silence so deep her thoughts sounded like spoken words in her head. Already, the forest was working its magic on her; she felt much happier.

Yet she had come to an obstacle, a roadblock. A wooden bar—yellow as that weird man's putrid makeup, and high as her neck—stretched all the way across the road. The roadblock had not been there before, and she wondered if the logging company had put it up to keep her out. The sign on the bar said no trespassing, go away nosy girl, stop hassling us with your stupid guilt trips. Well, not exactly, but something like that. It sure wasn't a friendly sign.

Ali stopped and got off her bike to catch her breath. She had been about to take a break anyway, but was disturbed by the roadblock. She realized she could get in trouble if she went on, yet she was not in the mood to give up. She had always been headstrong and, ever since her mother had died, had made it a point not to quit anything she started.

The sign was a square of hard cardboard, not metal. Feeling rebellious, she tore it off the bar and folded it and stuffed it in her daypack. If she got caught, she could always deny she had seen the sign. She hated to lie to anyone, but these were the same guys who were murdering her forest. It was not like they would arrest her or anything.

"They might," she said aloud. They might do exactly that. Then she would have to call her father, raise bail, appear before a judge, and maybe have her picture on the front page of the local newspaper. Worse things could happen, she decided.

Ali heard a truck approaching from the direction of town. She knew it was not a car because it was making too much noise. A minute later the gas guzzling, air polluting vehicle came around the bend and stopped in front of the roadblock. Mr. Ted Wilson—Sharla Wilson's dad, a so-so friend of hers at school—got out of the truck and smiled when he saw it was her.

Like Sam at the sandwich shop, Ted was one of the few adults in town who didn't mind being called by his first name. He was not paranoid about losing face or anything stupid like that—not like most of the teachers at her school, who had trouble seeing the students as real people, instead of hyperactive creatures that had crawled out of holes in the ground.

Because Breakwater was so tiny, she had been going to the same school since she was six, and the place was beginning to feel like a cage. It would be another year before she could move on to Tracer High, which was located in a town ten miles south of Breakwater. She was looking forward to the change. Except for hanging out with Cindy and Steve, she kept mostly to herself at school, spending her lunch hours in the library reading. She wasn't a snob—she hoped she wasn't—but she just wasn't interested in the same things as most of the kids her age. For example, she could not watch MTV without getting a headache, although she loved music. She was learning to play the piano, and her teacher said she was a natural talent. The only problem was, she did not own one; she had to practice on the one in Cindy's living room—usually while Cindy was watching MTV.

"Hi, Ali. What are you doing here? Or do I need to ask?" Ted said.

"Just out for a little ride, is all," she said innocently.

"Sure. You're going up to the logging site. What are you going to do this time? Tie yellow ribbons around the trees we have to cut down?"

"Red ribbons." She added, "You don't have to kill the trees, you know. You have a choice."

Ted was a friendly man, tall and thin, a bit of a scarecrow in his walk, with a face that somehow reminded her of a hero in a cartoon. His jaw was just a bit too strong, his gray eyes a little too round; nevertheless, he had a quick smile that was disarming, and he was always fair.

"It's my job," he said. "The world needs lumber. How could we build houses without it? Where would we get paper from? Besides, for every tree we cut down, we plant a sapling."

"It will take ten years for those saplings to grow," she began, before stopping herself, knowing it would be useless to argue with him. Ted knelt beside her.

"As you get older, Ali, you're going to discover many things in this world aren't fair. It's the way it is. The best you can do with your life is to try to fix those things—"

"Then I can ignore the roadblock and go up to the site?"

He held up his hand. "You didn't let me finish. You should work to fix things that can be fixed. You know as well as I that you're just going to get in the way at the logging camp. You're going to annoy the guys, and eventually somebody's going to have to grab you and stuff you in a truck and drive you down the mountain."

"I have my bike. I can get down myself, thank you."

"No, Ali." Ted stood and looked up the mountain. Clouds continued to hug the trees, gray ghosts drifting through branches, painting the entire area with gloom. Ted added, "The road's quiet now but in two hours there's going to be traffic. Lots of trucks barreling down here with full loads. Today we start our big push along the ridge. You know where that is. You're not going to be able to ride up there and then back down. You could force a truck to swerve to avoid you, and cause an accident."

Ali knew he was right. The road was narrow, the turns sharp. A truck could catch her by surprise. She was fooling herself when she thought she could make a difference.

Still, she did not want to go back home, not today. There was something special about today. She felt it in her heart, and she had learned to trust her heart ever since her mother had died. Sometimes, she felt, it was all she had left to trust.

She lowered her head and looked appropriately crushed.

"Okay," she said.

Ted gave her a suspicious glance. "Ali?"

She looked up. "I understand what you mean, about causing an accident and all. I don't want to do that."

Ted looked over her shoulder. "What have you got in your pack?"

She backed up a step. She hadn't stuffed the no trespassing sign down deep enough. "My poncho," she muttered.

Ted reached out and plucked the folded cardboard from her pack.

Ali added, "And a stupid sign that would probably have blown off the roadblock and littered the environment if I had not taken care of it."

Ted read the sign and sighed, and then folded it and put it in his pocket. He knew she had torn it off the roadblock, but didn't say anything. Again, he knelt beside her.

"Take care riding back down," he said. "Don't build up too much speed on the turns. The road is damp, you might slip."

She nodded. "Sure."

He patted her shoulder, stood and walked to his truck. However, he paused before climbing inside. "Ali, I don't say this to upset you, but you look more like your mother every day."

The remark did not bother her. People often told her that. "You went to school with her, didn't you?" she asked.

"From kindergarten to the last year of high school. She was a great woman." He opened his truck door. "Tell your father hello for me."

"I will. Thanks, Ted."

"Thank me by listening to me." He added, "Please move the roadblock while I pass. But be sure to put it back."

"I will."

The roadblock was light. She had no trouble pushing it aside as he drove past. He waved to her before he disappeared. She put the roadblock back like she promised. She could only assume that all the trucks that came down the mountain later in the day would have to stop and move it out of the way. All to keep people like her out. It seemed like a stupid system.

She had to make a decision. Ted was right about everything he'd said. She would just get in the way at the camp; she could get run over; they would cut down the trees no matter what she said.

Plus the hour climb had already tired her out. She'd slept lousy the night before. She'd had this nightmare where bats kept pinching her and telling her how tasty her blood was. She never watched horror films; she didn't know where the dream had come from.

Yet the feeling to go on persisted. She could not explain it; she simply felt she had to get to the logging camp.

"But I can't cause an accident," she said. Ted knew his business. Two hours from now the road would be jammed. If she continued up the mountain, someone would stop and order her back. They would not be as nice as Ted. She would probably get yelled at and feel bad the rest of the day. That would be no fun.

Ali came to a decision. The logging camp was not really farther up the mountain. The site was three miles west of where she stood. The road snaked around to get to it, going east and then north, before circling back. In a way, cutting across the forest would be like taking a shortcut to the camp, only it would be through the trees instead of on the road.

Not that such a hike scared her. She had grown up beside the forest; she trusted her knowledge of the area. And it would be nice to go for a walk after wearing her butt out on the bike.

Ali rode back a hundred yards and hid her bike off the road in a pile of bushes. No one would steal it; no one would even see it. Alongside the road, one spot looked pretty much the same as another. She was careful to memorize where she put it.

There was a Mars bar wrapper on the ground, beside her bike, and she picked it up and stuffed it in her pocket. She put people who littered in the same league as those who designed nuclear warheads.

She started hiking what she hoped was due west, slipping between the trees, stepping over the dew-covered grass, wishing she had a compass, but certain she would hear the lumberjacks when she got close to the camp. It was a massive forest; she knew enough not to underestimate it. If she got lost, she could die, and that would be no fun either.

Ali thought of Ted's last remark as she hiked. Like her mother, her hair had plenty of red in it, but her mom's had been much lighter, filled with a bright sheen that literally took Ali's breath away. In the sun, it used to look as if it were on fire. On the other hand, her mother's positive mood might have had something to do with that brightness.

Her mom had been a happy person, always joking and laughing, up until the week before her death. Had a part of her sensed she was going to die? Ali remembered vividly the last days of her life, how quiet and withdrawn she became. It was almost as if an evil stranger had sent her a letter announcing the soon-to-be accident. . . .

Ali fingered the tiny scar on her forehead, hidden by her hair, as she recalled that night. Then she angrily pushed the thoughts away.

"There's no point!" she scolded herself. She was alive and healthy. She had her father to love, her good friends—Cindy, Steve—to have fun with. Her mother was in heaven now, or in some beautiful place.

Restless, she resumed hiking, increasing her speed.

Tall for her age, Ali had been told since she was a baby that she was pretty, which made her pretty sure that she wasn't ugly. Still, it was hard for her to look in a mirror and not feel confused. It was as if she remembered herself looking different, somehow older and more important. Once she had tried to explain the feeling to Cindy and her friend had told her to stop eating junk food and see a counselor.

Sometimes she worried, when she stood in front of the mirror, that she tried to see herself *as* her mother. Cindy had told her that was another sign of mental illness, but Ali didn't know about that one. Her mom had been a true beauty.

Still, as Ted had said, she had a lot in common with her mother. They shared the same green eyes, the same small nose set in the middle of an oval face. They even had the same smile—wide, a little wild.

Of course she didn't smile much these days.

"Stop thinking about it!" she yelled at herself again.

Ali tried concentrating on the forest. She had not planned to hike; for that reason she had on her Nike's, not her boots. The shoes were lighter, they gave a better feel of the ground. As long as she didn't twist an ankle, she would be fine. And it was pleasant to feel the soft earth beneath her soles. Sometimes, just getting away from all the concrete and asphalt made her relax. . . .

Suddenly Ali froze in mid stride.

A chill passed over her, from the inside, not the outside.

She did not see anyone. She could not hear anyone. Indeed, seldom had the forest appeared so still. It was as if the birds and the insects had fled the area. Yet the sudden feeling of being watched was overwhelming. She moved in a circle, searching through the drooping branches.

"Hello?" she called.

Nothing. Except the feeling, something close.

"Who's there?" Her words hung in the air before dying in the dense woods. She called louder. "I have a gun!"

Like anyone in his right mind—even an ax murderer—would believe that a thirteen-year-old chick with an obsessive environmental outlook was carrying a handgun in her daypack. It would be better to keep her mouth shut, she decided, rather than yelling into the woods and telling whoever was stalking her exactly where she was.

She *did* feel like she was being stalked. Whoever it was, they seemed to be behind her, in the direction of the road. She tried to think how long she had been hiking. Twenty minutes? That meant the road was a half mile away, and the camp was at least two and a half miles distant.

"Oh no," she moaned. She regretted not having listened to Ted. She feared to go back the way she had come, but to continue forward meant she had to move farther from the road. Both choices scared her.

She was positive something was there. She trusted her intuition. It had been right so often before. She *sensed* a presence behind her. It was as if a magnetic field reached from deep inside her brain, and through the trees, and touched the . . . *creature*.

Or creatures.

Momma, Poppa, and Baby Bear?

No, something much worse.

She could not see them, but feared they could see her. Her white sweater was not helping matters. In the thick forest it was like a hello-please-don't-eat-me flag. Quickly, she reached for her olive-colored poncho. The thing was cheap vinyl, not warm, but at least it allowed her to blend into the trees. From past experience, she knew the poncho would not cover the collar of the sweater; she would still be easy to spot. So she pulled off the sweater before she put on the poncho.

The moment she changed clothes she felt a change in the mood of the creatures. They had paused to study her, but now they were anxious to catch her and eat her.

Ali heard a branch break. A bush crumple.

Dropping her sweater, she turned and ran toward the logging camp.

The next ten minutes were a blur. She felt trapped in the oldest of all nightmares: running from the unseen monster, the creature that kept getting closer no matter what one did.

Yet her terror gave her speed. She leaped over fallen logs, cut through thick branches, jumped over puddles. She ran flat out for a mile without even thinking of stopping.

It was not fair, she thought. She was a good person. She was trying to help the forest, and now she had *things* chasing her and wanting to eat her.

Ali scraped her leg on a dead bush, felt a branch rip a hole in her pants. She slipped on a rock, went down, got up, kept running, not even sure which way she was going.

A second branch cracked behind her. She heard a growl.

"No!" she cried as she kept running.

She entered a grass clearing and the noise behind her stopped. She was halfway across the meadow before she realized it. Slowing, she glanced behind, saw trees, just trees, standing tall and straight like guards whose only concern was to keep the clearing safe from intruders. Only they had let her in because they wanted to protect her.

Ali came to a complete halt, her breath roaring in her ears. She was not entirely sure why, but she felt safe in the meadow. The monsters appeared afraid to come out in the open.

She stood unmoving for several minutes, until her breath slowed and her nerves began to calm down. A ray of sun burst through the clouds, the warmth delicious on her face, causing her to relax further. In the distance, she heard the lumberjacks and their loud saws. Before the day began, she would never have imagined how happy she would be to hear such a sound.

She was still scared, though. She could not stay in the meadow. She had to get to the logging site. Ted could always give her a ride back to her bike.

What exactly was chasing her? She didn't believe in hairy monsters, not really, but a family of bears wouldn't have stopped just because she ran into a meadow.

She looked at the sun, wondered if it was the light that had caused the creatures to stop. If that was the case she had better keep going. Already the clouds were returning.

She hurried across the meadow and reentered the trees. They were not as thick in this part of the woods, and narrow beams of sunshine were able to reach all the way to the forest floor, lighting up the green moss and the yellow daisies. Up ahead, the sound of the lumberjacks grew louder; another mile and she would be safe.

Minutes later, the woods suddenly thinned and she came to a cliff. The drop was sudden, at least fifty feet, and a big surprise. She knew the woods but not this exact spot. The edge was made of sharp rocks and cracked boulders, and it looked like it could give way any second. In the distance, through the trees, she could see the outline of several logging trucks. They were still a half mile away, maybe more.

The cliff was a pain. In both directions, left and right, she could not find an end to it. She decided to go to the left, north. Although it was covered with a layer of dead pine needles, the ground appeared more stable in that direction. But with every step forward, she listened behind her. The sun vanished behind a cloud, and a gray arm stretched over the mountain.

She did not hear anything, she told herself.

The ledge narrowed. On her left a stone wall began to grow in height, until soon she was standing below *and* on top of a cliff. Two cliffs? What would she run into next?

The wall on her left was smooth, dark, probably made of granite. She could not see past its top. Unfortunately, the cliff on her right—the lower one—continued to grow more frail, and she found herself hugging the wall, afraid the whole ledge would fall apart.

How ridiculous it would be, she thought, to escape the monsters and get within shouting distance of the logging site and then die because of a stupid slip.

The gloom deepened. The side of the cliff was exposed. A slapping wind came from below, and she felt a chill in her arms and chest. Already, she missed her sweater.

Another minute, she told herself; she would find a way off the cliff. She imagined herself running into the logging camp. They would be happy to see her, they wouldn't get mad. After all, she thought, she was only thirteen years old, and they were not bad men.

Ali heard a sudden noise—a dragging sound, something heavy was being towed through the trees. A pebble fell from above, bounced past her face, almost stung her nose.

She froze, heard it again, the heavy breathing, or rather, a creature that normally breathed heavily, but which was now trying to move quietly. Slowly, she raised her head and looked up. A dark shape, much bigger than a man and far more hairy, was walking along the edge of the cliff.

It was forty feet away!

Ali tried to scream. She opened her mouth to let it out, but her throat felt as if it was filled with sand. All she could manage was a squeak.

She wondered what she should do. It didn't matter.

She wasn't given an opportunity to do anything.

The creature vanished behind the edge of the cliff and an avalanche of rocks came crashing down. It came all at once, not in bits and pieces. She wasn't given a chance to think; she had to react instinctively.

Beside where she stood was a small hollow, carved in the side of the cliff wall. As the first stone brushed the side of her face, she threw herself into it and covered the top of her head with her arms.

The noise was deafening. She felt as if the world were ending. Sharp rocks tore at her poncho, at her legs, pulling her down, to her knees, down into a cyclone of dust and dirt. The worst thing was, it wouldn't stop. The rocks kept coming, piling up all around, blocking out the trees, the sky, and she felt as if she was being buried alive.

The monsters didn't want to eat her, after all.

They just wanted her dead.

"Mommy!" Ali screamed.

The noise stopped. The rocks stopped. Everything went still. For a minute, she just breathed, let herself shake, even cried a little. She was alive, she kept telling herself. She was okay.

Everything was dark; she thought her eyes must be closed. But when she opened them, the dark remained. She blinked and rubbed her eyes and nothing changed. It took her a minute to realize the truth.

She was buried.

She was no longer standing, but sitting, her legs stretched in front of her. Behind her was cold stone; she assumed it was the granite cliff. Her daypack was twisted to one side, off her back. She could feel rock pressing into the bones of her spine. There was a burning pain in her right knee; her entire left leg felt numb. She tried to move her legs but found them trapped.

She stretched out her hands, felt around. She had maybe two feet of space in front of her, probably more to her sides. Only she could not reach far to her sides because she was pinned hard, like an ant under an avalanche of dust.

"Help!" she cried. "Help!"

She stopped. What if the monsters were prowling around outside? It would be better if they thought she was dead. She should sit quiet, give them a chance to wander off.

Ali waited. The darkness around her seemed to deepen, to close in. The silence also grew deeper. She could hear her heart, her breathing, but little else. It was as if she had been transported into deep space, beyond the galaxies, where there were no stars. Time went funny; she could not tell how much of it was going by, whether it had been minutes or hours since she had been buried. She felt like she couldn't breathe.

"It has only been minutes," she told herself.

But her breathing problem was real, she was not imagining that. She was buried in a tight space, not much bigger than a coffin. How long did buried-alive-people live?

She had to be realistic. She could not wait for hours for the monsters to leave. If no light was reaching her, then neither was any air. In less than an hour, she figured, she would smother to death.

"You have to get out of here," she told herself. "You have to get out now."

Okay, how? She couldn't think of anything.

She started yelling again. "Help! Help! Help!"

She screamed for perhaps five minutes before realizing it was hopeless. Before being buried, she had barely been able to see the logging trucks. She had not been able to see the lumberjacks. What were the chances that one of them had been looking her way—and been able to see her—when the rocks had started falling?

"Zero," she said.

Okay, no one was going to rescue her. What was the big deal? She was covered with a few small rocks. It was not like she was pinned under a boulder. She could move the rocks out of the way.

Ali set to work, picking up rocks and shoving them either left or right. Yet getting ahold of them was difficult. Most were buried under dirt, which she had to shove out of the way, and a lot of them were jammed under other rocks. In her cramped position, she had no leverage; as a result, the muscles in her arms began to cramp as her back tightened.

Worse, she began to breathe real hard. After ten minutes of work, she felt as if she were sucking on an empty scuba tank. No matter how deep she breathed, her lungs were not satisfied. Dizziness swept over her, and she saw black stars in the darkness.

She understood what was wrong. She remembered her science from school. She was breathing in more carbon dioxide than oxygen. Trees could do that, but not people.

Sadly, she had only begun to uncover her legs. She needed an hour, minimum, to dig herself out. And she had at most twenty minutes of air left before she would pass out.

The truth settled over her like a blanket made of despair.

She was going to die.

"No," she said. "No!"

But the darkness said yes.

"Help!" she screamed. "Help!"

This time she screamed until she was hoarse. But she suspected that a person could be standing five feet from where she had been buried and not hear her through the rocks and dirt.

Her body would never be discovered, she thought. Her father

would never know what had happened to her. Her bike would be found, though. People would think a crazy person had kidnapped her. Ted would tell the police about his talk with her. Such a nice girl, he would say. But stubborn, that Ali Warner, she wouldn't listen to a word I had to say.

Ali began to cry, to cough, and her coughing turned into choking. She couldn't breathe! The air tasted like swamp gas. When she drew it in, she wanted to vomit. Still, it was all she had; her lungs grasped the drained air as if it were a life preserver floating in the middle of a sea.

"I can't die," she moaned. "I don't want to die."

Then she felt it, the stick. It was nothing, really, a piece of wood, leaning against the wall beside her. She didn't even know why she bothered with it. She could not use it as a lever to move the rocks out of the way. It was way too flimsy for that.

Nevertheless, she picked it up and studied it with her fingertips. The stick was round, hollow—both ends were open. The feel of the wood was curious—it reminded her of some type of reed . . .

"It's bamboo," she said, amazed. She lived in the Northwest. Bamboo grew in the Caribbean, Hawaii; it did not grow on pine-covered mountains. With her oxygen-deprived brain, she must be hallucinating.

"No, it's real," she said as she stuck a finger down each end of the stick. It was definitely hollow, but she could not blow through it. Like all bamboo, it had places in it where it was blocked. That was too bad, because if the tube had been hollow, she could have pushed it between the rocks and dirt and out into the open air. Then she would have been able to breathe, and have time to dig herself out.

Her despair returned. To find something that could have saved her life, and then to not be able to use it—why, it was just too hard to take. She threw the stick aside in disgust and wanted to cry.

Yet a part of her refused to give up.

"Why is this bamboo here?" she yelled suddenly. There had to be a reason. She picked it up again, strained to think clearly. All she had to do was hollow it out. All right, she could not use her fingers. She could not use rocks. She could not use dirt. What did she have left?

Then she remembered. Her pocketknife! She always put it in her daypack when she went into the mountains. Opening the pack, she searched through it, and for a horrible moment she couldn't find it. But then—finally!—she saw the knife, dug into the bottom of the pack.

Her hands shook as she locked the main blade straight up.

Her father had given it to her the previous Christmas as a gift.

Her plan—it was really an act of desperation, she thought—was to aim the tip of the blade at the blocks in the tube; to shake the thing up and down and force the blade to cut into each block. Then she planned to shake the knife loose, ram it back in, and so on, until she cut all the way through the tube.

Unfortunately, she ran into a problem. Slipping the knife into the tube, the blade pointed down, she put her hand over the top end and shook hard . . . but the pocketknife stuck. She had to turn the stick over and pound the blade out. She worried that she might break the tube. Then it would be useless as an air pipe.

The pocketknife got stuck another four times, but then she got a break. The knife burst through the first block and stuck in the second block. That was good; that was part of the plan. But because the knife was stuck even deeper inside the tube, it made it harder to shake loose.

What did it matter? It was working!

Finally, she cleared all the blocks. It was a good thing. She was down to her last breaths. The air felt drained of oxygen. She suspected her face was as blue as a corpse's. She had to fight to keep from blacking out.

Ali shoved the tube into the wall that covered her legs. She hit a block—a big rock. She rammed it into another spot, hit another block. The third place she tried, the tube went in two feet before it blocked.

"Please. I need a little luck here," she told the darkness.

What she needed was a gap in the rocks that was only covered with loose dirt. It took her a dozen tries before she found such a hole. The tube appeared to slip all the way outside.

But no light appeared, no fresh air flowed in.

The bamboo tube was stuffed with dirt. Leaning over, she tried blowing it out. That worked about as well as her screaming for help.

Ali had no choice. She had to pull the tube out of the hole and pound the dirt out with the palm of her hand. But she kept one finger in the gap so she wouldn't lose it.

The dirt was jammed tight. It took her another two minutes to clear the bamboo. Then she rammed the tube back in the hole. Once again it went all the way through. The other end should be on the outside, she thought. Still, no air, no light.

Again, she blew on the tube. This time there was only a few inches of dirt stuffed inside, and the junk popped out.

Suddenly, there was light!

"Yeah!" she cheered. Greedy as a starving man for a meal, she leaned over and sucked on the tube. That cut off the feeble light but the taste of the fresh air in her lungs more than made up for it.

Ali drank from the tube for over ten minutes before her heart stopped pounding and her head cleared. Then she sat back and enjoyed the circle of light that now illumined her black grave. Only now it was not a grave.

"I'm not going to die," she whispered.

But she had plenty to do before she would be free. Returning to her dirt and rock digging, she worked around the bamboo stick. It didn't take her long to fall into a rhythm. She excavated for a minute, spent a minute breathing through the tube, then went back to digging. It took her only a dozen shifts before she had her legs free. As the blood gushed back into her numb left leg, she wanted to scream, it hurt so much.

Ali took it slow, rock by rock, one handful of dirt after another. The work did not bother her. She felt so grateful she had found the bamboo. But where had it come from?

An hour later she removed a rock and huge gobs of sunlight burst through.

Ali rolled on her side and peered outside. She couldn't see any monsters. Boy, she thought, it sure would be a drag to fight back from death's door and then end up in some hairy creature's stomach.

She worked faster, and a few minutes later the hole was big enough for her to climb out. The sky was still cloudy but to her it was the most beautiful sky in the world. She almost shouted out with joy!

But the monsters, she told herself, they might still be around. The best thing to do was to make a dash for the logging site.

Fixing her pack on her back, Ali resumed her hike along the ledge. But her right leg slowed her. The pants were torn away at the knee, and the skin underneath wasn't in much better shape. She wasn't bleeding at the moment, but she had plenty of dried blood up and down her leg.

The cliff finally dropped low enough that she was able to climb down into the trees and resume a straight line to the camp. Besides knowing that the loggers were in front of her, she began to hear Mercer River off to her right. The river flowed from near the top of the mountain—winding back and forth through the woods, and gaining strength from smaller streams—until it poured into the sea on the north side of Breakwater.

Had the day been clearer, she would have been able to see the highest point for hundreds of miles around, Pete's Peak. The peak was covered in snow year-round and reached a murderous altitude, but she often fantasized about hiking up there.

She wasn't sure why.

The monsters did not reappear, and she reached the camp not long after. She was lucky—the first person she ran into was Ted Wilson. He was working alone on a broken saw. He had tools out and looked absorbed in his task. But one glance at her torn pants and bloody hair—she had cut her head on top of everything else—and he dropped his saw and came running.

"What happened to you?" he asked.

Ali tried to act calm. She did not want her father to hear about her ordeal. He would get upset. Worse, he would forbid her to hike in the woods.

"I slipped and fell," she said. "I'm all right."

Ted studied the cut on the side of her head, then knelt and looked at her knee. His face darkened; he pointed to the leg. "That needs stitches," he said.

"No." Stitches would mean a hospital visit, and that meant her father would hear about her little adventure for sure. "It's nothing, it's just a cut."

Ted was doubtful. "I've hiked with you before, Ali. You're as surefooted as a squirrel. How did you fall?"

"I don't know."

Ted stood and took her hand. "I have a first-aid kit in the truck, I'll treat your cuts. Then I'll give you a ride back. I assume you ditched your bike by the side of the road and hiked here?"

"Yeah." She added, "Sorry I didn't listen to you."

"Don't be sorry. You have spirit. Few kids your age do."

Ted's truck was parked away from the others so she didn't have to face the gang of lumberjacks. Her plans for the day were ruined. She was emotionally and physically drained. She left her spool of red ribbon in her pack. She barely looked at the trees she had come to say goodbye to.

Ted cleaned her cuts with water and alcohol—which hurt, wow—and bandaged them with tape and gauze. While he worked, she asked if he could please keep what had happened private.

"As long as you promise not to hike in these woods alone anymore," he said.

"I want to promise you." She added, "But I've already broken one promise today. I don't want to lie."

"Ali . . ."

"I'll be more careful in the future. I can promise that. But this forest is where I go, you know, to forget about stuff."

He knew she was talking about her mother.

Ted gave her a ride back to her bike. His truck was bumpy but warm. On the way she asked if he had ever seen anything peculiar in the forest.

"What do you mean?" he asked.

"Oh . . . nothing."

"Did anyone chase after you today?" he asked.

"No."

"You're sure?"

She hesitated. "Yes."

When they reached her bike, she told him she felt strong enough to ride back to town. But he loaded it in the rear and insisted on taking her all the way home.

He dropped her off in her driveway. By then it was raining and she was glad to be home. As he lifted her bike out of the truck, he admitted he had seen something strange in the forest. Just the other day, in fact. He seemed embarrassed to talk about it.

"What did it look like?" she asked.

"I didn't get a real good look at it."

"Was it big? Was it hairy?"

"It was small and green."

"What was it?"

"I'm not sure. It was there one second and gone the next." He stopped and shook his head. "I must be imagining things."

"I know the feeling," she said.

CHAPTER THREE

Ali was in the house ten minutes when her father called from the road. He was a long-distance truck driver. His usual route ran from Breakwater to Los Angeles, to Santa Fe, then back again—three thousand miles altogether. Occasionally he drove to Florida to pick up freight. When he did that he would be gone for a week, and she would stay with Cindy.

"How's my Hunny Bunny?" he asked.

"Where are you?"

"Three hours away," he said.

"Great! I didn't think you'd be back until tomorrow."

"I've got to go back out this evening. All the way to Miami."

"No, Dad. We talked about this. You can't drive when you haven't slept. It's dangerous and, besides, it's against the law."

"No choice. Jerry's down sick. I've got to pick up his freight."

"Jerry's not sick, he's lazy. You're always doing him favors."

"We need the money."

"We have enough money," she said, unsure if that was true. Since her mother had died, they'd had financial problems. Her mom had worked for a software company downtown, and had earned the larger check. Ali added, "At least take a nap before you go back out. A few hours won't make any difference."

"We'll see." That meant no.

"I'll have dinner ready for you," she said.

"You don't have to do that."

"I want to do it, Daddy. Just drive safe."

"I'll see you soon, Hunny Bunny."

Three hours—that gave her time to shop for a special dinner for her father. Of course what was special to him was always the same thing: T-bone steak, a baked potato, and fried onions. Although she disliked steak and hated onions, she always ate with him. It made them both feel good to sit together for a meal. Then they could pretend they were still a normal family.

"We're still a family," she said as she hurried into the shower. Besides her cuts and bruises, she was covered with dirt.

Thirty minutes later she was outside and walking to the market. The rain had slowed to a drizzle, but she had her green umbrella with her, and let it twirl overhead like a leaf. She was going to miss the sweater she had lost, and the pants she'd ruined in the avalanche. She did not have many clothes that fit. She had grown six inches in the last six months, and her father was not in the habit of buying her clothes. Not because he didn't care, he just never thought about it, and she never brought up the subject. On the other hand, now that she was a full-fledged teen—now that boys were *sort of* looking at her—she found herself thinking about clothes more. What she wanted more than anything was a black leather coat, but because the leather was cut off the backs of dead cows—or poor dead sheep—she felt guilty every time she fantasized about it.

The market was fairly deserted. Ali was able to get a nice steak for half price. The man behind the counter said the store was having a special that day. She knew he was just being nice. He had gone to school with her mother as well.

Back home, Ali got busy. Besides preparing the steak and potato, she whipped up a batch of brownies for her dad. He had a sweet tooth; he could eat an entire pint of ice cream while watching TV late at night. Often he fell asleep in the chair with the TV on.

Her father came home an hour later. A big man with strong arms and a thick head of dark hair, he had a face that never seemed to age. Ali had heard the girls at school talk about how cute he was, and in fact he had powerful features; the firm line of his jaw almost looked chiseled. He had married her mother straight out of high school.

He picked her up from behind and kissed her on the back of the head. "I was going to take you out to eat," he said.

"Where were you going to take me?" she asked, not taking his remark seriously. Since her mother had died, they had eaten out maybe three times.

Her father sat down as she continued to fuss with the brownie batter. She still had to get it in the oven.

"Wherever you wanted to go," he said quietly. One look at him and she knew he was exhausted. The bags under his eyes looked like bruises. She put down the batter and reached for the phone.

"I'm calling Jerry. There's no way you're driving all night."

He stopped her. "It's my job, Ali. I'll be all right after I eat."

She argued but it was useless. He took pride in burning himself out to support them. She wished she could explain that he didn't have to prove anything to her. They were close, yet there were still things she couldn't talk to him about.

Like the night her mother had died. They never discussed it. To this day she didn't know exactly what had happened. The accident had knocked her out, thrown her clear of the car.

Yet over dinner she brought up the subject of bigfoot monsters, the mythical creatures that were supposed to haunt the forests of the Northwest.

"Why do you ask?" he said. "Did you see one?"

"People in town talk about them. I was just wondering if they're real."

"Most people will tell you they're only legends. But bigfoots have been reported all over the world, even in places as far away as China and Mongolia. Up north, where the Eskimos live, the tales of the abominable snowmen are probably the same as our bigfoots. With so many stories going around, I think there's got to be something to it." He added, "But I wouldn't call them monsters. Most people who've seen them say they're incredibly shy."

"But couldn't bigfoots be like people?" she asked. "You could have nice ones and rotten ones?"

"I never thought about it. I suppose you could."

They finished dinner and she helped him pack. On the way out he made her promise to get to Cindy's house by nine o'clock. Kissing him goodbye, she told him to drive carefully.

When he was gone, she cleaned up the kitchen and sat down to read for an hour before going over to Cindy's. She had already called her friend; she was expected.

But the house felt so empty. Outside the wind howled with a lonely ache. Inside the walls trembled with too many memories. Ali ended up packing her own bag and going over early.

Cindy met her at the door and led her to her room. Her parents had friends over for a video; they didn't want to be disturbed. Cindy's mother and father were nice people. They had let her sleep over many times since her mother had died.

Cindy was on to her the moment they were alone in her room.

"What happened to your leg?" she asked.

"My leg?" Ali asked.

"You're limping. What happened to it?"

Ted had seen her cuts but had not noticed her limp, nor had her father. "I fell."

"Did you go up to hassle the lumberjacks today?"

"Well . . ."

"Where did you fall? Let me see your leg."

"You can't see my leg."

"You're suddenly shy about your body? You're sleeping here tonight. I'll see it when you put on your pajamas."

"I'm putting them on in the bathroom."

"Why can't I see your leg?" Cindy insisted.

"I cut it. It's gross."

"I'm a gross-out kind of girl. How bad did you cut it?"

Ali realized Cindy was not going to let up until she saw her leg. Sitting on the edge of Cindy's bed—Ali slept on a foam mat on the floor—she rolled up her pants. The size of the bandage impressed Cindy.

"Cool," she said. "Did you have to go to the hospital?"

"Ted, Sharla's dad, bandaged it."

"So did you hassle the lumberjacks or what?"

"Not exactly." Ali stared down at her sore leg. The cut on her head hurt as well. While she had showered, it had begun to bleed again. But she had not put anything on it because then her father would have freaked out.

The trauma of the day's events came back to her right then. She felt like crying. Turning away, she stared at the wall. Cindy was a loudmouth, but she was sensitive. She came and knelt in front of Ali.

"What happened up there today?" she asked gently.

"I got attacked by bigfoot and his family."

"What?"

Ali told her the story. It took half an hour to explain. To her credit, Cindy listened without interrupting. When Ali was done, Cindy shook her head in amazement.

"You were lucky you found that bamboo stick," she said. "I would be picking out a coffin for you right now."

"That makes me feel a whole lot better," Ali said.

"Sorry. Actually, I'm amazed the way you kept your head."

"You believe me, don't you? Everything I just said?"

"Sure. That's too weird a story to make up."

"What do you think of the bamboo? Why was it there?"

"Forget the bamboo. What were the bigfoots doing there? They're not supposed to exist. If we could catch one, or even find a footprint, we'd be famous." Cindy got excited at the idea. "Hey, let's do that! Let's go back up, see if they left any prints. It rained today, the ground will be soft. I bet we can find something. We can photograph them, show the pictures to the police. We could get on TV!"

"Cindy. These bigfoots are *big*. They tried to kill me. We go back up there tomorrow, they might succeed."

"Nah. They were probably passing through. They do that."

"Up until an hour ago, you didn't even believe they existed. Now you're an expert on their migration habits."

"If you're afraid, I can swipe my father's gun."

"No guns. We're kids."

"Teenagers!"

Ali shrugged. "Whatever."

"Better to be living kids than dead kids."

"No. I hate guns. Your father shouldn't even have one in the house. And we can't just shoot them if we see them. It's their forest as much as ours."

"We won't shoot them unless they try to eat us. Look, you're the one who's talking about how dangerous they are. I'm not afraid of them."

"You're not the one they tried to bury alive."

"That must have been scary in the dark."

"It was—real scary," she said.

Cindy patted her shoulder. "You poor dear."

Ali thought further about what Cindy was saying. There was no bigger mystery in the Northwest than bigfoot, and they could be the ones to solve it. The possibility excited her as well.

"I wonder," Ali said finally.

"What?"

"I left my sweater up there, the one my mother knitted for me. You know, the white one?"

Cindy nodded. "I love that sweater. You don't want to lose it."

Ali considered further. "You might be right. If we could find the exact spot where they started chasing me, we should find footprints."

"Let's do it!" Cindy said.

"Maybe. But we shouldn't go alone."

"You want to take Karl?"

"Don't start that again." Ali paused. "Let's take Steve with us."

"Steve is a weenie. Bigfoot attacks and he'll run the other way."

"If they attack, believe me, we'll all run. But Steve is braver than he acts. I know him."

"Why don't the four of us go? Safety in numbers."

Ali yawned. "That's an idea. Let's talk about it in the morning."

"You want to sleep now?"

"Yeah. It's been a long day. Do you mind?"

Cindy did not mind. They got ready for bed and turned out the lights. As Ali snuggled in her blankets on the floor, she thought again of the bamboo stick. Of all the places it could have been, it had been right there to save her life. It was almost as if someone who could predict the future had placed it there.

But that was impossible.

Of course, so were monsters.

Sometime during the night, she dreamed.

She was in another world where there were no buildings or roads, no signs of civilization. And all the trees and grass and streams glowed with faint green radiance, as if filled with a magical light. Simply to open her eyes and bask in the light made her happy.

The most amazing part, however, was a group of floating islands in the sky. There were three or four straight overhead, and she could see dozens in the distance. They were inverted mountains: flat on the top, long and narrow on the bottom, covered with massive sheets of white snow. They drifted with the wind; solid clouds that never faded with the seasons.

Just by willing it she was able to lift off the ground and fly up to these islands. A movement of her hand one way, a bending of her fingers another, and she could change course and speed. The feeling of freedom filled her with joy. She was a bird, she was a human, and she was greater than both put together. More an immortal angel possessed of power and wisdom, with all the world and heavens to play in.

Yet on the horizon, far away, even in this enchanted realm, she saw a shadow. A growing shape of disease that could spread if not stopped, and consume all in its path. That darkness had a name—*Shaktra*.

It seemed to mock her as she flew above the world, higher even than the floating islands. It challenged her to not leave, but to remain and fight. To die if necessary, so that the magical realm could live and prosper. The Shaktra welcomed the battle with her, for it believed it could not be defeated.

And that, she understood, was why she had been born a girl.

CHAPTER FOUR

The next morning, while walking back to her house, Ali ran into Karl Tanner. He had a paper route; he was up early every morning. Occasionally—if she was up herself—she waved to him as he went by. Last week she'd made him hot chocolate, and put it in a paper cup that he'd squeezed into the cup holder on his bike. He seemed to like that.

She thought he liked her but was not sure. A quiet person, Karl was the smartest guy in the school. Last year he had gone all the way to the National Spelling Bee. Yet he seldom offered an opinion on anything. She liked that about him—the strong silent type thing.

Except when it came to her.

He was definitely handsome. Tall, with thick blond hair, he had blue eyes so piercing she imagined they could slice bread. He had muscles—he played on the school football team. Yet his manner attracted her more than his looks. He appeared *deep*. Of course she hardly knew him; it was possible that nothing of any importance went on inside his head.

"Hi!" Ali waved to him as he rode by. "Nice morning."

She had read that the weather was always a safe topic when it came to guys. Karl halted beside her. He had on a brown coat, and his cheeks were red from the morning air. His blond hair was longer than usual; she imagined that he had not cut it all summer.

"What are you doing up so early?" he asked.

"My dad's out of town and I slept at Cindy's." She added, "Her snoring would wake bigfoot!"

That wasn't very subtle, she thought.

Yet bigfoot was on her mind. A few minutes after waking that morning she had decided to try to get proof of his existence. The footprints should be there. The creatures wouldn't have stopped to brush them away. All she had to do was put together a team and find a decent camera. Why not invite Karl along?

Karl smiled briefly and offered her a newspaper. "This way you don't have to dig it out of the bushes," he said.

"You never throw it there. You're a good shot." If she was going to ask his help, she thought, she needed to hurry. He looked anxious to be on his way. She added, "I sure could have used a good shot yesterday."

"What happened yesterday?" he asked.

She told him the whole story. This guy she liked but didn't know that well—she poured out her guts to him. He listened closely, no longer in a hurry to leave. Halfway through the story, she realized how much she was trying to impress him, and she hated that about herself, but it didn't stop her. She went on and on about how calm she stayed while she was buried under the avalanche.

When she finished, he stood silently.

"What do you think?" she had to ask.

"You want to go back up there today and take pictures?"

"Yes. Cindy and I." She hesitated to bring up Steve. Karl and Steve were not the best of friends. She added, "Want to come? It could be the story of the century."

"Where exactly did you see these creatures?"

She described the area. "You know where I'm talking about?"

"Yes. That's high up. Can you go tomorrow?"

"We could. But the footprints would be fresh today. Also, it might rain again. I would hate to have them wash away. No one would believe me then." She wanted to ask: do you believe me? But was too shy. She added, "I guess we could wait for you."

"I have to help my dad at the factory right now." Karl's father owned a light fixture factory. The Tanners were the only rich family in town. Karl always wore the best clothes. He didn't need the money from his paper route, his father just wanted him to learn a work ethic. Karl continued, "I'll be busy until two. That wouldn't give us enough time to get up there and back. I think you're right, the footprints might not last. You and Cindy should just go."

Ali smiled. "You're not afraid bigfoot might eat us?"

"You have to be careful." His toyed with his bike pedal. "I better get going. Let me know what you decide. Leave a message on my phone. You have my number?"

"Yes." She hated to see him go, but supposed she had kept him long enough. "Karl?"

"Don't talk about it, I know. I won't, Ali. You can trust me."

"I do trust you. That's why I told you."

Ali went to Steve Fender's house next. Steve lived on her block, eight houses up. She had met Steve before she had met Cindy. He had stuck out his tongue at her. She had returned the favor. They had been three years old.

Steve had a difficult home life. His father came and went; it was hard to say which time was better. When he was at home, his dad yelled at Steve's mother and drank until he couldn't walk. But when he was away they both missed him.

Steve was short, slightly round. His idea of a good time was to go for doughnuts. He could eat four at once, with coffee. He was a coffee freak. He would go online and order strange brews from South America. Ali had to admit they were usually tasty.

Steve was an amateur astronomer. From memory, he could name a thousand stars in the night sky. He had made his own telescope; he had even ground the mirror by hand. He was also a genius with computers. He could hack into almost anybody's system, even big corporations. But he was not a jerk who secretly wrote virus software and tried to spread havoc. He did not abuse his talents, although he was not above playing games with friends. He once sent Ali an e-mail that loaded a program onto her computer that made everything she typed into the machine translate into Latin. For a while she had actually started to learn the language.

Ali was not sure if Steve's father was at home. Because she didn't want to run into the man, she didn't knock. Going around the side of the house, she peeked her head in Steve's bedroom. Like Cindy the day before, he was asleep on his back with his mouth open. She knew he liked her, in a girl-boy sort of way. Not that he would ever admit it.

"Wake up sleepy boy," she said gently.

Steve opened his eyes, looked at her, and rolled over, turning his back to her. "Come back in three hours," he mumbled.

Ali climbed into the room. It was messy but not as bad as Cindy's. She sat on the edge of his bed and spoke to his back. "We're going to get famous today," she said.

"I don't want fame. I want money."

"The two go hand in hand. Turn around, wake up. Yesterday I got attacked in the mountains by three bigfoots. Cindy and I are going back up there today to photograph their footprints. You're coming with us."

Steve rolled over and wiped his sleepy eyes. "Really?"

"Oh yeah. Let me tell you what happened."

He struggled out of bed toward the door. "I need some coffee first."

Steve returned fifteen minutes later with two cups of coffee. By then he had put on his pants and brushed his teeth. She sipped her coffee. It was scalding hot and tasted good going down.

"Talk," he said.

She told him the whole story, not leaving out the parts where she got scared and started crying. He interrupted a few times to ask questions—like how did she know there were three bigfoots and not one?—but otherwise he listened quietly.

"You want to take pictures of the prints?" he said when she was done. "That won't prove anything. With all the graphic programs available, people will say we faked them."

"I want to use the pictures to get the police to go up there."

"Sheriff Mackey eats the same breakfast as me. Only he's a million doughnuts ahead of me. He huffs and puffs getting out of his patrol car. There's no way you'll get him to hike up there to look at footprints." Steve added, "Plus he doesn't like Cindy and me."

"Why not?"

"We toilet papered his house last Halloween."

"Lots of people get their house papered on Halloween."

"Yeah. But Cindy put the paper too close to his jack-o'-lantern. The candle lit it on fire. The paper burned a weird design on his walls. It looks like a naked woman."

"I saw that! You never told me you did that!"

"We didn't want anyone to find out. But Sheriff Mackey suspects us"

Ali shook her head. "I can't believe you guys kept that secret from me."

"We all have our secrets, Ali."

She tried not to be offended. "Why doesn't the sheriff paint over the burns?"

"I think he likes them. But I know his wife doesn't. That's the main problem. Anyway, back to your footprints."

"Wait a second. You believe me, don't you? About what happened?"

"I think so."

"That's not a very strong yes."

"I just woke up and you're telling me about bigfoot. I have to adjust. Yeah, okay, I believe you."

"You better," Ali said.

"Sounds like a threat."

"Not at all. Will you come with us?"

"Sure. I have a camera we can use. It's the same one I use on my telescope. I have film. We can develop the pictures as soon as we get back. But if we can, we might want to print the film in another town, maybe over in Tracer. If Sheriff Mackey *does* go up there with us later, he'll try to steal all the credit."

"Who will we show them to?" she asked.

"Let's worry about that when we have something to show."

"Okay." She knew right then that he didn't really believe her.

Three hours later they were at the spot where she had ditched her bike. It had taken them longer to get started than Ali had wished. Cindy had been impossible to get out of bed, and then Steve had struggled on his bike up the steep road. He was out of shape. For lunch, he had brought a bag of doughnuts and a thermos filled with coffee.

The roadblock was still in place, minus its cardboard sign. None of them cared one way or the other—chances were they wouldn't see any lumberjacks.

They hid their bikes in the bushes and started to hike through the woods. Ali led the way, with Steve in the middle, Cindy taking up the rear. It did not take long to reach the spot where she had foolishly dumped her sweater. She was sure it was the right place.

But the sweater was gone.

"You might be confused," Steve said. "The forest looks the same all around here."

"No. I was here. Someone took the sweater."

"The lumberjacks don't come this way," Cindy said.

"Bigfoots don't wear sweaters," Steve added.

Ali pointed to the ground. "Look, you can see my footprints."

Steve and Cindy examined the ground.

"Yours are the only footprints here," Steve said.

"I'm not lying," Ali said.

"He's not saying you are," Cindy said. "But if you left your sweater here, who took it?"

Ali sighed. "It's possible the bigfoots took it out of curiosity."

"When we refer to more than one bigfoot, shouldn't we call them bigfeet?" Cindy asked.

"Oh brother," Steve said.

"Let's get to the cliff," Ali said. "You have to see the place where I got buried."

"We're not persecuting you," Cindy told her.

"I feel that, a little," Ali said.

"You just need a doughnut," Steve said, taking one from his bag.

Ali declined his offer.

Eventually they reached the cliff. Ali pointed out the mound of dirt and rocks that had buried her. But from the outside—with the gravel spilled over the edge of the path—it didn't look impressive, certainly not deadly. She saw the doubt on their faces.

"Where's the bamboo stick you breathed through?" Steve asked.

"I don't know," Ali said. She couldn't see it anywhere.

"Did you take it with you when you left here?" Cindy asked.

"No. I dropped it when I climbed out."

Steve kicked a large stone. "You're lucky these rocks didn't knock you out when they came down. It's kind of a miracle."

"Listen guys, I was trapped here," Ali said, annoyed. "You can see the hollow space in the stone wall. I pressed against it the instant the avalanche started and covered my head. That's why I wasn't knocked out."

Steve held up his hand defensively. "Okay. I can see that. But we're here for supersized footprints. Where are they?"

Ali pointed toward the top of the cliff. "We have to backtrack, climb up there. They attacked me from there."

"I just had an idea," Cindy said. "What if these creatures are supernatural? What if they didn't leave any signs behind because they aren't really physical?"

"You mean, like ghosts?" Steve asked.

"Exactly," Cindy said.

"But ghosts aren't real," Ali protested. "These creatures are. Look, we can argue all day. Let's climb up the cliff and see what's there."

"I hope we see something," Steve muttered.

Backtracking turned out to be difficult. They returned to where they had first encountered the cliff before it rose up, but the trees were thick. They had to circle far around before they were able to find a path through the forest. It took them an hour to reach a spot only forty feet above where they had been standing. By then Cindy seemed bored and Steve was outright cranky.

That all changed when they got to the cliff.

On the ground, in the soft mud leading up to the edge of the cliff, were large footprints. There were dozens of them, each at least two feet long, very wide, with four toes. Cindy and Steve got down on their knees to study them. Ali stood over her friends, feeling better about herself by the minute.

"Swear to me you didn't make these," Steve whispered.

"Steve!" Cindy snapped at him. "How dare you say that!" She glanced up at Ali. "You didn't make them, did you?"

Ali scowled. "With what? Look how deep these prints are. The creatures that made them must have weighed at least a thousand pounds."

Steve measured the depth of the prints with his index finger. It didn't even reach all the way into the heel; they needed a ruler. "Possibly. It would depend on how soft the ground was when they stood here," he said.

Cindy pointed out how the prints overlapped. "It looks like they were doing more than standing around," she said.

Ali smiled. "Of course, they were busy trying to kill me. Don't you guys owe me an apology?"

"I don't think so," Cindy said.

"We never actually called you a liar to your face," Steve said.

"Ha! You were talking about me behind my back!"

Steve took his camera from his daypack and adjusted the lens. "What do you need an apology for? You're going to be famous. These prints could confirm that bigfoot is real."

"What do you mean *could*?" Ali asked.

Steve began to snap pictures. Ali trusted his skill. He would cover every angle. Cindy got out of his way. They were all careful not to disturb the prints.

"Prints alone might not be enough," Steve said. "They can be faked. Now I know you didn't fake these. That would have taken a lot of work and equipment. Also, your prints are not mixed up with theirs."

"Then that's proof," Ali said.

"No," Steve said. "Hoaxes surround all supernatural phenomena. Just because you didn't fake these prints doesn't mean someone else didn't."

"But I saw the creature," Ali said.

"You caught a glimpse of something large and hairy before you were almost buried to death. Listen, Ali, stop worrying, *we* believe you. I'm talking about scientists. They'll have to come here and do all kinds of tests. We'll have to get them here right away. But I know what would help get them here, besides photographs."

"What?" Cindy asked.

"Hair from the creatures. The trees are thick here. At least one of them must have brushed against a sharp branch, scraped off a bit of hair or skin."

Cindy looked worried. "What if they're still around here?"

"Now she's scared," Ali gloated.

"I'm serious," Cindy said. "These big footprints are cool and all that but they won't help us if we're dead."

Steve adjusted the angle of his camera, glanced at the trees behind them, worried. But he kept snapping away. He would be finished with the roll of film in seconds. Ali was glad she had made him bring extra supplies.

"She has a point," Steve said.

"What do you suggest?" Ali asked him.

Wiping the sweat off his forehead, Steve again paused and looked behind him. The sun was bright and they had been exercising hard. In the distance, below them and to the right, they could just see the logging site, but Ali doubted the men could see them.

North of where they stood, to the left, towering over the woods like a powerful king above humble subjects, was Pete's Peak. The top had to be twenty miles distant; nevertheless, the mountain's sheer bulk blotted out a large part of the sky. The peak was sharp, clothed in white, a place of cold and ice that never faded.

For Ali it was almost as if it called to her.

She had to shake herself back into her body. Steve was talking.

"We shouldn't split up," he was saying. "But I think we should risk searching for a few hairs. You know the old saying: no guts, no glory. We might be able to follow their tracks. It's a shame we don't have any plaster."

"Why?" Cindy asked, not happy about his proposal.

"We could make a mold of one of the footprints," Ali said. "I should have thought of that."

"I did think of it," Steve admitted.

Ali laughed. "You didn't believe me! Don't worry, I forgive

you! Hurry and take your pictures. But don't you need to put a neutral object beside the prints? For scale?"

"I was going to suggest that," Steve said. "But since we don't have a ruler, I'm going to use you."

"Use Cindy. I'm having a bad hair day."

"It's your discovery," Cindy said. "You deserve to be the star."

Reluctantly, Ali moved behind the clearest footprint. Steve had her get down on her knees. "Smile," he said. "Think, two weeks from now this picture might be on the cover of *Time* magazine."

Ali knelt. Up close the prints were scary. Four toes? She wondered how tall the creatures were that made them. Ten feet? They would make great basketball players, as long as they didn't eat the refs.

"Whatever happens, we share the credit," Ali said.

Cindy snorted. "So she says now. Wait until the book contract offers come from New York. We'll barely get mentioned."

"She won't even remember how to spell our names," Steve agreed. Adjusting his lens for a close shot, he practically stepped on top of her and one of the footprints. Pulling her hair back, Ali tried to look older and smarter.

"Not true," she muttered.

"You're not smiling," Steve said.

"I don't want to look like a kid."

"You are a kid," Steve said. "Say bigfeet."

"Oh brother," Cindy growled.

"Bigfeet," Ali said.

Steve snapped another dozen pictures. Then he changed the roll of film and shot some more. He kept checking the angle of the sun; he had a good sense of lighting. Ali hoped she looked pretty.

Steve shot two more rolls. Altogether he took seventy-five photos.

"I wish I had my own dark room," he said. "I hate to let Harry at the photo shop develop them. When he sees what they are, he might make copies of the negatives."

"That's illegal," Cindy said.

"Tell Harry that and he'll be sure to make copies," Steve said.

"I thought you wanted to take the film down to Tracer?" Ali asked.

Steve nodded. "It might be worth the cost of a cab."

Ali studied the direction of the footprints. "I think the creatures headed back the way we came in," she said.

"I don't think it's a good idea to follow them," Cindy said.

"The prints are a day old," Ali said.

"Still," Cindy said.

Ali glanced at the sun. "I think today might be safer than yesterday." She told them about her experience with the meadow, how the creatures had stopped chasing her. She added, "If we run into them, we might just have to get out in the open, in the light."

"If we have time," Cindy said.

"Who knows, we might find some hair right away," Steve said.

They had no choice, they had to get off the cliff. They started back through the trees. Right away they lost the path of the footprints. Nor did they see any hair.

When they got down lower, however, Ali found another set of prints. They headed down the mountain, away from the peak, in the direction of the Mercer River. It was possible to follow the river all the way back to town, but it would be a long hike.

"I don't know about you guys, but I can't walk that far," Steve said.

"It's possible bigfoot likes the water," Ali said. "He might eat fish."

"Yesterday, he wanted to eat you," Cindy said.

"Let's at least walk down to the river," Ali said. "I know this area. There's a path we should be able to pick up. It stays mostly in the sun."

They found the path shortly. Overgrown with grass and weeds, littered with small stones, it did not make for casual hiking. Still, it was better than nothing.

They went on, the sun directly overhead. Ali kept one eye on the ground, the other on protruding branches. But she saw no more prints, no hairs. Perhaps they were wasting their time.

The sound of the river grew below them, on their left. The path wound lower, getting steeper. Between the trees they caught glimpses of the running water, until finally the path burst onto a narrow ledge that ran almost directly above the river. Fifty feet below, still feeding on last winter's melted snow, the water ran deep and powerful. In the distance was the thundering Cave Falls, where the Mercer River fell over two hundred feet in a single drop.

Ali had hiked to the falls before. This time of year they were often shrouded in whirling mist. When the angle of the sun was right, rainbows formed above the crashing foam. Yet even in the midst of the noise, Ali felt a haunting silence. The churning water seemed to talk to her, telling a tale of nature, of times before men and machines. She regretted that they would not see it today. The falls were at least a mile away. Steve's sore feet would never hike that far without major complaints.

The attack came without warning.

Cindy's water bottle was empty and she was thirsty. That was probably the reason she had wandered ahead of them. She wanted a drink from the river. Ali was also out of water, and for his part, Steve was exhausted. Ali hung back to keep an eye on him. But she wasn't that close to him, and the path continued to wind sharply. At any given instant all three of them were out of sight of each other.

Ali heard a muted cry behind her. Before she could turn, powerful arms grabbed her by the waist. The grip was vise-like; it could have burst her guts. She was not given a chance to struggle before she was lifted into the air and tossed over the side.

The water rushed toward her like a movie on fast forward. Her brain refused to accept what was happening. The river swelled like a tidal wave. Then came a cruel slap; she felt an icy sting. The sky and forest disappeared.

Underwater, tumbling, Ali saw light and shadows, felt intense cold. Yet it was the cold that shocked her awake. She was underwater! She had to get to the surface!

Catching a glimpse of blue, Ali kicked toward it. It took only seconds to reach the surface but it felt like ages. Her head burst into the bright sunlight and she gasped for air. She felt herself moving fast but did not understand where she was going.

Then she understood.

She was in the river, rushing toward the falls!

"Help!" she screamed.

It was like the avalanche all over again, but worse. She was so cold! Wiping her hair from her eyes, she searched for the shore. Below, her ankle hit a boulder and she felt a bone-jarring pain. On the ledge above, she saw Cindy running down the path, screaming at her.

"Swim toward the side!" Cindy shouted.

"Help!" Ali yelled back.

"The side! The falls!" Cindy yelled back.

Her friend could do nothing to help her. The pace of the river was faster than any thirteen-year-old could run. Cindy began to fall behind her, growing smaller. Then the river went around a bend and she disappeared altogether. Rushing toward almost certain death, Ali was once again alone.

She had fallen into the side of the river but the currents had yanked her into the center. Altogether, the river was a hundred feet across; not too large, not really, yet it was still wide enough to keep her from the shore—at least until it could throw her body over the falls and crush her on the hard rocks below.

Ali tried swimming for the shore, toward the same side her

friends were on, but her soaked pack and jacket felt like lead on her back and arms. Desperate, she reached down and unzipped the coat and unbuckled the pack, and watched them float away. But her improved maneuverability did not get her any closer to the shore.

In front of her, the sound of the falls grew louder.

Taking a deep breath, she put her face in the water and stretched as hard as she could with her arms, kicking her legs furiously. She had grown up by the sea; she was an excellent swimmer. Each summer, she spent hours at the beach. Unfortunately, nothing had prepared her for this. The fierce current cheated her of hope. She swam thirty feet toward the side, and got pushed back forty.

The water tumbled into a stone gully. That narrowed the river but also increased its speed. Ahead, not more than a quarter of a mile away, she could see foam blowing off the top of the falls. She had a minute, at most, to get out of the river before she would be killed.

Because the river had narrowed she was not as far from the shore. A few dozen vigorous strokes brought her to the side. But now the shore had transformed itself into an impenetrable wall. The smooth rock of the gully rose straight above her head. She could not possibly climb out!

Ali's hand caught a sharp edge. Her fingers, almost numb, reacted instinctively and gripped the protruding rock, and she threw out her other hand and tightened her grip, and for a moment she was able to stop herself from moving forward, although the force of the current was overwhelming. She did not know how long she could hang on.

"Oh boy," she gasped. Two days in a row: what were the odds of that? First she got buried and now something was trying to drown her. Nevertheless, she did not dwell on who or what had thrown her in the river. She had more pressing problems.

Her trap was an icy cauldron—the temperature of the water was barely above freezing. The falls were now only a hundred yards away. Raining mist blew off them like snowflakes in an arctic storm. The noise was deafening; she could not hear herself think. Plus the pressure of the current was relentless. She felt as if the cold hands of the entire mountain were trying to push her to her death.

She realized she had to make some tough decisions.

Cindy and Steve would not be able to rescue her. At best, they were only a mile away. It would take them at least thirty minutes to hike through the trees to reach her. Even then, they had no rope. Not that it mattered; she could not possibly hang on for even another ten minutes. Like yesterday, she was alone, she would have to save herself.

It was at that moment she spotted something promising. Hanging across the gully, a few feet above the falls, was a large dead tree. It must have fallen from the above ledge, perhaps last winter. The tree reached all the way across the river, a few feet above the water. But it was only in the center that a large branch hung down. The rest of the tree had been stripped clean by the current.

Ali thought frantically. To reach the branch, she would need to shove off from the side and swim like a madman—away from all hope of safety. Yet to stay trapped on this freezing side was hopeless. It was indeed a hard choice to make. If she missed the branch as she flew by, or if it could not support her weight, then she would go over the falls.

"But there's no choice," she told herself. "I'll die if I stay here."

Ali turned and braced her legs against the stone side. She knew she needed to swim straight out, get as much distance as she could from the side. The current would take her to the tree.

She shoved off. Immediately the current grabbed her. Here, so close to the falls, the river was narrow—thirty feet across at most; a first down on a football field. But that was not a bad thing. She was able to stroke only a dozen times before the branch loomed before her.

She had reached the center of the river.

Now she just had to catch the thing.

Ali reached up with both hands. Ten numb fingers grasping for life. Part of the branch slapped her hands. They were only strands; they sagged as she clawed at them. Cold horror swept over her. She felt herself slipping, the weak strands snapping.

The force of the water twisted her sideways. Water and wind rushed by. She could have been parachuting through a stormy sky. Still, she fought to catch something more substantial. Her fingers found a soggy branch. Yanking herself up, she let go of the strands and grabbed a second branch. Her feet continued to drag in the water, pulling her almost horizontal to the river.

Worse, she was so near the falls she could see over the edge. The white mist rushed toward her like steam blown from the cheeks of an ice monster. The crashing noise thundered inside her head. Her frozen body felt as if it weighed a ton, while the branches she clung to were like kite string. A few seconds more, she thought, and her hopeless situation would come to a bitter end.

Then she saw a rainbow, spread over the falls, a colorful half circle set like a bridge over the chasm below. It seemed to rise up as she stared at it, to touch her feet, to give her hope perhaps. For the last two days it had seemed the mountain had been trying to kill her, and now she felt as if it was trying to rescue her. Strength flowed into her from the colored light. Her frozen hands warmed and her head cleared. Suddenly, she knew she could make it.

Ali pulled herself up farther, took her feet out of the water. Kicking up high, toward the sky, she got one leg partway around the tree. Grabbing the tree and pressing it to her chest, she strained her leg to wrap higher, using the side of her ankle as a clawing hand. Again, unlooked-for strength flowed through her limbs. The damp wood slid below her like a fat metal tube. In a moment she was sitting on top of the tree.

The next few minutes were tense for Ali. It was like when she had found the bamboo yesterday, and not been able to use it at first. Safety was only a few feet away, but scooting along the top of the tree was not easy. The water had stripped away most of the branches, but there were still sharp stumps to contend with. She bumped into them with each foot forward that she took. To get past them she had to lift her butt off the tree, and loosen the grip of her legs, which increased her chances of slipping and falling. Twice she did slip, partway, almost giving herself a heart attack.

Finally, though, she reached the edge, and climbed onto the smooth stone. She did not stop to rest but hiked away from the waterfall and the deafening noise. The rainbow had faded. More than anything she longed to find a quiet place to sit down and warm her bones in the sun. But she worried about Steve. From the strangled cry he had let out, she knew whatever had grabbed her, had attacked him as well.

Ali had to wind through a maze of slippery gray stone until she found a semblance of a dirt path. The latter wound up and down, but she was not sure it was the same path she had been on earlier. She could hear the sound of the river, however, off to her right, although she could not see the water. She figured she couldn't get too lost.

Ali had been hiking for about fifteen minutes when she became aware that something was following her. Stopping on the path and turning, she stood as still as possible. For an instant she thought she heard footsteps; the sound quickly vanished. Then she imagined she heard heavy breathing.

She tried blocking out the noise of the river. Like yesterday, her belief that something was coming was largely internal. She was not even sure if she heard anything with her ears. She tried to convince herself that she was just imagining things. But that was hard to do when she had almost been killed two days in a row.

Then she heard a loud snort. It did not sound human.

She turned and bolted, down the winding path. The incline was steep; as she ran her feet spent more time in the air than on the ground. She ran like the wind—too bad her terror did not give her wings. Pounding footsteps and slobbery breathing had joined the loud snorts.

Not one but several creatures were chasing her!

The path suddenly ended back at the river, on a sandy beach. The shore was only fifty feet long, and blocked at the far end by an impenetrable wall of smooth stone. To get past it she would have to backtrack, in the direction of whatever was chasing her.

She was trapped!

Paralyzed by fear, she paced back and forth on the shore. An entire minute was wasted while she tried to figure out what to do next.

That was all the extra time she was allowed.

Three creatures emerged from around the bend.

Ten feet tall, they had broad shoulders and lengthy torsos, so long their legs were not much longer than a man's. They were more gray than brown; the hair on their bodies looked like flaking mud, or else they were incredibly filthy. With thick arms that reached to their knees, and legs like tree stumps, she had no doubt of their strength. Their blunt four-fingered hands looked like they could crush her skull with one snap.

The true horror was their heads. They had a dull cube shape. They could have been manufactured in the laboratory of a crazy scientist. Large yellow eyes glared out of the center of their huge skulls, and their wide and toothy mouths dripped green spit. Or maybe that was their blood. Maybe they were so hungry to eat her they had chewed on their long red tongues.

"I have a gun," she croaked.

They did not believe her, or else they did not care.

Or maybe they did not speak English.

They approached slowly, grunting, licking their teeth.

Ali backed up. She backed into the river.

She could not cross it; the current would sweep her away. Nobody knew that better than she. Yet that was probably her only chance—to jump into the water, hope they couldn't swim, and float down to the dead tree and pray for another miracle at the edge of the falls. Either way, if she lived or died, it would be better than being eaten by these creatures.

She sniffed the air. It stank.

They had bad breath on top of everything else.

Keeping her eyes on the creatures, she stepped into the river. Water swelled around her calves. The creatures kept coming, fanning out, making sure she could run neither right nor left. She moved deeper; the icy liquid rose to her waist, the current was cruel. She could not believe she was able to remain standing. But if she had been hoping that they were scared of the water, it was a vain hope. The first creature stepped into the river, and the second one quickly followed.

Only the third one stayed on the shore. Not as tall as the others, he had his mouth shut and was not slobbering. He seemed to want to study her more than eat her. Yet he was not doing anything to save her.

Ali waded out farther; the water reached her chest. The current was as strong as it had been earlier. Yet she stood against it without bending. How was that possible?

All of a sudden she felt incredibly heavy. The water rushed around her as if she were a statue made of marble. Even the cold was unable to penetrate her skin. She did not understand what was happening. Like when she had struggled on the log above the falls, a strange power swept through her body. The creatures stopped to stare at her and suddenly she was not afraid of them.

On impulse, she bent over, stuck her head underwater, and grabbed a rock from the floor of the river. Coming back up, she took aim at the first creature. She loved baseball; she played for hours every summer with Steve and Cindy. She especially liked being the pitcher. Yet she had never thrown a ball the way she threw this rock. It flew from her hand like a bullet and hit the closest creature right in the face.

He staggered back and fell on his butt with a loud splash.

"Better leave me alone!" she shouted, dunking down for another rock. This one she aimed at the other creature in the water. He stood there stupidly and took the stone in the gut. The blow must have hurt. He let out a yelp and doubled up in pain.

Ali reached down for a *huge* rock. This one was so big it must have weighed fifty pounds, yet she had no trouble lifting it. Taking aim at the creature on the shore, she let it fly—and fly it did. The stone flew a hundred feet through the air before it smashed into the creature's leg. The impact was loud—she thought she heard its leg snap. It sure let out a loud cry. Limping back up the path, it called to its friends in monster language.

The others had seen enough. Chasing after their injured friend, they disappeared around the bend. Ali heard them growling for several minutes before the forest fell silent. She felt confident they would not be back any time soon.

Ali got out of the water. It was a day of miracles. The sun shone bright and felt good on her face. Yet the cold continued not to bother her. Even her wet clothes did not make her shiver.

Filled with amazement and relief, she hiked away from the river and sat down in a meadow filled with long grass and yellow daisies. Peeling off her soaked sweatshirt and pants, she lay down in the grass and let the warm sun sink into her stiff muscles. The minutes drifted by; her breathing began to calm down.

For some reason, in that moment, she forgot all about her friends. She closed her eyes. She felt so at peace. . . .

CHAPTER FIVE

When she opened her eyes it felt much later. Looking up, she could not find a cloud in the sky. The sun seemed unusually bright.

Ali stood and put on her clothes. They were completely dry. She must have slept for hours—it was the only explanation. She had been dreaming . . . something about a magical realm. No, that had been last night.

Why did the dream only come back to her now? She remembered the green light glowing inside every tree and plant and blade of grass, the joy of soaring through the air—most of all the enchanting ice mountains that drifted across the sky, cold white glaciers in the heavens.

There had been a scary darkness at the end of the dream, although she could not remember exactly what it had been.

But she remembered Steve and Cindy, and the thought alone should have brought anxiety. Something had thrown her in the river—probably one of the bigfoots. There was an excellent chance the same creatures were after her friends this very minute.

Yet, unlike before her nap, she was suddenly not worried about

Steve and Cindy, and she puzzled over the lack of concern. It was not that she didn't care about them—she was just certain they were fine. The conviction ran deep. It was another one of those gut feelings she occasionally got, like yesterday, when she knew something was following her without hearing or seeing anything.

It was then Ali saw the tree.

It stood at the edge of the meadow. A fat redwood amid a family of skinny pines. Why hadn't she seen it before? Redwoods were rare in the forest, and this one was extraordinary. It was no taller than a three-story building, yet it had the circumference of a small house. Was there such a thing as dwarf redwoods? It did not look as if the tree had burned down before, or been chopped down and regrown.

Walking toward the tree, Ali felt a tingling sensation at the back of her neck. The redwood drew her much as the top of the peak had drawn her the previous day. She was not surprised, when she got closer, to see that there was an opening on the side.

The hole was round and narrow, set three feet above the ground. She thought she could squeeze inside but wasn't positive. She sure would hate to get stuck with her butt sticking up in the air. But she figured she had to risk it, and finally poked her head in the opening.

"Hello?" she called. "Any bears in there?"

She half expected to hear a flutter of tiny feet. A few squirrels, at least, should have made the tree their home. All was silent, however. Indeed, her words seemed to be swallowed by the inside of the tree.

Ali pulled her head out and looked around. She still did not understand how she could have missed the tree before. Although short, it was still the single most impressive object in all the woods. But here it was, there was no denying that it was real. As real as the creatures that had attacked her.

Ali crawled inside—what the heck, head first—her back down

low. The bark of the tree was six feet thick. Then the hole burst through into a hollow space, a dome shaped room in the center of the tree. Yellow light shone through from the outside.

Ali was in awe. The domed ceiling was smooth; it could have been cut with fine tools, polished over many years. Covered with sawdust, the floor felt springy under her feet. The interior was perfectly still, the peace as soft as her mother's smile had been; and the air was fresh, not the least bit stale, rich with its redwood aroma; and she could hear nothing except the sound of her breathing and her heart. Even the noise of Mercer River, close at hand, could not be heard.

Ali sat in the center of the room, her legs crossed, her back to the opening. She felt safe inside the tree. For some odd reason, she did not fear that anything would *dare* to attack from the outside. More, she felt at home, as if she had visited the tree before, in her dreams perhaps, or even in a body that was not her own. The peace of the chamber sunk into her chest like a hot drink. She was not sleepy, but she felt the urge to close her eyes.

So much peace, inside and out. The silence was so strong she half expected it to speak. What was also true, she realized with a start, was that she wished to speak to it. What a strange idea, to have a conversation with nothing.

"Hello Mr. Tree," she said softly. "Who are you?"

There was a long pause. She waited for an answer. Once again, she knew it was silly, trees did not talk, but she expected this one to talk to her.

But the answer, when it came, was not in words. Nor was it a voice inside her head. Deeper than that, it was like a gentle feeling in her heart, spoken in a language that was not her own; an ancient language made up not of set words but of musical sounds and sensations long ago forgotten by mankind. Yet she understood it.

"I am your friend. I am here to help you."

Ali paused, stunned. "Am I imagining this?"

"No. I am real. I am as real as you."

Her heart beat faster. "You are not there. I do not hear you."

"You cannot hear me, true, but I am here."

Ali stopped and shook her head. "I am talking to myself."

"Do you believe that?"

"Yes. I am sitting in a tree and talking to myself."

"That is fine, then talk to yourself. I will still help you."

"No. People who talk to themselves are crazy. I should get out of here."

"Do you want to get out of here?"

"No." She paused. "I like it here."

"Why?"

"It is quiet, peaceful."

"It is peaceful because you are with an old friend."

"Hey, maybe I shouldn't be here. My friends might be in danger."

"Do you think they are in danger?"

She paused. "No. It's weird, but I know they're safe."

"They are safe. You can stay for a while and we can talk."

She relaxed further. "Okay. But who are you?"

"You may call me what you wish."

"But don't you have a name?"

"I have many names, as do you."

"My name is Ali Warner. That is the only name I have."

"It is the only name you remember. But I remember you by another name."

"What?"

"Alosha."

"Alosha," she repeated. "That's a pretty name."

"I think so."

"What does it mean?"

"That is a secret. An important secret that you must figure out for yourself."

"Why don't you just tell me?"

"If I tell you then it won't be a secret."

"Come on."

"You will have to learn a great deal about yourself before you are ready to know what it means. I can tell you this—you are very important. But you know that already."

"What are you talking about?"

"What did you do this afternoon?"

"You mean, with the bigfoots?"

"They are not bigfoots. They are trolls."

"No! There are no trolls!"

"And there are bigfoots?"

Ali stopped. "I see your point. Both are imaginary creatures. But trolls are even more imaginary. They're only in books and stuff, like elves and dwarves."

"There are elves and dwarves."

"Gimme a break. I can't believe that."

"What is there to believe? You spent the morning fighting three trolls and now you think you are talking to a tree."

"But you are a tree."

"I am a tree now."

"Wait a second. If my name is Alosha, what's your name?"

There was a long pause. "You may call me Nemi."

"I have never heard that name before. What does it mean?"

"No One."

"Your name means No One?"

"That is one of its meanings."

"What are the others?"

"That is a secret. For now."

"Then I'm talking to no one?" she asked.

"In a manner of speaking."

She nodded. "Then I *am* talking to myself."

"You are talking to Nemi. What do you wish to ask?"

"Okay. I have a few questions. These trolls, what are they doing in this forest?"

"They are invading it."

"What? Why?"

"Trolls are part of the family of elementals. Dwarves, elves, fairies, trolls, leprechauns—they are all elementals. And they are mad at humanity for ruining the Earth. To stop them, they have decided to wipe everyone out." Nemi paused. "There is another reason."

"What is it?"

"That is also a secret."

"You have so many secrets. What kind of friend are you?"

"I am your best friend."

"Really?"

"Yes."

"So you like me and stuff?"

"I like you and lots of stuff."

Ali opened her eyes, looked around. She had forgotten that she had closed them. "Am I dreaming?"

"No."

The answer was hard to pick up. She closed her eyes again, spoke to the being inside the tree. "I'm not so sure about that. Lots of weird things have been happening with me lately."

"I know."

"You do?"

"I know everything about you, Alosha."

"It feels weird to be called that."

"How so?"

"Like, I remember the name but don't really remember it. Know what I mean?"

"Yes. It was your name before you were born."

"No way! I didn't exist before I was born!"

"You did. And you will exist after you die."

"Really?"

"Really."

"That is so cool. How old are you, Mr. Nemi?"

"Nemi is fine. I am very old. Older than the stars."

"No way. Really?"

"Yes. So are you."

"Wow. How come I don't remember any of this?"

"It is part of being human."

"Will I remember in the future?"

"Hopefully."

"These elementals—where are they coming from?"

"They have always been here, in a sense, all around you. But now they have entered your dimension."

"What do you mean, my dimension?"

"Do you watch TV?"

"Too much."

"When you watch TV, you look at a single screen. Yet you can change channels and enjoy different shows. It is the same with your Earth. On one channel humanity goes about its business. People build roads and buildings, they cut down trees and pollute the water. Men and women meet and get married and have babies and life goes on. But that is only one of Earth's channels. If you switch stations, you see the elementals. They live here as well. This is their world as much as humanity's. Do you understand?"

"I think so. But what are they doing on our channel? I mean, in our dimension?"

"I told you—they are here to wipe out humanity."

"That isn't very nice of them."

"They don't feel you have been very nice to the Earth. Even though they are in another dimension, the damage you do in this dimension affects them."

"That's awful. How come no one knows about this?"

"Few people know how to change the channels on the TV inside their heads. They don't believe in elementals or in other dimensions."

"Why do I get to learn about this?"

"Because you are very important."

"To what? The world?"

"To the war that is about to take place. You are here to stop it."

"No way. I'm thirteen years old. I'm on summer vacation. I can't stop a war."

"You are the only one who can stop it."

"But what am I supposed to do?"

"For now, you have to stop the elementals from entering your dimension. Even though they are all around you in their dimension, they are entering your dimension through a magical gate called the Yanti."

"Where is this Yanti?"

"On top of the mountain. You have to go there and close it."

"It is freezing on top of the peak. The air is thin. I can't go up there."

"It is your choice. But if you don't humanity will be wiped out."

"That's not fair, Nemi. That's too much responsibility to put on my head."

"It is neither fair nor unfair. It is what it is. Through the Yanti the elementals are able to enter your dimension. The war is starting here, in this forest, in your hometown. But soon it will spread to other parts of the world. What is necessary is to delay it, at least for the time being. Most of the elementals will still want to wipe out humanity, but if they can be stopped for now then you can make other plans for the future."

"Do some of the elementals like humanity?"

"Yes. Many more are undecided what to do with people. But enough of them want to go to war so there is bound to be trouble. You have to get to the Yanti."

"What does it look like?"

"You will see when you get up there."

"What do I do with it when I get to it?"

"You will know."

"You have a lot of confidence in me."

"True. Look how well you have done the last two days."

"What do you mean?"

"You have survived two major tests: the test of earth and the test of water. You got buried in the earth and you did not panic. You figured a way out. The same with getting thrown in the river. You kept your head and you saved yourself from drowning."

"Those were tests? Who is testing me?"

"Nature tests you."

"But the bigfoots . . . the trolls made those things happen. Are they part of nature?"

"Everything is part of nature. The sun and the moon and the stars are parts of nature. The tests were going to happen no matter what the trolls did. And there are more tests to come."

Ali swallowed. The first two had been bad enough.

"What are they?" she asked.

"Nature is made up of elements. They are seven: earth, water, fire, air, space, time, and the seventh one—that is secret."

Ali interrupted. "That is what people used to think. Now we know better. I learned that at school. There is oxygen, gold, lead, hydrogen, mercury—over a hundred different elements. They're on a thing called the Periodic Chart. I can show you my science book if you want to see it."

"I know about the Periodic Chart. What I am telling you is deeper. Everything in nature has a particle of these elements in them—some more, some less. It is by controlling them that you will learn magic."

Ali got excited. "I've always wanted to learn spells and potions. I've read books about them."

"That is not magic, that is fiction. Real magic is always connected to the elements. When you master them you gain powers. See what happened to you in the river today. The rushing water could not knock you over. You were able to pick up heavy rocks. That is because you have already passed the tests of water and earth."

Ali was delighted with the news. "You mean I'm a superhero now?"

"You will not be strong all the time. But when the need is there, your powers will appear." Nemi added, "Hopefully."

"What do you mean, hopefully?"

"Maybe not all the time you need them."

"That's kind of scary."

"It's a scary world."

"Let's talk more about these elementals. How many have invaded this forest?"

"A few. But in two days there will be a full moon. That is when the Yanti will open all the way. An entire army of elementals will come through then."

"What will they do?"

"Kill people."

"But people will fight back. The army will be called in."

"More elementals will appear, and there will be a big war. It is hard to say who will win, and it doesn't matter in a way. The world will be in ruins, in both dimensions."

"Say I get to this Yanti in the next two days. When I close it, won't the elementals who are already here in our dimension be trapped?"

"No. They will shift back into their own dimension. The forest will be free of them." Nemi added, "Unless you want some to stay."

"I was thinking about that. I'm not sure what the elementals are doing is wrong. Lumberjacks are destroying this forest. I want someone to stop them."

"Things are out of balance in your dimension, that is true. But a war is a poor way to bring balance." Nemi added, "Think of the men who work on the mountain. They have families. Do you want them hurt?"

"Of course not. But someone needs to teach them a lesson."

"What lesson do you want to teach them?"

"I don't know, something."

"You think about my question. You might get an answer to it before the day is through. You think about the task that has been put before you."

"Do I have to go up there alone?"

"You may take whomever you wish. I can only advise you— you have to make your own decisions. You don't have to go at all. It is entirely up to you. But if you do go, be wise and be careful. The forest is now a dangerous place to be. Certain elementals will do everything in their power to stop you from reaching the Yanti. Many of them are much more dangerous than trolls."

"When will I face the other tests?"

"Soon."

"And each test I pass, I gain more power?"

"Yes."

"What if I fail one?"

"You will die."

"That's a pretty severe punishment."

"You are an unusual girl. A lot depends on you. If you do not reach the Yanti in time, there will be few left alive, on both sides. Think about that as well." Nemi added, "Now it is time for you to find your friends and return home."

"But I don't want to leave. I feel happy with you."

"I am always happy to be with you. But if you are to reach the Yanti in time, you must make preparations."

"One last question. Two days from now, exactly when will the Yanti open all the way?"

"When the moon is straight overhead. That will be late at night. At that moment, the moon will begin to burn."

"What do you mean?"

"If you have the courage to go on this quest, you will see for yourself."

Ali fidgeted where she sat. Her eyes burned; she wiped away a tear before it could touch her cheek. Here she was talking to no one and it broke her heart to leave.

"Can I talk to you again, Nemi?" she asked.

"I am always nearer than you think. Go, Alosha. Be brave."

Ali opened her eyes and stood. She looked around the inside of the tree. There was no one there, not even a ghost of a person. Yet she felt as if Nemi touched her heart in farewell. She was reminded of her mother's love. She wished she had remembered to ask Nemi about her. Maybe next time.

"Thank you," she said.

Ali climbed out of the tree and hiked toward her friends.

She found Cindy and Steve twenty minutes later, at the same spot on the path where she had been thrown in the water. When she walked up, they were both sitting on the ground and going through his daypack.

Cindy appeared unhurt, and Steve did not look bad, although he had a bruise on the side of his head and a spot of blood near his left eye. Seeing them alive, Ali let out a squeal and leaned over and gave them a hug. Intuition and talking trees aside, it was good to see with her own eyes that they were all right.

"They didn't eat you!" she exclaimed.

"You didn't drown!" they cried.

Ali stood back up. "There was a tree hanging over the river. I was able to grab it and escape the falls. Then I . . . well, I can tell you later. I'm just so happy you guys are okay!"

"I was looking all over for you!" Cindy said. "I figured you went over the falls and finally gave up hope. I just got back to Steve a few minutes ago."

"I just woke up," Steve muttered.

Ali was shocked. "You were knocked out all this time?"

"Must have been." Steve shook his head in disgust and pointed to his pack. "My camera's gone, and all the rolls of film."

"What happened?" Ali asked.

"I don't know," Steve said. "One moment I'm walking behind you and the next I got hit on the head."

"You didn't see what it was?" Cindy asked.

"I didn't even hear it coming," Steve said, getting up slowly. His eyes were clear and he was not wobbly. "But it must have been strong to put me out so easily, and lift you and throw you so far."

"I know what happened," Ali said.

"You do?" Steve asked, puzzled.

"Yes." Ali offered Steve her arm for support. "But let's talk about it later."

CHAPTER SIX

A funny thing happened to Ali on the trip back to town. She tried to imagine telling her friends about her battle with the three trolls, and her conversation with the tree, and a lightbulb went off in her head.

They would think she was crazy.

Bigfoot was one thing. Lots of people had seen the creatures. But an army of invading elementals? That was too much for any reasonable person to accept, never mind the fact that she was supposed to be the "chosen one" who was destined to defeat the magical army. She could just picture Steve and Cindy's faces if she started to explain such a scenario. They would not laugh, they would rush her to a doctor.

So on the way home she said nothing. The others did not care. They were all exhausted. By the time they reached town, Cindy and Steve did not even bother to quiz her about what she had seen. They each just wanted to get to their houses and rest.

Yet Nemi's explanation haunted her as she entered her house. She knew for a fact the trolls were real; since they were, everything else he had said was probably accurate. The world was in danger, she thought, something had to be done. But why had he placed all the responsibility on her head?

She hated to ignore what he said for another reason, one that she was almost too embarrassed to admit. She trusted Nemi, she trusted his love. More than anything else, that is what she had felt inside the tree. She wanted to talk to him again soon, have him approve of her.

She did not know what to do.

Filthy from her adventures, Ali jumped in the shower and let the hot water pour over her head. Clean at last, she dressed in her bedroom while she let a frozen dinner heat in the oven. She hated pre-packaged meals but felt too weary to cook.

She threw her dirty clothes in the wash. In two days she had lost a sweater, a coat, a daypack, and ruined one pair of pants. She couldn't keep this up; she would have nothing left to wear. She felt especially bad for Steve. He loved his camera; it had taken him two years to save for it. His parents had even less money than her father did.

The phone rang. It was Cindy.

"Did you hear what happened to Ted Wilson?" she asked.

"Tell me," Ali said.

"A tree fell on him. He's in the hospital, in a coma." Cindy added, "The doctors don't think he's going to make it."

"How could a tree fall on him?" Ali asked.

"I don't know. The logging company is investigating the accident. They have closed down their operation for the time being." Cindy added, "I guess you got what you wanted."

"This is not what I wanted," Ali cried, remembering her arrogant remark to Nemi about teaching the lumberjacks a lesson.

Cindy heard the pain in her voice. "I didn't mean it that way."

Ali was shaking. "Look, I can't talk right now. Let me call you later, okay?"

The second Ali set down the phone, she was out the door. The town had only one hospital, Breakwater Memorial. Her father always said he wouldn't go there unless he was dying, and then only if he wanted to speed up the process.

Ali rode her bike to the hospital. Parking it outside without locking it, she hurried inside and asked directions to intensive care. She figured that was where Ted must be. But when she reached the area she ran into an old and wrinkled nurse with a face as stiff as her starched uniform. She told Ali that only family was allowed inside.

"But I'm a good friend of Ted's," Ali protested.

"Those are the rules," the nurse snapped, sorting a stack of files. "Now, please, I'm very busy."

There was no point in arguing. Ali stepped into the hallway outside intensive care. The interior walls had many windows; she could still see into the nurse's station. A few minutes later, Ted's family came out from one of the back rooms, his wife and Sharla, her not-so-nice pal from school. They were a mess: Sharla was crying and the wife was white as a sheet. They spoke to the nurse a minute, then the woman led them into the hallway. Ali ducked around a corner. The nurse was giving them directions. Ali watched as the three of them walked down the hallway and disappeared.

Ali seized the opportunity, not even sure what she was doing. Dashing back to the nurse's station, she hurried to the room the others had exited. These were not real rooms, however, more like sterile cubicles separated by glass and curtains.

Peeking inside, she saw Ted lying in bed with a dozen wires and tubes attached to his battered body. The sight broke her heart. Two days ago he had been a vital man and now his skin was the color of a corpse. It did not seem fair.

Ali entered the room, stood beside Ted. A monitor above his head beeped with an annoying rhythm. The room stunk of alcohol and pain. Ted's head was heavily bandaged; it looked as if his right arm was broken. Purple bruises covered his eyes and his breathing was ragged. Ali felt sick to her stomach.

"Oh Ted," she whispered, taking his lifeless hand. It was cold; he did not react to her touch. But it was when she touched him that she understood why she had come. Nemi had said she had magical powers. Was it possible—was it too much to ask—that she could heal him?

Gently, Ali put her left hand over his forehead and her right above his heart. She did not know what she was doing; she had never done it before. But she felt it was the right thing to do. She prayed that some kind of magic would flow through her hands and make him wake up.

Ali closed her eyes and tried to concentrate. She thought of how much she loved Ted. Most of all she tried to feel the power that had swept over her that afternoon when she had fought the trolls.

Minutes went by. The monitor kept beeping.

Nothing happened. No power came.

Ali opened her eyes and stared down at Ted. She spoke to him in a soft voice, knowing he could not hear her.

"I'm sorry about what happened to you. I'm sure you were not stupid enough to let a tree fall on you. A troll must have got you, or else it was one of the other elementals. I'm sorry I can't heal you. But seeing you like this, I know now what I have to do. I think that's what Nemi wanted me to see. Tomorrow, I'm going to climb the mountain. I'm going to find the Yanti. Until I get back, I need you to hang on. You're not to die." She lifted his hand and kissed it and her eyes burned with tears. "Don't die, Ted."

She did not know how long she stood there like that. When she looked up, Sharla was at the end of the bed, staring at her. Sharla had a stern face at best—she was a real wrong-right kind of person. There was no in-between for her. If you made a mistake in her book of rules, she let you know it.

"What are you doing here?" she demanded.

Ali put down Ted's hand. "Nothing," she muttered.

"You're hurting my dad!"

"I'm not hurting your dad."

Sharla turned. "Nurse! Nurse! Ali's fooling around with my dad!"

The nurse appeared, and Ted's wife, and it did not go well for Ali. The nurse grabbed her by the arm so hard one would have thought she had been caught trying to drink Ted's blood. Ali was dragged out of the cubicle and into the hallway. She did not put up a fight. In a way, Sharla was right—she had no right to be there.

"Get out of here!" the nurse shouted, shoving her so hard that Ali almost fell on the floor. Yet she did not try to defend herself.

"I'm sorry," was all she said.

Leaving the hospital, Ali collected her bike and rode home. Of course the house was dark and empty. It had been that way forever, it seemed. Right then she missed her mother so much that she felt like curling up in a ball on her bed and crying.

She called Karl instead. She needed to talk to someone, she figured. But why she chose him—over Cindy and Steve—she was not sure. She asked if he could come over. She must have sounded upset.

"I'll be there in ten minutes," Karl said.

He took five minutes. When she answered the door, it was getting dark outside. He wore a blue sweater that matched his eyes. His messy blond hair looked as if it had been combed by the breeze.

She invited him in and made tea—the strong caffeinated stuff. He let her fuss with the drinks without asking any questions. Karl was good that way; he had more patience than the rest of them combined. Finally, though, they were both seated at the kitchen table and she had to talk. How to begin?

"I talked to a tree today," she said. "And I had a rock fight with three trolls."

He sipped his tea. "Tell me what really happened."

"That's what happened."

He saw that she was serious. "Start from the beginning."

She told him everything, in as much detail as she could. He did not simply listen this time, like he had in the morning. He quizzed her at length about the trolls. They were how big? Why did they run away? He asked even more questions about her conversation with the tree. You heard him without hearing him? How were you sure it was not a dream?

She tried her best to explain what it felt like to sit inside the tree: the feeling of silence, of comfort. The only things she didn't tell Karl were her secret name and the name of Nemi. For some reason she felt funny about saying that.

When she was done he sat silent for a long time.

"What do you want to do?" he asked finally.

"Do you believe me?" she asked.

"Yes."

"You said that before and didn't mean it."

"Why do you say that?" he asked.

"Because you would have come with us today if you thought there was a chance we could photograph bigfoot's tracks."

"True."

"So why do you believe me now?"

He hesitated. "Your story is too weird to have been made up. Plus Cindy and Steve saw the tracks. Some type of large creature must have made them. And you and Steve were attacked by something. You didn't just trip and fall. Also, I heard about Ted from my dad. He talked to three of the men who work up there. Even they said it was no accident, that Ted was attacked by some type of creature. That's why the logging company pulled its people out." Karl added, "But they think it was a bear."

"It was a troll," Ali said.

"I'm sure it was. I'm sure it was a troll that knocked Steve out and threw you in the river. Since these things are facts, why shouldn't I believe what you say now?"

Ali appreciated his logical mind. She leaned forward and gave him a hug. "Thank you," she said. "I was so scared you were going to laugh at me."

"Not at all." He added, "I always knew you were special."

She blushed. "What are you talking about? You hardly know me."

"I've watched you this last year. You know how to take care of yourself."

She lowered her head. "I had to learn that. I had no choice."

"Sure you did. You could have sulked and acted like a little girl when you lost your mom. Instead you grew up overnight."

"Thank you." She added, "I think you're pretty special."

Karl allowed a faint smile. "I'm just another kid whose father controls his life. There's nothing special about me. But let's get back to my question. What do you want to do?"

"I want to stay here in my house and pretend none of this is happening. But after seeing Ted tonight I feel like I have no choice but to try and find this Yanti. It has to be closed."

"Did the tree say how you would close it?"

"He said I would know how."

"It's on top of Pete's Peak?"

"At the very top. What's the elevation there?"

"Almost fourteen thousand feet."

"Do I need oxygen to go up that high?"

"No. But you'll get winded easily. Hiking uphill is the worst. Close to the top, you'll take five steps and have to stop and catch your breath."

"I have to do it."

Karl nodded. "I understand. There are other problems. Pete's Peak is so steep it never attracted serious skiing. The mountain was never developed as a tourist attraction. The end of the road only takes you to within twenty miles of the top. That's a long way to hike uphill and through a forest. You won't be able to do it all in one day. That means you're going to have to camp out. Do you have a tent?"

"No."

"A warm sleeping bag?"

"No."

"Do you have a warm jacket?" he asked.

"I did. It washed away in the river."

"You can't go up there without equipment. The top is packed with snow year-round. You're going to need boots and crampons."

"I have boots. What are crampons?"

"They're spikes that go on your boots. They let your feet dig into the snow. You need an ice ax as well."

"Can I do it? Seriously?"

"Yes. But not without help." He added, "I'll help you."

"Are you saying you'll come with me?"

"Yes."

She felt a wave of affection for him. "Thank you. I was going to ask Steve and Cindy. Do you think that's a good idea?"

"The more the better. Call them."

Ali hesitated. "Steve doesn't bother you?"

"No. Do I bother him?"

"He doesn't know you is all."

"He'll get to know me over the next few days. We have a ton of planning to do. Have them come over now."

Ali got on the phone. Steve happened to be at Cindy's house. They agreed to come over right away. While she waited with Karl, she made a pot of coffee for Steve, and put out a plate of cookies. Cindy and Steve were both sugar freaks. She was hoping to soften them up so they would go easy on her.

A vain hope. Her friends arrived, and she had barely begun to explain what had happened after she had climbed out of the river when they jumped on her.

"Is this a joke?" Steve asked.

"I'm not in the mood for this," Cindy said.

"Everything I'm telling you is true. I was attacked by three trolls."

Cindy looked at Karl. "Have you guys been drinking?" she asked.

"Give her a chance to explain," Karl said.

Ali continued. If Karl had not been there, silently supporting her, she doubted she would have continued to the end. She had barely finished describing how she drove off the trolls when Steve started staring into his cup of coffee and Cindy began polishing her nails. It was obvious they didn't believe a word she said.

When she finished there was a long silence.

"Well, say something," Ali said.

"So *you* are a superhero now?" Steve asked.

"Only *you* can save the world?" Cindy asked.

"I'm just telling you what I was told," Ali said.

"By a tree?" Steve said.

"A talking tree," Cindy added.

"It didn't actually talk," Ali said.

"A telepathic tree then," Steve said.

"That none of us has ever seen before," Cindy said.

"You never believed in bigfoot before yesterday and today you saw huge tracks and were attacked by something huge," Ali said.

"But bigfoot is not a troll," Steve said.

"He's not a dwarf or an elf either," Cindy said. "I don't think he's an elemental."

"He's definitely not in the book," Steve said sarcastically.

Ali's cheeks reddened. "Karl believes me," she said in a small voice.

"I do," Karl said. "Because I know Ali and she's not a liar. Because of the tracks you guys saw. Because of your knock on the head, Steve, and Ali's getting thrown in the river. And because of Ted Wilson. Something put him in a coma."

"A tree fell on him," Cindy said.

"He's been a logger all his life," Karl said. "A tree didn't fall on him."

Steve shook his head. "I need proof. If you're so strong, Ali, let me see you snap this chair in two."

"My powers will only come when I need them."

"Convenient," Cindy quipped.

"You need them now," Steve said. "If you're trying to convince us to go with you to the top of the mountain."

"I'm not going up there," Cindy said quickly.

"Don't go then, I don't care," Ali said, annoyed. "Karl and I will go."

"You're going?" Steve asked Karl, a note of jealousy in his voice.

"I think we should all go together. From what Ali says, the forest is a dangerous place now. We'll be stronger together."

"But how can you believe all this?" Cindy asked Karl.

"I just told you why I believe her," Karl said.

"But there are no elementals!" Steve exclaimed.

"Then you explain what happened to Ali and Ted," Karl said. "And to yourself for that matter."

Steve did not like having the tables turned on him. "I can't explain it. But just because I can't doesn't mean our entire view of the universe has to be rewritten." Steve paused and studied Karl. "You're really going with her?"

"Going to start packing tonight," Karl said.

"That's insane," Cindy complained.

Karl shrugged. "What if the world really is in danger?"

"I suppose I could go," Steve said suddenly.

Cindy turned on him. "Now you believe her? Just like that? Or do you have another reason for wanting to go?"

What she was asking, Ali knew, was if Steve was going because he hated the idea of Ali being alone in the mountains with Karl for two days. No one spoke for a moment. Finally Steve shrugged.

"I'm not doing anything the next two days," he said. "Just eating doughnuts and drinking coffee. I may as well get some exercise and help save the world."

"This is crazy!" Cindy said. "We're thirteen years old! Our parents aren't going to let us hike up there in a million years."

"We can't tell them," Karl said. "I have thought about this. We have to convince our parents that we're staying at each other's houses. I have a cell phone—it should work on the mountain. We should be only gone four days. We can check in with our parents if we have to."

"Cindy, you can say you're staying with me," Ali said. "I'll tell my dad I'm at your house. I'm doing that already, anyway. Steve and Karl can say they are staying with each other."

"I don't want to do this," Cindy said. "It's too dangerous. What if more trolls attack?"

"I thought you didn't believe in trolls?" Karl said.

"I'll believe in them if they try to kill me," Cindy said.

"I can handle them." Ali added, "I don't mean to sound like I'm better than you guys. I don't feel that way." She touched Cindy's leg. "I need you, Cindy. You're my best friend. How can I save the world without you?"

Cindy stared at her, then burst out laughing. "Do you know how insane that sounds?"

Ali smiled. "Yeah. But it might be true. That's the scary thing."

"How bad is Ted?" Steve asked.

Ali lost her smile. "Real bad. They say he's going to die."

"He's such a nice man," Steve said.

"There could be lots of Teds if we don't go," Karl said.

They all looked at Cindy. She shook her head.

"This is crazy," she said. "The only way I can go is to not think about how crazy it is." She added, "But I suppose I could get my camping gear out."

"You'll come?" Ail asked.

"Yes."

"Great!" Ali cheered, and gave her a hug.

"Don't I get a hug?" Steve asked.

Ali gave him one as well. "This is exciting! We're going to have fun!"

"If we don't freeze to death," Steve said.

Karl nodded. "We'll all need camping gear. For that reason, I don't think we can leave at dawn. Ali, I know, needs some stuff from the stores. We might have to wait until after nine, after the stores open."

"Do you have money to buy a bunch of stuff?" Steve asked Ali.

"I have money, I can help," Karl said.

Ali looked uncomfortable. "Let me figure what I can get away with. How about you, Steve?"

He shrugged. "I need to dig around in the garage, see what's there. We're going to have to buy food as well."

"How about water?" Cindy asked. "Do we have to carry it? That could be heavy."

"I have a portable water filter," Karl said. "We can get water from the river, purify it. I don't think we have to carry it. Another thing—if we get a late start, let's take a taxi to the end of the road. With heavy packs on our backs, it will be hard to ride our bikes up there."

"That's a great idea. It will save time," Steve said.

"A taxi will be expensive," Cindy said.

"I'll take care of that," Karl said.

"Wait. I want to visit the tree on the way up," Ali said. "You guys should see it."

"Going to the tree will take us out of the way," Karl said. "We would have to tell the taxi to wait for us at the road while we hiked to it. *That* could get expensive."

"I agree," Steve said. "I don't want to hike any farther than I have to."

"But don't you guys want to see it?" Ali asked.

"Sure, if we didn't have a two-day deadline," Karl said.

Steve stood. "Let's discuss it tomorrow. I've got to get home and pack."

Cindy also stood. "I better go as well. But one last question, and I know Ali's going to hit the roof. If the woods are crawling with elementals, shouldn't we bring a gun?"

"No," Ali said. "Absolutely not. Guns are bad."

"They're only bad in the hands of bad people," Cindy said. "I told you, my father owns a gun."

"I can protect us," Ali said.

"Some of us would like to be able to protect ourselves, thank you," Steve said.

"It's illegal for someone our age to carry a gun," Ali said.

"Where is the law against shooting a troll?" Cindy asked.

"We need a rifle is what we need," Steve muttered.

"We're not bringing any guns!" Ali said, exasperated.

Karl raised his hand. "Let's not argue about this now. We have so much else to do. It's another thing we can talk about in the morning."

Their meeting broke up. Ali was left with mixed feelings. She was happy her friends were coming, but feared their motivations were confused. Steve was going so he could hang out with her. Cindy was coming because they had pressured her into it. Only Karl seemed to understand how serious the situation was.

She felt funny accepting his help. She disliked taking charity. Of course she needed a jacket and a sleeping bag. She would freeze without them. In the morning she would go to the bank and

see exactly how much she had in her savings. It was possible
Cindy or Steve could loan her a few things. Her mother had always been against getting in debt to people. She used to say that
when you owed people, you lost a part of your freedom.

Her mother had been so wise.

Ali wished she had asked Nemi about her.

CHAPTER SEVEN

The next morning Ali was up at dawn. She had slept poorly. She had kept looking at the clock. The deadline Nemi had set plagued her. She had checked on the Internet. The moon would be straight overhead at two in the morning the following day—which, technically, would actually be the day after tomorrow. Whatever, they had only forty-two hours left to reach the top of the peak.

She was not the only one up early. She had hardly come out of the bathroom when Karl called. He wanted to take a cab to Tracer and shop for hiking equipment.

"What size are you?" he asked.

"I went through Steve's garage with him last night. We found two old sleeping bags and he had an old jacket in his closet. It's torn but I think I can sew it and make it work."

"You're still going to need crampons and an ice ax. What size are your boots?"

"Five. Cindy is a four and a half. I don't know what kind of boots Steve wears."

"I'll call him," Karl said.

"Is there a sporting goods store in Tracer open at this time?"

"Sort of. It belongs to a friend of my father's. He's going to open it early for me, but he has promised not to tell my dad what we're up to. The guy's cool."

"That's great. What time do you think you'll be back?"

"Not sure. Besides shopping, I have to get Barney Adams to cover my paper route. I have to show him the houses. I can get together with you guys at around ten, I think."

"That late?"

"Sorry. We can't go up there unprepared. Anyway, you and the others buy food and pack. But watch what Steve buys—I don't want to eat doughnuts and drink coffee for the next few days."

"I'll keep an eye on him," Ali said.

Karl said goodbye and Ali examined the sleeping bag she had from Steve's garage. It smelled—she could not imagine sleeping in it unless it was washed. Throwing it in the machine, she took a harder look at the jacket. The coat needed serious work; there was a two-foot rip in the back. Reluctantly, she decided to let Steve and Cindy handle the food buying. She called Cindy to get her going.

"What time is it?" Cindy mumbled into the phone.

"Six."

Cindy groaned. "I'm not cut out for this hero stuff."

"Get up and shower, you'll feel better. Then get over to Steve's house and wake him. Gerson's is open twenty-four hours—go there. Use your own money. I'll give you some later after I go to the bank. Remember, you're buying food for four people for four days. Don't get any junk."

"How about candy bars?"

Ali loved chocolate. "Get protein bars. The tasty kind."

"How about potato chips?"

"I don't know."

"Ice cream?"

"Cindy! We're not carrying a refrigerator on our backs. Get food that doesn't need to be cooked."

"We're not going to make any fires?" Cindy asked.

"No. We don't want to draw any attention to ourselves."

They exchanged goodbyes. Ali set to work on her jacket. Steve had got it from his dad, who had got it from his dad. It looked like a World War Two jacket. The faded material smelled like history.

She figured she had two hours. Her mother had taught her to sew. She would shorten the sleeves, she decided, take in the shoulders, repair the tear. Getting out the sewing machine, she hoped Cindy was able to wake Steve. Last night, searching in his garage with him, he had begun to express doubts about what they were doing. The truth was neither of her friends believed her.

Ali worked non-stop until eight, when she got a frantic call from Cindy. "You won't believe what just happened to Steve and me!" she said.

"What?"

"We got robbed! Now we have no money to buy groceries!"

"Who robbed you? Wait a second, did you bump into a weird short guy with an Irish accent?"

"Yeah! How do you know him?"

"Same way you do," Ali muttered.

"He took our watches! My purse and Steve's wallet!"

"You know Mr. Fields's pawnshop? It's on Hadley. Meet me there in five minutes."

"Why are we going to a pawnshop?" Cindy complained.

"Trust me, he'll be there."

Ali left the house and got on her bike. Breakwater was so small—everything was five minutes away. She was not sure where Cindy had called from, but she reached the pawnshop before her friends. Paddy O'Connell was coming out the front door when she pulled up. He nodded politely to her as she came up the steps.

"Top of the morning to you, Missy," he said.

"Hello Paddy." Ali felt strong, *real* strong—she guessed this must be a crisis. Grabbing Paddy by the arm, she pulled him close. "You just robbed my friends! You robbed me the other day!"

Paddy tried to shake loose, was shocked when he felt how strong she was. "My pardon, Missy, but you are hurting my arm."

"I'm going to break your arm if you don't give my friends back what you stole!"

He stared up at her with his bright green-gold eyes and his wide mouth trembled. He had his lousy makeup on again, she saw. "Excuse me, Missy, but I think you have mistaken me for another. I'm not a thief, I assure you, only a stranger to these parts."

Ali tightened her grip. "Don't lie to me!"

Paddy gasped in pain. "Surely we can talk about this, Missy? If you would only let go of . . ."

She shook him; his hat almost came off. "Did you steal from them or not? Tell me the truth or you will be missing an arm!"

"Well . . . no, yes, sort of. You're hurting me!"

"You're a thief! That's what you are!"

He was indignant. "I'm not a thief!"

"Then what are you?" She pulled him closer. She could feel his breath on her face, and he sure must have been able to feel hers. His breath was not unpleasant, however, not like the trolls.

It smelled like shamrocks.

Paddy did not answer, only looked more miserable. She must have really been hurting him, she realized, and softened her grip. A bead of sweat broke on his forehead. It rolled over the side of his nose, onto his cheek, and as it did so it washed away a portion of his makeup. Ali was shocked to see he had green skin.

"You're a leprechaun!" she gasped, letting go of him and taking a step back. Paddy quickly rubbed his face, trying to cover up the green blemish.

"A leprechaun, Missy? There are no leprechauns. This is a world of men and women, boys and girls. What nonsense are you saying?"

She pointed at him. "You came through the Yanti! You're from the elemental kingdom!"

He looked shocked. "You know of the Yanti?" he whispered. "Who told you?"

"It doesn't matter. You're a leprechaun, admit it."

Paddy glanced down at his sore arm. "Well, kind of, yes. But it's no business of yours what I am. When I met you, I didn't ask what you were."

"But you stole my money. Why? Don't you have a pot of gold lying around somewhere?"

Paddy was insulted. "If I had a pot of gold, I wouldn't be here. I only came here to seek my fortune. I don't see the crime in that."

"Wherever you're from, you must know it's a crime to steal. In our dimension we have jails for people . . . for creatures like you."

Paddy looked positively terrified at the mention of the word jail. "But I cannot go there! I cannot be locked up! You do not lock up leprechauns! I will die if you put me in jail!"

"Then you have to stop stealing or that's where you will end up."

He lowered his head. "I hear you, Missy. Paddy will never steal again. Now if you will just let me get about my business . . ."

She blocked his way. "You're such a liar, you'll say anything. What do you need so much money for?"

He hesitated. "To eat. To buy gold. What else?"

He no longer had his pillowcase with him but there was a small brown bag tied to his thick black belt. She pointed at it. "Give me that," she said.

He backed up and covered the bag with his hands. "No, Missy."

She grabbed his arm again, feeling quicker as well as stronger. The sensation of power was delicious. Yet she was not in a mood to waste time with Paddy. Reaching down, she snapped the bag free; it crunched like a bag full of change in her fingers, and she did not need to open it to know it was stuffed with gold coins. Paddy looked as if he would cry.

"That's me gold!" he whimpered.

"I'm going to keep your gold for the time being." A wild idea came to her. She added, "I'll give it back to you after you help me."

"No!" he squealed, trying to grab it back. But she held it out of reach. He was pretty short and not much of a leaper. His black boots did not help matters; they looked awfully tight. Then again, maybe leprechauns had small feet.

"You don't get your gold back until you do what I ask."

Paddy looked so sad one would have thought he had just been told he was going to be executed. "What do you want?" he asked quietly.

Before she could reply, Cindy and Steve appeared. They immediately started yelling at Paddy about how he had stole their money. Ali had to step in front of him for his protection. She was not afraid of him running, though. Not as long as she held the gold. She took a minute to calm her friends.

"He has the money and he's going to give it back," Ali said. "Aren't you, Paddy?"

He frowned. "When I get me gold back."

"No," Ali said firmly. "You give them the money now. Plus Steve's wallet and Cindy's purse, and their watches."

Paddy glanced at the pawnshop. "Paddy already sold their stuff, Missy."

"Then you unsell it," Ali snapped.

"You took me gold!" he complained.

"His gold?" Cindy said.

"Who is this guy?" Steve asked.

"He's not a guy, he's a leprechaun," Ali said.

Cindy and Steve both went to laugh but then they looked a little closer at Paddy. Cindy reached out to wipe the makeup off his face. Paddy growled and brushed her hand away.

"Paddy didn't give you permission to touch, lassie," he said.

"Trust me, under all that makeup, he has green skin," Ali said. "I think our little friend here is the first of the elementals to reach Breakwater. Isn't that right, Paddy?"

The leprechaun sulked. "Paddy doesn't have to answer your questions."

"Yes, you do," Ali said. "You remember how strong I am? You don't behave and you go to jail."

Paddy trembled visibly. Ali did not trust him, but it was clear he was being honest when he said his kind could not be locked up. There had been real terror in his face when she had grabbed him.

"Paddy is the only one here," he said.

"The only leprechaun or the only elemental?" Ali asked.

"The only one I know of," he said evasively.

"Okay." She pointed toward the pawnshop door. "Go get their things back."

He turned and opened the door. "If Paddy can, he will."

"And I want the cash," Ali called after him. When he was inside with Mr. Fields, she turned to the others. "Do you believe me now?"

"He could just be a midget," Steve said cautiously.

"He's the weirdest looking midget I ever saw," Cindy remarked.

"You guys are impossible," Ali said. "But I don't care about that right now. I want to make a change in plans. I want to bring Paddy with us."

"Are you crazy?" Steve asked.

"He'll steal us blind the first chance he gets!" Cindy said.

"I think I can keep him under control. He's already afraid of me. But think, he came out of the Yanti. He must know where it is, what it looks like, maybe even how it operates."

"But you know it's at the top of the mountain," Steve said. "The tree told you."

"A reliable source," Cindy muttered.

"It's not that," Ali said. "He must know about the various elementals, and we're about to head into a forest filled with them. He might be able to give us information that could save our lives."

"You've taken his gold," Steve said. "You've threatened him with prison. Why should he save your life? It's more likely that he'll lead the elementals to you."

"I'm willing to take that chance," Ali said. "I think the advantages outweigh the disadvantages."

"I love all these decisions you're making for us," Cindy said. "And only yesterday you were my friend."

The comment hurt Ali. Was there truth in it? It was their lives she was risking as well as her own. They should have a say in her plans.

"I'm sorry," she said. "We can vote on it. I've given you my reasons for taking him. But if you think it's too dangerous, say so."

"I think it's too dangerous," Steve said.

Cindy considered. "He might be able to tell us stuff we don't know."

"He might lie to us and mislead us," Steve said.

Cindy smiled. "He's kind of cute, though."

Steve groaned. "Now she has a crush on a leprechaun."

"I don't have a crush on him! He's different is all." Cindy paused. "I say bring him."

"Brave choice," Ali said.

Steve frowned. "What if he doesn't want to come?"

"I'll make him," Ali said simply.

It turned out to be far from simple. Paddy returned with Steve and Cindy's things. He even forked over the cash he had picked from their pockets. Then he wanted his gold back—he demanded it. Perhaps he was not as afraid of her as she thought.

"It doesn't belong to you," he said. "If you keep it you will be the thief, Missy, not Paddy."

"I will return it to you after you do me a small favor," Ali said.

He was suspicious. "A favor?"

"You are to come with my friends and me to the top of the mountain. You're to take us to the Yanti. Then you can have your gold back."

Paddy's eyes bugged out of his head. He shook his head violently. "You can't go up there! A nice girl like you, Missy! Lord Vak's coming soon—he brings many of his people! They'll slice you to pieces!"

Ali stopped. "Who's Lord Vak?"

"See! You know nothing of what you speak, Missy. You don't even know who Lord Vak is. No, Paddy will not go up there. You can keep me gold."

His words shook Ali. Again, she thought to threaten him with prison. Yet Steve had made a good point. Threats were a lousy way to start a working relationship. Also, she remembered something Nemi had told her.

"Say I get to this Yanti in the next two days. When I close it, won't the elementals who are already here in our dimension be trapped?"

"No. They will shift back into their own dimension. The forest will be free of them . . . Unless you want some to stay."

"You have been here only a few days, Paddy," she said. "But already you've made a bag of gold for yourself. I imagine leprechauns are pretty industrious. In our dimension we would call you guys self-starters. But I think it'll be harder for you to make money here if there are thousands of leprechauns. The competition will be terrible. Do you see what I mean?"

His bushy eyebrows frowned. "Not sure, Missy."

Ali knelt so she could talk to him face to face. "I'm going to close the Yanti with or without your help. But when I do I can choose which elementals will remain in this dimension. If you help me, I'll make sure you're the only leprechaun left on this side."

Her proposal interested him. He put a hand to his chin. "What if you don't make it up there? What if Lord Vak catches Paddy helping you and cuts off me toes?"

"He won't catch me. I have powers."

Paddy frowned. "Are you a fairy?"

"I'm a human being. But I fought three trolls yesterday and defeated them easily."

He was thoughtful. "Paddy heard a bit about that. But Lord Vak is smarter than trolls, and more powerful. Will your powers work on him?"

"Yes," Ali said.

"I don't know about . . ." Cindy began.

"Shh!" Ali snapped, before turning back to Paddy. "Think how much money you'll make as the only leprechaun in the United States? Why, you might end up with your own talk show."

"Shows talk?"

"Never mind. You'll get rich no matter what you do." She suddenly handed him his bag of gold. "Take this back as a sign of good faith."

His face brightened. He weighed the gold in his hands, perhaps to see if she had stolen any while he was in the store. He nodded his huge head.

"Paddy will go with you," he said. "But you must give your word that Paddy will be the only leprechaun left on this side when you close the Yanti."

"Agreed. You must give me your word you will do all you can to help us reach the Yanti safely."

"Agreed." He reached in his pocket and drew forth a silver flask. "Let us drink to our bargain."

Ali wrinkled her forehead at the flask. "What's in that?"

He took a gulp and sighed with pleasure. "Whiskey." He offered her the flask. "Drink, and the deal will be sealed."

"You have my drink for me."

" 'Tis not the custom of a leprechaun to drink for another."

"I'm not a leprechaun. You can have my drink."

He paused and gave her an unusual look. "Very well," he said, having another gulp. Then he closed the top and put the flask back in his pocket. He held out his hand. "Paddy will be needing a few dollars for supplies."

"We're buying the food," Steve said. "We'll buy enough for all of us."

He shook his head. "Paddy prefers to buy his own things. Be needing whiskey for me stomach and tobacco for me pipe."

"The Surgeon General has warned that smoking is harmful to your health," Cindy said. "And excess alcohol can lead to cirrhosis of the liver and a host of other medical problems."

"Cindy," Ali said patiently. "He's a leprechaun. Tobacco and alcohol are probably good for him."

" 'Tis true," he said, his hand out. "Can't travel without drink and smoke. A few dollars please, don't be stingy."

Ali nodded to Steve. "Give him forty. I'll pay you back after I go to the bank."

"Sixty," Paddy said quickly.

"Forty," Ali replied firmly. "You're to meet us back here in one hour. If you're not here on time, our deal is off. I still don't trust you, Paddy. None of us do. You will have to earn that trust. Do you understand?"

He saw that she was serious. "Aye, Paddy hears you, Missy."

Steve gave him the money and he walked off in the direction of the liquor store. Cindy nodded her approval. "You handled him well," she said.

"I agree," Steve said. "Except at the end. I think it was a mistake to let him out of our sight before we take off."

"I did that on purpose," Ali said. "If we can't trust him in town, we won't be able to trust him up on the mountain. But if he's back here when I told him to be here, then at least he has shown good faith."

"How do we know what good faith is to a leprechaun?" Steve asked.

CHAPTER EIGHT

The rest of their preparations went well—except, in Ali's opinion, they took too long. At the market they shopped carefully. Ali insisted they stock up on nuts and granola, two light items that were easy to eat on the run. They also bought two loaves of bread, a pound of dried fruit, and several cans of tuna. Steve insisted they get a few giant Hershey bars, and Ali was not hard to convince. Quick energy, Steve called the candy. But Ali drew the line at potato chips, which annoyed Cindy.

"The bags are mostly air. They'll take up too much room in our packs."

"I'm willing to carry them," Cindy said.

"But then you wouldn't have room for more important items," Ali said.

Cindy sighed. "I feel like I'm in the army."

"We'll probably all lose some weight on this trip," Steve said, already munching on a chocolate bar.

"I doubt it," Ali and Cindy said at the same time.

Paddy was waiting for them outside the pawnshop when they walked up with their groceries. He had a couple of bags of his own. Ali insisted on looking inside. Four quart bottles of whiskey, three bags of tobacco, and two pounds of beef jerky. Ali thought his last item was a wise choice and told him so. She wished they had bought some.

"Aye, Missy," he said. "You don't want to be doing any cooking in them woods. Lord Vak and his people can spot a fire miles away."

"Can't we at least make coffee in the morning?" Steve asked.

Paddy slapped Steve on the leg. He seemed to be getting into the idea of going on an adventure with a bunch of humans. "Laddie, you don't need coffee when you have whiskey!" he said.

"But we don't drink," Cindy said.

Paddy frowned. "You don't drink? You have to drink to live."

"We're kids," Ali explained. "In our dimension no one is supposed to drink alcohol until they're an adult. Even then it is considered a bad habit. All we drink is water and soda, mostly soda."

Paddy was dumbfounded. " 'Tis a strange land."

"Tell us more about Lord Vak," Steve said.

Paddy glanced around and lowered his voice. "Let us speak of him when we're sure we're alone," he said.

Grocery bags in hand, they headed for Ali's house, with Ali pushing her bike. The weather was mixed—clouds came and went, as did the sun. She hoped it did not rain on them during the night. They did not have a tent. She wondered what Karl was up to, if he had completed his tasks.

Along the way Ali asked the leprechaun if he was comfortable in his black boots.

"Aye, Missy," he said. "Paddy's worn them all me life."

"They haven't worn out?" she asked.

He blinked; he did that when he was confused. "What does that mean?"

Ali wondered if anything ever wore out in the elemental kingdom.

"Nothing," she said.

Ali stopped at her bank on the way home. She had three hundred and twenty dollars in her savings. She had earned the bulk of it baby-sitting. Withdrawing the lot, she gave half to Steve for the groceries. He was obviously embarrassed to accept the money but took it anyway.

Karl was not at Ali's house but he had left a message. He was still showing Barney Adams his paper route, but said he would be done by ten-thirty. He told her to be ready. He was not delaying them, Ali figured. They still had to arrange the food in their packs.

The backpack Steve had found for Ali was much larger than her daypack. When it was full, and on her back, she had a hard time walking. Steve adjusted the strap around her waist.

"How does it feel?" he asked.

"Heavy. I don't like it."

"It feels heavy because it is heavy. Backpacks are that way, when they're full." He added, "But I can take more of the food if you want."

"No," Ali said. "We each carry our fair share."

"I am in the army," Cindy groaned, struggling with her own backpack.

Karl appeared shortly afterward. He took one look at Paddy, doing his nails on the couch, and pulled Ali aside. To make matters worse Paddy had washed off his facial makeup. As green as a dollar bill, he gave Karl a lot to take in at once.

"Who's that?" he asked. "Or should I say, *what* is that?"

"That's Paddy. He's going with us."

Karl glanced back at the leprechaun. Still on the couch, Paddy was painting his toenails green. His feet were as hairy as his arms. Ali was not looking forward to seeing the rest of him.

"Is he a leprechaun?" Karl asked.

"Yes."

"How did you meet him?"

Ali gave him the short version. "I think we can trust him," she said in conclusion.

"But everything you just told me says we can't trust him," Karl said. She had never seen him annoyed before. Once again, she glanced at Paddy. He had his hairy foot almost into his mouth, blowing on the nail polish to dry it.

"He's a crook, I know," she said. "But I don't sense any cruelty in him."

"You don't know that for sure. In the legends leprechauns are always tricksters. You've already told me what a liar he is."

"All these stories about leprechauns and other elementals— how do we know any of them are accurate?"

"Most myths are based on some fact. I believe the books. Let's leave the guy behind. I'm sure Steve doesn't want to bring him."

"I hate to go into the woods without any idea what we're going to face. Paddy can teach us a lot. That's another reason I want to visit the tree. I have questions to ask."

"The tree will take us more than two hours out of our way."

"I think the delay will be worth it."

"I've hiked these mountains with my father. The going gets tougher the closer you get to the top. Remember the snow."

"Did you ever go all the way to the top?" Ali asked.

"Close. But we turned back. That tells you how hard it is. We've already got a late start. Ali, we need every hour we have left."

His words made sense. Time was crucial, and to return to the tree would be like backtracking. Yet a part of her felt uncomfortable leaving without checking in with Nemi.

"Let me think about it some more," she said.

It was eleven before they were ready to leave. Karl had bought four pup tents in Tracer—cheap plastic things that could hold one person. They were light and they would keep the rain off. Ali insisted on paying him for the tents and the crampons he had picked up. He refused the money.

"I charged them on my dad's card," he said. They were alone in the living room for the moment. Cindy and Steve were out on the street, helping load the taxi. Paddy was in the bathroom. She just hoped the leprechaun knew what toilet paper was for. He had already showered and asked to borrow her hair dryer. Of course he was probably going to steal it after he was through with it.

"But I have enough. I want to pay," she told Karl.

"Let's talk about it when we get back."

"Is Barney okay with the paper route?" she asked.

"You know him. He has the memory of a pumpkin. He might miss a few houses. It's not the end of the world."

"Not yet," she added.

He nodded gravely. "I don't think the others know how serious this trip is."

"They will if Lord Vak attacks."

"Who's he?" Karl asked.

"Paddy mentioned him. I don't know who he is but he sounds nasty." She paused, troubled. "He sounds familiar, too."

"What do you mean?"

"Like I've heard his name before."

"Where?"

"I don't know." She added quietly, "Maybe before I was born."

Karl stared at her. She hoped she was not freaking him out.

The taxi driver's name was Frank. He was originally from New York. He looked like he had been scraped off skid row with a greasy spoon. Besides not having shaved in days, his clothes were dirty; they could have been plucked from a Dumpster. Ali supposed they would look no better after a few days on the mountain.

Frank seemed to know how to mind his own business. One look at Paddy and he didn't bat an eye. Steve told him that Paddy was from Los Angeles—like that explained why he was three feet tall and green.

"Paddy's been in a cult," Steve went on, motioning for the leprechaun to keep his mouth shut. "We just got him out. We're deprogramming him—he's doing a lot better."

Frank burped and got behind the taxi wheel. "Been to Los Angeles. Strange place," he said, nodding.

Karl sat up front with Frank. The rest of them were in the back—a tight fit with their backpacks, not to mention the leprechaun. Paddy practically sat on Ali's lap. He gazed out the window as they started up the mountain. She wondered if he had ever been in a car before. For that matter, she wondered where he had learned to speak English. Could elementals hear human beings from their own dimension? Could they see them? There was so much she didn't know.

Again, she smelled Paddy's breath—Ireland in the summer, the odor as fresh as a field of grass and flowers. For all his lies and tricks, there was something innocent about the leprechaun. She studied his green and gold eyes as the trees flew by. He could have been a small child seeing a forest for the first time; he appeared hypnotized.

Maybe it was her imagination, though. Karl's warning came back to haunt her. She would have to keep an eye on the leprechaun.

They came to the roadblock, parked, and got out and stretched. Karl moved the barrier aside. The others were watching Ali, waiting for her to push the talking tree issue. With the taxi driver out of earshot in the cab, Steve made his feelings clear.

"I'm not hiking to the tree," Steve said. "Karl's right, we'll lose too much time. Now that we've met Paddy, we believe you about the invading elementals."

"Yeah," Cindy said.

"You didn't believe me before?" Ali asked.

"No," Cindy and Steve said at the same time.

Ali saw she could not push the issue. "Okay. We'll keep going," she said.

They got back in the taxi and continued up the mountain. Eventually they reached the logging site, found it empty. Ali had half expected to see the three trolls playing with the lumberjacks' equipment. She wondered if the beasts would run the next time they saw her. The higher they drove, the less powerful she felt.

At the logging site she made them stop, however. From that part of the mountain she figured she could see Nemi's tree. Getting out of the taxi with a pair of binoculars, she stepped to the edge of the road and focused in the direction of the meadow where she had taken her long nap. Impatient, the others gathered at her back.

"What are you looking for?" Karl asked.

"Reassurance," she whispered.

She did not get it.

In the spot where she remembered finding the tree, she saw what looked like a large pile of ash. It was gray and flaky, stacked like a ghostly pyramid that could be destroyed by a gust of wind.

"Oh no," she gasped. Her heart sank when she saw the ruin; she felt tears coming. It had meant so much to her to find Nemi. And now he was gone.

"What is it?" Steve demanded.

From such a distance, it was impossible to be sure, but it did not look as if any other tree in the same area had been touched by the fire.

"The tree—it's been burned down," she said, handing the binoculars to Steve. She pointed out where he should search. He found the pile of ash, but was unsure what he was looking at.

"That could be ash," he said, giving the binoculars to Karl.

"What else could it be?" Ali asked.

Steve frowned. "I'm not sure."

"It sure looks like ash to me," Karl said, studying the area through the binoculars. "I think I see burned bark."

"Let me see!" Cindy demanded.

Karl handed Cindy the binoculars, spoke to Ali. "What do you think happened?"

"I can't imagine," Ali said.

Cindy got excited. "Maybe this is a case of spontaneous human combustion. You know, when people suddenly catch fire for no reason and burn to cinders?"

"Cindy," Steve said.

"What?"

"This cannot be a case of spontaneous human combustion."

"Why not?"

"This was a tree, Cindy. It was not a human being."

"I know that! But what if there was another person inside the tree, talking to it, and he or she caught fire, and burned the tree down?"

No one wanted to answer that one.

Karl was thoughtful. "It's odd how the trees right next to it look fine. Maybe it's like Ali said—it was no ordinary tree. It probably did not burn down the same way another tree would."

Ali wiped her eyes. She did not want them to see how badly she was shaken. "Why did it burn down at all?" she asked.

"If it was a magical tree," Steve suggested, "if there are such things—then maybe this was its way of going elsewhere."

"Where?" Cindy asked.

"Beats me," Steve said.

"Do you think someone intentionally burned it down?" Karl asked Ali.

"I guess the trolls could have got it. Or other elementals—they might have known about it, seen it as an enemy. But . . ."

"What?" Karl asked.

Ali shook her head. "I thought it would have been able to protect itself. It was so wise."

"A tree can't do much to protect itself," Steve said. "It can only stand there."

"Or it can fall on you and kill you," Cindy said.

Ali was annoyed. "A tree didn't fall on Ted and he's not going to die."

"Okay, don't get mad," Cindy said. "I was just talking."

Karl put his hand on Ali's shoulder. "There's nothing we can do here," he said. "We'd better keep going. Whoever was in the tree—I'm sure he would want you to go ahead with your mission."

Ali felt terribly alone. Nemi had swept into her life like a dream, told her she was fit for brave deeds and magical acts. Now that he was gone would the magic leave her as well?

They got back in the cab, drove farther up the road. The others chatted easily but Ali sat silent, lost in thought. Her resolve to reach the Yanti was not as strong as it had been a few minutes ago. She had wanted to close the Yanti to make Nemi proud of her, she realized. Now there would be no pat on the back at the end of the job; it made her sad. At the same time she realized how childish she was being. Closing the Yanti could save the whole world. She had to push her small desires aside, do the job and shut up.

She felt she had done little else since her mother had died.

They came to the end of the road, got out. Unpacking took only a few minutes. Karl tried to give Frank a tip, but the guy waved away the extra cash.

"That's okay, Karl," he said. "The hundred on the meter is enough."

That sounded like a lot to Ali.

Frank left. As the taxi went out of sight, and the noise of its engine faded in the distance, the silence of the forest deepened. At last, she thought, they were cut off from civilization. They had cell phones, true, but it was not as if they could call anyone if they were attacked.

Finally, their adventure was about to begin.

CHAPTER NINE

A path led away from the end of the road, and there was an out-house. They all used the latter, Paddy included. He seemed to like human toilets. A comfort to the bum, he called them.

Karl had remembered to bring a map. Before they left the road, he spread it out for them to study, pointing out landmarks.

"It's just after twelve," he said. "It'll be light till nine. We have nine hours to hike. Before then I want to reach this spot, it's called Overhang. It's a great place to camp. The cliff sweeps overhead—it'll keep the rain off us if the clouds are pouring." He added, "And it's an easy place to defend."

"If we're attacked, you mean?" Steve asked him.

"Yes."

"But we have nothing to defend ourselves with," Steve complained.

Karl and Cindy exchanged a look. Ali caught it.

"What?" she asked.

"Nothing," Cindy said.

Karl pointed to a line on the map. "This path is called Treeline.

It starts twenty feet behind us. It follows the ridge above the Mercer River. We should stay on it for today."

"If there are elementals in these woods," Ali said. "They might be on the path. Maybe we should avoid it."

Karl shook his head. "We can't. We'll lose too much time trying to cut through the trees. They're thick around here. We have to risk the path."

"How far is Overhang?" Steve asked.

"Twelve miles from where we stand," Karl said. "It's at an elevation increase of four thousand feet. Right now we're more than a mile above sea level. The higher we go, the harder it will get to breathe. Twelve miles in nine hours doesn't sound like a lot but we'll be lucky to reach Overhang by nightfall."

"It sounds like a lot to me," Steve said.

"'Tis a nice place to sleep," Paddy remarked.

"You were there?" Ali asked.

"Yes." Paddy added quickly, "Maybe."

"Paddy," Ali said. "You have to be straight with us. We're partners on this adventure. Haven't you ever had a partner before?"

"Aye. Clyde McDogal. We were partners two years, until he stole me gold."

"He was the only partner you ever had?" Ali asked.

"Aye. A born thief. Gone my own way since Clyde."

"A bad role model," Cindy muttered.

"Won't we have to break for lunch?" Steve asked Karl.

"We can take short breaks," Karl said. "But nothing more than a few minutes." He gestured to the trailhead behind them. "We better get started."

They lifted their packs onto their backs. Karl gave Ali a hand. Once again she found the weight difficult. Karl knew more about packs than Steve. After he adjusted her shoulder straps, she at least felt balanced. Paddy, for his part, carried his whiskey and tobacco in two brown paper bags. She suspected he could out-hike any of them.

They said goodbye to the road. The first part of the trail was a delight. The dense trees formed a tunnel, twenty feet overhead, the branches wrapped together like old friends. An occasional drop of water, from the drizzle and the dew, splashed their faces. The path was dark—light barely filtered down from the sky—but the dim added to its mystery. The ground rose slowly; they did not have to fight for breath.

The others walked ahead. Ali, thinking to save her energy, stayed in the rear with Paddy. His paper bags had handles but she feared they would wear out. She told him as much.

"Paddy can always put the bottles in me pockets," he said.

"Your pockets are that large?"

He patted his coat. "Aye. All leprechauns have large pockets."

"How many leprechauns came through the Yanti with you?"

"Two others, Missy."

"What are their names?"

"Mickey and Frankie."

"Friends?"

"Distant relatives, Paddy would say. Not the best of friends."

"Have you seen them since you got to town?"

"No."

"Do you think they're in town?"

"Don't know and don't care."

"Do you mind answering my questions?"

"You're the boss. Have to listen to the boss."

"Why do you call me the boss?"

"It is what you are. You have the power."

"Did I hurt your arm when I grabbed you this morning?"

"Aye. A bit stiff it is."

"I'm sorry. I won't hurt you again."

"Matters not."

"What does matter to you, Paddy? Besides gold and food?"

He glanced up at her, his eyes bright beneath his bushy eyebrows. "Humans do not know leprechauns. Leprechauns do not know humans. It is that way, Missy, you cannot change it, even with all your questions."

"But I want to understand you."

"Why?"

"Because we're traveling together. We should get to know each other."

"Why?"

She wanted to know him better to see if she could trust him.

But she did not want to say that.

She noticed something odd about their conversation. Since entering the woods, Paddy had begun to speak in shorter sentences, more abruptly. He was not the smooth-talking salesman that had first approached her outside the supermarket. She suspected it had something to do with him reentering his natural habitat. After all, leprechauns were supposed to live in the woods, not the city.

"Tell me about Lord Vak. Who is he?" she asked.

"King of the elves. A powerful warrior."

"I thought elves were sweet little creatures who just liked to play in the woods?"

"They are friendly until you make them mad. Then they can be nasty." Paddy added, "They're not so little."

"Are they bigger than you?"

"Yes. Most are."

"Bigger than me?"

"Some."

"They carry weapons?"

"Aye. Bows and arrows. Sharp knives. When they're angry they don't mind killing." He added, "They're angry now."

"At humans?"

"Aye. Lord Vak has vowed to wipe them out."

"Why? I mean, why now? Humans have been polluting the Earth for a hundred years."

"Don't know, Missy. Leprechauns try to stay out of such business."

"Does Lord Vak control the Yanti?"

"Aye. Him and Lord Balar."

"Who is Lord Balar?"

"King of the dwarves. Grumpy old beard."

"I thought dwarves and elves were usually enemies?" The comment was kind of silly, she realized a second after she said it. The various fantasy books she had read could not be taken literally. Yet Paddy nodded at her question.

"Sometimes they are enemies, sometimes they are friends. But they have agreed to fight together against the humans."

"But you don't know what's stirred them up?"

"No, Missy. Never spoken to them."

"Who let you go through the Yanti?"

Paddy hesitated. "Lord Balar and his people."

"Why did they send you?"

Paddy lowered his head. "Don't know, Missy."

"Paddy?"

"Aye?"

"You're lying again."

His head jerked up. "No, Missy. Paddy does not know."

"Did they want you to report back in?" she asked.

Paddy chewed on his lower lip, not answering, his head still down.

Ali could see he was ready to clam up. She changed the subject. "Have Lord Vak and Lord Balar ever fought in the past?" she asked.

"Many times. There was the Tree War and, a hundred years before that, the Rock War."

"Were you alive during these wars?"

"Aye. Paddy has been alive a long time."

"How long? How old are you?"

"Do not know, Missy. Do not count the years."

"What was the Tree War over?"

"The dwarves ran out of coal. They needed wood for their furnaces. That is what they said. They began to cut down trees in the elves' forest. The elves fought back."

"Who won the war?"

"The elves. Lord Vak drove the dwarves from the woods. He killed Lord Balar's son, Makle. Cut off his head."

"That must have angered Lord Balar?"

"He was already angry. He just got more angry. But the elves won—what could he do? He lost Makle and half his kingdom."

"Did he ever find more coal?"

"After a time."

"What happened in the Rock War?"

"The elves hired the dwarves to help them build castles in their woods. The dwarves worked many years, raised many stone buildings."

"Then what happened?" Ali asked.

"They wanted to live in them. They wouldn't leave. Lord Vak drove some out, but not all. In that war he almost lost his son, Jira. But later, in the Tree War, Lord Vak won back all that the elves had lost." Paddy added, "Lord Vak is clever."

"Is Lord Vak close to Jira?"

Paddy gave her a look. "He was."

"Was?" she asked. "I thought you said he *almost* died?"

Paddy continued to stare. "Jira died later."

"How?"

Paddy shook his head. "Lord Vak never got over losing Jira."

He had not answered her question, but she decided to let it pass.

"Did the leprechauns fight in these wars?" she asked.

"Tried not to. Did not want to get involved."

"Did the fairies fight in these wars?"

"No."

"Do the fairies want to wipe out humanity?"

Paddy gave her another strange look. "Don't think so. Except for the dark fairies. They would hurt all people if they could."

"Who are the dark fairies?"

Paddy shuddered. "Best we don't speak of them."

"But . . ."

Paddy raised his hand, made a sign as if to ward off evil.

"We do not speak of them," he repeated.

"Okay." His reaction made her uneasy. Once again, it was as if she remembered part of the history he related. Certainly the names Lord Vak and Lord Balar sounded familiar. If only she could ask Nemi these questions!

Paddy's mention of the dark fairies reminded her of her dream two nights ago: the shadow growing on the horizon; that strange word—*Shaktra*. She wanted to ask Paddy about the latter but feared he would get spooked again. Maybe later she could bring it up.

"Tell me about the good fairies," she said. "Are they on humanity's side in this upcoming war?"

"Fairies do not take sides. They are like leprechauns."

"Are they really like leprechauns?"

He stuttered. "Well, they are the same and they are not the same, if you see what Paddy is saying. A few fairies have great powers, more than any of the other elementals." He nodded to himself. "Those are the ones you have to watch out for."

"Do fairies and leprechauns get along?"

"After a fashion. Best to keep a distance from fairies, though, that's what my pa used to say. Never know what a fairy will do if it's in the mood."

"Have any fairies come through the Yanti?"

"Don't know."

"How many trolls have come so far?"

"Don't know. Heard about the three who attacked you."

"Who told you?"

He froze. "Heard is all."

"Paddy?"

"Don't remember! It's not important!"

He was lying, it probably was important. What did she expect? He had been an elemental all his life. Why should he suddenly side with humans now that war was coming? Karl might be right, he could betray them all.

"Paddy?" she said.

"Aye?"

"I talked you into coming with us. You might feel like I forced you. But if you want to leave us now, you have my permission."

He looked distressed. "Missy not like Paddy anymore?"

"I just want you to have the freedom to stay or go. That's all."

He was sad. "Paddy's not welcome anymore. Said the wrong things." He turned around, took a step back down the path. "Go now, Missy. Sorry."

She stopped him. The others had pulled farther ahead. The two of them were alone. The trees hung low where they stood. If she stood on her tiptoes, she could have touched the branches. A drop rolled off the leaf of a vine, touched her face. Another fell on Paddy's cheek. Or was that a tear? She did not know if leprechauns cried.

"No, I'm the one who's sorry," she said. "I didn't mean to hurt your feelings. It's just that what we're doing is important. I have to get to the Yanti and close it before lots of people, on both sides, are killed. Do you understand?"

"Aye. Paddy understands." He stared up at her with his big colored eyes and blinked. In that moment he could have been a huge animated doll, something she had been given as a present at Christmas. That was part of her problem, she realized. She did not see him as a person yet. Or maybe he was right and humans simply could not understand leprechauns.

Yet she heard sincerity in his voice when he spoke next.

"Paddy will not hurt Missy," he said.

Ali smiled and leaned over and gave him a hug. "I believe you, Paddy."

She meant it, at least at the moment.

The path led out of the green tunnel and into the open forest. The ground began to climb steeply. Ali heard Mercer River on their left, the same river the trolls had thrown her into. It was below them in a deep gorge, out of sight behind rocks and trees. But she knew they would have to visit it soon to refill their water bottles.

The hours went by. Ali began to sweat, they all did. Up front, Karl continued to plow ahead. They were in danger of losing sight of him. Steve and Cindy had to keep stopping to catch their breaths. Ali felt tired as well. What a difference the altitude made! A slope that would have been a cinch to climb at sea level drained away their strength. Finally, with Cindy and Steve falling way behind, Ali called to Karl to slow down.

"Time for a break?" he asked as he strolled back down the path. He had on hiking shorts; his legs were muscled, very tan.

"Yes," she said, easing the pack off her back. Paddy bent to catch it but Ali stopped him. Now the leprechaun was anxious to please; she couldn't figure him out. One thing was clear, though, the hike was not tiring him. He looked the same as always.

Karl nodded in the direction of Steve and Cindy, who had stopped fifty yards back. Steve, in particular, looked beat. "I think I should take his backpack," Karl said.

"You can't carry two backpacks," Ali said.

"Do we have a choice? Steve's slowing us down, and we've just begun. He's only going to get worse."

Ali glanced at the others. Steve had taken out a chocolate bar and was munching away, and Cindy was drinking a can of Coke. Heaven knew where that had come from. She made a mental note to tell her friend not to litter.

"It'll embarrass him if you carry his stuff," Ali said.

"I can carry it," Paddy said.

Ali chuckled. "What's worse? To be embarrassed by the hotshot guy at school or by a leprechaun?"

"I'm not such a hotshot," Karl said.

"You are and you know it," Ali said. She spoke to Paddy. "The exercise doesn't bother you?"

"No, Missy. Not as long as I have me drink and smokes to give me strength."

Ali thought a moment. "Okay, Paddy, I'll ask Steve if he wants to give you his backpack. Even if he doesn't, I appreciate your offer."

"I can take Cindy's backpack then," Karl said.

Ali groaned as she looked down at her own backpack. "You can take mine. Just teasing! How far are we from Overhang?"

"At least seven miles."

"We've only walked five? You must be wrong. Look at your map."

"I just did."

Ali groaned again. She held up her empty water bottle. "We need to hike down to the river."

"Not here, the gorge is too steep. A mile up ahead there's a better place."

"You really know these woods. I thought I was the only one who came up here."

Karl nodded. "Last summer I was up here every other weekend."

"Why didn't you tell me? We could have gone together."

"I didn't know you loved the forest so much or I would have."

A few minutes later Steve and Cindy caught up. Then they needed to rest again. Cindy looked hot and sweaty; Steve was gasping. He dropped his backpack the moment he stopped. Paddy bent to pick it up.

"What're you doing?" Steve asked the leprechaun.

"He wants to carry it for you," Ali said.

Steve was relieved and unhappy at the same time. "I don't want it to get out that I needed help from a leprechaun."

"Like one of us is going to bring it up at school," Cindy said, wiping her hair from her eyes.

"Would it be okay if I took your backpack?" Karl asked her.

Cindy had it off in a second. "Sure, if you want."

Karl accepted the backpack, let it hang on the side of his own. At the same time, Ali took his map and studied it, feeling depressed. Her watch said it was three-thirty. The sun had moved a long way through the sky. If only they had gotten an earlier start!

"We have to pick up the pace," she said.

"What?" Steve gasped. "I was hoping we could slow down."

Ali gave the map back to Karl, said, "We'll take a longer break a mile from here, when we stop for water. Karl and I'll take the bottles down into the gorge and fill them up. You guys can rest then."

Steve and Cindy nodded wearily, too tired to debate the issue.

They started out again. Ali reached into her supplies and took out a bag of dried figs. She ate three handfuls of almonds as well, washing them down with some of Cindy's Coke. Next she tried a chocolate bar—that was the best part. The exercise had her starving. She ended up eating two candy bars. The almonds and chocolate were great together.

Karl was strong; the extra backpack did not slow him down. He kept up the pace. Paddy was not doing too badly, either. He lit his pipe as they hiked, blowing round smoke rings up into the trees.

"Is that safe?" Ali asked. "You said we shouldn't make a fire. Couldn't the other elementals in these woods spot the smoke?"

"No one blows smoke rings like a leprechaun," he replied. "They'll just think it is one of us wee folk, out for a stroll."

She hoped he was not lying.

They reached the spot where Karl said they could hike down into the gorge. The slope still looked steep to Ali. The moment they halted, Steve plopped on the ground and closed his eyes. Cindy sat and stared off in the distance with a dull look in her eyes. Only Karl and Paddy were full of life. Karl wanted Ali's water bottle.

"I'll hike down with the leprechaun," Karl told Ali. "That'll give you a rest, too. Remember, we're still only halfway to Overhang. And that's a lot less than halfway to the top of Pete's Peak."

"But after Overhang we have only eight miles to the top?" Ali asked, handing over her bottle. She *did* need to sit down, she feared, her legs were trembling.

"That eight miles will feel like eighty," Karl said.

Karl left with Paddy. They disappeared into the gorge. Ali sat near Cindy, but her friend had already closed her eyes. Soon Cindy was asleep beside Steve. Their breathing rose and fell with the faint breeze. Ali closed her eyes as well.

A minute later she opened them.

There was a noise behind them, back the way they had come. Thick scampering feet and foul breathing—sounded like trolls to her. Yet the noise was extremely faint—the creatures could have been either far away or else trying to be quiet.

Ali stood, not bothering to wake the others. They looked so peaceful, and she doubted either of them had the energy to backtrack.

All of a sudden she felt stronger. Her muscles were like steel. Was this a crisis?

She started back down the path. Overhead, the clouds had returned. In the absence of sunlight, the forest appeared black and white, empty of color. She wondered if the shade would give the trolls the confidence to attack. She wished she had quizzed Paddy more about the creatures, found out their weaknesses. She thought to shout for Karl and the leprechaun, but did not want to lose the element of surprise.

At the same time she was not scared. Concerned, yes, but she had handled the trolls before. Maybe all they had to do was see her face and they would run. Then again, they might run straight to Lord Vak and Lord Balar and tell them exactly where the stupid humans were hanging.

Ali did not even know if the elf and dwarf kings were in her dimension yet. They might not come through until the moon was full.

"When the moon is straight overhead. At that moment, the moon will begin to burn."

Such an odd phrase Nemi had used.

Ali hiked down a quarter of a mile, staying on the path. Twice she heard footsteps off to her right, once on the left. But the trees were like curtains, and she saw nothing.

She sensed the creatures retreating at her approach, however. She was not sure that was a good thing. Why had Lord Vak sent elementals through the Yanti before his army? They must be scouts, she thought, or spies. For all she knew Lord Vak already knew what she had planned.

"We could hike all the way to the top and be killed," she told herself.

Ali hiked back to her friends, but came up off the path, on the right side, to further check out the area. As a result she returned without their knowledge, and heard Steve and Cindy talking about her. Ali was not one to spy, especially on friends, but felt it was best if she knew their true feelings about their adventure. Standing behind a tree and feeling guilty, she listened closely. On top of everything else, since passing the tests of earth and water, her hearing had improved. They were still exhausted, they were talking quietly, but as far as her ears were concerned, it was as if she sat beside them.

"It's gone to her head," Cindy was saying. "Ali was never egotistical before but now she talks to me like I'm her slave."

"You're not exaggerating a little?" Steve said. "She has a lot on her mind."

"I'm sure she does. But I notice the last few times she talked to you, it was like she was giving you orders. I mean, it's not like we're getting paid to do all this work."

Steve sighed. "I don't like it. But we've got to support her. Something weird is definitely going on up here. That green guy, Paddy, he sure don't look human."

"But is he really a leprechaun? See, we're not even sure of that."

"Whatever he is, he gives me the creeps," Steve said.

"I'm more worried about the trolls, or the bigfeet, or whatever they are. Ali acts like she can protect us from them, but I haven't seen any signs of her magical powers."

Steve agreed. "That's what gets me the most. She keeps talking about stuff that only she knows about. That makes it impossible to argue with her."

"Why didn't you tell her that back at her house?" Cindy asked.

"I did. Sort of."

"Not! You agreed to come on this trip for one reason only. You're jealous of her and Karl hanging out together."

Steve got heated. "Why would I be jealous of him?"

"Because he's good looking. Because he's got money. Because he's smart. Because she likes him."

"She doesn't like him. She hardly knows him."

"Who was the first one she called to talk to about the talking tree?"

Steve sounded disgusted. "What was that all about? Karl hadn't even seen the footprints, and she tells him this totally far out story, and he believes it."

"Maybe he's just acting like he does," Cindy said.

"Like us?" Steve asked.

Cindy did not respond, and Ali felt she had heard enough. Naturally, their remarks hurt, and she was angry, but before storming out from behind the tree and yelling at them, she tried to see the situation from their point of view. They hadn't actually seen the trolls, they had not talked to the tree. Yet she didn't think she was acting like a princess. Those comments were unfair. But to challenge them on it, she would have to admit she had been spying on them, and that would just cause more hard feelings.

For the time being, for the sake of their goal, she decided to let it be.

Ali hiked back down the path a bit, circled around, then came back up. Steve and Cindy acted like they had just woken up, and she hid her own feelings well. Paddy and Karl appeared a minute later.

Karl had been unable to find his water filter before they left, but he had iodine tablets. He put one in each of their bottles. It made the water taste like . . . well, iodine. But he said it was better to be safe than sorry.

"The water's probably okay to drink straight but we don't want to get sick up here," he said. "The iodine will kill any bacteria."

"Where did you go while we were sleeping?" Cindy asked Ali.

"Just looking around." She hated lying but didn't want to alarm them. If they knew trolls were stalking them, they might freak. She decided to tell Karl later, though. One of them would have to stand watch while the other slept.

Karl stared at her suspiciously.

"Why were you looking around?" he asked.

Ali shrugged. "No reason."

They resumed their hike. The ground continued to rise; they got no breaks. Once again Steve and Cindy fell behind, Steve in particular. Even without a backpack, he was dragging himself up the mountain. Ali found herself stopping more often than she wished to keep an eye on him. They could not let anyone get out of sight, not with the trolls nearby. Karl continued to push the pace.

Six o'clock came and went. The sun moved toward the horizon; the shadows of the trees lengthened. A couple of times the woods thinned and Ali was able to see all the way down to Breakwater and the ocean. She was stunned to see how high up they were. Her town resembled a collection of toy figures set out on a field, and the sea looked like another sky, only turned upside down.

Even as she watched, the clouds returned once more. The ocean turned dark and Breakwater seemed to shrink further. The higher they went, the cooler it got. She was sweating but she knew when they stopped to camp she would be cold.

At seven o'clock, with two hours of light still left, Steve plopped down and didn't get up. Ali called to Karl to stop, then ran back to check on Steve. She cursed herself for having talked him into coming.

"How are you feeling?" she asked, as she knelt by his side. Cindy stood above, lost in her own exhausted zone. Flat on his back, Steve had closed his eyes and was breathing heavily. Ali's earlier anger evaporated. How could she be mad at them when they were working so hard to help her?

"Wonderful," he said.

"You need to rest." She added hopefully, "It's not much farther to Overhang." Actually, it was another two miles. Maybe Steve knew that. He opened his eyes and shook his head wearily.

"You guys go on, I'll catch up later," he said.

"We're not leaving you," Ali said. But she could see he was finished for the day.

"What's wrong with camping here?" Cindy asked.

Karl heard the question as he walked up with Paddy.

"Here's no good," Karl said, checking the sky. "It's too open. It's going to rain tonight. We'll get drenched."

Steve sat up, embarrassed. "If I could rest for ten minutes," he said.

Ali did not like his coloring; he was a ghastly gray. "We've gone far enough for one day," she said.

Karl crouched beside them. "I'm sorry to sound like a drill sergeant," he said. "But the less distance we cover today, the more we'll have to cover tomorrow. Like I said, we'll be higher up then. It will get even harder."

Steve struggled to get up. "I can do it."

Ali stopped him. "No. We'll get up earlier tomorrow, before dawn if we have to. We might be more used to the altitude by then."

"People usually feel weaker the second day," Karl said.

"You're full of good cheer," Cindy muttered.

Karl looked up at her. "Excuse me, it's just the way it is."

Cindy plopped down near Steve's head. "It doesn't matter, I can't walk any farther. You guys go on, I'll stay with Steve. We'll be all right."

"It might be a good idea," Karl agreed.

"No," Ali said. "We stay together. These woods are dangerous."

"We haven't seen any danger," Cindy said.

"It's here, I feel it," Ali said. "Paddy?"

"Missy?"

"Do you think it's safe to camp here?" she asked.

He set down the paper bags and scratched his huge head. "Off the path a bit might be more to my liking," he said. "Nothing like a shallow cave or a clump of bushes to hide in. Pull up a bed of dried leaves and close the old eyes. Aye, that's how leprechauns like it."

Karl stood, unhappy. "I'll scout around for a place," he said, and walked off.

"Thanks," Ali called, before turning back to Steve. She stroked his hand. "Don't be embarrassed."

He shook his head. "I hate being the weak one in the group."

"I like it. It takes the heat off me," Cindy said.

Ali glanced back the way they had come, down the winding path and the endless trees. She could not see or hear the trolls but knew they were near. Also, she sensed something else approaching—a heavy shadow, like the coming night, if a shadow could be called a thing. Once again, her dream came back to her. The Shaktra had appeared near the end of it, mocking her, calling her out to battle. But even in the dream she had not understood what it wanted, or even what it was. She had only known that it hated.

Ali suspected that it would be a long night.

CHAPTER TEN

They set up camp two hundred yards off the path, in a spot Karl had discovered. The place was partially sheltered, with high rocks on one side and thick trees on the other. It was not a cave, however; it was still exposed in two directions, and already that looked like it might be a problem. A nasty wind had begun to blow out of the east, and because they were afraid to build a fire, Ali worried that they were going to have a cold sleep.

They used the cell phones, called everyone they were supposed to. Ali felt guilty lying to her dad. He was somewhere in New Mexico. He sounded exhausted.

The pup tents Karl had bought were easy to set up. They assembled all four in a row. She felt bad they didn't have a tent for Paddy, but he brushed off her concern.

"Rather sleep in a coffin than in one of those," he said.

The sun had set by the time they sat to eat dinner. They brought out a bag of nuts, a loaf of bread, and opened two cans of tuna. Unfortunately, for some reason, the fish tasted old. Ali tried having a bowl of granola with water poured over it—yuck!—and quickly set it aside. She was surprised when Cindy took a bag of barbecued potato chips out of her backpack.

"I should have known," Ali said. "Give me some."

Cindy offered her the bag. "I should make you beg."

Paddy was generous with his beef jerky. He passed around his supply. Ali would never have imagined that beef jerky and potato chips would taste so good together.

Pretty soon they were all chewing away. In the west the light faded, while in the east a white glow appeared. With the mountain in the way, they could not see the moon directly, but they all knew it was only one day shy of being full.

Overhead the clouds wrestled the stars. Looked like the stars were going to lose. The wind continued to be a problem but it wasn't awful.

When Paddy had finished eating, he opened a fresh bottle of whiskey and filled his pipe. He offered the drink and tobacco to the rest of them but got no takers. Easing back onto a rock, he returned to blowing smoke rings into the trees, a hobby that continued to make Ali nervous. Yet it appeared as if Paddy felt at home in the group.

"I wish you wouldn't do that," Karl told the leprechaun.

"It's okay, I think," Ali said quickly.

"Others might see them," Steve said.

"Paddy says they'll just think it's a leprechaun," Ali said.

"Are leprechauns second-class citizens where you come from?" Cindy asked Paddy.

"Don't understand the question, lassie," he said.

"Why do you call me lassie and Ali, Missy?" Cindy asked.

"Missy has the power. She's the boss."

"Paddy," Ali said.

"What I mean is, are leprechauns looked down upon?" Cindy asked.

"Aye. Short. Everybody has to look down to see us."

"That's not what I mean," Cindy said.

"What she's saying is, how are leprechauns treated by other elementals?" Ali said.

Paddy puffed away. "Treated like leprechauns, aye, that is what we are. But if you ask who is friendly to us folk, I say none. Elves take care of elves. Dwarves take care of dwarves."

"What about the fairies?" Ali asked.

"There are nice fairies. There are mean fairies. Hard to tell them apart just by looking at them. My pa used to say, the only good fairy is a sleeping fairy."

"Why is that?" Steve asked.

Paddy's eyes lit up. "When they sleep, you can take their stardust."

"You mean, steal it?" Cindy said. "That's not right."

"They have plenty, why not share some with us leprechauns?" Paddy asked.

"What can you do with fairy stardust?" Ali asked. Paddy had a drink of whiskey before answering the question.

"Many things, Missy. Fly for one."

"Have you ever flown using the stuff?" Cindy asked.

Paddy thought it was a silly question. "Leprechauns can't fly. Only fairies fly, and only if they have enough stardust."

"How does it run out?" Ali asked. "On fairies, I mean?"

"Don't know, it just does. Disappears quick when they are up in the air."

"Where does it come from?" Ali asked.

"Fairies."

"No. Where do they get it?" Ali asked.

He hesitated. "Don't know, never asked them."

Ali had a sudden inspiration. "Is it made from gold?"

Paddy stared at her a long time. "Maybe. Maybe not."

Ali nodded to herself. Leprechauns craved the stardust, and

tried to steal it, because it was related to gold, and was just as valuable, if not more so. The fact excited her for reasons she did not understand. And the fact that the *fact* had come to her, out of the blue, also thrilled her. One thing for sure, the stardust was important, she would have to learn more about it.

"The elementals want to get rid of us because we're destroying the Earth," Ali said carefully. "If they succeed—if there is a war and they win—what will they do next? Will they stay in our dimension?"

"Paddy not sure, thinks so. The elves want to turn the world into a forest. The dwarves have an eye on your cities. All that concrete and asphalt excites them—makes their beards grow faster. If you ask Paddy, those two will be fighting over your world in no time."

"How would the leprechauns feel about that?" Karl asked.

"No one cares how leprechauns feel. Whatever happens, happens. We go about our business, keep to ourselves."

"How about the trolls?" Ali asked. "Are they friendly with elves? Dwarves?"

"Trolls have no friends. Feed them and tell them what to do and they do it. Don't feed them and they eat you. Trolls are as dumb as rocks."

"Do they turn into stone in the sun?" Ali asked.

"Don't like it, for sure. Their skin gets hard."

"But they have to be in direct sunlight?" Ali asked.

"Aye."

"What do they hope to win in this war?" Ali asked.

"Trolls do not hope. They eat, they sleep." Paddy added in a softer voice, "Eat boys and girls if they're available. If Lord Vak allows it, and he has."

"This Lord Vak sounds like one angry dude," Steve said.

"Aye. Lord Vak is very powerful," Paddy said.

It was time to rest. They were exhausted. Barely saying goodnight, Cindy and Steve crawled into their tents and went to sleep. Paddy pulled up a pile of leaves for his back and a rock for his head. Tilting his green hat over his eyes, he also went straight to sleep. Ali was left with Karl to clean up. The moon had finally come up over the eastern ridge. Even without a fire, they could see each other clearly.

"I'll take the first watch," Karl said, as he put the nuts and bread back in Cindy and Steve's backpacks. He had mostly equipment in his own pack: the crampons and ice axes.

"That's not fair. You're as tired as I am," Ali said.

"Sure. But you're the boss, remember? Besides having to hike, you have all that responsibility. It must wear you out."

Ali blushed. "I don't feel like the boss."

"Someone has to be. It can't be me."

"Why do you say that?"

He nodded toward Cindy and Steve. "They're your friends. They hardly know me. They certainly haven't accepted me yet."

"I think you scare them with the pace you set."

"I just want to get you to the top on time."

Ali looked in the direction of Pete's Peak. Standing in the middle of the forest, they could not see the top of the mountain. All day, they had got only glimpses of it. But she continued to feel as if it called to her. One thing was certain, when they left the shelter of the trees, they would be exposed. Whoever or whatever was in the forest would see them.

"Can we make it in time?" she asked.

"It's going to be tight. Tomorrow, we'll be hiking deep into the night."

"Is that safe? At the top with the snow?"

"It's very dangerous," Karl admitted. "But the moonlight will help."

Ali sighed. "There's another danger. When you went into the

gorge with Paddy, I heard trolls behind us. I never saw them but I'm positive they were there."

"Stalking us?" he asked.

"Looks like it."

"Have you heard them since?"

"No."

"How come you didn't tell me earlier?"

"I wanted to get you alone. I didn't want to scare the others."

Karl scanned the woods. With the bright moonlight glistening on every branch and leaf, the forest appeared enchanted, wrapped in a snowy white spell. They could have stumbled into a fairy tale, Ali thought. They had all the necessary characters present: trolls and leprechauns, talking trees and dark fairies. The only problem was that she was never going to live happily ever after. Her mother was dead; she was never going to have another mother.

"Don't keep secrets from me. I need to know," Karl said.

"I won't do it again."

He paused. "Am I being a jerk?"

"Why do you say that?"

He shrugged. "I have no idea how you see me."

"I have no idea how you see me."

He grinned. "You have the power, Missy. I have to like you."

She smiled, too, but it was a sad smile. "That's not a reason to like someone."

He did not reply, just lowered his head. Did he think she was scolding him? She had not meant to. She supposed she still had to learn how to talk to boys, particularly to ones she liked. To escape the uneasy moment, she bid Karl a hasty goodnight and crawled into her tent, wiggling into her sleeping bag. The wash at home had done the bag a world of good; it no longer stunk.

She did not seal the pup tent opening.

The wind continued to blow; she left her coat on. She watched as Karl stepped to the edge of their camp and sat on a boulder, his back to her. In many ways, she thought, he was as important to their adventure as she was. From the start he had taken charge. They would have been lost without him.

Ali closed her eyes, tried to sleep. She was exhausted, yet sleep did not come easily. For some reason, her right arm ached. The skin on the back was tight; it felt on the verge of tearing. Of course it wasn't just *some* reason that made it hurt. It always bothered her when she thought about that night.

The night her mother died. Her twelfth birthday.

She remembered so much and so little. She had been driving home at night with her mother, from a play at school. She had been one of the stars in the play, *Frogs and Freaks*. She had been the main frog, in fact, Princess Wartly. She was not sure where the play had come from, but had heard a student at school from years before had written it.

The story was about a bunch of frogs who ruled the world, and a group of freaky creatures who were trying to steal the toad's power. Steve was in the play as well—a giant ogre who always needed his back scratched.

After the opening night, on the way home, she chatted excitedly with her mother. Being onstage was a new experience for her. She loved having the warm lights on her face, and thrilled at how the audience followed her every word. Her mother shared her excitement. She promised Ali she would go to every performance.

"You don't want to do that," Ali said. "You've seen it—you know what's going to happen next. You'll get bored."

Her mother took her eyes off the road, glanced her way. "Nothing you do bores me," she said.

Ali snorted. "Yeah, sure. What about when I scream at you?"

"When do you scream at me?"

"All the time, in my head. I'm just too polite to do it out loud."

Her mother reached over and took her hand. "You are more than polite."

"I'm also a great actress? A better liar?"

Her mother chuckled. "No, I'm talking about something else."

"What?"

Ali never forgot the change in her mother's face right then. Their talk was light, frivolous—nothing they were saying really made much sense. They were just goofing off. Yet when her mom looked over at her, it was as if her eyes were suddenly connected to a river that was capable of washing away the pain of the world. In that instant, it was as if the person who had given birth to her and raised her was more than human.

Her mother reached over and tugged gently on her left ear. "You're my daughter, Ali. You always will be. And you have magic."

That was all Ali remembered. Except the flash of red light; it had come from every direction at once. She had never heard of red headlights before.

Then she woke up in the hospital, and her father was sitting beside her and telling her that everything was all right. But his eyes were bloodshot; he looked like he had aged twenty years since she had last seen him. Her head and arm were bandaged. The skin on her arm felt like it was on fire.

"What's wrong with me?" she mumbled.

"You got a bump on the head and you burned your arm a little," her father said. "You're going to be fine."

"Where's Mom?"

He blinked, several times. He tried to stop her from seeing his tears. She saw them anyway, and then he didn't have to answer her question.

Nothing was all right. Nothing was fine.

"She's dead," she said, and knew it was true.

Her father told her the story. It was a short story.

There had been an accident. She had been thrown from the car. Her mother had not been so lucky, and the car had caught fire. Her father didn't say so but it seemed her mother had been burned to ash. When they buried her, three days later, all they had was a vase full of ashes. They put the tiny vase in a big coffin, and watched as it was lowered into the ground. The people at the burial home had sure saved money on the cremation, she thought bitterly.

That was all Ali knew.

CHAPTER ELEVEN

Mommy," she whispered as she tossed in her sleeping bag.

Ali awoke with a start. Her voice had startled her. Had she been asleep? Strange, she did not remember passing out. Yet it felt much later.

Ali climbed out of her tent and stood. Karl continued to sit on the boulder, his back to her. His head was down now, though. He might have been asleep.

The moon had risen high in the sky. She must have been asleep for several hours. The woods were bright, it was like daytime. Yet the light could be wiped out in a second by the shifting clouds.

Staring at the sky, Ali saw the clouds as vast kites made of cold mist. She was supposed to have control over the water element. Could she pull their strings? Or were they under the control of another? The clouds seemed to haunt the sky. It was as if they had entered the human dimension from the elemental kingdom. The cold wind blew and she shivered.

Ali realized Paddy was missing. But even as she searched for him, he reappeared. He could have been sleepwalking, or maybe he had just gone to pee. He stumbled back into camp, his eyes half-closed, and plopped down on his pile of leaves. A second later he was snoring peacefully. But he talked to himself as he slept, occasionally mumbling the name *Lea*, and it made her wonder if he had a girlfriend in the other dimension.

Ali walked over to Karl. He raised his head as she neared, looked at her. "What are you doing up?" he asked in a quiet voice.

"Your turn to sleep. What time is it?"

He checked his watch. "Two-fifteen."

She sat beside him on the boulder. The moonlight suited him. It took away his tan but made his clear blue eyes gleam all the brighter.

"I don't even remember falling asleep," she said.

"You were tossing a lot."

"You were watching me?"

"I was keeping an eye on the whole gang," Karl said.

"Did you see Paddy leave and come back just now?"

"I saw him leave. That was a while ago." Karl glanced over his shoulder. "Did he just come back?"

"Yes."

"I must have dozed for a few minutes."

"That's okay, you're exhausted. Let me stand guard."

Karl stood and yawned. "Wake Cindy or Steve before dawn. They have to do their fair share."

"I will," she said, although privately she thought it would be better to let her friends rest. She did not feel tired anyway. Her right arm continued to ache, though.

"Wake me if you hear anything. Anything at all."

"Sure," she promised.

Karl patted her shoulder. "Goodnight Ali."

"Goodnight. Sweet dreams."

Karl crawled into his tent. Ali stood and walked silently around the camp. Better to move, she thought, keep warm. But the jacket

Steve had given her was thick and comfortable, and it had a hood. She was glad she had taken the time to fix it. It was not like she could afford a new jacket. She wondered if her father would notice the switch.

Ali thought about her father then—the long lonely roads he traveled to support them both. He could be halfway across the country by now. She wished there was more she could do for him. He was a great man, he had not deserved to suffer so much.

The moon vanished. Just like that, the clouds stole it away, and the forest was plunged into a deep gloom. Again, she felt as if the clouds taunted her. She and her friends were at a mile and a half elevation. The clouds couldn't have been that much higher. Yet they looked far away, untouchable.

The rain came a few minutes later. For a moment the wind stopped to let it fall. Then the drizzle was grabbed by the breeze, and whipped into her face. More than anything else she wanted to climb back into her tent and try to stay dry.

Ali feared the night, though, now that it was so black. She knew she had to stand guard. She feared the things Nemi had told her, especially about the elementals who stalked the forest, looking for humans. It was still not clear to her why they had suddenly decided to attack after all these years. They hadn't even tried to talk to humanity about the pollution. People deserved a chance to change their ways.

"Listen to me, I didn't think so a few days ago," Ali said to herself. Last week she had wanted to scream at the lumberjacks. Now she just hoped Ted got better.

The rain did not get heavier but it did manage to work its way deeper into her hair and skin. She began to get real cold. One shiver led to another; soon she was trembling like a leaf. Even walking did not help. It was then she decided she had to do something drastic.

Ali did not know how to call on her power. The first time—with the trolls—it had just come. The second time—when she had grabbed Paddy—the same thing had happened. But now she sat on the boulder and willed it to come.

"Now," she whispered.

It was not long before her call was answered.

A strange heaviness grew in the pit of her stomach. Yet the sensation was not unpleasant. It was almost as if that part of her body got thicker, more dense. She felt a strength there, a power that seemed to tell her without words that it could be moved. But moved where and for what reason?

She had an answer to that question.

"Rise above and form an umbrella over my head," she said.

Ali felt the energy spread out. There was no magic light, nothing to see or hear, but it was definitely there. She felt as if her body expanded with the power, until she was ten times bigger. Of course she remained the same size, but she had to tell herself that was true. Otherwise, it felt as if she *was* the invisible umbrella.

More important, the rain stopped falling on her head.

"Cool!" she gushed as she saw how the rain came within fifteen feet of her head before pouring off to the side. The force field—she did not know what else to call it—was dome shaped. She willed it to expand further, to cover her friends, and was delighted to see it obey. The drizzle no longer fell on their tents, nor even on Paddy.

Still, the force field did not feel separate from her. Only then did she realize her power came from inside, not outside. She wished Nemi was with her to see what she was doing.

Then something odd began to happen. At first she wondered if it was connected to the use of her power, but then dismissed the idea. The clouds came lower, swooping in like a bank of fog. That was not so unusual, but when they began to flash with lightning she got worried. Because this lightning was not accompanied with thunder. And it was red.

"Red lightning?" she said aloud. "There's no such thing."

A dark figure flew out of the clouds. Ali caught only a glimpse as it swooshed by. Bat shaped, it appeared as tall as she, with wide black wings and a skull-like head. At its center burned a red light. It shook its claws and that red light caught fire. A laser bolt shot past Ali's head and struck the tree behind her. The bark exploded in flame and a large branch crashed to the ground.

"We're under attack!" Ali shouted.

The cry was not necessary. The noise of the toppling branch woke everyone. The gang was on its feet in seconds. But they were dazed, they did not understand what was going on. Ali did not know what to tell them.

Three more figures came out of the clouds. They flew just above the trees. The red light at their centers swelled like exploding light-bulbs. More laser bolts flew toward the ground. Ali ducked—all the guys did, including Paddy. But Cindy was too stunned. A bolt caught her on her left shoulder and she went down with a loud cry.

"Cindy!" Ali cried, rushing to her side. Cindy's shirt was on fire. Quickly, Ali put it out and grabbed Cindy and dragged her behind a tree. The creatures had disappeared for a moment but Ali knew they would be back. "Can you walk?" Ali shouted at Cindy.

Cindy nodded, grimacing in pain as she held her arm. "What are they?" she gasped.

"Do you know?" Ali shouted at Paddy, as he leapt behind the rocks.

"Dark fairies, Missy!" he shouted back, peering into the foggy night.

"What should we do?" Steve asked, reaching for a stick.

"Run!" Paddy said.

"We can't run! Cindy's hurt!" Ali called, as she leaned Cindy against a tree. Ten feet to her left, another tree had caught fire. Red smoke poured into the glowing clouds, creating a ghastly soup. "How do we stop them?"

"Use your powers!" Paddy advised.

"Yeah! Use your powers!" Steve agreed.

The creatures came again, six this time, a hideous line of giant bats in the burning night. Not sure exactly what powers she had at her command, Ali stepped from behind the tree and tried to raise the magical umbrella that had protected them so well from the rain. The energy field expanded; she felt it stretch out like an invisible wall before the swooping monsters. Once more, for the third time, she saw them twitch their claws and watched as the red light blossomed at their centers.

The red bolts fell on her friends; her shield did nothing to stop them. Apparently she could deflect water, but not fire. Trees cracked and exploded all around Ali. She felt incredible heat on her head, reached up and discovered the hood of her jacket was on fire. Karl put it out with his hand before it could catch her hair. His handsome face, caught in the glow of the burning trees, looked stunned. Yet he had not collapsed in terror, none of them had. Ali thought that was a miracle in itself.

"We cannot stand here and take this pounding!" he said.

The figures disappeared into the glowing clouds. They were like dive-bombers, just getting ready for another deadly run. Ali searched for Paddy. He was still behind the rocks, looking none too happy.

"What do they have in their hands?" she shouted at the leprechaun.

"Fire stones!" he shouted.

"Tires?" Cindy asked.

"Not Firestones," Ali said. "Fire stones."

"Aye," Paddy said. "Fairy magic, very powerful."

"How do they work?" Ali asked.

"Don't know. Dark fairies don't tell their secrets. Can you not stop them, Missy?"

"I'm trying," Ali replied, searching the ground for suitable rocks. The strategy had worked with the trolls. Of course here her targets were smaller and moving fast. She saw a couple of medium-sized rocks and picked them up.

The six dark fairies returned, burning shadows in the fiery night. Ali saw their fire stones start to kindle and took aim. A red bolt exploded the bush near her leg and she let go with the rock. Her arm was a rocket launcher—there was so much power in it.

A perfect shot, the rock hit the center fairy in the head and the creature plunged from the sky and vanished behind the trees. The creature's partners let out ear-piercing shrieks and wheeled to the sides and disappeared in the clouds.

"They're running!" Steve exclaimed.

"Don't think so, laddie," Paddy said.

The five dark fairies returned, coming at them from several directions. That made it much harder to hide behind the trees. In fact, they couldn't hide. The red bolts sizzled within inches of their faces. A spark touched Ali's ear; she felt as if a firefly was trying to sneak in her brain. Her friends cried out—she assumed someone else had been hit. There was too much confusion, too much fire!

Ali let fly her second rock, missed completely. The monsters retreated into the eerie fog. More trees had caught fire. Flaming smoke poured into the evil clouds.

"Who was hit? Was anyone hit?" she demanded.

"They burnt me hat!" Paddy said, disgusted, his charred hat in his hands. "Pa gave me this hat."

"They're coming at us from all sides!" Karl said. "Use the backpacks as shields!"

The idea was smart; they each reached for a backpack. Even Cindy had recovered enough to defend herself. But Ali could not hold a backpack and fight at the same time. She was the only offense they had. She would have to risk it, she decided. Bending over, she gathered three more rocks.

The dark fairies would not give up. Again, they came. Again, red bolts fell all around them. This time she got off a good shot. But it only stunned the creature—the fairy did not fall from the sky. For the first time Ali began to feel that their situation was hopeless.

Karl must have figured the same. He pulled her aside as the monsters momentarily flew out of sight. The backpack in his hands was in ruins. It was her's—all that was left was smoked granola and fried almonds. Even if they survived the night, there would be nothing for breakfast in the morning.

"We have to split up," he said. "It's our only chance. You're the strongest. Take Cindy with you, try to reach Overhang. I told you, the place is easy to defend. I'll stay here with Paddy and Steve, try to hold them off."

"With what?" Ali gasped.

"It doesn't matter! Just go! If we can't stop them here, then we'll split up. I've let Steve study the map, and Paddy knows these woods better than any of us. Let's all try to meet at Overhang in one hour."

Ali was anxious. What he said made sense, but it felt wrong in her gut. Yet she could not think of another plan. "We could all get lost in the woods," she said.

"It's better than dying." He picked a fresh backpack off the ground. She thought it was his. "Take this, take Cindy. Sneak out of here right after their next pass."

She accepted the backpack. "You have to take care of Steve."

"I'll do what I can," Karl promised.

The dark fairies returned with a vengeance. They came straight down upon them, aiming for their heads. Once again, Ali set aside her pack to get off a shot. But her rock exploded in midair—the creatures had zapped it.

Thankfully, on this run at least, no one got hit. Nodding to the others, Ali picked up the backpack, grabbed Cindy by the arm, and snuck out of camp.

Ali had only a vague idea of where they were going. The map of the mountain was clear in her head, but that was not the same as saying she knew the area. Plus, with the moon gone, it was hard to see. Could fairies see better than humans in the dark? She wished she had asked Paddy before she had left.

Cindy's shoulder was hurting but she didn't complain. Ali admired her courage. She held Cindy's hand as they hurried north. But she dared not use a flashlight, or cross over to the path.

They stumbled through the woods, running into each other as often as they ran into trees. Behind them the light of the fires changed into a haunting red mist as the clouds came between them and their friends. Ali thought she heard someone scream in pain.

The hike was a nightmare. The clouds hugged the woods. The trees were like disembodied spirits that kept blocking their path. Or else *they* were the spirits, trapped in a bad dream with no exit. Ali kept expecting to run into more dark fairies.

"Do you know where we're going?" Cindy asked, gasping for breath. In their terror, they had forgotten about the altitude but it had not forgotten about them. Ali felt light-headed from the thin air.

"Sort of," she said, adding, "The main thing is to keep moving."

"I'm worried about Steve," Cindy said.

"Karl and Paddy will take care of him."

"How do we know the leprechaun didn't lead the dark fairies to us?"

"Paddy wouldn't do that," Ali said. Then she remembered how Paddy had left the camp. And Karl had not been sure how long the leprechaun had been gone.

The drizzle let up some, which was good and bad. A strong rain would have put out the fires. But not having cold water splashing in their faces gave them one less thing to think about. When they could no longer see the fires behind them, they stopped to catch their breaths.

"Why are there good fairies and bad fairies?" Cindy asked.

"Why are there good people and bad people? I don't know. How's your shoulder?"

"It's burned. It hurts like crazy."

"I have Karl's pack. He was carrying a first-aid kit. When we reach Overhang, I'll put something on it."

Cindy looked around in the dark. "We're never going to find anything in this mess. We're probably going to have to wait for the sun."

Ali had thought the same thing. The idea was not appealing. Dawn had to be at least two hours away, maybe three. Could the dark fairies attack when the sun was up? Paddy would know.

They started off again. They had not gone far, however, when the crazy night caught up with them in an unexpected way. Directly in front of them, through the clouds, the forest glowed a sober red.

"We've been hiking in circles!" Cindy cried.

"Maybe," Ali admitted.

"There's no maybe about it. We have to turn around."

"No. Then we'll be even more lost. If the camp's in front of us, then we should go to it to get our bearings. I want to check on the guys anyway."

"What if the guys are gone?" Cindy asked. But what she was really asking was: what if the guys are dead?

Ali sighed. "I don't know."

The next few minutes were some of the longest of their lives. They half expected to find the guys lying on the ground, burnt to ash by the dark fairies. But when they reached the edge of the camp, Ali was relieved to see the guys were gone, with no sign of them around.

Yet there was a troll trapped in the center of the fire. He looked like the one Ali had hit the other day on the leg with a rock. Pacing back and forth, trying to escape the flames, the creature limped badly. To her surprise, she saw the troll had her white sweater tied around his neck.

"So that's where it went!" she exclaimed.

"What?" Cindy asked.

"He has my sweater."

Cindy squinted. "What does a troll need a sweater for?"

"Like I would know?" Ali added, "I don't see the guys."

Cindy hesitated. "Do you think the dark fairies carried them off?"

"They didn't look big enough to lift a bunch of boys."

"Spiders are not big but they're strong for their size."

"True. But we're talking about fairies, not insects."

"What should we do?" Cindy asked.

Ali didn't answer. She watched uneasily as the fire closed in on the troll. Already sparks were landing on his hairy hide, and his yellow eyes shone with terror. She should have no sympathy for him, she thought. He and his pals had tried to kill her twice and he was, after all, only a troll. Like Paddy said, they were big stupid beasts that ate everything in sight. Still, it was hard to stand by and watch him die. She said as much to Cindy.

"What?" Cindy cried. "You want to save him? He's a monster!"

"I didn't say I want to save him. I just said it's not easy to watch him burn to death." She added, "Maybe we could save him."

"I'm not risking my life to save a troll!"

"Then I'll save him," Ali said.

"How?"

"I don't know how."

"But why?" Cindy asked.

"Because he's alive! He doesn't want to die!" Ali added, "He's like you and me."

Cindy studied the troll. "He might be like you, but he's certainly not like me."

Ali pointed. "Look, I can climb that tree behind him, crawl onto a branch above him. Karl has a rope in his pack. I can drop the rope down and he can climb to safety."

"Excuse me? That tree is about to catch fire. You get up there and it'll collapse and you'll land beside the troll. Then he can enjoy one last glorious meal before he dies."

Ali stepped forward. "I'll think of something."

Cindy grabbed her arm. "Ali, you'll die!"

She smiled. "Funny, but all of a sudden I'm sure I won't die. At least not today."

Ali circled around the camp and the bulk of the fire. The tree she had spoken of was near the rocks Paddy had used for his pillow. But Cindy was right—several of the upper branches were already on fire. It made Ali wonder if she needed a new plan.

Or did she simply need faith? Nemi's words came back to haunt her.

"When will I face the other tests?"

"Soon."

"And each test I pass, I gain more power?"

"Yes."

"What if I fail one?"

"You will die."

This was the third test, she realized, it had to be, the test of fire. She had to face the fire, she had to show no fear. Well, maybe she could show a little fear. Getting buried alive and thrown in the river had scared the heck out of her, and she had still passed those tests. She believed Nemi, that the situations had been set up by nature. The main thing to do was to save the life of the troll while staying alive.

More branches caught fire above her. Hopeless, that way, she thought, the tree.

Ali stood on the rocks, above the camp. Between her and the troll was a wall of fire. But if she took a running start, and flew through the air, the flames probably wouldn't hurt her. Then what? Like Cindy said, she could get trapped beside the troll.

The question was: how much did she trust herself?

"In the end I'm the one who has to take the tests," she said.

Ali choked on the smoke. Her lungs felt full of cinders. She could not stand here all night debating with herself. The troll had a space of ten feet left to survive in. His hide would catch fire any second.

Ali turned, jogged back a few steps, and then ran forward. Her speed carried her off the rock ledge, through the air. Throwing her arms over her face, she closed her eyes as she soared through the flames.

Ali felt the hot singe of the fire wall pass by. Reopening her eyes, she crouched low so she would roll when she hit the ground.

Her landing was far from smooth. Her right hip hit the ground hard, and she rolled too far. She almost ended up in the fire. To her surprise, it was the troll that stopped her.

Lying on the ground, her hair only inches from the flames, she looked up into his frightened eyes and wondered if she should say thank you or let out a scream. He had a powerful grip on her shoulder.

Yet it was the troll who spoke first.

"Fairy?" he asked in a voice that sounded like a man in its deep tone, but which was a hundred percent little boy in its innocence.

"No, I'm a girl." She added, "I'm here to rescue you."

The troll helped her up. He pointed to the fire, and then to his arms. "Hurts," he said sadly, and once again he sounded like a lost little boy with the vocal cords of a giant.

She petted him; he was dirty and smelly. "You poor dear. We've got to get you out of here."

"Fire stop," he said.

"That's what I'm going to do. I'm going to stop the fire," she said.

Since she had seen the trapped troll, she had been wondering if she had the wrong idea about her control over the water element. Sure, it had been fun to make an invisible umbrella. But was it possible to pass the test of fire with what she had learned during the test of water?

Rather than stopping the rain from pouring, could she make it pour?

"Maybe I should have tried it out before I got myself trapped," she wondered aloud. She knew that was not true, though. She had to face the fire like she was, putting everything on the line, including her own life. She said to the troll, "I need to sit for a minute and close my eyes. I'm going to make it rain."

He nodded anxiously. "Rain hard."

Good advice, a drizzle wouldn't save them. The heat from the flames made the camp feel like an oven. Ali pulled off her jacket as she sat down, trying to concentrate. But even behind her closed eyelids, the fire could be seen. Smoke filled her nose and she had to cough. They had seconds left to live. How was she supposed to concentrate?

In that desperate moment, a surprising calm settled over her. The heat of the flames, the smoky air—they all seemed suddenly far away.

The truth hit her like a thunderbolt.

There was no need to invoke her magical powers!

She had already passed the test of fire, she realized, when she had decided to risk her life to save the troll. Already fire was under her control! She could do with it what she wished!

Ali opened her eyes and stood. The troll stared at her, at the sky.

"Not raining," he said, worried.

She grabbed her jacket and smiled and offered her hand. "I'm going to tell the fire to let us by. Don't worry, it will obey me."

He did not hesitate, he took her hand. Her fingers, in his massive grip, felt lost. But he was gentle; he seemed to believe everything she had to say.

Ali turned toward the fire and held out her free hand. "Let us pass!" she snapped.

The miracle happened all of a sudden, the fire parted. The flames could have been alive; it was as if they arched their spines to avoid them. Holding onto the troll's hand and staring straight ahead, Ali stepped over the smoking ground. In a minute they were clear of the fire and standing beside Cindy.

"Does he talk?" Cindy asked, eyeing the troll nervously.

"Yes," Ali said.

"Is he going to eat us?"

Ali let go of the troll's hand. "Well?" she asked him.

The troll patted her on top of the head. His palm was bigger than her entire skull. "No hurt," he said.

"What about me?" Cindy demanded.

The troll licked his dark teeth and Ali saw a hint of green spit.

"Hungry," he said.

"No," Ali said. "I saved your life. You're not to eat me or any of my friends. Do you understand?"

He nodded. "Nice girls. No eat."

"Some of our friends are boys. No eat them either," Ali said.

He nodded. "Nice boys. Nice girls."

Cindy fanned her face. "I don't know about you, but I'm cooked. Let's get out of here."

"Just a second," Ali said. "I have to save the trees."

Cindy was exasperated. "Why don't you save the whole world while you're at it?"

Ali caught her eye. "That's what I'm trying to do," she said evenly.

Cindy stared back, for a moment, perhaps trying to make a point, then lowered her head and said, "How did you walk through that fire anyway? That was a neat trick."

"I'll tell you later," Ali said, walking away. "Give me a minute alone."

"What if he attacks me?" Cindy called after her.

"How do you know he's not a she?" Ali called back.

Not far from the flames, she sat to concentrate. Maybe it was not necessary, the sitting, but closing her eyes seemed to help. Again, she felt the heaviness fill her body, and she let the power stretch out above her head. But this time she let it rise up high, above the clouds, into the clear sky where the moon shone throughout the night. For a second she thought she saw the moon, but it might have been her imagination.

Then Ali brought down the power.

She willed it toward the earth, pressing on the clouds from above, as if they were giant wet rags she could squeeze with a magical hand.

It began to pour.

She opened her eyes and smiled as the rain washed over her face. The cold no longer bothered her. The fire would be out in a few minutes, and then she would turn off the water and rescue the guys.

Earth, water, fire—all three were at her command now. Sure, the dark fairies had started out the night on the winning side, but they were going to be toast when she got through with them.

CHAPTER TWELVE

In a hurry to reach Overhang, feeling confident in her powers, Ali decided to risk a return to the path and head north from there. She did not use her newfound abilities to push away the clouds, however, but after the brief hard rain, the clouds cleared on their own and the moon came out. The forest that had been a nightmare an hour ago was now a place of magic again.

Cindy walked in front with Ali, the troll trailing thirty feet behind. The rain had improved his smell but he was still a noseful. Ali had decided to let him keep her sweater for the time being. She didn't want to handle it until she was close to a washing machine. The troll slobbered as he walked and occasionally belched, but he was remarkably well behaved.

"I have a question," Cindy said when they had hiked for a few minutes.

"I can guess it," Ali muttered.

"Why have we invited a troll to join our expedition?"

"He's strong. He's on our side now."

"He could kill us while we sleep!"

"I don't think so."

"What if you think wrong?"

"Cindy, you think. The troll is an elemental, like Paddy. He probably knows stuff we need to know."

"You act like trolls have a sense of loyalty. That's a pretty big assumption. Your saving his life might mean nothing to him."

"I'll ask Paddy about troll loyalties when I see him."

"You can't go to a leprechaun to get advice about a troll. That's like asking a lion if a tiger is safe to wrestle with."

Ali chuckled. "Hey, that's pretty funny."

"Thank you. Have you asked why he has your sweater?"

"Good question." Ali stopped and called to the troll. The creature lumbered up beside them, his huge yellow eyes glowing in the dark. She pointed to the sweater. "Did you find that in the woods?" she asked.

He nodded. "Found," he said.

"You found it when you were chasing me the other day?"

He nodded. "Hungry."

"You were hungry the other day? That's why you chased me?"

"Huh."

"Is that yes?"

He nodded. "Huh."

"Why did you keep the sweater?" she asked.

The troll touched it lovingly. "Pretty," he said.

"You kept the sweater because it's pretty?"

"Huh." He pointed to her. "Pretty."

Cindy giggled. "He thinks you're pretty like the sweater."

Ali blushed. "I'm not pretty to a troll."

The troll kept gesturing to her and the sweater. "Pretty," he said again.

Cindy cackled. "The troll has a crush on you!"

"Stop that!" Ali snapped. "It's a misunderstanding." She spoke to the troll. "Do you have a name?"

"Huh."

"What's your name?"

"Fart."

Cindy clapped her hands. "Perfect!"

"Calm down, would you? Fart, do you have another name?"

He was confused. "Fart. Fart."

"Do you have a Christian name? A last name?"

"He's a troll, not a person. Of course he doesn't have a Christian name," Cindy said.

"I was just asking." Ali felt frustrated. "We can't call you Fart. It's not a nice name." She got an idea. "What if we call you Farble?"

The troll nodded. "Farble Fart."

"No, just Farble. How do you like it?"

The troll thought a moment. "Mean?"

"No, it's not a mean name. Oh, I see what you mean. What does the name mean?"

The troll nodded. "Huh."

Ali considered. "Well, Farble means . . . he who is strong and brave. Yeah, that's what it means."

For the first time the troll smiled. With his green spit, yellow teeth, and bad breath, it was a rather gruesome affair. But Ali felt encouraged.

"Farble. Farble," the troll repeated. He liked the sound of it.

"Farble," Ali said, pointing to her chest. "My name is Ali. And this is Cindy. Ali and Cindy. Do you understand, Farble?"

"Cindy. Ali." He nodded. "Geea."

"Geea? Where does he get that? No, my name is just Ali."

For some reason he touched her sweater. "Geea."

"Ali. Ali." She tapped her chest. "Ali."

"Huh." Farble nodded and tried to give her back the sweater. She stopped him.

"You keep it for now," she said.

Farble's eyes glowed brighter. Maybe he thought she was giving it to him as a present. He hugged the sweater to his chest. "Geea," he said.

Ali turned to Cindy. "How's your arm feeling?"

"Don't even ask."

"I ask because we have to get to Overhang as fast as possible and I'm worried about you hiking for an hour straight."

Cindy shrugged. "We have no choice."

"We do. Farble can carry you."

"What? He stinks!"

"Fart," Farble said.

"Please, your name is Farble. Cindy, we've hiked ten minutes up the path and already you're breathing hard. The guys could still be in danger. I feel bad enough taking this short break. We can't have another. Let Farble carry you. You can always wash off later in the river."

"But what if Farble doesn't want to carry me?" Cindy complained.

The troll appeared to understand. Bending down, he picked Cindy up. He was ten feet tall; she looked like an infant in his arms.

"Hey!" Cindy cried.

"Cindy," he said. "Farble."

Ali laughed. "It's you he likes! Come, we have to hurry!"

Her vow to hike steadily proved impossible to keep. The terrain grew steeper. She was forced to stop several times to catch her breath. Her powers had deserted her again. She didn't like it that there had to be a crisis for her magic to work. But maybe there was a reason behind the rule.

It was nice to see Cindy at ease in Farble's arms. The troll was so careful with her, Cindy even dozed. To Ali he seemed more like a friendly giant than a man-eating monster.

But she knew she had to be on guard against trusting an elemental just because he looked cute. They were here to wipe humanity out. Still—like when she decided to enlist Paddy's help—there was something inside her that told her to bring the troll.

She needed to understand the elementals better if she was to heal the gap between them and humanity. Even if she managed to reach the Yanti in time, and close it, she knew the problems between the two dimensions would still exist. Nemi had told her as much.

Cindy stirred in Farble's arms. "You never told me how you walked through the fire?" she asked Ali.

"It was the test of fire. I told you a little about them while we were hiking. With each test I pass, I gain control over that particular element."

"What did you do to pass this test?" Cindy asked.

"Rescued Farble."

"And that gave you control over fire?"

"I think so," Ali said.

"But you had to have control over it to rescue him in the first place?"

"I think it was enough that I braved the fire for Farble."

"Sounds mystical to me." Cindy shook her head and added, "I think I liked you better when you were just my best friend."

Cindy was teasing, sort of, but the remark hurt Ali. Did becoming powerful mean she would lose her friends? Did people who discovered magic always have to pay a price?

Ali pushed the pace. The moon, although bright, was sinking toward the horizon. The sun was less than two hours away. Karl's map was not in his pack, and she had to steer by memory alone. But with the clouds gone she at least had landmarks.

She remembered that Overhang was half a mile west of the

path, and she knew that Karl had planned to veer to the left when they reached the top of the second ridge, which was just ahead. She kept praying that the guys had reached Overhang and were safe.

That hope faded as they crested the next ridge. Up ahead they saw flashes of red light. Seeing the weapons of the dark fairies at work, Cindy climbed down from Farble's arms. The red flashes could only be directed at the guys.

"The guys must already be at Overhang," Cindy said. "The dark fairies must have them trapped there."

"Probably," Ali agreed.

"Can you do anything to help them from here?" Cindy asked.

"I don't know." Ali closed her eyes and willed a tongue of flame to whip across the valley and strike the dark fairies. She imagined it clearly in her mind, put all her energy into it.

Nothing happened.

"We have to get closer," she said to Cindy. "I'm pretty sure I can at least deflect their fire stones."

"You might want to get your hands on some of those stones," Cindy suggested.

They hurried on. Cindy's idea stayed with Ali.

The weapons could come in handy, she thought.

The terrain finally gave them a break; they got to go downhill for a while. Cindy half jogged alongside Ali, with Farble loping behind. Except for twice saying how hungry he was, the troll did not complain.

They approached Overhang from the east. Ali kept them in the shadows, close to the rock wall. They could see the dark fairies up ahead, hovering like a swarm of black bees above the rocky ledge. Cindy was probably right—the guys had reached Overhang only to get trapped inside.

Ali knelt and picked up a rock.

"What are you going to do?" Cindy whispered.

"Get some of those fire stones," she said.

Without the pressure of the fire bolts sparking her hair, Ali was able to take careful aim. Even before she let go of the rock, she felt the power build in her muscles. Her stone flew like it had been shot out of a cannon. The closest of the dark fairies took it in the head and dropped like a swatted fly.

"Let's go!" Ali shouted as they ran forward. Of course the fairy's friends saw what she had done. The creatures were on them in seconds, hissing above like a swarm of black wraiths hatched from an evil tomb.

Inside, Ali reached for her power, felt it whirl through her entire body and then spin above her head like a cyclone made of living energy. There was a new element in the force field; it was much different than the one she had invoked before to keep out the rain. It glistened with ghostly fire. Tiny orange suns cracked and burst all around like boxes full of sparklers that had been tossed into the air.

The fire element was indeed under her command. Ali was not surprised when the dark fairies' red bolts were deflected harmlessly off to the side.

Yet it was odd how quickly the dark fairies realized what she had done. *That* surprised her. They fired only two shots before stopping. It was as if they had seen that trick before.

Still, they followed, a hundred feet overhead. The sound of their anger made Ali nauseous. Farble, also, appeared frightened. She had to hold his hand to get him to come.

The wounded fairy lay in a crumpled pile on top of a large boulder. It twitched as they approached, raised its head, but it was clear it could not fly. Its left wing was twisted at an awkward angle and a sickly purple fluid leaked from the side of its egg-shaped skull. The light of its eyes glowed a wicked red, but even that light faded in and out as they drew close.

The creature appeared a cross between a human, a lizard, and a bat—probably closest to the last. Coated with black scales, the fairy had claws instead of fingers, and a long dark tongue that lashed out as they came near.

"Death!" it hissed at them in a foul voice.

"Yeah, right. You're going to die, Snake Face," Cindy said.

"Shh!" Ali cautioned. The fairy had dropped its fire stones. They lay in the dirt at its feet, smoldering like hot coals that needed only a splash of fuel to ignite.

But above, the flock of dark fairies drew closer. They saw what she saw, and probably guessed what she was up to. They could swoop in at any second, rescue their fallen partner and the deadly weapons.

Why did they hesitate? They must be afraid of her.

Letting go of Farble's hand and easing the pack off her back, Ali knelt and picked up a rock. The dark fairies—there were four now—hovered above her energy umbrella. She could feel how high up it reached; it seemed they could as well.

They hissed as she stood and cocked her arm to fire. Quickly, they withdrew farther, like bees moving away from a poison flower. Was that how they saw her? Could she use their fear of her against them?

"I'm taking the fire stones!" she shouted. "In exchange you can have your friend back!"

They hissed, and their translucent wings moved in a dizzy blur. But they did not change position. Ali kept her rock ready.

"Cindy," she said quietly. "Go get the stones."

"Me? What if Snake Face tries to bite me?"

"Cindy," Ali said with a note of impatience. "I don't know how long I can hold them off. Take the backpack and kick the stones into it and let's get out of here. Hurry!"

Cindy stepped forward and used her feet to shove the stones into the pack. They were not large; they could have fit in the palm of their hands. Ali was not even sure if they were hot. Nervous, Cindy shoved a fair amount of dirt into the pack as well. Then, to top things off, she kicked a clot of mud in the wounded fairy's face.

"That's what you get for burning my arm!" she shouted.

Cindy hurried back. Farble patted her on the back and Cindy smiled. Her rock still held ready, Ali began to lead her friends away from the scene.

"Stay away from us!" she shouted. "If you come back again, you'll all die!"

The dark fairies buzzed loudly. But they did not descend to lift their partner away until Ali and her pals were almost out of sight. She was sure of their fear now, but she wondered if that was enough to keep them away.

Overhang was the perfect name for the ledge that stood above their heads. The mantle jutted out from the rock wall like a petrified flying saucer that had crash-landed on the side of the mountain a thousand years ago. Ali could see why Karl had insisted they reach it before nightfall. Maybe if she had listened to him, the attack of the dark fairies could have been avoided. It was a perfect place to take shelter.

Now they just had to see if the guys were all right.

Ali's heart pounded as they hiked up the final few feet.

A head poked over the ledge above them. "Hello down there?"

"Steve?" Ali cried. "Is that you?"

"It is I. Karl and Paddy are resting behind me. Do you need a hand?"

"Sure," Ali said, reaching up for help. She had Karl's pack on her back again; it was heavy. But Steve suddenly withdrew his hand.

"What the heck is that?" he gasped, looking past her.

"That's Farble, he's a troll. Help me up."

"We're not going to tell you his real name," Cindy snickered.

"What are you guys doing with a troll?" Steve wanted to know.

Ali sighed. "It's a long story."

*   *   *

Finally, they were all together again, alive, and in one piece. Ali supposed they had a lot to be thankful for. Yet the night had taken its toll.

Karl had taken a hit to the stomach. The burn was more serious than Cindy's. Ali marveled that he had been able to make it to Overhang with the dark fairies on his trail. Sitting with him in the shadow of the ledge, she opened the first-aid kit to treat the wound.

"What you really need is a doctor," she said.

"You'll do fine, Nurse Ali."

"I'm no nurse," she replied, thinking of Ted in intensive care. Was he still alive? Taking out the disinfectant, she leaned closer. "Does it hurt?"

"Only when I think about it."

"Which is every two seconds?"

"Right," Karl said. "Can I ask you something?"

"Sure."

"Why do we have a troll for a friend now?"

"I saved his life in the fire. I think he can help us."

"He doesn't want to eat us?"

"He has been behaving himself. But I think we better feed him soon."

"Sounds like a relationship built on trust," Karl muttered.

"You have to get to know him. His name is Farble."

"I heard he had another name."

"That Cindy. Sit still, I have to clean this mess," she said.

The center of his jacket had been burned to a crisp. He was lucky he'd had it on, and that it had been thick. Otherwise the bolt from the fairy could have burnt his guts. She peeled away the charred remains of the coat to get a better look. His skin had already begun to blister.

"What happened after we left?" she asked.

"We kept getting pounded. They hit Paddy's whiskey bag. The bottles exploded like gasoline. We wanted to give you guys the best head start we could, but we couldn't remain at the camp. So we split up and ducked into the fog. We would have been dead without the cover. For a while—for me at least—it seemed I had lost them. But when I got here, they were waiting for me."

"Waiting for you?"

Karl frowned. "It was weird, it was like that. They were hovering outside. I was lucky to get inside. Had to fight my way in."

"How did Steve and Paddy get inside?"

"Steve was here when I got here."

"He got here before you?" she asked.

"Yes."

"Wow. It shows you the energy fear can give you."

"Yeah. He was lucky. He didn't have a scratch on him. Paddy came a few minutes later. The fairies hit him a couple of times but that leprechaun is tougher than he looks. He helped us defend the place until you arrived and saved us."

"I didn't save you." She sprayed his stomach with the disinfectant and he jerked. "Okay?"

"No problem." He took a painful breath and added, "Sure you saved us. We saw what you did from up here. That took guts."

"It took more magic than guts. How did you guys defend yourselves?"

"Rocks mostly."

"Nothing else?"

"No." He hesitated. "Sticks."

"So you took the hit in the stomach here? I thought you got it back at the camp."

"They hit me a few minutes before you got here. With me down, it was looking pretty scary. I didn't think Paddy and Steve could hold out much longer."

"How much supplies were you guys able to save?"

"None."

Ali gasped. "What?"

"We don't even have our water bottles."

"The sleeping bags?"

"They caught fire with Paddy's whiskey. I'm sorry, Ali."

"Don't be sorry, it's not your fault." She paused, thinking frantically. "Can we make it to the top without supplies?"

"You saved my backpack. We have the crampons, the rope, and the ice axes. Sure, we can go a day without food. Water's the problem. You need tons of it to hike at this altitude."

"What about the river?" she asked.

"We'll leave it behind after a few more hours of hiking."

"There's snow higher up. We can melt it for water."

"We need fire to melt snow."

She thought of the fire stones, told him about them.

He nodded. "That might work. But we won't have anything to get down with. No food, no sleeping bags, no cell phones." He gestured to his ruined coat. "Nothing."

"Do you want to turn back?"

"Do you?" he asked.

Again, she thought of Ted. "I can't. I have a responsibility."

"To see this through to the bitter end?"

"I know that sounds dramatic, but yes, I have to see it through. The tree told me that I was the only one who can do it. And I believe him."

"The tree was a him?"

"You know what I mean, Karl. But none of that applies to you guys. You're hurt. You should go back."

He stared at her a long time. "You've changed in the last few days."

"You mean, the powers I've gained?"

"It goes deeper than that. You're like a different person."

She smiled. "Better or worse?"

"You scared those creatures tonight. I told you, I was watching from up here. You scared me, Ali."

She lost her smile. She saw that he was serious. Another friend that looked at her funny. Here she had thought how cool it would be to have magical powers. The price of her abilities was adding up quick. She could end up even more lonely than before.

"More reason you should go back," she said.

He shook his head. "I think it's a reason to stay."

"Why?"

"Because I think you're going to be on the winning side."

CHAPTER THIRTEEN

The others were still resting when Ali stood and hiked from the stone ledge of Overhang and down into the trees. The clouds had cleared. In the east a faint light had begun to appear, and Venus shone like a hard diamond against the black-blue sky. The cold, crisp air was too invigorating to sleep in—at least to Ali, but then again she had a lot on her mind.

In her hands she carried the fire stones. They were not hot.

She did not know how she stumbled across the pond. Suddenly it was just there, at her feet, and she decided it was as a good place as any to sit and think. Kneeling near the water, she was pleased to see how clear and still it was—an almost perfect mirror of the sky. If anything, Venus looked brighter in the pond. The light of the planet flickered over the icy surface like the gleam in an angel's eye.

"The planet of love," she said to herself.

Ali picked up the fire stones and casually rubbed them together.

A red bolt of energy erupted and stabbed the pond.

A gusher of steam exploded into the air.

"Ouch!"

"What?" Ali gasped. Did someone say ouch? The bolt had shocked her silly, but not as much as the miraculous way the water settled back down. Why, within seconds it was as calm as when she had walked up to the pond.

"How is that possible?" she whispered.

A voice spoke in her mind.

"I have a little magic of my own."

"Nemi!" she squealed.

"Hello, Alosha."

She clapped her hands together. "This is great! This is just what I needed!" Quickly, she closed her eyes so that she could hear him better.

"To shoot me with your fire stones?" he asked.

"Don't be silly. Nemi, I thought you were dead!"

"You mean, you thought I was a tree?"

"No. Yes!" She added, "I don't know who you are. You never told me."

"Why worry about me? You don't know who you are."

"Ah. Is that a test question?"

"As a matter of fact it is. That is the seventh test."

"Why don't you just give me the answer and save us both a lot of trouble?"

"That would be no fun. You will find out. But first you must conquer air, space, and time."

"So I have a hurricane to look forward to? Or will it be a tornado? We don't get too many of those in the Northwest."

"Air is a mysterious element. Consider what is carried through the air—the greatest of all human inventions."

"I don't understand," Ali said.

"That is why it is called a test." Nemi added, "The tests don't have to be in order. You might solve one before the other." Nemi added, "You just have to stay alive."

"How can you be so encouraging and so dark at the same time?"

"It is the way I am."

She had to smile. Yet the smile did not remain.

"I have so many things on my mind," she admitted.

"That means the test of air is around the corner." Nemi added, "What troubles you?"

"Lots of stuff. The gang almost got wiped out last night. The dark fairies could come back at any time. We have no food or water. Everything feels like it's falling apart." She shook her head. "I feel like I was the wrong person to trust with such an important mission."

"Aren't you being too hard on yourself? You have done well so far, considering the obstacles. You are still alive, that is a miracle in itself." Nemi paused. "Something else troubles you."

"Yes."

"You feel something is wrong that you're not seeing."

"Yes. How do you know?"

"I am a smart tree. Or a smart pile of ash, however the case may be."

"Would you stop that!" She quieted. "Why do I feel this way, Nemi?"

"Do you want me to take your test for you?"

"Sure. Take them all. They're too hard."

"You joke. You know I can't do that. But you have learned to trust your feelings. There must be something important that you are missing. It could be right in front of your face."

"And that's the test of air?"

"It might be," Nemi said.

"I don't know why I like you so much. You sound like a New Age psychic."

"You are the one who's talking to a pond."

"You're so frustrating!"

"Imagine how I feel about you."

She paused. "I guess I must look pretty stupid to you."

"You are not stupid at all. You are close to passing a very hard test."

"What if I don't pass it?"

"You know the answer to that."

"I will die? Will my friends die, too?"

"Some things I cannot say."

Again, she wanted to ask about her mother. But she knew she should change the subject. Nemi did not want to talk about death—he was telling her as much.

"Do you know Lord Vak and Lord Balar?" she asked.

"Yes."

"Are they evil?"

"Is the president of your country evil? Lord Vak and Lord Balar have their own interests. Sometimes that blinds them to the interests of others."

"Is there another reason besides the pollution that they are attacking the human race? I know you said before that it was a secret, but I need to know."

"You do not need to know the answer to that question to find the Yanti and close it. But it is true, later you will need to know."

"Can I trust Paddy and Farble?"

"You decide."

"No! Tell me!"

"Trust yourself. Remember, I am not your master and you are not my slave. You must make your own choices."

"Why are you here then?" she asked, feeling overwhelmed.

"I miss you," he said.

Three simple words. They touched her so deeply.

"I've missed you, Nemi. Promise me you won't go away again."

"I told you, I am always around." He added, "What else troubles you?"

"The dark fairies. Were they always so evil?"

"No."

"What happened?"

"They made poor choices. They wanted power more than anything else."

"They seem to know me."

"Why do you say that?"

"They reacted quickly when I was trying to steal their fire stones, and at the same time they seemed afraid of me."

"An astute observation. They know you well."

"How?"

"You will see."

"Am I more powerful than they are?"

"Power cannot be put on a scale and measured. Sometimes the greater a person's power, the weaker they are."

"Are you talking about me? I've been worried about that. My friends have started to treat me different. I don't want to lose them."

"Don't lose them."

"But how?"

"Be wise. Wisdom is a great power. It is the first thing the dark fairies lost long ago."

"They are disgusting, but there is something that scares me even more. And I haven't even met it." Ali paused. "What is the Shaktra?"

Nemi sounded surprised. "Where did you hear about that?"

"I dreamed about it. What is it?"

There was a forever pause.

"Something very painful. Something very personal."

"Nemi," she began. But he interrupted.

"You do not want to know what it is, and you will not know for some time. Your task, at present, is the Yanti. Focus on that."

She wanted to pressure him for more information, but feared what she might hear. "I will," she promised.

Nemi's tone was gentle in her mind. "It is time for you to go back to your friends."

Ali felt so much peace in his company, and so much pain at the thought of leaving. "Can I talk to you again before I reach the Yanti?" she asked.

"Not in this way, Alosha. But I told you, I am always near."

Ali stood. Nemi said he was not her master. He probably would not like her bowing to the pond. She touched the water instead, raised the finger to her lips. It was almost as if she could taste the sweetness of his personality in the cold liquid.

"Don't go too far," she whispered.

CHAPTER FOURTEEN

They got an early start. With no breakfast to eat, no showers to take, there was nothing for the gang to do but wake up and get going. They didn't even have to shoulder their backpacks. Karl's pack was the only one left and he insisted on carrying it, his burnt stomach notwithstanding. He said his wound felt much better.

"Now it only hurts when I breathe," he told Ali.

Cindy was hurting from her burn but refused to complain. She could be tough when it counted. Ali was proud of her, proud of them all. No one even talked about turning around.

They resumed their hike up the mountain, always up, even before the sun rose. But now they were starting a half mile west of Treeline Path, and Karl said there was no point in heading back to the trail.

"It doesn't go to the top," he explained as they stopped for a quick breather. "It cuts far east, circles the mountain, and then starts down again. It comes out somewhere on the backside of Pete's Peak, I'm not sure where."

"Do we follow the river for now?" Ali asked.

"Yes. As long as we stay near it we'll have water. But it doesn't go to the top, either, of course. We'll have to leave it when we reach the snow line."

The snow was near, a thousand feet above. Already they were approaching the treeline. The pines and firs had thinned since yesterday.

Pete's Peak stood above like an ice sculpture carved by an ancient race of giants. Up close the peak was daunting, the sides so sheer Ali could not imagine scaling them. But by the day's end they would have to be near the top, and by two in the morning they had to reach the summit.

"What's our elevation now?" Ali asked.

Karl glanced at the map. "Ten thousand feet. That's an important height. Above it breathing becomes much harder."

"You're depressing me," Steve said.

"We have to know what we're facing," Karl said.

"I don't know about that," Steve disagreed.

They started again, the river on their left, a hundred feet below. It was not as wide as it had been at lower altitudes, but it still packed a punch. Ali would have hated for any of them to fall in the water. She figured the current would sweep them all the way to the falls before there would be a chance to get out.

Without a path to follow, the way was rough. They kept running into clumps of trees and steep rocks; they were constantly backtracking. However, they made surprising progress before the sun came up.

Then they had a major problem.

As the first rays of the morning sun licked over the woods, Farble ran behind a tree and cowered. Paddy, who showed no love for their new traveling companion, shook his head in disgust.

"What else can you expect from a troll?" Paddy said. The leprechaun was in poor shape himself. Besides missing his hat, his green bow tie was in tatters and the back of his coat was burned.

"The sun is hardening his skin?" Ali asked, concerned.

"Aye. Troll skin burns then hardens," Paddy said. "Best we leave him behind, Missy. Never know what a troll will do. Before we left this morning he pawed Paddy and told me he was hungry."

"He's not going to eat you," Ali said impatiently.

"Leprechauns are a delicacy for trolls. The moment you turn your back, he'll try to put poor Paddy in his stomach."

"Paddy sounds like he knows what he's talking about," Steve said.

"I think we need Farble," Ali said, watching the troll tremble behind the tree. She felt a pang of sympathy; here Farble was threatened by fire again.

"We need him like we need a dark fairy to laser off our warts," Steve said.

"He'll only do more harm than good," Paddy agreed. "Leave him be, Missy."

"Karl!" Ali called. As always, Karl was a few steps ahead. "Do you still have that umbrella in your pack? And that sunscreen?"

"We need that sunscreen for our faces," Cindy complained. "I don't want to get burned and get wrinkles and look old."

"How old are you?" Paddy asked.

"Thirteen," Cindy said.

Paddy shook his head in amazement. "You're but an egg, lassie."

Ali got the umbrella and sunscreen from Karl and walked over to the troll. So far Farble had avoided any direct contact with the sun's rays, but it was only a matter of time before he was caught out of the shade.

She knew it would be an even worse problem for him once they were above the treeline. Of course they would all be exposed up on the slope. Anyone could see them, from miles away. The thought continued to haunt her.

"Farble," she said softly. "Are you okay?"

He shook his head. "Scared."

She came closer, touched his thick arm. He needed a bath before she could even think of putting on the sunscreen. She showed him the lotion, however, and opened the umbrella to demonstrate how it could shield him from the sun.

"This lotion can stop the sun from hurting your skin," she explained. "And the umbrella will keep the sun off your face and shoulders. But what I need you to do first is take a bath."

His big head wobbled. "Bath?"

"Yes, a bath. You need to wash off this mud so the sunscreen can work. Go down to the river, sit in it a few minutes up to your neck, then shake off and come back here. Hurry, we don't have much time."

Farble nodded and lumbered down to the river, limping all the way. His leg must still be hurting, she thought, feeling a pang of guilt. She turned and waved to the others. She could tell they were talking about her.

Farble was back in a few minutes. Most of the dirt had washed away, and he smelled a whole lot fresher. He knew how to shake off better than a dog. Already his skin was pretty dry. He sat patiently in the shade while she rubbed the lotion on his gray hide. Even sitting, his head was taller than her's.

"Farble, I need to talk to you about something," she said as she worked the sunscreen into his arms. He appeared to enjoy the massage; she doubted he had ever got one before. She was glad the lotion was rated a full fifty. The label said it would block the sun completely.

On humans, she thought. No doubt his hairy hide would make it less effective.

It was interesting to study his body up close. He did indeed have plenty of hair; it was not just flaky mud. The fibers were thick but surprisingly soft. His skin, also, was much smoother than she would have imagined. Yet it was the muscles under his skin that fascinated her. Because they felt as if they were all one piece, solid, hard to separate. As if he were a tree trunk rather than a breathing animal.

His huge yellow eyes looked up at her as she rubbed on the lotion.

"Talk?" he said.

"Yes. You saw part of what happened last night. We were attacked by dark fairies and they destroyed our food. We have nothing to eat."

He nodded. "Hungry."

"Yeah. We're hungry, and I know you're hungry too. The point is we have nothing to feed you. We're all going to be hungry on this trip. But that doesn't mean you can eat any of us. Especially the leprechaun, Paddy. He's not for lunch."

"Dinner?" Farble said hopefully.

"No. You can't eat him period. But after we're done with our trip, I'll find you something tasty to eat." She paused uneasily. "What do you like to eat?"

"Babies," he said.

Ali frowned. "Human babies?"

Farble nodded. "Babies and leprechauns."

"How about a big rare steak?"

"Steak?"

"Yeah. They come from cows."

Farble nodded. "Cows. Steak. Good."

"I'll get you a big steak when we get back to town," she said, as she continued to apply the sunscreen. It took time to cover all of him, and when she was done the tube was practically empty. But by then he was able to stand in the sun and not cringe. Showing him the best way to hold the umbrella, she took off her sunglasses and put them on the end of his nose. Of course, with his massive skull, it ruined the glasses trying to fit them over his ears. But he seemed to like them so much, she didn't mind the sacrifice.

In the distance the others snickered. She had to admit Farble looked pretty funny. But she smiled and patted him on the shoulder.

"Now you could walk around Breakwater and no one would notice," she said.

He nodded, happy with all she had done for him. She noticed that he continued to keep her sweater tied around his neck.

"Farble," she said before they returned to the others. "Did you push me in the river the other day?"

He shook his head. "No hurt."

"But you chased me that afternoon. You admitted that already, and besides, I saw you. I threw that rock at your leg. Remember?"

He nodded, ashamed. "Hungry."

"That's all right, I understand. But earlier that same day—about an hour earlier—did you or your friends push me in the river?"

He shook his head. "No hurt Geea."

"Ali. My name is Ali. Listen closely, Farble, this is important. Could your friends have pushed me in the water when you were not there?"

He shook his head. "No."

She was puzzled. "Did you or your friends hit Steve on the head by the river?"

He shook his head.

"Are you sure?"

He was confused. "No."

He must be mistaken, she thought. Who else could have attacked them? The creature that had flung her in the water had been strong. And Steve had taken a nasty blow to the head. He had been knocked out, his camera taken.

Funny about that, though. Steve did not get much of a bruise from the attack. His face looked fine this morning. What was even more odd was how quickly he had reached Overhang once the dark fairies attacked. Of course, he had been scared. Frightened people often did amazing things.

Why was she suddenly doubting Steve?

They resumed their torturous hike, as the sun rose higher into the sky. They had lost their water bottles, but Karl had a couple of steel cups in his pack. They were able to drink from the river when they wanted; however, their hunger came quick and hard. The exercise was to blame; they must have been burning a thousand calories an hour.

Like before, Steve tired quickly. Ali demanded that he let Farble carry him. Even with one hand on the umbrella, and a bum leg, the troll appeared to have strength to spare.

"I'm not letting that smelly carpet carry me," Steve complained.

"He doesn't smell so bad since he took a bath," Ali said.

"He won't drop you, I can vouch for that," Cindy said.

"No," Steve said, annoyed.

"Look at you, we've hiked only two hours and you're exhausted," Ali said. "An hour from now you'll be flat on your back. Don't you see, we can't afford that? We have to keep moving and we can't leave you behind. You have to swallow your pride."

"What if the guys at school find out about this?" Steve asked.

"Who's going to tell them?" Ali asked.

"I might," Cindy said brightly.

"Oh brother," Ali groaned.

Steve glanced at the troll, then at Paddy. "What do you think?" he asked the leprechaun.

"If he doesn't take a bite out of you, laddie, I suppose it could do you no harm," Paddy said.

"You're a big help," Steve grumbled.

"I think he's safe," Karl said.

"You didn't say that last night," Steve said.

"I wasn't in such a hurry last night," Karl said, wiping the sweat off his brow and looking at Ali. He tapped his watch.

"I don't know," Steve said, sulking.

Farble surprised them all. He stepped forward and reached out a hand to Steve. "Help," he said.

"See, he wants to help you," Ali said.

Steve glanced at the peak and then back at the troll. "You try to bite me and I'll take away your umbrella," he said.

Farble shook his head. "No hurt."

"Okay," Steve said. "But only for a few minutes. Just till I catch my breath."

The troll picked Steve up and nestled him in one arm like an overgrown child. They resumed their climb. Steve ended up holding the umbrella over Farble's head. Ali thought they looked cute together.

Later, they were about to leave the trees behind when Paddy suddenly stopped. Sniffing the air, he glanced at Farble, who quickly set down Steve—his few minutes had grown into a laid-back hour—and also sniffed the air.

The leprechaun and the troll looked worried.

"What is it?" Ali asked.

"Elves," Paddy said.

Karl looked around. "Where?"

"Close," Paddy said. He spoke to Farble. "Behind us?"

The troll stared back the way they had come. There was nothing to see but the river and the forest. Farble nodded in response to Paddy's question, however.

"Elves," Farble said.

"Do you see them?" Ali asked.

"Not easy to see elves in the woods, Missy," Paddy said. "Move fast, from tree to tree. They'll be here before you know it."

"What should we do?" Ali asked.

"Run," Paddy said. "Fast. Up the mountain."

"I don't think I can run," Cindy said, soaked in sweat and out of breath. She had been talking about trading places with Steve just before Paddy and Farble had caught the scent.

Paddy hopped from foot to foot, anxious. "The troll can carry you, lassie. Best we be gone."

Farble nodded, scared. "Elves. Coming."

"Can't we talk to them?" Steve said. "I thought elves were supposed to be reasonable."

"They're invading our dimension to wipe us out," Karl told Steve. "I don't think talking with them will help."

"*Us* talking doesn't help," Paddy said. "Time to be on our way."

Ali looked back the way they had come, hesitated. If they left the shelter of the trees, they would be easy to track. "How many elves are behind us?" she asked.

"Don't know!" Paddy said. "Enough! Let's go!"

"Six," Farble said.

"Are you sure?" Ali asked the troll.

"Six," the troll repeated.

"That isn't too many," Ali muttered.

"He's a troll!" Paddy complained. "He can't count up to six. He can only count to two—the number of leprechauns he can eat at one time. Missy, we must run!"

She held up her hand. "Wait. If there's only six, we might be able to handle them. I have the fire stones."

"Cool," Steve said, nodding. "Blast the suckers."

"No," Ali said. "I'm not going to kill them."

Paddy was close to a nervous breakdown. "Either kill them or run from them, Missy! Do one or the other!"

"Why not kill them?" Cindy asked her. "If they try to kill us?"

Ali considered. "Because they're not like the dark fairies. They're not evil. This whole war—I think it's just a misunderstanding."

"That might be true," Karl said. "But if the elves are as intense as Paddy says, then I doubt we'll be able to clear up that misunderstanding before we're dead."

She nodded. "But I hate to run up into the snow. We could get bogged down up there, and Paddy says the elves are great archers. They could pick us off from a distance, one by one."

"That's why you have to kill them," Steve said, getting more scared.

"Better them than us," Cindy said.

Just then an arrow flew out of the trees and struck Farble's umbrella. Another arrow followed; it hit a tree beside them. The gang ducked behind the rocks and trees. Crouched near a boulder, Ali peered down the mountain. Still, she could not see a thing.

"Fire off a few shots, let them know we're armed," Karl said, kneeling nearby.

Ali already had the fire stones out. "I can't start a fire. There's no clouds to put it out," she said.

"For once let's not worry about the environment!" Steve shouted.

More arrows flew over their heads and landed harmlessly behind them. But the elves were not out for target practice. The arrows were meant to kill. They had been lucky so far, she realized, but their luck could not last forever.

Ali caught a glimpse of movement; it gave her a target. Standing up and rubbing the stones together, she willed the beam to follow the course her mind set. The stones were like high-powered lasers, she imagined. She was the battery. She was confident she had more juice than a typical dark fairy.

The bolt that erupted from her stones was awesome. The red beam tore the air and struck a boulder in front of the spot where she had seen movement, and the rock exploded as if dynamited. The noise was deafening. Dust rained down on them, as the boom echoed across the mountain.

Her friends cheered, and for a moment the forest went still. But then another wave of arrows flew overhead. "I was hoping it would scare them away," she hissed, ducking back down.

"Kill a few and they'll get scared," Karl said.

She looked at him. "I didn't come up here to kill."

"You came up here to stop a war. Sometimes that involves killing."

She tried to hand him the stones. "You do it then."

He shook his head. "I don't have your power." He paused. "Ali?"

"What?" she asked.

"Paddy's right. You have to make a decision. We either stay and fight or else we run. There can be no in-between."

She sighed. "I know."

It was then her gaze was drawn to the river. They had not considered trying to cross it. The current would sweep them away in seconds. But what if they had a tree to walk across? A downed tree, after all, had saved her life at the falls. She hated killing a living tree but it was better than killing elves, or her friends for that matter. Tapping Karl's arm, she pointed at the river.

"We need to get in the gorge. All of us," she said.

"No. They'll trap us down there."

"No. I'm going to make us a bridge."

Karl was confused but then understanding dawned and he smiled. "Good plan," he said.

Trying to stay under cover, the gang scampered into the gorge. It was not steep at this altitude. Indeed, they had already walked down to the river a number of times during their morning hike.

Unfortunately, the elves refused to let up. Another wave of arrows followed. One hit Karl's backpack, and a second one flew between her legs as she dashed across the open space. A few inches to either side and she would have been crippled.

"We can't swim across this water!" Steve cried, terrified by the raining arrows.

"We're trapped!" Cindy said, despairing.

"We're not trapped and we don't have to swim." Ali pointed to a tree that stood twenty feet above the river. "I'm cutting down that pine. Stand back!"

Because the branches were weighed heavily on the side of the river, she was confident the tree would fall over the water. But to get a clean shot at it, she had to climb out of the gorge, once more exposing herself to the arrows.

Ali decided to give the elves something to worry about for the next few minutes. Raising the stones, she fired off another shot, blowing up a clump of bushes and a mound of dirt. The debris showered over the slope and the noise probably told anyone who was listening exactly where they were. Well, she thought, it couldn't be helped.

Ali jumped onto the rocks and studied the tree. The base was thick—better to have a precision cut than another explosion, she thought. Holding tight on the stones, she concentrated on how she wanted them to perform. She was rewarded when a narrow beam of light poured out and she was able to cut the tree like a slice of bread. In fact, she cut it so clean that it didn't move when she was done, although the stump had been severed from the rest of the trunk. She had to give it a stiff kick.

The tree toppled across the river. The dust, when it landed, was like a blast from a sandstorm, but she was too relieved to care. She shouted to the others.

"Get across! Hurry!" she said.

Karl was the first across, followed by Cindy and Steve. Paddy went next, but Farble was having second thoughts. Ali had to climb down into the gorge and take his hand.

"Are you afraid?" she asked.

He nodded sadly. "Can't swim."

"You don't have to be able to swim. We're not going in the water. Come on, I'll walk behind you. You'll be safe with me."

Farble believed her. Whatever she said, it was gospel to him. It made her wonder. Why did he keep calling her Geea?

The troll leaped onto the fallen pine—with a quick look behind to make sure she was coming—and lumbered across. The wide trunk was as easy to skirt as a real bridge. Ali was across in seconds. It was only on the other side, however, that she saw the arrows the elves had put in the tree.

For the first time she got a glimpse of the enemy. They stood above the gorge on the other side. Clad entirely in green, they had long yellow hair that reminded her of gold crowns set in the sun. With human-shaped heads and large eyes and gentle mouths, their faces appeared as soft as children's.

The sight of them reminded her of something Paddy had said.

"Is Lord Vak close to Jira?"

"He was."

"I thought you said he almost *died?"*

"Jira died later."

"How?"

Paddy had changed the subject then.

The name Jira was even more familiar to her than Lord Vak.

She pushed away the thought. She had more pressing concerns. The gang was far from safe. Across the river, the elves carried bows and arrows. Two of them pointed at her as she studied them through the branches. They lifted their weapons.

Ali raised the fire stones, took aim above their heads. The blast went lower than planned. Maybe a part of her wanted to hurt them, after all. The two elves lost their caps; they almost lost their heads. They ducked out of sight.

"The tree, Ali!" Karl shouted.

"I know," she said. This time she didn't bother to be precise. Aiming the stones at the tree's center, she fired a hard blast. The red laser tore through the wood, sending out a rain of charred splinters, cutting the trunk in two. The pieces collapsed into the water and the current dragged the logs down the mountain and out of sight.

Ali felt a stab of regret. It had hurt to cut down the tree.

The gang ran into the trees, finally safe on the west side of the river. But they had not gone far when they were forced to stop and catch their breath. They didn't even get to enjoy their rest. Paddy brought up more bad news.

"Elves have axes. They can cut down their own trees, make their own bridges," he said.

Steve must have been feeling cocky after seeing the way she had sliced and diced the tree. "If they cross the river, Ali will take care of them," he said.

Paddy shook his head. "You believe a troll when he says there were only six? There were six right behind us but more will come."

"Are you saying they were only scouts?" Karl asked.

"Aye. The noise will bring others. We must get away from this place."

"How do you know there are more elves in the woods?" Ali asked.

The leprechaun was frustrated. "Paddy guesses. But it's a good guess."

"The moon was almost full last night," Ali persisted. "Do you think the Yanti opened further, and more elementals were able to come through?"

Paddy nodded. "Possible, Missy."

"Have you spoken to the elves since you came through the Yanti?" she asked.

"Leprechauns and elves don't often speak."

"Paddy?" Ali said.

"Aye! Saw a few before I made me way to town. Matters not, all this talk. Let us leave this place, Missy!"

"We should keep going," Karl agreed.

Ali considered. "I'm still afraid of getting caught on the open slope. If there are more elves, they'll see us up there and track us down."

"Do we have a choice?" Karl asked.

"Do we?" Ali asked. "You've studied the map more than anyone. Is there another way to the top?"

"Sure. We can circle around to the backside of the mountain. But we'd lose a whole day."

"But with the fire stones, you could waste a hundred elves," Cindy said.

Ali shook her head. "No way."

Paddy nodded vigorously. "Elves also have magic. Cannot count on stones to save us. Lord Vak and his people are smart. Stones might not work when we need them."

Ali spoke to the leprechaun. "Do you know another way to the top besides hiking up the slope in front of us?"

Paddy hesitated. "No safe way. No, Missy."

"Sounds like an evasive answer," Steve muttered.

Before Ali could press the leprechaun further, Farble spoke.

"Cave," he said.

Ali turned. "What cave?"

Farble gestured up the mountain. "Cave. Dark."

"You know of a cave that leads to the top of the mountain?" Ali asked.

Farble nodded. "Cave. Sleep."

"You have slept in the cave during the day when the sun is out?" Ali asked.

Farble nodded. "Dark. Nice."

Ali stared at the leprechaun. "You know about this cave." It was not a question.

Paddy shook his head. "No, Missy."

"Paddy!"

He was a mass of nerves. "Cave is filled with dwarves! Worse than elves! They hate leprechauns! Cut off the head of any they see!"

"Have you been in this cave?" she demanded. "The truth!"

"No, Missy. Only heard of. But dwarves are there, truly."

"Is this cave like one long tunnel? Or does it have different branches?" Ali asked.

"A vast cave it is, Missy. A place to get lost in. Better to walk outside in the sun, risk the elves."

Ali was thinking. "But if it is a vast cave, we might be able to avoid the dwarves."

Paddy took her hand, pleaded. "Missy, listen to Paddy! In the dark, dark creatures have power."

She caught his meaning. "There are dark fairies in there?"

He nodded miserably. " 'Tis where they live."

"The ones we fought last night?"

"Aye. Paddy does not want to see Missy die in there."

"I'm not going in there," Cindy said. "I had enough of them last night."

"It doesn't sound like my kind of place," Steve agreed.

Ali looked at Karl. "What do you think?"

He shrugged. "It has advantages. If the elves are going to chase us up the slope, it would be a nice way to disappear. But . . ."

"But it sounds dangerous," Ali said.

"Yes," Karl agreed.

Ali spoke to the leprechaun. "Would the elves follow us into the cave?"

Paddy seemed resigned to the fact that they had a crazy leader. He spoke in a defeated voice. "Elves do not like caves. Elves smarter than Missy."

Ali turned to Farble. "Show us this cave. I'll decide what to do when we get there."

"*You'll* decide?" Cindy said.

"Our vote doesn't count anymore?" Steve asked.

Ali hesitated. "I just want to keep us safe is all."

"You just want to get to the Yanti," Cindy corrected her.

Ali did not reply. The Yanti *had* begun to obsess her. Was it a mysterious object or a secret doorway? After talking to Nemi again, she still was not sure. Yet she imagined it was something she could hold in her hands, maybe even wear on her body. She hoped it was made of gold and inlaid with beautiful jewels.

Yet her longing for it surprised her. She was not normally one who got attached to *stuff*. She never wore jewelry at home or at school. There was simply something about the Yanti—just the *sound* of its name—that drew her. Even talking to Nemi had not freed her of the desire for it.

But perhaps Cindy was right and her goal had become more important to her than the lives of her friends. She hoped that was not the case. She stared at her friends. They stared back.

"The Yanti is the reason we set out on this trip," she said. "Of course I want to get to it. I need it to stop this invasion. But you guys owe me nothing. I'm grateful you've come with me this far. But if you want to turn around and head home, it's fine with me."

There was a long silence. Finally Steve spoke.

"We turn around, the elves might get us," he said.

"Or the dark fairies," Cindy added. "We couldn't get back to the road before sunset."

"Personally, I still think there's safety in numbers," Karl said.

Ali agreed. "I think so, too. But I don't want to *force* any of you to follow me." She added, she could not help herself, "I don't want any of you to feel like you're my *slaves*."

It was not a showdown; however, it came close. Steve and Cindy exchanged uneasy glances, but did not speak. Ali turned back to Farble.

"Lead us to the cave," she told the troll.

CHAPTER FIFTEEN

Finally, they left the trees behind. Right away they ran into a foot of snow. Soggy from the heat of the sun, it did not crunch under their feet so much as splat. The stuff was melting fast. The water from the snow soaked the ground beneath, slowing their feet with mud. Another two weeks of sun, Ali thought, and it would be altogether gone from this altitude. Too bad she couldn't wait until then to save the world.

The river ran on their right now, galloping down the snowy slope like rain pouring over the side of a white roof. Far below, in the trees, Ali sensed movement but did not see any elves. But Paddy and Farble assured her there were plenty.

"They gather their forces," the leprechaun said.

"But you said they won't go in the cave?" Ali asked again.

"Aye. Paddy said that."

Farble seemed sure that the cave was on their side of the river. But Ali knew it would be a mistake to think of the river as impassable. As Paddy had pointed out, the elves had axes. They could make their own tree bridges. Worse, two thousand feet above them, the river was going to vanish. Ali hated to think what it would be like to hike up the mountain with them on one side of the water, the elves on the other—with the elves just waiting for the river to shrink to a stream. Again, it made her want to take the cave.

Yet the cave terrified Paddy. Leprechauns, she thought with a sigh. Even when they told the truth, they never told the whole truth. What was he hiding? She noticed that he no longer walked beside her, and did not meet her eyes when she looked at him.

Farble carried Steve and Cindy, one at a time, giving each one a breather every twenty minutes. Well, actually, Steve was getting the most mileage out of the troll, but he probably needed it.

Ali had to stop regularly to catch her breath. She missed her sunglasses. The glare of the sun was blinding. No matter how much she drank, she was constantly thirsty. Plus she had a headache. Without bottles, what would they do when they left the river behind?

"It's tough, isn't it?" Karl said, as they both stopped to rest.

She forced a smile. "I can make it."

Karl nodded, gestured to Paddy and Farble, who continued to walk ahead. "Those two have more endurance than all of us put together."

"They're lucky. Farble's helped a lot."

"But what if war *does* break out? Are we sure they will remain on our side?"

A disturbing question. Ali had not thought about it that way.

The cave appeared suddenly, which was a surprise given that the square entrance was big. However, the opening pointed due west, and was tucked behind an outcropping of rock. They might have missed it if Farble had not stopped them.

Still, its size raised questions in Ali's mind. Why was the cave not on the map? Over the years, hundreds of people had hiked to the top of Pete's Peak. Someone must have seen it before. Or did it mean the cave was new? Standing near the entrance, she brought up her doubts to the others. It was an example of how tired they all were that no one seemed to care.

"Well, it's here now," Steve said.

"Yeah. And I don't like the look of it," Cindy said.

"What do you think, Karl?" Ali asked.

He had sat down to rest, unusual for him. His burnt stomach must have been bothering him more than he let on. "The entrance looks kind of square," he said. "It might have been cut out."

"When? By whom?" Ali glanced at the leprechaun. "Paddy?"

He was disgusted they had even brought him to the cave. "Dwarves like caves. Dig out many with their steel tools."

"But was this cave here a few weeks ago?" Ali asked.

"Don't know. Paddy wasn't here then."

"Do you know, Farble?" Ali asked.

The troll shook his head.

"But you're sure this cave goes to the top of the mountain?" she asked.

Farble nodded. "Close."

"It goes close to the top?" The troll nodded. Ali continued, "Does it come out on the backside of the mountain?"

Farble nodded. "Nice cave."

"Is this guy telling you what you want to hear?" Steve said.

"I don't think Farble lies," Ali said.

"He might be wanting to please you," Cindy said. "You have to be careful how you question him. For all we know this cave leads to a sewer in town."

"I sort of doubt that," Ali muttered. Her friends did have a good point, though. She studied the troll. "Farble, do you know how to get around inside the cave?"

He nodded. "Lost."

"See," Steve complained.

"You got lost inside the cave?" Ali asked.

Farble nodded. "Lost."

That was not what she wanted to hear. It made her decision more difficult. Karl spoke up.

"If this cave opens on the other side of the mountain," he said, "then there should be a breeze blowing through it from one side to the other. If we do come to a fork in the cave where there are several ways to go, we should be able to tell the right way by the freshness of the air."

"I'd like to see that," Steve said.

Karl glanced at him. "It's not as hard as it sounds. Anybody can smell fresh air."

"Wait a second," Cindy said. "The main reason to go in the cave is to avoid the elves, right? Well, I don't see any of them chasing us up the mountain. I say we stay outside where at least we know where we're going."

"Aye," Paddy said.

"I agree with the cheerleader and the leprechaun," Steve said.

"I'm not a cheerleader yet," Cindy said. "Just a wannabe."

The discussion might have gone on for awhile if they hadn't become aware of two large heads poking out of the cave. As a group they quickly ran away from the entrance. They ended up a hundred yards down the mountain.

All of them except for Farble. Because the two big heads belonged to two trolls. Ali supposed they were the same two who had attacked her at the river. They looked the right size, a head taller than Farble.

Farble, carrying his umbrella and sporting his sunglasses, walked over to his friends and struck up a conversation. Just three trolls standing in the shade on a nice afternoon, checking out a pal's oily skin and cool glasses. But since Farble could take direct sunlight without frying, his friends must have thought something special had happened to him.

Ali did not have it so easy. Her friends were rebelling.

"No way we're going in there now," Steve said.

"There could be a whole herd of trolls in there," Cindy said.

"'Tis always a bad omen to see trolls at the door," Paddy agreed.

"Hold on a second," Ali said. "We don't know if there are more than three trolls on this whole mountain. Three's all we've seen so far."

"You're really determined to go in that cave," Steve said, disgusted.

He had a point. Like the Yanti, the cave called to her. Enter Ali, it seemed to whisper in her ear, and you will be shown real magic, even dark magic, if you're ready for it. She understood the source of the call. She felt the cave was where she was destined to face her last four tests. Either she would pass them far beneath the earth and claim the Yanti for her own, or else she would die trying and never be heard from again.

Best to get it over with, she thought.

Ignoring Steve, Ali called to their troll. "Farble!" He came lumbering over, and she patted him on the shoulder and asked, "Do you still want to stay with us? Or would your rather go off with your friends?"

Farble gently squeezed her arm. "Ali."

She smiled. "That's great. But we have a problem. Your friends are blocking our way. Could you ask them to please let us pass?"

Farble nodded and walked back to his friends. The three trolls talked a couple of minutes and then Farble returned. He pointed to his sunglasses and his umbrella.

"Want," he said.

"They want umbrellas and sunglasses to get out of the way?" Ali asked.

He nodded. "Sunscreen."

"We're all out of sunscreen and umbrellas. Maybe we could give them a couple of pairs of sunglasses." Ali turned to her friends. "Guys?"

Steve put his hand to his glasses and took a step back. "These have Polaroid lenses. They cost me fifty bucks. I'm not giving them up to a couple of smelly trolls."

"Same here," Cindy said.

"You bought your sunglasses at the drugstore for two bucks," Ali told her.

"It makes no difference. I don't want to go in that cave. None of us do," Cindy said.

"I do," Karl said, handing over his sunglasses.

"Thanks." Ali took them and gave them to Farble.

"I thought we agreed that we'd all have a say in what we were going to do?" Steve said, although he must have known they had reached no such agreement. He continued, "Three don't want to go in the cave, two do. You're outvoted, Ali."

"Farble likes the cave. He has a vote the same as the rest of us," Ali said.

"What!?" Cindy and Steve screeched.

"My poor head," Paddy said, looking ill.

"We have a deadline. We cannot keep stopping to argue," Ali said. "Cindy, give me your sunglasses."

Cindy practically threw them at Ali. Ignoring her, Ali handed them to Farble, who seemed unaffected by their argument. She spoke to the troll.

"Tell your friends this is all we have to give them," she said.

Farble left to deliver the message. He was back quickly. He pointed to Paddy.

"Hungry," he said.

Ali frowned. "They're hungry and they want to eat Paddy?"

Farble licked his lips and nodded. "Leprechaun."

Paddy's headache got a lot worse. He had to sit down. "Oh Missy. Negotiating with trolls. It's not done."

Ali shook her head. "No way. Farble, you tell your friends

they're making me angry. And if they don't let us pass, I'll use my fire stones and cook their hides."

Farble's huge yellow eyes grew wide, and he hurried back to his friends. This particular conversation lasted a while, and was quite animated. Ali wondered what it would be next. Finally, Farble returned.

"Names," he said.

"Huh?" Ali said.

"Want names," Farble said.

"New names? Like I gave you a new name?"

He nodded. "Pretty names."

"This has got to be a first," Cindy said.

"If I give them new names, do they promise to let us pass and never bother us again?" Ali asked.

Farble nodded. "Like Geea."

Ali was not sure if they wanted pretty names like Geea or if they personally liked her. But since she had almost killed them the last time they had met, she doubted it was the latter. With Farble by her side, she walked over to meet the trolls. They lowered their heads as she neared, although they continued to drip green spit out their mouths. Ali tried to sound friendly.

"I hear you guys want new names?" she said.

They both nodded vigorously. Standing near his friends, acting incredibly proud, Farble pounded his chest. "Farble," he said.

"So what are your names now?" she asked, thinking she might make the new ones rhyme with the old ones.

"Spit," the one on the left said.

"Snot," the one on the right said.

"Oh boy," Ali said. She had to rack her brain for a minute, but then she had it. She pointed to the troll on the left. "Spit," she said, "from now on you shall be known as Sprite. That means, 'He who is tasty and refreshing.' " She paused. "Do you like it?"

Sprite positively glowed. He nodded and patted her so hard on the back that she almost fell over. She had to put up a hand to stop him. She turned to Snot.

"And you shall be known as Snickers," she said. "That means, 'He who is chewy and crunchy.'"

Sprite and Snickers were the happiest trolls on Earth. They pounded their heads as if they were coconuts to split open, then bumped their butts together out of sheer joy. Ali was relieved. She wished her friends were as easy to please.

Ali returned to the gang. Again she argued for the cave. They could hide from watchful eyes. It could be a shortcut to the top. They could avoid most of the snow. They might find water underground. They would need less water if they were out of the sun. The argument seemed logical to her.

They hardly listened, she saw that. While she had been talking to the trolls, they had resigned themselves to the fact that the new and improved Ali Warner had to get her own way.

She didn't like the feeling she got from her friends as they walked past Sprite and Snickers and into the cave. Paddy had spoken of omens. Perhaps their anger was a bad omen. It seemed a bad way to start the darkest leg of their journey. She wondered if it would come back to haunt them.

CHAPTER SIXTEEN

The entrance was wide, but they had hiked only a hundred yards inside when the walls and ceiling narrowed. A grown man would have had trouble walking upright. Ten-foot-tall Farble had to stoop to keep from bumping his head. But the troll didn't appear to mind the awkward position. Ali was sure someone had dug out the cave. Its strange roughly-hewn-square shape continued. Nature just didn't form such sharp angles.

But there were no bricks on the walls, no tiles on the floor. The interior was as black as empty space, silent as a closed coffin. They had to stay close together to walk, which was difficult with the narrow walls. Ali hoped Karl had put new batteries in the flashlight before they had left home. The glow of their only light seemed to die against the walls and floor—the material sucked the life out of it. Ali was not sure what the material was; not simple rock, no, it was too smooth, much too dark. It reminded her of hardened lava, which made sense in a way. Scientists said Pete's Peak had been an active volcano as recently as two hundred years ago.

Only the floor of the cave was different.

Grainy sand, black sand, it seemed to stick to the soles of her boots.

The cave went neither up nor down; it appeared determined to cut straight across the inside of the mountain. They were thankful for a flat surface. It gave them a chance to catch their breath. Also, the farther they walked, the warmer it got, and they were able to take off their jackets.

The increase in temperature surprised Ali. She knew most caves got colder the deeper you went into them. She wondered what it meant.

For a short spell Paddy ended up in the back with Ali. She took the opportunity to question him. "Do you have a mountain like this in your dimension?" she asked.

"Aye. Tall one like this."

"Is it exactly the same?"

"Nothing is the same here. Nothing stays the same there."

"What do you mean?"

"Missy must know."

"I don't know." He didn't answer so she tried another question. "If we have a big oil spill in our world, say down at the beach, does it show up in your world?"

"Aye. Something bad shows up. Doesn't have to be oil."

"I don't understand," she said.

"Humans hurt this world, it hurts ours."

"But the damage could take another form?"

"Aye."

"What if you guys damage your dimension? Does it hurt our world?"

"Don't know, and don't care."

"Are you still mad at me for dragging you in here?"

"Missy has the power. Paddy's just a leprechaun."

"I don't feel that way. I value your opinion."

He gave her a look as if to say: gimme a break.

"I do, really." She added, "Thanks for sticking with us."

He waved his hand. "Paddy is here. Tries to help."

"Why do you want to help us?"

"Missy and Paddy have a deal."

"You want to stay in our dimension, right?"

"Aye."

"And build up a big pot of gold?"

"Aye. Paddy has never had much."

"I'm sorry to hear that." She hesitated. "Do you have a wife? Kids?"

"No gold, no wife."

"Is that why you want gold? So you can get a wife?"

Her questions might have gotten too personal. The leprechaun lowered his eyes. "Paddy used to being alone," he said quietly.

She changed the subject. "This cave is square-shaped. Do dwarves like that shape?"

"Aye. Dwarf caves always square, like their brains."

Ali smiled. "Is that a leprechaun joke?"

"Aye. Paddy can joke."

"I'm sure you can. Maybe when this is all over we can trade jokes. But I need to ask you more about the dwarves. This cave wasn't made in the last few days. Dwarves must have built it in the past."

"Don't know, never asked."

"Is it possible elementals came into our dimension many years ago? We have so many stories about them in our books."

"Don't know, and don't care."

"Did you ever talk to an elemental that had been here before?"

"Leprechauns don't ask questions. Mind our own business."

"You said that Lord Balar was angry at Lord Vak. But they have joined forces to attack humanity. Is that right?"

"Aye. Elves and dwarves fight together for first time."

"Are you sure they intend to fight together? Could they just be acting like they're together?"

"Not understand, Missy."

"This is a dwarf cave. You're afraid we might run into dwarves. But you also said the dark fairies live here. Is it possible the dwarves are working with the dark fairies?"

The idea shocked Paddy. "Dark fairies have no friends, only enemies."

"Then who is letting them come through the Yanti?" she asked.

He hesitated. "The dark fairies . . . they must come from somewhere else."

"Where?" Ali asked, surprised. Nemi had said nothing about another entrance into humanity's realm.

Paddy averted his eyes. "Best not to talk about."

"Do the dark fairies work for the Shaktra?" she persisted.

She had hit the wrong button, or else the right one. The leprechaun fell silent and absolutely refused to speak. She had got out of him all she could for the time being, she thought. Quickly, he moved up front to walk beside Karl and she was left alone with her questions.

What was the Shaktra? Was it a powerful elemental? Or something else?

Ali turned her mind to her last conversation with Nemi. He had said he could not help her with her next test, yet he had given her hints on how she might face it.

"Air is a mysterious element. Consider what is carried through the air—the greatest of all human inventions."

What was the greatest of all human inventions? Atomic energy? No, that was a brilliant invention but one couldn't say it was great. Atomic bombs killed people; besides, there was all that radiation to worry about. Rocket ships? Rockets had taken people to the moon and back, an amazing feat. Only, rockets were the one thing on Earth that did not travel through air.

Ali felt frustrated. Nemi had been purposely vague, she had no doubt. He didn't want to hand anything to her on a plate. For that matter, he did not seem overly worried if she got killed trying to reach the Yanti. Perhaps there was no such thing as death to him.

Back to the riddle. What was carried through the air? Dust? Pollen? Kites? Balloons? Airplanes? Planes were cool, they brought people from all over the world together. But what did they have to do with her?

Absolutely nothing. It was driving her crazy!

Ali tried to remember more of their conversation.

"Something else troubles you."

"Yes."

"You feel something is wrong that you're not seeing."

"Yes. How do you know?"

Something wrong that she was not seeing? She could not see air. But what did it mean? What had he said near the end?

". . . You have learned to trust your feelings. There must be something important that you are missing. It could be right in front of your face."

"And that's the test of air?"

"It might be."

Ali tried to match the clues. Something carried on the air. Something she was missing. Something right in front of her face. All related to her feelings, which she was supposed to trust.

"This is the stupidest riddle I have ever heard of," she said aloud.

Then she had it. The answer, it came to her in a flash. The stupidest riddle she had ever heard of? What did she hear? What did all of them hear all the time?

Words. Language.

Language was the greatest of all human inventions. It was because of language that civilizations had formed. Language was carried through the air, between people. What words were right in front of her face that were troubling her? The question could have only one answer.

They had to be words that were not true.

Nemi had been telling her that someone was lying to her.

The test of air was unlike the other tests she had taken. She was not going to be swept away by a hurricane or lifted off to Oz in the center of a tornado. The test of air was the test of hearing what was true and what was false.

Unfortunately, the solution to the riddle raised even bigger questions.

Who was lying to her? Why were they lying to her?

Would they all die if she didn't figure out the answers?

All of them except one? The one who was lying to her?

Ali's thoughts swam. Her friends couldn't be lying to her, could they? Farble was too stupid to lie. Wasn't he? Paddy lied all the time, but so did all leprechauns. Or did they?

Ali had a headache. Falling back a few steps, she let the others walk ahead. Her trust was shaken to the core. All of a sudden she was not sure if she wanted any of them for traveling companions.

They came to a fork in the cave; or rather, they ran into three metal doors, set one beside the other, arranged in a shallow semicircle. Perhaps to accommodate the doors—they were larger than those on normal houses—the cave swelled in size. The metal was dark and slightly dusty, cold to the touch, and all three were simple rectangles, devoid of special markings, although each had a domed curve at the top. Ali wondered if the doors led to other sets, if tunnels covered the entire interior of the mountain.

They stopped for a break. They had been walking underground for two hours and they were thirsty. Of course there was nothing to drink. Except for Karl, they sat against opposite walls near the three doors and stared at each other.

Their impromptu break was a sign of how exhausted they all were. Obviously they had to go through one of the doors to continue on their way and—it was almost a joke—they didn't even have the strength to study them. Or perhaps they all assumed Karl would check them out. Basically, he was the one leading them forward.

"Turn off the flashlight since we're not walking," Ali told Karl. He went to obey but Cindy freaked out.

"I don't want to sit here in the dark!" she said.

"We should save the batteries," Karl said.

"Why do you always take her side?" Cindy asked.

"This isn't about sides. If the light runs out, we're all in trouble."

"Leave it on then, we won't sit here long," Ali said.

"So now you're deciding how long our breaks are going to be?" Cindy said.

"You want the light on, I told him to keep the light on," Ali said. "What else do you want me to do?"

"I don't want anything from you," Cindy grumbled.

"Oh brother," Ali muttered.

"Stop it," Steve said. "We have bigger problems. Or am I the only one who's worried about the three choices we have in front of us? Which door leads out of here?"

Karl, who had never sat down, tried opening the door on the right. But the black handle refused to move; it appeared locked. Yet it was interesting—there was no place to insert a key. Karl tried the door in the center, and they were relieved to see it swing open. Especially when the door on the left also refused to budge.

"We might not have a choice after all," Karl said. Stepping through the door—which appeared to simply extend the cave they were in—he stood silent for a moment, occasionally holding up his palms to feel the air. He even sniffed a couple of times, softly, before striding back through the door and walking over to Farble, who was sitting near Ali. Karl spoke to the troll.

"Does the central door lead outside?" he asked.

Farble nodded. "Outside."

"Karl!" Steve exclaimed. "We've been over this with Ali. Don't ask Farble to confirm what you think. First ask him what *he* thinks."

"He's probably agreeing with you because he wants you to like him," Cindy said.

Karl nodded. "My mistake. But I'm pretty sure the middle passageway is the right one. It has a faint breeze in it. You can feel it."

"What difference does it make?" Cindy asked. "It's the only door that's open."

"It makes a huge difference," Karl said. "If I didn't feel fresh air, I would hammer on the other doors until we got them open." He added, "I wonder if we shouldn't do that anyway."

"With what?" Steve asked. "Our heads?"

Ali forced herself to stand, and stepped through the central door. Like Karl, she could definitely feel a faint breeze, although the air continued to be warmer than expected. Because the open door was two feet thick—and solid metal—she didn't see the point in Karl's last remark. If the doors were locked, they were locked, they were not going to break through them. She tried each one to be sure, and it was as if the knobs had froze in place centuries ago.

Ali glanced at Paddy. "Do dwarves make doors like these?" she asked.

He hesitated. "No."

The answer surprised her. Did dwarves avoid domes at the top of their doors? "Who does? Elves?" she asked.

"Paddy has never seen doors like this before."

Again, his response surprised her—particularly since the doors did not have an elaborate design. They were thick, though, she had to admit that much, and they were heavy. The central door swung smoothly, the hinges did not even creak, but because of the sheer mass of the door, she had to lean into it to get it to move.

After ten minutes of rest, they continued on, through another square tunnel that seemed to lead nowhere. But just before they left the area, Ali lagged a little behind and tore a button off her shirt and set it in the crack—on the floor—where the door would fit if someone tried to close it. The button was on the large size and it was made of wood. It was possible—not likely, but possible—it could help wedge the door open if the breeze, or even a dwarf, tried to close it. She was paranoid of the door closing on them. Yet she was afraid to leave anything substantial behind— like a scarf—in case the dwarves saw it and used it to track them. One good thing about the button, it was painted black, and was hard to see on the floor of the cave.

Ali quickly caught up with her friends, and as they moved on, the cave began to angle upward, which Ali took to be a good sign. They had to go up sometime if they were to reach the top of the mountain.

Unfortunately, the altitude came back to haunt them. The air was no thicker inside the cave than outside. The increase in the slope demanded more effort. They got winded fast, especially Steve. Because Farble was bent over, trying to keep his head from hitting the ceiling, he was unable to carry Steve. And they only had the one light; they could not split up. They ended up having to take more frequent breaks.

Another couple of hours dragged by; these two were deadly. Ali didn't know their altitude, but it must have been over twelve thousand feet. The floor kept getting steeper. As a group they would walk fifty feet, then stop and breathe for five minutes. Soon they were taking ten steps and stopping.

Despite Karl's warnings, Ali could never have imagined the altitude bothering them so much. It felt as if they were hiking through an airless cavern on the dark side of the moon. Even when they did stop, Steve could not catch his breath. In the dim light, his skin shone with a blue tinge. He was slowing them down, and the clock kept ticking.

Ali wondered if taking the cave had been a mistake.

They came to another fork in the road, and the cave grew extremely wide—it was almost as if they entered a small cavern—because here there were *seven* doors to choose from, all neatly arranged in a *deep* semicircle. The doors were similar to the previous three, made of metal, with featureless handles in place of knobs, and with neatly designed domes on the tops. However, there was one major change. Each door was a different color. Starting on the far left, there was a red door, followed by an orange one, a yellow one, a green one, a blue one, a violet one, and on the far right there was a white door.

The colors intrigued Ali. She immediately stepped forward and tried to scratch at the blue paint—on the fifth door—to see if it would come off, and almost broke a nail for her efforts. It was as if the color was intrinsic to the door, not just a coat of paint that had been brushed on.

The Fifth Door. She had called it that in her mind without thinking.

The Blue Door. Something about it intrigued her.

She noticed there was no dust on these doors.

As a group they tried the doors, but only two opened—the red and yellow ones. Ali felt a stab of disappointment. She was not sure why. She had wanted the fifth door to swing wide. But five of them appeared locked and, once again, there was no place to insert a key.

Beyond the open doors, the red and yellow ones, the caves looked identical.

Identical to the cave they had been hiking in. At least, up until it had expanded.

"It looks like we have a choice this time," Steve said.

Ali finally turned to Farble. "Which door leads outside?" she asked.

The troll pointed to the yellow door.

"Are you sure?" she asked.

Farble nodded his head.

"Have you been this way?" Ali asked Farble.

The troll shook his head.

"Oh no," Steve groaned.

"Have you been through the red door?" she asked.

The troll nodded. Then shook his head.

"Are you confused?" Ali asked.

Farble glanced at Steve and nodded. "Sorry," the troll said.

"But he liked the yellow door. That was his first choice," Karl said.

"It means nothing," Cindy said.

"I disagree," Karl said. "I think we confuse him when we ask a lot of questions. His first choice might count for a lot. Also, I think the air is a bit fresher in that cave. It feels cooler. Plus the yellow door is more in the center."

"What if both doors lead to the outside?" Ali said.

Karl nodded. "That's possible. But if I were a dwarf and I was designing the layout of my tunnels, and had only one door that led to the outside, I would put it more in the center."

"Now we're getting into dwarf psychology," Cindy muttered.

"The green door is the central door," Ali pointed out.

"Yes. But it's locked," Karl said. "The yellow door is the next best thing."

"You don't want to *pound* the green door open?" Ali asked. "You considered that at the other doors."

Karl shrugged. "I was being foolish. These doors are thick. We're not going to force them open."

"I wonder why only two are open?" Ali mused.

"Why are *any* of them open?" Cindy said.

"We have to make a choice," Steve said, still trying to catch his breath. "We have come too far to go back to the entrance."

Ali turned to Paddy. "Do you know?" she asked.

He hesitated. "No."

"Have you been in here before?" she asked.

He lowered his head. "Missy asked that before. Paddy said no."

The cave they had just hiked trailed behind them like a gully into a bottomless pit. Yet the two caves before them—through the two doors—leveled out. Ali wondered if they were already near the top of the mountain. It seemed too much to hope for.

In the end, Ali knew she was the one who would have to choose. Like Karl, she felt the cave through the yellow door had fresher air. But the difference was slight—for all she knew they could be imagining the difference. Yet there was something mysterious about the first cave, behind the red door. It was identical to the other one, in appearance, but like the green and blue doors, it drew her. Almost like a voice, talking softly inside her head.

Magic, Ali. Black and white magic. Let us show you.

Yet the voice did not belong to Nemi.

She was not even sure if it was real.

"I think we should take the red door," Ali said.

The entire group stared at her.

"Why?" Steve said.

"I have a feeling about it," she said.

Karl was worried. "That's not a good reason to choose it."

"It is to me," Ali said.

"I agree with Karl," Steve said, stepping toward the yellow door, feeling with his outstretched palms. "The troll's first choice probably has some meaning. I think I feel a faint breeze coming out of here."

"You didn't say that a minute ago," Ali said.

"I didn't feel it then," Steve said.

"Let's flip a coin," Cindy said. "Got a gold one, Paddy?"

"We're not flipping a coin," Ali snapped. "I sense something about the first door—the red door. We have to check it out."

"If you sense something's in there, we should avoid it," Karl said.

"Yeah. It might be a swarm of dark fairies," Cindy said.

"I can handle them," Ali said.

"I wouldn't get overconfident. Not down here," Karl said.

"I don't like the red door!" Paddy suddenly blurted out.

The gang turned to the leprechaun. Ali stared hard at him. "You just said you don't know anything about these doors. Why don't you like it?" she demanded.

Paddy would not look at her. "Heard stories, Missy. Evil stories."

Ali sharpened her tone. "Who told you these stories?"

Paddy stuttered. "My pa . . . others."

"Other leprechauns?" Ali asked.

Paddy shook his head, then nodded. "Yes, Missy."

"Then we definitely should not take it," Karl said.

Ali shook her head. "I don't know."

Cindy spoke up. "You wanted to bring Paddy along so you could ask his advice. Well he's telling you the red door is a bad way to go."

Ali knelt in front of Paddy, forced him to look at her. "I need to know what's wrong with the red door. Tell me everything you know. Because I want to go that way."

Paddy looked unhappy. "They said it was bad."

"How did they know? Had they ever seen it?"

He was vague. "Maybe, maybe not."

Ali stood, feeling frustrated. Her attraction to the red door remained. She spoke to the others. "Look. We can hike some distance into the first cave. Say a mile or two. If it doesn't look like it's going the right way, we can come back here."

Karl was not happy. "How will we know we're going the wrong way? We won't know anything until it leads us outside."

"I agree," Steve said.

"You can't simply ignore what Paddy's saying," Cindy added.

"Trust me," Ali said.

None of them looked like they trusted her, even Farble, who did not appear to like the smell of the red door. But once again they could see she had made up her mind.

They walked through the red door, into the first cave. Once more, just before leaving the area, and unseen by the others, Ali wedged another one of her buttons in the door's frame near the floor. More than the previous door, she didn't want anyone closing the red door behind them.

The new cave looked the same as the old cave. They kept walking. There was no talking. They were not fighting a hard upward slope, but all the exercise was still wearing them out. Their thirst was entering the danger zone. Ali did not understand why a person needed more water at altitude. Maybe it had something to do with the dryness of the air. She was not merely craving liquids, she felt heat in her chest and had begun to get sharp stabbing pains in her head. Her lips felt like dried scabs; they cracked and bled under her thirsty tongue.

Worse, Karl's flashlight had begun to dim. The light was more yellow now than white, and the beam only lit the area around their feet. When Ali asked Karl about the batteries, he assured her they were new.

"But we've been in this cave over five hours," he said. "I wouldn't be surprised if the batteries do run out."

"What do we do then?" she asked.

"Feel our way forward. Hope we don't step into a bottomless hole."

Funny he should say that. An hour after they had stepped through the red door, they came to a deep chasm. They bumped into it suddenly—Cindy almost stepped out into empty space. Steve grabbed the back of her shirt at the last second.

The gorge was a hundred feet across. Even with their failing light, they could see the other side clearly, and another cave where their one left off. The latter looked like a square hole in the wall because the walls on both sides of the chasm seemed to stretch forever in every direction. Karl took a pebble from his pocket and tossed it over the edge. They never heard it hit bottom.

Yet there was a bridge, made of rope and wooden planks, hanging uselessly on the far side. Ali knelt and studied two metal hooks that had been hammered into the floor. She realized the ropes had been tied to the hooks. There were threads of rope lying close to the hooks, as if a knife had been used to cut the bridge. Had it been recently? Did it have anything to do with them? Ali stood and peered over the edge.

"I wonder how far down it goes," she said.

"It could be miles," Karl said.

"What does it matter? We have to go back," Steve said.

"What a waste of time this whole cave thing has been," Cindy said.

"Not so fast," Ali said. "What if this is the way out? Farble, did you ever come this way?"

The troll had to think, not his strong point. Finally he shook his head.

"Are you sure?" Ali asked.

Farble nodded.

"So I made a mistake," Ali muttered.

Steve groaned and sat down on the floor near the edge. "I thought we didn't have time for mistakes," he said.

"What time is it?" Karl asked.

"Six-fifteen," Cindy said, checking her watch.

Ali shook her head. "That's impossible. Last time I looked it was six-forty. Your watch . . ." Ali did not finish—*her* watch said six-fifteen.

"What is it?" Cindy asked.

"I have the same time as you," Ali said.

"What's the big deal?" Steve asked. "You read your watch wrong. It probably said five-forty."

"Yeah," Ali agreed, although she felt far from certain. She was paranoid about the passing time—she didn't see how she could have made such a mistake. She turned to the leprechaun. "Could there be magic in this cave?" she asked.

The leprechaun was ill at ease. "Magic, yes, there could be some type of magic here. But leprechauns . . ." He stopped in mid-sentence.

"What is it?" Ali demanded.

Paddy tilted his ears back the way they had come. "Hear something."

"What?" Karl asked.

"Sounds like . . ." Paddy grimaced; his face would have turned white if it hadn't been so green. "Dwarves!" he cried.

"I don't hear anything," Karl muttered.

"Me neither," Cindy said.

Yet Farble also looked scared. Clearly the elementals had more acute senses. Ali trusted that they were indeed hearing dwarves.

"Is the sound getting louder?" she asked. It was possible the dwarves were in one of the other caves, closing in on the fork they had just left behind, perhaps preparing to hike to the main entrance. Paddy dashed that hope.

"They're singing! They're coming this way!" Paddy exclaimed.

"If they're singing, they must be in a good mood," Steve said.

"Dwarves are never in a good mood! They sing as they go into battle!" Paddy was beside himself with fear—worse than when the elves had attacked. He practically bounced off the walls. "They're going to kill us!"

"Stop that!" Ali snapped. "No one's going to kill us. They can only approach through this narrow cave. I have the fire stones. I can always fire off a few shots and scare them away."

Paddy's face was a mass of nerves. "The stones will not work here! Not for you! No fairy magic works on this side of the red door!"

Ali frowned. "Why didn't you tell me that before we came in here?"

"Missy would not listen to anything!"

"Wait a second," Ali said. "Say the stones don't work, it doesn't matter. I have other powers."

"They are fairy powers!" Paddy yelled at her. "They won't work here!"

"But I'm not a fairy. I'm a girl," Ali said.

Paddy was angry on top of his fear. "Missy does not know what she is. What can Missy do now? How will she save poor Paddy?"

Then they heard it, with their human ears, the deep rhythmic chanting of the dwarves. To Ali it sounded like echoing thunder, heard through the deep valleys of ancient mountains and forgotten times. The chant sounded very old, and sad too, as though it were more about death than life, more about darkness than light.

"Maybe we can talk to them," Steve said hopefully.

"Dwarves don't talk! Dwarves kill!" Paddy cried.

"Wouldn't they at least talk to a fairy?" Ali asked, still reeling from the leprechaun's words. Was she a fairy? Was this the seventh test? No, she had not passed the other three, it made no sense.

Freaking out, Paddy started banging his head on the wall and talking to himself. "Dwarves will not talk to Paddy! Dwarves hate Paddy! Off with the leprechaun's head! We're going to take your head!" He hit his head again. "My poor head!"

Ali caught a strange note in his voice. Was she finally beginning to hear truth? The leprechaun was acting like he had already talked to the dwarves. She grabbed his arm as he went to hit his head some more.

"Stop that!" she ordered. "Stand here and talk to me. How do you know they'll cut off your head?"

"They're dwarves!"

"True. But you must know these dwarves to be this scared. You must have talked to them. What did you talk about, Paddy?"

"Paddy never . . ."

"Don't lie to me! We could all die in the next few minutes! You tell me what you know and you tell me now!"

Paddy looked so miserable she almost regretted yelling at him. Almost but not quite. Because it was obvious that he had been keeping a big secret from her. Why, he couldn't even look at her! She grabbed him by the chin and forced his eyes to meet hers.

"You made a deal with them!" she swore. "What kind of deal?"

"No!"

She shook him violently. "Tell me!"

"To turn you over to them!" he cried. "But Paddy did not do it!"

Ali let go of him and took a step back in disgust. "So that's how it's been? From the very beginning, you've been a traitor."

Her words wounded him. "Paddy not know you in the beginning!"

Ali shook her head. "I don't care. Karl, get ready to throw this traitor over the side."

"With pleasure," Karl said, grabbing the leprechaun by the hair. Paddy squealed but could not shake loose.

"Wait! Wait!" he cried. "Missy hurts poor Paddy's arm in front of the pawnshop and Paddy sees she has fairy magic. Paddy knows she's the one the dwarves search for. So Paddy makes a pretend deal with Missy. Missy must be pretending, too! Missy doesn't even drink to seal the deal!" He was close to tears. "Paddy doesn't know Missy is a nice fairy! Paddy knows nothing!"

Ali finally heard truth in his words. She gestured for Karl to ease up. "Are you saying that once you got to know us you liked us and decided not to tell the dwarves about us?"

Paddy nodded frantically. "Paddy gave the dwarves nothing!"

"You wandered away from camp last night. Did you see the dwarves then?" Ali asked.

"Aye. Paddy told them he didn't know where you were. That's why they'll cut off me head!"

"He's lying," Karl said. "The dark fairies attacked right after he returned."

"That's true," Cindy said.

"How do you know?" Steve asked her. "You were asleep."

"So were you!" Cindy said.

Behind them, down the dark cave, the chanting grew louder.

"Paddy didn't bring the dark fairies! They just came!" Paddy shouted.

"How did they know where to find us?" Ali asked.

"They know you! They can see you!"

"How?" Ali insisted.

"Paddy doesn't know! Poor Paddy only knows he did nothing wrong!"

Again, she heard truth. She considered. "Let him go."

"Ali?" Karl complained.

"We have more pressing matters to worry about. Let him go." Yet she knelt in front of Paddy as Karl released the leprechaun. "Did the dwarves promise you gold if you gave me to them?" she asked.

He was filled with shame. "Aye. Promised me a whole pot."

"You wanted it so that you could get to be with Lea?"

His eyes widened at the name, but he nodded. "Aye. Paddy lonely all the time."

Ali squeezed his shoulder. "Were you lonely when you were hiking with us?"

Finally, he looked her in the eye. She was not sure what he saw there. What was a nice fairy to a lonely leprechaun? But he brushed the tears from his own eyes and shook his head. "Missy is kind," he said. "Paddy should have known from the beginning. Paddy is sorry that he lied to Missy."

"That's okay, I forgive you." Ali stood and turned to the others.

A faint orange glow could be seen in the depths of the cave. Dwarf torches, no doubt. The others saw the light as well. She continued. "We have to get to the other side of this gorge."

"How?" Karl gasped.

"I would rather surrender," Cindy said.

"Dwarves don't take prisoners," Paddy said.

"Isn't there a law against that?" Steve asked.

"We take the rope, make a lasso at one end," Ali explained. "There are steel hooks on the other side, same as this side. We get the rope around one of those, we can climb across."

Karl looked doubtful as he studied the far side of the gorge. "It would take a lucky shot to catch one of those hooks."

"More the reason we should start shooting now," Ali said. "Come on, get the rope out. I'll do it if you can't."

She might have put it more politely. Karl gave her an annoyed look.

"I can do it," he said.

Of course the *annoyance* was not because she had snapped at him. They were all looking at her, no doubt thinking if they had taken the yellow door, they would be outside by now. She didn't know what to say—they were right. For that matter, she didn't know why her intuition had prodded her to take the red door. Perhaps she had misread it, and was confused about many things.

Karl surprised even himself. He caught a hook on the other side on his fifth try. Pulling the rope taut, he tied it to a hook on their floor. Naturally, on the other side, the rope was not tied, and that made the crossing that much more dangerous. That's why Ali insisted on going first.

"I have to see if the rope will support our weight," she said.

"Some of us weigh more than you," Karl said.

"Not to mention a certain ten-foot-tall troll," Steve said.

The dwarves were near. Ali could make out individual torches in the distance, and the noise of their chanting seemed to shake the inside of her skull. "We don't have time for another argument," she said, getting down on her knees. "I only need a minute."

"Be careful," Cindy said, kneeling beside her.

"I thought you hated me," Ali said.

Cindy was worried, but forced a smile. "How can I hate my best friend?"

Getting onto the rope, figuring out how to hang, was the hardest part. But Ali knew there was no way she would be able to stay on top of the rope. Crawling onto her back, she stuck her head over the edge and grabbed the cord and pulled herself three feet out, at the same time wrapping her legs around the rope. Well begun was supposed to be half done, but she did not know if that applied in life and death matters.

Her long maroon hair hung below her head like a red flag waving from the window of a spaceship. Nemi had talked to her about the test of space. She had never realized what he had in mind. She thought if she let go she would fall and never hit bottom. Her soul would be trapped forever in darkness, and, like a dark fairy, she would never have another chance to find the light of wisdom.

She realized that was her fear talking. The tests were about nothing but fear, and courage. She remembered reading once that all babies were born with two fears: the fear of darkness and the fear of falling. The gorge gave her a chance to face both at the same time.

"How are you doing?" Karl asked as she scooted farther onto the rope, leaving the ledge behind.

"I love it," she whispered.

"Do you feel like you're about to fall?" Cindy asked.

"Don't say the F word," Steve said.

"I feel fine. Let me concentrate," Ali said.

The distance was not far, a hundred feet. If the rope had been strung a hundred feet between two ladders in her backyard, she would have covered it in less than a minute. As it was she moved very slow.

Even before she reached the far side, she realized she had been selfish to go first. The dwarves were closer than she had figured, and there was slim chance all her friends would be able to get to safety in time.

Ali's hand bumped into stone. She had made it across. Reaching out, above and behind her head, she grabbed a steel hook and pulled herself onto the ledge. When she got to her feet, she saw a herd of dwarves approaching behind her friends. Their beards were long, their axes shiny, and their torches seemed to burn the night. Ali didn't understand why they looked so angry.

"Hurry!" she shouted.

Cindy went next—no, it was Karl. Tucking the flashlight in his belt, he told Cindy he needed to get across to secure the rope on the other side. Ali could have done that, she thought, if she'd had more time. But time was the sixth test, after space, and it looked like it was about to run out for all of them.

The dwarves clanged their weapons as they bore down on them.

Her friends started to panic.

Karl was only a dozen feet over the gorge when Cindy climbed onto the rope. Cindy was five feet out when Steve reached for the cord. Then there were Paddy and Farble, who were naturally itching to get to the other side. The leprechaun was banging his head on the wall again and the troll was howling as if he were on fire.

Steve had barely got his feet away from the edge when Paddy leaped onto the rope. The leprechaun's impact caused the entire cord to shake. Karl almost lost his grip and Cindy let out a cry.

Now there were four of them, at one time, hanging over the abyss. It was madness, Ali thought. The rope was not meant to hold so much weight.

Karl almost made it. He was reaching for her hand when Farble decided he could take no more. The dwarves were only twenty feet behind the troll when he jumped onto the rope.

It was hard for Ali to blame Farble for what happened next. No doubt the dwarves would have hacked him to pieces the second they reached him. They had fire in their eyes, or maybe it was just the reflection of their torches.

The troll weighed more than the rest of them put together. When he climbed onto the rope, it was too much, way too much, by about a thousand pounds.

The rope snapped.

It broke on Farble's end. In one deadly swoop, the gang fell like the wrong half of a pendulum and smashed against the wall on her side. Because he was hanging at the very end of the rope, the impact was hardest on Farble. The troll hit the wall and lost his grip. Then he was falling, screaming like a wounded animal as he disappeared into the deep.

Paddy didn't fare much better. The impact from hitting the wall must have stunned him. Or else the closeness of the dwarves caused his nerve to fail. Whatever, five seconds after Farble lost his grip, the leprechaun was falling. It broke Ali's heart to hear his last cry.

"Missy!" he screamed.

Then he was gone. Just gone.

Karl had slid several feet down the rope, smashing into Cindy's head, who in turn had slid into Steve. The three of them were clumped together near the center of the rope like the tangled victims of a car crash. Yet they were still alive, Ali told herself. They could be saved.

Maybe. The front line of the dwarves stood only a hundred feet away, on the opposite side of the gorge. Ali could see eight of them but there could have been hundreds. They were short and stout, three-and-a-half-feet tall at best, with strong bodies and heavily armored limbs. On their heads they wore steel helmets, and in their eyes Ali saw the darkness and pain of their underground lives. With long coarse beards, they stared at her friends and whispered among themselves, probably debating how the invaders should die.

Ali wanted to shout at them that this was humanity's world.

Desperate, Karl was climbing back up the rope, trying to reach the ledge where Ali stood. Never had she seen such a look of terror on someone's face. Straining with his arms and feet, he accidentally kicked Cindy in the face. Indeed, he hit her so hard that she lost her grip and slipped. But Steve caught her as she fell, grabbed her by the waist with one hand, even as he fought to hang on to his own life.

"Help Ali!" Karl cried as he neared the top. Kneeling, she gripped a steel hook embedded in the floor and stretched dangerously over the side. Again, she cursed herself for having put her friends in such a frightening position. If she could not save them, she vowed, she would die trying.

Across the chasm, a dwarf with gold-lined armor lifted his battle ax. He caught Ali's eye and she knew in that moment she was looking at Lord Balar, master of all dwarves. His long beard was snow white and his dark eyes burned hotter than a red sun. Paddy had spoken of the dwarf's anger and Ali saw it all—an aged ruler bitter with battle scars and personal loss. It would be useless to beg for his mercy, she knew, yet she cried out anyway as he swung his ax over his head.

"Don't!" she shouted.

Her word did nothing, her fairy magic was useless. The sharp blade flew across the abyss, a shining razor in the cursed darkness, and hit the rope. The dwarf's aim was perfect, it was horrible. The ax cut the rope just above Karl's outstretched hand.

The rope broke, her friends fell. They were within reach one second and the next they were mere stick figures, twisting and turning, shrinking in the endless night, until they finally disappeared into a grave that she knew in her heart had no bottom.

Across the way, the dwarves cheered. More axes were raised.

Ali stood and ran. She had no light, she could not see where she was going. She ran from nowhere into nothing. She didn't care. Her heart was ruined; it could never be healed. In that moment she could have been a dark fairy. All she wanted was darkness.

CHAPTER SEVENTEEN

Trapped in a nightmare, time lost all meaning to Ali. She only knew she had to keep running. She hit the wall, she fell, she got up and ran some more. Her feet tripped her, she got up. The darkness not only surrounded her, it filled her. Each gasping breath she drew in only added to her quotient of darkness. Her heart and lungs were choked with it.

Honestly, she thought, she *was* the nightmare. There was no other way to explain what had happened in her life. Her friends were dead, her mother was dead. Everything she touched died! There was no one left to care for. No one left to care for *her*. There was nothing to do but run.

She wondered if she was losing her mind.

Ali didn't know how long she went on like that, chasing the endless length of the cave that for all she knew could suddenly open onto another gorge and hurl her into the pits of the Earth. Yet a time came when her lungs could no longer suck enough oxygen from the thin air. Crumpling like a rag doll drenched in oil, she sagged onto the hard floor and closed her eyes.

"Help Ali!"

She tried not to remember the faces of her friends in that second before the rope had been cut and they had plunged to their deaths. She tried not to recall how their eyes had turned to her, to the great Ali Warner and her fairy magic. How they had silently begged her to work a miracle. Because she had been unable to do anything for them.

She had not even been able to say goodbye.

To her friends or to her mother.

She could not stop thinking about it.

Eventually, her breathing slowed and her heart ceased to pound and she was left with nothing to do but sit and wait. Of course there was nothing to wait for and there was no reason to sit. Yet she could think of no reason to get up either. There was nowhere to go.

Since they had entered the cave, she had noticed the volcanic sand that made up the floor. The grainy texture reminded her of the black beach she had gone to with her parents in Hawaii two years ago. That had been a wonderful day, the sun bright in the sky, the warm water rushing onto the shore like the loving arms of an old friend. She had lain on the beach for hours on end with her mother and let the waves run over her from foot to head.

One glorious day in the life of Ali Warner.

Her watch glowed a faint phosphorescent green in the dark—she was able to read it. Five-forty-five—a half-hour earlier, if the watch could be believed, than when they had reached the chasm. But she didn't believe it—the stupid watch must be broken. She didn't believe anything anymore.

Ali felt the darkness close in. She no longer craved it. Suddenly it seemed to her a living being, a hungry creature whose stomach she'd had the bad luck to end up in. An ancient monster that would devour her at its leisure, over the next two hours or the next two hundred years. No, she did not like the darkness at all.

She laid on her back and tried to close her eyes again. She could not be sure if they were open or closed, not really, not in such a dark place. Sweat formed on her forehead and she wiped it off. She was surprised how hot it was. The temperature had risen at least twenty degrees since her mad dash through the cave.

She felt like a loaf of bread in a stone oven. Soon the yeast in her guts would expand and she would rise up like a little dough-girl. Or else she would die and her spirit would rise up from her body and would join her friends. She felt so exhausted, it didn't matter what happened anymore.

They came for her then.

They flew on a hissing wave, like vampiric bats that had grown large and strong on the blood of mortals. Their eyes glowed a hateful red in the dark. Her own eyes must have been open to see them. But their eyes moved fast, as did their wings, and this time they swooped down upon her without fear. She was not even given a chance to take the fire stones from her pockets. Not that they would have worked here, *on the other side of the red door.*

Three caught her: by her hair, her legs, her arms. Her stones were taken away. They did not care that they hurt her. As they flew down the cave, away from where her friends had fallen, a claw closed over her throat and she had trouble breathing. Yet they did not choke her. They wanted her alive.

It was not long before they entered a vast underground cavern. Its size boggled her imagination. The floor of the dark space could have been miles away. Yet she could see it, even from such a distance, because it was traced with lines of burning lava. The lava choked the air with a stink of rotten eggs, which she knew from school to be sulfur fumes. The ghastly red glow was a horror. She felt as if she was being dragged into a world of demons.

The dark fairies took her lower. They flew in the direction of a giant hive that stood at the center of the cavern like a honeycomb stuffed with sewage instead of sweets. The structure was gray, pocketed, and the buzz that came from it made her want to vomit. Around the hive flew a thousand dark fairies. They moved through the air like lizards with wings, or black flies with minds. With such a complex home in place, Ali knew it was impossible that they had only arrived in her dimension a few days ago.

But was she still in her own dimension?

Maybe when they had passed through the red door, they had entered another.

Or maybe this was hell, she thought, and she was here because of what she had done to her friends. It was possible she would be here a long time.

The fairies brought her inside the hive, into a shallow area perched high above the volcanic lake. The place could have been another cave, or a jail cell, or a torture chamber. From the ceiling hung sharp metal hooks, and the skeletons of a dozen victims who had been there before her. Most appeared to be young children, and probably all had died long ago. Hung upside down like slabs of beef, the sockets of their skulls seemed to cry out to her as she came near, and she did not know how much more she could take.

But her three companions were just getting started. Grabbing her by the feet, they tied her upside down on one of the metal hooks. They pinched her as they worked, and grinned with pleasure at the sight of her tender limbs. They had fangs for teeth, and long purple tongues with sharp tips. They were going to eat her alive, she thought.

Soon they left her alone, though, and flew out the opening and disappeared into the swarm of fairies that seemed to endlessly circle the hive. There were no bars on her cell, no guards, but she would have needed wings to escape.

Ali checked her watch. Five-thirty, fifteen minutes earlier than the last time she had looked. What was wrong with it? Or was the time distortion due to the cave? What time was it outside? Had she already failed Nemi?

Hanging upside down, the pressure of the blood in her head was painful. She knew she could not stand it long before she would pass out. Fortunately, they had not tied her hands and she was able to swing up and grab the hook beside her. Only it had a skeleton attached to it; the bony feet practically poked her in the eyes. She wondered how long ago the kid had been killed.

Her arms grew tired. She had to let go, swing down, let the blood rush back into her head. But that quickly grew unbearable so she swung back up. The routine was torturous; the dark fairies probably wanted it that way. She felt herself despairing. Tears burned her eyes, but they rolled upward, into her hair, instead of onto her cheeks, and they brought her no relief.

She checked her bonds. The rope the fairies had used was like thick spider-web; it was sticky to touch, and very strong. Without a knife, there was no way she was going to get through it.

Then she had an idea. What if she tied her hair onto the nearby hook? It would hurt to have it constantly pulled on, but anything would be better than what she was doing.

Swinging up and grabbing her hair into a long bunch, she worked on a knot. It was not easy—one hand had to hold the hook while the other fiddled with her hair. But after a few minutes she had her knot, and a hammock of sorts. Too bad her body and hair were the only things holding it together.

The tug on her hair was awful. Her scalp felt as if it were being peeled from her skull. She could only breathe and bear it. Escape was impossible. She wondered if the dark fairies would eat her alive or wait until she was dead.

Then she came, the queen. Ali knew she was the big bat without knowing how she knew. The fairy wore no special ornaments, no gold or silver crown. The creature flew straight into the torture chamber and landed five feet in front of her. Ali saw that her head was injured. Red veins pulsed beneath its translucent skull, reminding Ali of the lines of lava on the floor of the cavern. It was the same fairy she had wounded the night before.

"Do you know me?" the dark fairy asked. The voice hissed like a reptile, like the previous night, yet there was an intelligence behind it. Ali knew she would have to be careful what she said.

"I know you," Ali said.

"What is my name?"

"Snake Face."

That was not being careful. Annoyed, the creature came close, spoke in a deadly voice. "You joke. You used to like to joke. Or is it that you really do not remember?" The fairy paused. "What is my name?"

The name simply came to Ali, seemingly out of nowhere. "Radrine."

The dark fairy seemed satisfied. "What is your name?"

"Geea." Again, she did not want to speak the name Nemi had given her. She felt the name had power, and this beast would surely misuse it. Radrine nodded at her reply.

"Your memory is long, I am impressed. Especially since you are now human. That is one reason I have come to question you. Why did you become human?"

Ali hesitated. "To stop the war."

Radrine mocked her. "All by yourself, Geea? Have you grown so powerful as a human being, or merely so deluded? Come now, what was your real reason?"

Ali twisted and arched her back to make herself more comfortable. The effort did not help. "Funny, but I can't think of another reason right now," she muttered.

Radrine came near and spoke softly. "I can make you think of another reason. I can torture you in a hundred ways. Or I can let you go. It is your choice, Geea."

Ali did not need fairy magic to hear the lie. "You will not let me go."

Radrine gloated. "But there are so many ways to die. I could make it quick and painless, or slow and messy. I could make you beg, Geea."

Ali refused to give her the satisfaction. "That will never happen."

"Perhaps not." Radrine paused and stepped to the opening. Beyond her the interior of the cavern glowed like a vision of a prehistoric world. The fumes continued to bother Ali—she could not stop coughing. Far below a mound of lava erupted and a geyser rose up like a flame born of a dragon's breath. The fire seemed to please Radrine, although Ali could not see her face. With her wings pulled close to her scaly body and her bony back to Ali, Radrine spoke in a soft voice. "Tell me about the Yanti. You possessed it a long time, before even Lord Vak had it."

The remark told Ali a great deal. Clearly knowing Radrine's name had convinced the creature that her human captive had all her previous memories back. Ali wished that was the case. Had she really been a fairy? And an important one at that? If she moved carefully, she thought, she might be able to find out a lot about the elemental kingdom.

For all the good it would do her.

Radrine was familiar to Ali—her voice, her movements, her manner of speaking. Yet she remembered the dark fairy differently. The creature had been pretty once, Ali was sure of it.

"You know plenty about the Yanti," Ali said, making an educated guess.

"But no one knows its secrets like you." Radrine glanced over her shoulder. "Lord Vak is ready to use the Yanti to bring his army into this world. No doubt he will succeed. But he cannot tap its full power. A code was placed upon it, I suspect, a mystical formula. The Yanti does not always obey his will, nor, I think, would it obey mine if I had it with me now." Radrine fluttered her wings and took a step toward her. "What did you do to it, Geea?"

Ali was not sure what a mystical formula was, never mind which one she had placed on the Yanti. "Why should I tell you?" she asked.

Radrine smiled, her teeth very sharp. "Because you are my prisoner, and I can do whatever I want to you. You were a fool to try to face me on this side of the red door. Indeed, you surprised me, coming here. The old Geea would never have made such a mistake. What's happened to you? Has taking human form made you stupid?"

Ali did not like being mocked. "Being human has taught me a lot. The elementals cannot win this war. Humanity has jet fighters, machine guns, huge tanks, atomic bombs. The elementals will be wiped out in a matter of days."

Radrine laughed softly. "You are mistaken, the end will not come in days. The war will be long and bloody. Humanity has physical weapons, true, but lacks magical powers. Both sides are equally matched. But in the end we want the dwarves and elves to be destroyed, as much as we want humanity wiped out. Did you not know? The whole world can glow with radioactive dust and we will be happy. Because it is then we will move fully into the third dimension, and take over, and make all who have survived our slaves."

The third dimension?

The yellow door had been the *third* door. And it had been open. Radrine's words stunned Ali. She understood now why Paddy had said everyone hated the dark fairies. "You'll need the power of the Yanti to take over the whole planet," she said, making another guess. "I don't think Lord Vak's going to just give it to you."

"He cannot hold onto it if he has no hands!"

"You're not strong enough to kill him," Ali said, not sure how strong anybody in this upcoming war was, least of all herself. Yet she felt she had to continue to play the role, see what she could learn. Radrine took her insult in stride.

"Perhaps. That is why I will let the humans destroy him."

"They'll destroy you as well!"

"Really? How will they find me on this side of the red door?"

"They'll find you," Ali said, feeling the hopelessness of her words.

Radrine came near. Ali felt her breath on her cheek, so cold, even with the torture chamber so hot. The fairy raised a nail and traced the outline of Ali's eyebrows. She spoke in her ear, a hissing whisper that recalled to Ali nightmares she had never known she'd had.

"I used to admire your eyes. So much power in them, such beauty. I am pleased to see that even as a human they are powerful." Radrine's nail came lower and brushed her lashes. "But what if I were to pluck one out? Eat it in front of you? Would you still be beautiful, Geea?"

Ali had to fight to stay calm. "I would still be who I am," she said.

"You are brave. You were always brave. I grant you that."

"Thank you."

"Tell me the code you placed on the Yanti?"

"No." Ali turned her head so her eyes met Radrine's. To her surprise she saw that there were still traces of green in the fairy's eyes, hints of beauty in what were now largely holes into horror. Yes, a part of her did remember Radrine as much different than the foul creature who stood before her. She also remembered that she had sworn to herself that she would never bow to the monster. Ali added, "You waste your time and mine."

Radrine lost her smile and suddenly reached up with her sharp nail and cut Ali's knotted hair close to her skull. It was like being scalped—her hair swung from the hook and Ali swung upside down. The dark fairy stared down at her and spoke in a quiet voice that no longer hissed.

"There is a difference between us. I have time to waste . . . you have none." She moved toward the opening, her dark wings slowly unfolding like the black thoughts of people who have been born bad. But she glanced back once more and Ali was surprised to see a trace of sorrow on her otherwise cruel face. Radrine spoke. "You should have listened to me long ago, Geea. I asked you to join the Shaktra then but you said no. Now it is too late for that, don't you think?"

Ali did not know what to say. She still did not know what the Shaktra was, although it was clear it was not the queen of the dark fairies. It appeared that Radrine worked for it.

Radrine's regret quickly vanished and was replaced by a fangy grin. "I will let you hang for an hour. Then I will return, for dinner. Maybe you will be unconscious by then, maybe not." She added, "I look forward to the meal. I've always wondered what royal meat tastes like."

Radrine turned and flew away.

"If I'm awake, I'll be sure to spit in your face," Ali muttered, to no one.

This was it, the test of time. She understood that. It had not come before and it was not going to come later. Because there would be no *later*, that was the nature of the test. Nemi had not told her but she should have guessed. The test of time was the test of death, when all time would grind to a halt.

Ali felt bad she had not passed the test of air. The test of space had been painful enough, crossing over the gorge with only a rope to keep her from falling, and then having to watch her friends die. But cornering Paddy on his little lies had been nothing—she had never discovered the *big lie* hidden inside the group. Now she never would. That was the problem with failing the test of time, class was dismissed. Plus she still didn't know who she was. That bothered her more than she would have imagined. To die and not even know what her secret name meant. How sad.

Ali swung up and grabbed the hook beside her. The one she had tied her hair to. The one with the bony foot of the kid who had died before her. Her arms were weaker than they had been before Radrine's visit. Talking with the dark fairy had exhausted her. The creatures were like vampire bats. Just being around Radrine had sucked the life out of her. Ali could only hold on a few minutes before she had to let go. Of course then all her blood went straight to her head and she thought she would pass out.

So she swung up again, up and down.

It could not go on long.

She thought of her father, alone on the long roads—and how he would be even more alone when he returned home. She thought of her friends' parents, how they would search for their children and never find them. Even Paddy and Farble—they must have had someone who would miss them. So much pain, she thought, and all because of her single lousy decision—the red door instead of the yellow door.

So much for her intuition.

Ali stared at the wooden buttons on her green shirt. She had chosen the shirt at the start of their adventure because she had thought the color would help her hide in the woods if they were attacked. The shirt had been cheap. She had bought it at a small store in town when they were having a half-off sale. But she remembered distinctly that the shirt had had *seven* black buttons.

Now there were *six*, she could count them even hanging upside down. The number made no sense. She had dropped two buttons, one at each of the doors they had passed through. That was a fact, she could have sworn to it.

Yet the shirt had six buttons. Not five, not seven.

She studied it closer. Only one button had been torn off.

What did it mean?

Why did her watch now read exactly five o'clock?

More questions. They would have annoyed Paddy, if he had been alive to answer them. They probably would have annoyed the skeletons who hung beside her. Questions were for the living. Why did she keep asking them now? She would be dead soon, they could not help her escape.

Still, it bothered her, the extra button, her confused watch.

Ali tried swinging up again. She had stayed down longer than she had planned and the blood in her brain felt like it would burst her eardrums. Only this time she could not get up, she did not have the strength. Telling herself not to panic, to rest a minute, she took a few deep breaths and tried again. No luck, her back was too weak, the muscles of her arms too tired. It looked like she would have to stay upside down.

The pressure grew swiftly inside her head. Her heart pounded in her ears, even in her eyes—they felt as if they would pop. Her breathing grew hoarse—her lungs sounded like they were filling with fluids. She felt pain, everywhere, in every joint and bone.

Radrine would have to eat alone.

She was going to black out.

Then maybe she did pass out, she wasn't sure. When she woke up the pain was less. It had not stopped, but it felt far away, as if it were happening to a friend and not to her. But she could still hear her breathing, it sounded awful. It could have belonged to an animal that had caught a disease and was now being put to sleep. The noise was louder than her heartbeat. In fact, she couldn't hear her heart in her ears anymore. She could not even feel it in her chest.

Ali opened her eyes and got a surprise. She was sitting at the edge of the torture chamber, staring out at the endless legions of dark fairies, as they flew in their mindless circles around the immense hive. She saw the boiling lava far below, and the stinking red gases that whirled like tornadoes lit by fires that should have burned out long ago. The scene was a wonder, she thought, but it was far from wonderful.

Her attention was drawn upward, and she saw a cave on the roof of the cavern. She wondered if it went all the way to the top of the mountain, if the dark fairies had not taken it when they had come here, to this place, where nightmares were more real than scary stories and demons lived and breathed and plotted in darkness. Yet suddenly she could not remember how she had come to be there.

She turned and saw a girl hanging upside down beside a bunch of skeletons. The girl's hair was a deep maroon—most of it swung from another hook on the ceiling. The girl swayed as she hung, slightly, back and forth, and Ali could hear her labored breathing, but even that seemed to be slowing down, growing quiet. It was only after staring at the girl for several minutes that she realized it was her.

"No," she said, to no one. Because there was no one there.

She felt afraid, and terribly alone.

Again, she thought she blacked out.

Then she was on the black sand beach in Hawaii with her mother. They were lying halfway in the water, halfway on the sand, and they were having a wonderful time. Their position was scary, but that only added to the fun. Because if a wave came in too strong, it would wash over their heads, and they would have to close their eyes and hold their noses until it retreated. But the warm water felt like joy, she would not have cared if it had carried them both out to sea.

She looked over at her mother and caught her mother staring at her. Her mother had such beautiful red hair, it lit up the black sand. Smiling, her mother reached out and clasped her hand.

"You have magic, Ali. Did I ever tell you?" she said.

Ali laughed and asked her what that was supposed to mean.

"You will see," was all her mother said.

Then she was in the car with her mother, the opening night of the play, her twelfth birthday. They were driving home and she was telling her mother how much fun it had been to play Princess Wartly, the heroine of *Frogs and Freaks*.

"It was so neat to have the stage lights on my face. I never knew how hot they were. And I couldn't see anybody past the first row. It was like the audience was hardly there. At the same time I felt them all the time. Like they were in love with my character. Do you know what I mean?"

"I know exactly what you mean, Ali. I felt that way."

She laughed. "You just say that because you're my mom."

Her mother shook her head. "I think everyone was wild about you tonight. I could feel the love in the audience." She added, "I'm going to go to every one of your performances."

"You don't want to do that," Ali said. "You've seen it—you know what's going to happen next. You'll get bored."

Her mother took her eyes off the road, glanced her way. "Nothing you do bores me," she said.

Ali snorted. "Yeah, sure. What about when I scream at you?"

"When do you scream at me?"

"All the time, in my head. I'm just too polite to do it out loud."

Her mother reached over and took her hand. "You are more than polite."

"I'm also a great actress? A better liar?"

Her mother chuckled. "No, I'm talking about something else."

"What?"

Her mother reached over and tugged gently on her left ear. "You're my daughter, Ali. You always will be. And you have magic."

Then there was a burst of intense red light and the night went crazy. The light came from every direction at once and flooded the inside of the car, and seemed to be made of fire, only worse. Turning to her mother, feeling pain in her right arm, Ali tried to scream. But before the cry could leave her throat a bright green creature smashed through the window and grabbed her by the arms, and lifted her up high, into the night air, where she caught a glimpse of the burning car below, a dark figure beside it, and the white moon above.

Then they were flying, away from the street a short distance, behind a row of trees. There the creature set her on the ground, on a lawn, although it continued to support her from behind. Ali realized her head was bleeding and that her arm had been burned. She tried to turn around to see who had saved her.

"Stop!" the creature commanded, in a soft musical voice. "Do not turn around."

"Who are you?" Ali asked. Through the trees she could see the car engulfed in flames, the red smoke pouring into the sky. Yet all around her, cooling green *and* blue lights played. They were coming from the creature at her back.

"You do not know," it said.

"I know that." Ali tried to turn again. Its grip tightened, stopping her. Ali felt as if she was not being held by physical hands, but by some type of force field. "Why can't I see you?" she demanded.

"You will, in time."

"When?"

"When you understand the mystery of time. Then you may turn and look upon me and know who I am."

On the other side of the trees, the gasoline tank exploded and the fire grew more intense. Ali felt panic. "Is my mother all right? Can you save her?"

The creature came closer and spoke in her ear. "It is a mystery."

She wanted to weep; she felt so scared. "I don't understand."

The creature hugged her, and for a moment it felt completely human. "That's because you're sleeping. You're dreaming about the past and the future. All you have to do is wake up." The creature seemed to speak inside her head. "Wake up, Alosha. And turn around."

Ali awoke with a painful breath. The air that entered her lungs was filled with fumes and heat, and her entire body ached, especially her head, which pounded with blood. For several seconds she didn't know where she was. Then she saw the dry skeletons swinging beside her, and the open door that led into the cavern where the fairy hive stood, and the red glow beyond. She was not dead, she realized, not yet, but she would be soon if she didn't come up with a plan.

Yet she had hope now.

She had listened to the one behind her.

The bonds that held her feet to the hook had not changed since her last inspection. The fairies were not fools—they knew how to tie up their prey. She could well imagine all those who had come before her trying desperately to undo their bonds. But had any of them tried to unscrew the hook itself? Looking up, Ali saw that it had definitely been screwed into the ceiling. . . .

What had been screwed in, she thought, could be screwed out.

Ali began to twist herself right and left, using her outstretched arms as levers, clockwise and counterclockwise, trying to build up some momentum in either direction. But she noticed that when she went clockwise, the hook turned slightly. Leave it to the dark fairies to put their screws in backward.

Ali stopped and concentrated on trying to spin clockwise. The screw at the end of the meat hook twisted some more. She spun it around once, all the way, twice. A crack appeared in the stone beside it and black dust rained down on her eyes. Excited at her progress, she practically yanked her body into a pretzel shape. For a moment she forgot all about the fumes in her lungs and the blood in her head. She just kept turning, and the hook kept turning.

Then she fell to the floor, which fortunately was not too far away. Rolling on her side, she felt such incredible relief not to be hanging upside down that she burst out laughing. She had to remind herself that she was not free yet.

Ali checked her watch. Four-thirty; it was over an hour *before* her friends would reach the gorge. The truth hit her like a laser bolt. On the other side of the red door—the side she was on now!—time flowed *backward*. She was amazed she had not realized that sooner, and what it meant.

She could still rescue her friends!

She had an immediate problem, however. Even sitting upright with a clear brain, she could not get free of the sticky rope that tied her to the hook. Rolling several times over on her side, she tried scraping the material against the rough stone edges of the wall. It took her several minutes of hacking, but eventually the rope snapped and she was able to pull off the stuff and stand. That brought another wave of relief, to actually stretch toward the ceiling and get her blood moving in the right direction.

Ali stepped to the opening and peered out. The cave she had entered the cavern through was about two miles away, and between her and it were a thousand dark fairies and a mile-deep volcanic fissure. Okay, she thought, those were not small obstacles.

What to do? She could not fly, and even if she could, she was not going to be able to fly past so many of the enemy. It was not like the dark fairies wouldn't notice. What she needed was to bum a piggyback ride off someone who knew the hive inside out.

"Radrine," Ali said aloud, and smiled. She was glad the evil queen was returning for dinner. Especially when she studied the space above the stony entrance and found a perfect place to hide. Picking up the hook and wiping off more of the sticky goo, she climbed into position. She could hardly wait to see the surprise on Radrine's face.

The wait felt long. She spent the time thinking about the bright green being that had rescued her from the burning car. Time was indeed a mystery. She wondered what it would be like to run down the tunnel and warn herself not to take the red door. She just hoped she got that far.

Ali heard a noise below. A dark shape entered the torture chamber. Ali watched as Radrine stepped farther inside and then froze when she saw the cracks on the ceiling where the hook had come unscrewed—not to mention her missing dinner. Ali didn't give her time to shout for help. Leaping from her hiding space, she landed on the fairy's back and shoved Radrine forward onto the floor.

"Dinner is not ready yet," Ali said as she gripped Radrine's neck and smashed the fairy's face into the floor. Ali had no idea how strong a dark fairy was. Not wanting to take any chances, she banged Radrine's head a few more times to soften her up. Yet she knew the queen must still be weak from her earlier injury. Her creepy translucent skull didn't look like it would be safe in a game of football. Also, Ali didn't want to knock the fairy out altogether. Radrine was going to be her transportation, after all. Kneeling hard on the back of the fairy's wings, she slipped the metal hook around Radrine's throat.

"How are we feeling now?" Ali asked brightly.

Radrine made a hissing noise. "You're choking me!"

Ali eased up with the hook, but kept it around her neck. "You realize I can kill you at any moment?" she asked.

"You'll never get out of here alive."

Ali tightened her grip. "You didn't answer my question."

Radrine gasped. "Yes!"

Ali lightened up. "I'm glad. It's important you understand where you stand with me. And you're wrong, I'm going to get out of here, and you're going to help me. You're going to fly me back to the same cave where your pals took me prisoner."

"Impossible."

"Okay. Maybe you're right and I'm wrong. I might as well kill you now." Ali started to choke her again. Radrine twisted her head to the side.

"Stop! You can't escape past my minions!"

"Good point. We're going to have to go out the back way, with me on your back, so to speak. Being human and all, I can't fly." Ali paused. "Can we go out the top of the hive?"

"No. We'll be seen." Radrine coughed and spat on the floor. "We'll have to go out below."

"Is there another cave that leads up to the one where I was captured?"

"It's not a cave. It's a gorge."

Ali was stunned. "Where my friends fell?"

Radrine was bitter. "I know nothing about your friends."

The fairy was telling the truth, Ali realized. Of course, because time flowed in strange directions inside the mountain, her friends hadn't fallen into the gorge yet. This minute, they were still alive. She thought if the dark fairies had favorite TV programs, they sure would have a hard time figuring out when they were on.

"All right," Ali said, slowly standing beside the dark fairy, careful to keep the hook around Radrine's neck. "You lead and I will follow. But if you make one move to alert your minions, I will break your scaly neck. Understood?"

Radrine turned, caught her eye. "You think you have won, Geea. You are wrong."

"Time will tell," she replied.

Ali grabbed her hair off the hook before they left, stuffed it in her coat pocket. She did not want to leave the dark fairies any souvenirs. She could only imagine what kind of spells they might try to cast if they had a piece of her.

CHAPTER EIGHTEEN

What happened next blew Ali's mind. She followed Radrine as the fairy walked to the back of the chamber and twisted a rock on the wall. The rear wall swung open, and they entered what for all the world could have been an elevator, only it had no walls, no ceiling. Standing on the platform, Radrine moved a knob at their feet and the lift began to descend at high speed through a long black tunnel. The outside light flickered through openings in the hive like a spinning siren. Ali felt a hot wind; they could have been going down a thousand floors.

"Why do you need an elevator when you can fly?" Ali asked.

Over her shoulder, Radrine gave her a strange look. "You know why."

Ali figured it was best to hide her ignorance.

They fell for a long time, and when the lift finally stopped Ali knew they were far below the hive. She suspected they were miles beneath the mountain itself, if they were even in the same dimension as the mountain. They stepped into a narrow corridor lit by flaming torches. Here the air was almost impossible to breathe. It was not thin like she had experienced at altitude, but the smell reminded her of a filthy oil refinery.

Ali took time to grab a torch as they walked the long corridor. Now she had her hands full. Radrine mocked her.

"Can't see in the dark as a human?" the dark fairy asked.

"I see well enough to keep an eye on you. Where are we going?"

"To the gorge. Isn't that what you want?"

"How are we getting there?"

"You know," Radrine said.

Of course she had no idea. She felt fear, however. Did forgotten memories try to rise and warn her? The door at the end of the corridor opened and Ali saw the beginning and end of an ancient nightmare.

The space was gigantic, larger even than the cavern that held the fairy hive, and it was filled with fire and fumes. Yet the latter was the least of its dread. Because beyond its stark appearance was a feeling of despair, of a hopelessness so deep and lasting that no hope or prayer could touch it. Ali peered down into the abyss and thought she saw insect-shaped creatures, many miles away, flying lazily through the forsaken sky.

"What are they?" Ali gasped, not wanting the fear and ignorance to show but unable to stop it. This time Radrine nodded as she glanced back at her.

"You don't remember, Geea," she said. "Interesting."

Ali hardened her voice. "You don't know what I know."

Radrine followed her gaze, down into that awful cauldron. The heat scorched them where they stood. But how much hotter it must be down there, Ali thought.

"Even we do not disturb them," Radrine said softly.

"Then why do we go this way?" Ali demanded.

Radrine shrugged. "It was you who brought us here."

Now came the tricky part, when Ali had to trust Radrine to fly her back to the cave. Fortunately the fairy's wings attached high on her shoulders, and she was able to grip Radrine around the waist while still keeping the hook around her neck. Ali made Radrine carry the torch, and she pulled Radrine's head close before they took off.

"Try to drop me and I snap your neck," Ali said.

"Kill me and you die." Radrine glanced down and added, "Or worse."

Ali tightened her grip with the hook and the fairy gasped. "I may not remember everything since becoming a human, Radrine. But I do know that you're a coward. Fly straight and smooth and maybe I'll let you live."

Radrine got the message. They took off above the pit and the fairy did nothing to shake her off. Ali was relieved because she suspected the creatures who flew below them hated humans above all creatures.

Ali was never to forget that flight. Radrine did not speak and Ali could not. Not in the face of the pain of that place. She closed her eyes but she could not close her heart. Anguish filled the void; the only sound was the occasional distant wail of a lost soul.

The despair followed her even when Radrine reached the bottom of the gorge and began to fly straight upward.

"You're heavy," Radrine panted.

"You're never supposed to tell a human girl that. You might give them a complex, make them anorexic."

"Is that a curse?"

"Something like it," Ali said.

Slowly, the stink and heat of the pit receded as they climbed higher into the heart of the mountain. Soon all they had was the light of her torch to guide them, but that did not seem to bother Radrine. Yet it was obvious the fairy was straining to reach the cave.

Ali had to make a decision, she realized. She feared to leave

Radrine alone to fly back to her minions and sound the alarm. She needed to tie up the dark fairy; she needed rope. As the bisected cave and the broken bridge came into view, Ali put her head close to Radrine's.

"Land on the side where the bridge hangs down," she said. That was on the far side, farther away from the fork in the caves.

Radrine was surprised. "How will you cross the gorge?"

"Let me worry about that."

Radrine did as she requested and soon they were standing on the ledge where hours before—no, in a few hours *from* now—her friends would fall to their deaths. Ali let go with the hook and the fairy sagged to the floor from exhaustion. Radrine looked up at her and sighed. Ali had already taken the torch back.

"Are you going to grow wings next?" Radrine asked.

"Lie facedown on the floor."

Radrine shook her head. "I am a queen. You are not going to tie me up."

"You're my prisoner." Ali put the sharp end of the hook to her neck. "If I don't get to tie you up, I'll have to slit your throat."

Radrine saw she was not joking. Spreading her wings to the sides, she lay facedown on the floor. Ali cut a piece of rope from the hanging bridge and began to bind Radrine's wings backward, at which the fairy protested.

"That hurts," she said.

"Like I had a fun time in your hive?" Ali said.

"That was different," Radrine said.

"How so?"

"We're the bad guys. You're supposed to be merciful."

"There are times for mercy, and this is not one of them." Ali knotted the rope behind Radrine's neck as the fairy wobbled on the floor. She talked as she worked. "You know that I'm hiking up to the top of the mountain to get the Yanti back. I'll be running into Lord Vak and his troops later tonight. I don't want you or your minions showing up. You want to take this advice, Radrine. Since becoming a human, I've been getting back my powers slowly. But I'm a lot stronger than last night when you attacked us. If you ignore me and do try to steal the Yanti back, I'll kill you." Ali yanked the fairy's wings back real far. "Do you understand?"

Radrine gasped. "Yes! Not so hard!"

Ali finished her knot and stood. "You look like a bug that's been stepped on."

"You sound like a human that doesn't know what she's walking into."

"I know," she replied, but there was doubt in her voice.

Ali cut off another length of rope from what was left of the bridge and attached the hook to one end. She did not have Karl's skill when it came to lassoing, but eventually she caught hold of one of the floor hooks on the other side. Securing her rope to the floor, she groaned inwardly at the thought of taking the test of space all over again. What made it worse was that, with the torch, she would only have one free hand.

But when she was out over the gorge, she was pleasantly surprised to discover she was not afraid. Once she passed a test, she must have control over the element. To some degree, at least—she was pretty sure she did not know how to fly yet.

Ali paused when she reached the other side. She looked back at the dark fairy. She could see Radrine in the flickering light of the torch, weary and wounded from the beating she had received, but far from defeated. It made Ali wonder, about lots of things.

She checked her watch. She had plenty of time before the others reached the fork in the cave, assuming her watch was not lying to her. She called out to Radrine.

"Remember my warning," she said.

"Remember mine, Geea," Radrine said.

Ali turned and walked into the cave.

* * *

The big question—for which she had no answer—was what was she going to say to herself? Naturally, she would steer the group away from the red door, but then what? Would there be two Ali's for the remainder of the adventure?

She had a sneaking suspicion that none of the above would happen. The reason was the number of buttons on her shirt. The buttons were part of the time paradox, perhaps the answer to it. She still had six buttons instead of five because even though she had already taken the red door and had had tons of adventures her friends knew nothing about, she had yet to drop the second button—*as far as her friends were concerned*. It was the number of buttons that connected the old self to the new her. At least that was how she saw it, but she could be wrong. Her intuition wasn't always right. Going the wrong way had taught her that much.

"But I had to go the wrong way to learn that," she said to herself as she hurried through the cave with her torch in hand. "I had to face the tests. So I didn't really go the wrong way, after all."

The return hike, to the colored doors, was hard on her. She still needed water in the worst way and her stint in Radrine's jail cell had worn her thin. But she hoped when she reached the red door, and got on the other side, that time would start moving forward again and she could rest a bit. The upcoming meeting with herself—she didn't know how to think of it—continued to weigh on her mind. She just hoped the *new* her would not be as stubborn as the *old* her had been.

Finally she reached the red door, and was glad to find it closed but unlocked.

Naturally, the door had been closed when they had reached it the first time.

She stepped *over* to the other side, and went to shut the door behind her.

But her eyes strayed downward. To the corner of the door frame.

She was shocked—but not surprised—to see her button gone. Of course—*now*—she had not yet left it.

Her watch began to move forward.

Ali closed the red door and sat down to rest, her back against the stone wall.

She probably dozed; she thought she heard herself snoring.

After what seemed forever, she heard the mutter of her friends talking. Quickly, she put out her torch and hid it on the other side of the red door. Then she crept forward in the dark, using the wall for a guide. There was a yellow glow up ahead from Karl's flashlight. Her friends were close to the doors! Her body trembled with excitement!

Her theories could be all wrong. Maybe when she met herself face to face the world would explode. She had seen a science fiction movie where that had happened once.

The gang reached the seven doors, paused to gaze at them.

Ali stepped out of the shadows to greet them.

They did not see her. Wow.

"Is it because I'm still in another time, ahead of them?" she asked.

They did not hear her.

She guessed that meant the answer was yes.

Or perhaps the reverse was true. She was behind their time.

She studied her watch, particularly the second hand. It was moving forward, quickly, and Ali took that to mean she was definitely behind them—time wise—but that she was probably catching up on them. She was not sure if the latter was true, but at least it gave her hope their time lines would synchronize at some point. Hopefully soon!

Ali watched as the gang studied the doors, found the two that opened. Standing like a ghost with her back to the wall, she listened as they questioned Farble about which way to go.

She glowed with pleasure at how great it was to see her friends alive again!

Most of all, she studied herself. It was unlike gazing in a mirror. She looked like a stranger. She did not like her hair, hardly recognized the proud expression she wore. The line of her mouth, too, it was so hard. Did she always look this way? It was a frightening thought.

The next few minutes were tricky, she told herself. She had to use the button, and at the right time. Timing was everything when dealing with a time paradox, she thought.

"We have to make a choice," Steve said. "We have come too far to go back to the entrance."

Ali watched herself turn to Paddy. The movement was disorientating.

Darn, she didn't look as pretty as she thought she looked!

Ali decided to think of her new self as Alison. After all, that was the name on her birth certificate. Yet it was a name Ali had always refused to go by.

"Do you know?" Alison asked the leprechaun.

"No," he said.

"Have you been in here before?" Alison asked.

"Missy asked that before. Paddy said no."

Ali watched herself stop to think. She could almost hear Alison's thoughts, as the red door called to her with the soft voice of a witch. She saw the resolve harden her face.

"I think we should take the red door," Alison said finally.

"Why?" Steve asked.

"I have a feeling about it," Alison said.

Karl was annoyed. She had not noticed before how annoyed he was. "That's not a good reason to choose it," he said.

"It is to me," Alison said.

"I agree with Karl," Steve said, checking out the yellow door's entrance. "The troll's first choice probably has some meaning. I think I feel a faint breeze coming out of here."

"You didn't say that a minute ago," Alison said.

"I didn't feel it then," Steve said.

"Let's flip a coin," Cindy said. "Got a gold one, Paddy?"

"We're not flipping a coin," Alison snapped. Ali was shocked at how arrogant she sounded. It was awful to watch herself act so bossy. Alison added, "I sense something about the first door—the red door. We have to check it out."

"If you sense something in there, we should avoid it," Karl said.

"Yeah. It might be a swarm of dark fairies," Cindy said.

Good for you, Ali thought.

"I can handle them," Alison said.

"I wouldn't get overconfident. Not down here," Karl said.

"I don't like the red door!" Paddy suddenly shouted.

Ali watched as Alison turned on the poor leprechaun, and grilled him, and hardly listened when he tried to warn her. It was a lot to take in. Ali found it hard to believe that she did not even stop to consider what might be behind Paddy's words. Alison just saw him as a liar, a coward. What arrogance!

Finally Alison pronounced her decision.

"Look. We can hike some distance into the first cave," Alison said, trying to sound reasonable but determined to get her own way. "Say a mile or two. If it doesn't look like it's going the right way, we can come back here."

Again, Ali was struck by Karl's annoyed reaction. She had not really noticed it the first time.

"How will we know we're going the wrong way? We won't know anything until it leads us outside."

"I agree," Steve said.

"You can't simply ignore what Paddy's saying," Cindy added.

"Trust me," Alison said.

Famous last words, Ali thought.

The gang prepared to pass through the red door. Ali acted fast. Slipping out of the shadows, she stepped through the open *yellow* door, into the center of the *third* cave. She watched as Alison reached for a button on her shirt to tuck into the corner of the *first* door frame.

Right then Ali tore off the *same* button on her shirt and let it bounce on the floor.

On the floor of the *third* cave. Just beyond the *yellow* door.

Alison paused and looked over, *and she saw the button!*

Why was Alison able to see it when she couldn't see her?

Ali was not sure. She had just hoped Alison would.

Yet when Ali had been stuck in Radrine's prison cell, it had been the buttons—and *not* her watch—that had reacted to the *two* time frames. She suspected it might have had something to do with where she had placed the buttons when she had hiked the length of the cave. The first set of doors they had come to were still a mystery to her, but it was possible they had something to do with time. There had been three, after all, and there were always three dimensions to time: past, present and future.

It was a mystery she would have to solve later.

Stepping away from the group, Alison walked over and picked up the button. Almost, Ali reached out and touched herself. At least her long hair, seen from behind, looked better than she had thought. But she would have to do something about the front, maybe get bangs.

At least *Alison* still had her hair. Radrine had cut off hers.

Ali watched herself study the button, the confusion on her face. Actually, they were both confused. Because when she had dropped the button for Alison to see, the button on Alison's shirt had suddenly vanished. Now it was in Alison's hand, and it must have been freaking her out because she had not even torn the button off her shirt.

"Take the yellow door! Take the yellow door!" Ali shouted at herself. Maybe a part of Alison heard her, at least inside. Alison continued to stare at the button, thinking. The others were already a dozen feet into the first cave.

Then Ali saw something miraculous; they probably both did. For a few seconds the button in Alison's hand glowed with a faint green and blue light. The light was warm and hypnotic; neither of them could take their eyes off it. Suddenly it focused into a beam and Ali saw it pierce Alison's eyes and enter her brain. Shaking her head as if she had just been awakened by a slap, Alison looked around for the others.

"Take the yellow door! Take the yellow door!" Ali shouted at herself.

Alison called to the others. "Wait!"

The gang turned around and came back.

"What is it?" Cindy asked.

Alison hesitated. She looked at the button again.

"Are you changing your mind?" Steve asked.

Alison swallowed. "Let's take the yellow door."

"How can you change your mind?" Karl asked.

Alison thought a moment, then shrugged. "I'm a girl. I can do that."

The gang was agreeable. Ali shouted out with joy. Yet Alison paused to peek once more into the first cave, on the other side of the red door, just before she closed it. Did Alison suspect what she had just missed? The skeletons and the demons? Ali would have relished telling her twin that some tests were better taken only once.

The cave began to climb, not steeply, but bad enough. Once more they were forced to take frequent breaks, and their thirst grew swiftly. Ali felt so dry she would have traded everything she owned for a glass of water. But all she had were the clothes on her back, and no one could see her anyway.

Ali stayed close to Alison, feeling like a shadow, checking out the time on both their watches. She did not think the split between them could go on much longer. She noticed, as time passed, that the times of the two watches were coming closer together. She was now only nine minutes behind Alison, she seemed to be gaining a minute on her every ten minutes. In an hour and a half they should come into sync.

"What will happen then?" Ali wondered. She was still worried about a major explosion. What a mess that would make of their plans.

They passed what appeared to be a group of six tunnels—three round entrances opened on either side of the main cave. These possessed no doors, and without exception, they seemed to lead slightly downward. The gang passed them by without hardly a pause. It was unlikely any of them led to the outside.

Yet they intrigued Ali.

Ali found herself struggling to keep up. To her surprise, Steve seemed to have gotten a second wind. He walked up front beside Karl, with Paddy and Farble in the middle. Ali found herself in the back with Alison and Cindy, the three of them—or the two of them—huffing and puffing together like they sometimes did during PE class. But Ali was more exhausted than her double, who had not had to hang upside down for hours and then fight with Radrine. Yet she feared to fall behind, to be away from Alison when the two times met.

She watched as Alison glanced over at Cindy.

"How are you doing?" Alison asked.

"I would rather be home in front of the TV, drinking a vanilla shake," Cindy said.

"Please don't talk about food or drink," Alison snapped.

Cindy nodded. "Here we're near the end of this amazing adventure and it's all I can think about. I guess that means I'm a shallow person."

Ali saw that Alison was about to agree with Cindy. The closer their time zones came to each other, it seemed the more she could read Alison's mind.

"Be nice to her," she told Alison. Her double paused and glanced over her shoulder. Ali smiled and waved but Alison didn't notice. Yet Alison acted like she had heard something.

"It just means you're hungry," Alison said sweetly.

"Probably," Cindy agreed.

Alison paused. "Cindy?"

"What?"

"I want to apologize," Alison said.

"For what?"

"For being so bossy. For acting like I know everything. I've been a real pain in the butt these last two days."

Good girl, Ali thought. She felt like a guardian angel handing out sage advice over her double's shoulder. Everyone in the world should have the chance to see themselves from the outside, she thought. They probably wouldn't like what they saw.

"True. I accept your apology," Cindy said.

"You don't want to yell at me first?" Alison asked.

"I'm too tired."

Alison continued. "I think it was something I had to learn, that I could make mistakes. It was a test in its own way. That's why I think I had to go the wrong . . ." Alison caught herself.

"You had to go the wrong what?" Cindy asked.

"Nothing," Alison said, puzzled by her own remark.

Definitely her double must be hearing her thoughts to make such a slip. Ali took it as an encouraging sign. She didn't want to rejoin her other half and end up schizophrenic.

The next hour and a half was a killer, for Ali more than any of them. Again, the time she had spent in the dark fairy's hive had taken more out of her than she had realized, and the slope of the cave kept getting steeper. Try as she might, she could not get enough air in her lungs. She thought of wrapping her arms around Alison's waist and asking to be towed along.

Ali knew they were getting near the end of the tunnel, however. The air had cooled and she could smell the waiting snow. After all she had gone through inside the mountain, it would be good to get outside.

A light appeared up ahead. With a shout of excitement the gang rushed forward. Alison followed at first, but then began to lag behind. Ali herself had no choice but to plod along. Her head ached and her muscles burned—she was completely spent. But she managed to pull behind her double and recheck Alison's watch. Their time zones were now only seconds apart.

Perhaps Alison sensed that. She stopped in mid-stride.

Ali put her hands on Alison's shoulders, much as the bright green being had touched her after the accident, one year ago. The light at the end of the tunnel seemed to increase, or else it was the same light from that mysterious night, come to revisit. The walls of the cave shimmered with a green radiance—with hints of blue—and a wave of silence swept the length of the tunnel.

Ali felt herself split in two. She was as much in Alison's mind as her own. The green being had probably felt the same when she had held her. Yet she spoke to Alison and her double finally heard her with her own ears. The seconds on the watch continued to tick. Almost time, but not quite yet. . . .

"Stop," Ali said. "Do not turn around."

"Who are you?" Alison asked, stunned by the voice, the invisible grip.

"You do not know."

"I know that." Alison tried to turn. Ali felt the power of the earth element flow through her arms and she was able to stop her double. All her tiredness fled, and she was filled with a surge of wonder and joy. Her double struggled in her arms. "Why can't I see you?" Alison demanded.

"You will, soon."

"When?"

"In a few seconds. What is happening now is true magic. You have passed all the tests, even the test of time, and you are about to understand who you are."

"No. I have several tests left to take."

"No. I took them for you."

Alison sucked in a deep breath. "Who are you?"

"You."

"Who am I?" Alison asked.

Ali came closer to Alison and spoke in her ear. The feeling of holding herself went beyond déjà vu. She did not simply remember the green being, she *was* her. Wasn't that the answer to the greatest mystery of them all?

"It is a mystery," she told herself.

Alison wanted to weep; she trembled with fear. "I don't understand."

Ali hugged her, and for a moment she felt one with her double, and one with the green being that had saved them that night. Of course there was no Ali, Alison, or green being. Time truly was a mystery. There was only one.

Their watches finally synchronized, down to the last second.

"That's because you're sleeping," Ali told her double. "You're dreaming about the past and the future. All you have to do is wake up." She whispered in Alison's ear. "Wake up, Alosha. And turn around."

Her double turned and their eyes met. Ali did not see her, however, nor did her double see her. They were suddenly both gripped by the same vision of the green being who had rescued them from the fire that dark night. They both remembered the creature's face. The magical light that flowed from her enchanting eyes. The hypnotic colors of the jewels in her golden crown. And most of all the love that radiated from her gentle heart. They both remembered who they were.

She had saved herself that night.

She *was* Alosha, queen of all the fairies.

CHAPTER NINETEEN

When Ali Warner came out of the cave, she was whole again. The cave opened on a snow-packed ridge that overlooked the rear of the mountain, a forest she had only seen pictures of, and read about in books. She thought it fitting to see a new world when she had just been given a new understanding of herself.

With the moon rising on one side and the sun already set on the other, the peak was bathed in various colored lights: red, white, and orange—blended together like different flavors spread over a gigantic snowcone. A narrow ridge led away from where they stood, toward the top, with sides as steep as a witch's hat. The ridge was long and sheer. Ali estimated they had three miles left to hike, perhaps two thousand feet still to climb. They had not gained as much altitude inside the cave as she had hoped.

Yet the cave had done them a favor. The elementals who had already come through the Yanti were probably on the front of the mountain, waiting for their partners to enter the human dimension before joining forces to attack the town. Hiking up the rear, her gang did not have to worry so much about being spotted. They would have the advantage of surprise when it came time to take the Yanti back from Lord Vak.

Ali felt as if her body was charged with atomic energy. Even though the trees were miles below, she could see individual leaves on the branches, and hear the birds as they snuggled into their nests for the night. She had all of Queen Alosha's powers at her disposal, and she knew they would not leave her until this night was finished, if indeed they ever left her again.

The others stood around her, coughing from thirst and the dry altitude. Yet the view had taken their breath away as much as the thin air. As the twilight blended into night and more stars emerged, Ali had to ask herself if she had ever seen a more glorious sight. The view alone had been worth the journey.

Still, there was much to do, and not all of it would be pleasant.

Karl stepped to her side and nodded toward the peak. "We can make it before the moon is straight overhead. But we need water and we need it now. Can you melt some snow with the fire stones? I can put some snow in my cooking pot if you want."

Ali nodded. "Give me your pack, I'll do it."

"You need to rest as much as we do. Let me help."

"No. The altitude suits me. I feel great."

Ali took his pack and retreated to the cave opening. She wanted to hide as best she could. The glow of the fire stones would be visible for many miles.

She hated to use an instrument of the enemy to make water. But even though she could feel her powers alive inside, she did not know how to use them all. They were in a hurry, they had to drink. The fire stones it would have to be.

Ali sorted through Karl's backpack before she brought out the stainless steel pot he had brought along. There was fresh snow all around; she only had to reach out and grab a handful. Yet the snow was probably older than it looked. The last major storm to go through Breakwater had been in April. Still, there was no pollution this high up. The water would be fine.

She had much better control over the stones than before. While her friends sat and rested, she squeezed out a narrow beam of laser light and heated the side of the pot. In less than a minute she had a warm quart of water, which she offered first to Steve. He drank it down in five seconds.

"I could use two more of those," he said, handing the pot back to her.

Ali smiled. "There's plenty where that came from."

For the next half hour she made water and let the others drink their fill and regain their strength. Farble needed the most fluids. She made him ten pots before he nodded his big head in satisfaction. She was so happy to see him alive, sitting not far from Paddy. She felt so much love for all of them.

Except for one. The traitor.

She knew who it was now. She remembered everything her twin had gone through, in and out of time. The clues had been there all along, she just hadn't recognized them. Now all the pieces of the puzzle were in one place, in her head, and the picture they showed her was not pretty.

Karl came up to her as they stood and stretched and mentally prepared themselves for the final push. She had given him his pack back, and he had the rope in his hand.

"I think we should tie ourselves together," he said. "We can loop the rope through our belts. That way if one of us slips and begins to slide down the side of the ridge, we can save them."

"That's a great idea. Do you want to lead the way?" Ali asked.

"I probably should. I have the most experience."

"Tie me behind you, and give us space from the others. I need to talk to you alone."

"About what?" Karl asked.

"Let's talk when we're up on the ridge. It will be safer."

He was confused but he turned to do what she asked.

Before Karl strung them together, Ali took the leprechaun aside and spoke to him alone. "Is the Yanti at the very top?" she asked.

"Aye Missy."

"Did you actually see it when you came into this dimension?"

Paddy looked nervous. He stared at her strangely. He was extremely sensitive, in his own way. Perhaps he suspected she had undergone a major change inside.

"Didn't see it, Missy. Paddy came out of the cave, walked down the snow." He added, "Didn't talk to a soul."

"You talked to the dwarves, Paddy. Then and last night." She raised her hand when he went to protest. "Don't worry, I know all about your deal with the dwarves, and I know you had a chance to turn on us last night and you didn't. I trust you, Paddy, I really do. But I need to ask you another question."

Paddy trembled. "How does Missy know these things?" he asked.

She smiled to reassure him. "Missy learns quick. You say you came out of a cave on the top. Was it at the front of the mountain? On the town side?"

Paddy nodded. "Aye. Opened at the front. But Paddy does not like dwarves. They . . ."

Ali interrupted. "I told you, you don't have to worry about that. What I want to know is, could the Yanti have been *above* the cave you came out of?"

Paddy considered. "Aye. Must have been near for it to work."

She patted him on the top of the head. "Thank you. You have been worth your weight in gold on this adventure."

Paddy's eyes gleamed. "Could Missy get Paddy a large pot of gold when the adventure is finished?"

Ali laughed. "We'll see."

Karl roped them together. Steve ended up behind Farble, in the rear. He was not happy about it, but Ali had made sure he ended up there.

"Why do I have to hike behind the troll?" Steve demanded.

"It is for your own safety," Ali said. "You're the most tired and stand the most chance of slipping off the ridge. Farble weighs as much as all of us put together. He can act as an anchor for you."

"He did carry you halfway up the mountain," Cindy reminded Steve.

"He carried me a few minutes, big deal," Steve complained.

Farble nodded his head and looked happy it was dark.

They started up the ridge, with Karl and Ali taking the lead. With the sun gone, the temperature dropped swiftly. Their breath came out like puffy clouds. The cold and the altitude did not bother Ali. She noticed the top layer of snow—which had softened in the sunlight—freezing again beneath their feet. The ice made for slippery hiking.

As their leader, Karl hiked with his ice ax held ready. The rest of them depended on their crampons—the metal spikes they had fitted onto the soles of their boots—to keep from slipping. Ali had never used them before—it took her awhile to adjust to the spikes. With each step, she had to dig her foot into the snow, and make sure she had a safe grip, before she raised her other foot.

Only three miles to the top, she reminded herself, but it would be a hard three miles, especially for the others.

Yet the sight of Pete's Peak, glistening like a diamond in the glow of the full moon, drew them on. They had gone through so much to get this far. It seemed none of them was ready to quit.

Ali pulled a short distance ahead, with Karl, and spoke to his back.

"I want to talk but I don't want you to turn around," she said quietly. "I don't want the others to know we're talking. Okay?"

"Sure," he said. "What's up?"

She spoke in a low voice. "We have a traitor in our group."

Karl froze. "What?"

"Don't stop, keep walking, I'll explain."

Karl resumed hiking. "That sounds crazy."

"There's a list of facts I need to share. None of them means much alone, but when you add them all together you'll get the picture. First off, Steve is the traitor."

Karl shook his head. "No way."

"Listen! The day after I was buried by the trolls, Cindy, Steve and I came back up the mountain to take pictures. You know all this. We were after bigfoot and we thought if we got some photographs we would get famous. After we shot a few rolls of troll prints—thinking they belonged to bigfoot—we hiked down to the river. Cindy was about a hundred feet in front of me and Steve was not far behind me. Then I heard this cry—I thought it was Steve. In fact, it was Steve. But I was not given a chance to turn around. Someone lifted me up and threw me in the river."

"Farble and his friends," Karl said.

"No. I spoke to Farble. He and his pals were not at the river at that time. Let me continue. After I got out of the river—and after I spoke to the tree—I found Cindy with Steve. He was sitting in the middle of the path with a bump on his head. His film and camera were missing."

"So?" Karl said. "The trolls hit him on the head and stole his stuff."

"How would trolls know enough to take his camera and film? You've seen Farble. He's nice enough for a troll but he isn't that bright."

"They probably took the stuff out of curiosity, like Farble took your sweater."

"Maybe, but I don't buy it."

"What are you saying? That Steve threw you in the river and then faked the blow to his head?"

"Yes. He was right behind me. When you think about it, it's the most obvious explanation."

"But you said the creature that lifted you up was powerful?"

"He was."

"You're losing me," Karl said.

"Just listen. The night the dark fairies attacked, Steve was the only one who didn't get hurt. Plus he was supposed to be totally exhausted, and he got to Overhang before you. Even when he got there, the dark fairies did nothing to keep him out."

"You don't know that for sure. You weren't there."

"You were there! You told me these things yourself!"

Karl slowed almost to a crawl. He seemed to be thinking.

"That did make me wonder," he admitted.

"Of course it did. Steve's a traitor. He must have been working with the dark fairies all along."

"But how?" Karl asked.

"They have been here longer than I thought. He could have contacted them anytime in the last year."

"But why?"

"I don't know, maybe he's one of them."

"Ali," Karl said in disbelief.

"You have to trust me on this. We can't let Steve near the Yanti. You see that stone mound on top of the peak? The Yanti's on top of that, above a cave that opens on the front of the mountain. I spoke to Paddy about this. What I want to do is let Steve get as far as the base of the mound. Then I want to tie him up and leave Farble and Paddy to guard him. You, Cindy, and I can go on from there."

"What if you're wrong?" Karl asked.

"I'm not wrong," Ali said. "But even if I am, there's no harm done. I can apologize to Steve later. But if I'm right, the decision could save the world."

Karl nodded. "I guess it's better to be safe than sorry."

"My feelings exactly," she said.

They plodded on. Their water break outside the cave had given them fresh energy, unfortunately it did not last. Besides being steep and narrow, the ridge was made of a lumpy mixture of ice and rock. The combination was deadly. Twice Steve slipped and had to be hauled back up by Farble. Once Cindy tripped and rolled over the side. Ali barely caught her in time. If they hadn't tied themselves together, the last leg of the journey would have been a disaster. Ali was grateful for Karl's foresight.

They took endless mini-breaks. They would hike ten steps forward and then stop to catch their breath. With her powers, Ali didn't have to struggle, but she worried about the others.

They got mad at her when she refused to make more water.

"We can't use the fire stones up here on the ridge," she said, during a short break. "We're too exposed. It would be like shooting off a flare. The elementals might see us."

"I thought you said they were all on the other side of the mountain," Steve said.

"Most of them are, I think, but you never know," Ali said.

"But I'm dying for a drink," Cindy complained.

"Yeah. The altitude has me totally dehydrated," Steve said.

"Aye. A little sip would go down nicely right now," Paddy said.

Farble nodded hopefully, his green spit dry around the outside of his mouth.

Ali shook her head. "The fact that we're standing in bright moonlight is bad enough. I won't do it. Suck on some snow."

"Snow's cold," Karl warned. "It can give you cramps."

"A little won't hurt," Ali said, bending over and grabbing a handful. She hated to be so bossy—like the *old* Ali—but felt she had no choice.

They set out again. The night wore on and the peak waited. This close to their goal, the top of the mountain blotted out half the sky. As the moon rose above the shadow cast by the peak, Ali felt transported back in time to the last ice age, when people had huddled around fires and the elementals had probably roamed both dimensions.

They reached the base of the mound at one in the morning. The full moon was almost straight overhead by then, a brilliant white eye that seemed to glare down at them impatiently. Ali remembered Nemi's words to her inside the tree.

"When the moon is straight overhead. At that moment, the moon will begin to burn."

After all she had gone through, she was still not sure what that meant.

The mound that towered over them was at least two hundred feet tall, roughly circular in shape, with sheer sides made of cracked and fitted stones that might have been put in place by nature and time, or else set and cemented by a small army of dwarves. Ali could not tell which it was and she supposed it didn't matter. They had to climb to the top and it was not going to be easy. Snow and ice gripped the stones. There were too many places to slip. One mistake and the fall to the bottom would kill them.

Ali feared to hike around to the front of the mound, worried that guards might have been placed at the entrance of the cave Paddy had spoken of. She suspected elves could be waiting for Lord Vak to come through the doorway the Yanti would create. The mound was thick, however, at least two hundred feet across, and she was not afraid the elves could hear them talking.

While the others rested in the packed snow at the base of the mound, Ali pulled Karl aside and spoke in a low voice. "When I was getting the pot out of your pack, I saw a roll of duct tape," she said. "Why did you bring it?"

"My father told me to bring tape whenever I went on a hike. He said you'll always end up using it, for one reason or another."

"Have you used it on this trip?" she asked.

"Not yet. What do you have in mind?"

Ali glanced toward the others. They were so exhausted from the hike, they just sat in the snow like discarded mannequins. Even Farble, who had not carried anyone the last leg because of the danger, looked beat. Ali thought she might be able to use their exhaustion to her advantage.

"I don't want to get into a big fight with Steve in front of Cindy," Ali said. "I'm going to accuse him of being a traitor and then I want you to slip in and tape his mouth shut. End of argument."

"Do you still want me to tie him up with a piece of the rope?"

"No. Use the duct tape on his hands and feet. That will hold him. I want to save the rope for the mound." She glanced straight up at the rock wall at their backs. "Can we do it?" she asked.

Karl was grim. "We're taking a big risk. I'll go up first, throw the rope down to you and Cindy."

"No. You fall and you'll die. At least if you're tied to Cindy and me, you stand a chance."

Karl shook his head. "I know more about climbing than you. If any of us falls, he or she will pull the others down. Let me take the risk."

Ali patted his shoulder. "You're so brave. But since we started out we've shared every risk, and I think we should keep it up until this is all over. You can lead us up the wall but I want us tied together."

"You're making a mistake."

"It won't be my first one," she said.

They returned to the others. Ali didn't waste time before hatching her plot. Standing above Steve, she pointed a finger at him. "You traitor!" she said. "I know you've been working with the dark fairies since we started this trip! You're planning to steal the Yanti!"

Steve looked up at her and blinked. "Huh?"

Ali gestured to Karl. "Tape his mouth! Farble, hold Steve down while Karl binds this traitor!"

Karl and the troll were quick to obey. Before Steve could defend himself, his mouth was closed with tape. Farble gripped Steve's arms and legs while Karl wound the tape around Steve's torso, doing a more thorough job of it than Ali had asked for. Steve's eyes bulged in disbelief.

Cindy and Paddy were slow to respond, the accusation was such a shock. But both finally got to their feet.

"What are you doing?" Cindy snapped at Ali.

"I told you, Steve's a traitor," Ali said. "Farble and Paddy are going to hold him here while we check out the Yanti."

Cindy snorted. "Steve's no more a traitor than I am! Let him go!" She took a step toward Steve. Ali blocked her path.

"No!" Ali said. "I don't have time to explain. You have to trust me. Steve's been working against us from the moment I told you guys about the trolls."

"No way!" Cindy said.

"It's true," Ali said.

Paddy looked worried. "Missy, are you sure? The laddie's not too bright, but Paddy has not noticed a bad bone in his body."

Ali spoke to the leprechaun. "I'm sure, Paddy. You remember how I knew things inside your head that you thought were secret? In the same way I know Steve is a traitor."

Paddy was curious. "Missy's using her fairy magic?"

"Exactly." Ali turned to her friend. "Cindy, I know this seems crazy but after we check out the Yanti, I'll explain everything. Okay?"

Cindy was upset. "Steve's our friend. He's done nothing wrong. You can't treat him this way." Again, she tried to rescue Steve. This time Karl blocked her.

"Ali's explained everything to me in detail," Karl said. "Please, this is not easy for any of us, but you have to believe her."

Cindy gave up trying to get past them and paced in the snow. "I want to know the reasons now, before we climb this stupid wall." Pointing a finger at Steve, she shook her head angrily. Ali saw tears in her eyes. Cindy continued, "He didn't get a chance to defend himself. That's not right."

"I know," Ali said quietly, trying to calm her. "If we had more time I would give him that chance. And I will, once we have the Yanti in our hands. But for now I don't trust Steve. He's going to have to stay here with Farble and Paddy." Ali put an arm around Cindy. "Think of it this way. Steve's a klutz. If he tried to climb up the cliff with us, he would probably slip and kill us all. It's better he stay here."

The logic soothed Cindy, somewhat. "You make sure that troll doesn't squash him," she said.

"No one will hurt him while we're gone," Ali promised. Giving Cindy a hug, she came and knelt beside Steve. Karl was still applying the duct tape and Farble seemed content to hold Steve all night.

Exhausted from the struggle, Steve had stopped squirming and sat defeated. Ali gestured for Karl and Farble to back off so she could have a word with him alone.

"I don't know how long we'll be gone," she said. "But we'll release you when we get back. Then you can make your case. Until then I want you to sit here patiently and not give Paddy and Farble a hard time." She turned to the troll and added, "And Farble, don't eat Steve or the leprechaun while we're gone."

Farble looked disappointed but nodded his big head. Paddy pulled up a small rock beside Steve, determined at least to keep their prisoner company. Steve glared at her. She didn't know what else to say to him.

Ali stood and stared up at the cliff that waited for them. The moon was only a few degrees away from the center of the sky. They did not have much time.

"Let's get this over with," she said.

CHAPTER TWENTY

The climb to the top did not take nearly as long as Ali had feared. Two hundred feet was less than the length of a football field, even if it was straight up. Nevertheless, the minutes the three of them spent on the wall were some of the longest of her life.

Once again, she herself was not in danger. It was the others she had to worry about, even those below, in case Karl or Cindy fell on them. With her supernatural strength, she was easily able to dig her feet into the snow and rocks. She almost tore the crampons off her boots, she dug so hard. The tiniest crevasse gave her plenty to hold on to. She imagined, even if she did slip, that the fall could not hurt her. The power of all the fairies combined continued to flow through her blood.

Twice she kept Cindy from falling, grabbing her with the strength of an elephant and the reflexes of a cat before Cindy even had a chance to cry out. Ali didn't want any loud shouts, this side of the mound, not with elves possibly around the corner.

Karl showed his skill. He kept a steady pace and didn't slip once. Ali thought he must have had a ton of experience on such snowy walls. It was a very good thing they were tied to him, she decided.

Then they were at the top, and a surprise greeted them.

The roof of the mound was a perfect circle, flat as a parking lot. There was no way it had been carved out by nature in the last ice age, or in any time before that. Plus there was no snow, not a trace, and the ground, although seemingly made of the same volcanic sand they had run into much of the way, was as white as a Caribbean beach. Ali had no explanation for the color of the ground, but she quickly felt how warm it was. She took off her coat and hat. The heat appeared to radiate from the center of the mound. Pointing in that direction, she spoke to the others.

"Something over there is keeping the snow melted," she said.

"I hope it's the Yanti," Cindy said. "Do you know what it looks like?"

"Not really," Ali admitted. Once again, she had only vague memories, but at least now she remembered that it was something she used to wear.

Karl squinted toward the center. "I see some kind of structure."

Ali nodded. "Let's go see."

Structure was too kind a word for what they found. At the center of the mound was a crude framework made of bamboo sticks, like the kind that had saved her life when she had been buried alive on the ledge. There were four thick posts, bound together at the top by a roof of finer sticks, and then tied tight by many yards of green vine.

Yet the hut had not been built to live in, or to keep the rain and snow off. The framework was only four feet high and it stood above a three foot wide, perfectly round, hole. Ali suspected the hole went all the way into the center of the mound and joined the cave Paddy had spoken of, the one through which he had entered their dimension.

Lying flat on top of the bamboo sticks, directly above the hole, was a seven-sided gold band, with a gold triangle inside, which in turn had a tiny diamond in the center of it. The entire band was perhaps two inches across, but the most curious thing about it was, the three pieces—the band, the triangle, and the diamond—were unconnected. There was only air between them.

Ali knew it was the Yanti. She *remembered*.

She remembered that the pieces were in fact connected, by an invisible force.

But there was even more she could not remember.

A white string, perhaps made of silk, dangled off one side, and a gentle warmth radiated from the medallion in all directions. The heat was a mystery; it was no greater close up than it had been at the edge of the mound. Indeed, she was sure the Yanti would not be uncomfortable to touch.

Ali went to pick it up.

But she noticed her companions were not by her side. A wide circle had been traced in the white sand around the bamboo hut. A crude circle—it could have been drawn with the tip of someone's foot. Yet it appeared as if the line had the power to block Karl and Cindy. They stood on the other side of it, seemingly frustrated.

"What's wrong?" Ali asked.

Cindy held up her palm and felt the air between them. "It feels like a force field. You didn't notice it?"

"No," Ali said.

"We can't reach the Yanti. Only you can," Karl said. "Pick it up and bring it here, I'd like to see it."

"Yeah. Is it pretty?" Cindy asked.

Ali glanced at the Yanti. The medallion was lighter than most gold, and shiny, as if it lay glistening in warm sunlight and not beneath the cold rays of the moon.

"Well?" Karl said.

"Well what?" Ali asked.

"Are you going to show it to us?" he asked.

Ali had trouble taking her eyes off it. "Sure. But I think I'll leave it where it is for the moment," she said.

"Why?" Cindy asked.

"Yeah," Karl said. "Aren't you supposed to get it out of here before the Yanti opens an interdimensional gate and all the elementals pour through into this world?"

"You have a point," Ali said, thinking.

"Why won't you let us see it?" Karl asked again.

She turned away from them, giving her full attention to the Yanti.

"There's time. Be patient," she said.

Ali heard a movement at her back, a stifled cry, a click of metal. Then she heard a voice she knew well, one she had heard plenty of in the last two days. But it was a voice that had aged and grown bitter in the space of seconds. He still sounded like the young man they had known all their lives, and at the same time he sounded like the wicked creature that had dwelled inside him since the day he had been born.

"I'm afraid there isn't time, Geea," Karl said. "Pick up the Yanti and bring it here."

Ali turned and found Karl gripping Cindy with one hand, and in his other hand he held a gun, and it was pointed at her head. He smiled as she turned, his face filled with satisfaction. He tapped the side of Cindy's head with the tip of the barrel.

"The Yanti, please," he said. "Bring it here."

Cindy struggled in his arms. "Karl! What are you doing? Let me go! What are you doing with my dad's gun?"

"Don't fight him," Ali said. "Just relax, there's nothing to fear."

Angry and confused, Cindy stopped struggling and went still in Karl's arms. It must have been obvious to her that he was stronger than any thirteen-year-old boy had a right to be. Fear darkened Cindy's face, even in the light of the bright moon. She seemed to sense that there was more going on than met the eye.

"Can you help me?" she asked Ali. There was a note of pleading in her voice.

Ali nodded. "I will, I promise."

Karl grinned. "You can help her by handing over the Yanti. It is all I want. Then I'll let you girls go." He added, "Otherwise, I'll put a bullet in her brain."

Ali ignored the threat and nodded to the line in the sand at their feet. "Lord Vak must have set up this barrier. That's why you couldn't reach the Yanti before. But when I started talking about it, you saw a way to get to it."

Karl spoke in a slick voice. "What better way to get to the Yanti than through the great Geea? It was yours before it belonged to him. I knew it would welcome you back, and that no magic of Lord Vak's could keep it from you."

"How long have you known who I am?" she asked.

"You would do better to ask how long I've known who I am!" He paused. "Don't you remember me?"

Ali stared. The face was different, of course, and the voice only approximated his old voice. Still, the truth of his secret identity came back like a cold slap.

"You are Drugle," she said. "One of my advisors. You were on my court, in the elemental kingdom, and you argued with me to join with the rest of the elementals and attack humanity."

"I was your *chief* advisor, Geea. For a long time I gave you excellent advice. But then I came to see you were too weak to be a powerful leader."

"You mean I was too nice," Ali said.

"Whatever. You were no one to follow. As time passed, I realized I had to take my own counsel, seek out my own allies. This war must go on, Geea. Even though I take the Yanti now I am not going to stop Lord Vak and Lord Balar from bringing through their armies. This war is necessary to clear the way for my friends and me."

Ali heard Radrine in Karl's words.

". . . . *But in the end we want the dwarves and elves to be destroyed, as we want humanity wiped out. Did you not know? The whole world can glow with radioactive dust and we will be happy. Because it is then we will move fully into the third dimension, and take over, and make all who have survived our slaves.*"

"You work with Radrine," she whispered.

"True."

"You work for the Shaktra."

Karl was momentarily surprised at her knowledge of the name, but then nodded. "Your memory is coming back, Geea. A shame it returns too late." He pressed the gun into Cindy's ear. "The Yanti, hurry, I grow impatient."

"Ali!" Cindy cried. "I don't understand! What are you guys talking about?"

"Shh. It will be all right," Ali said, once again ignoring his threat. She wanted to learn as much as she could while she had the chance.

Ali took a step toward them, a step away from the Yanti. Above, a halo appeared around the moon, which was strange because the sky was clear and dry. As she studied it, a second one appeared, huge ghostly circles that magnified the light of the moon. The top of the mound was now almost as bright as it would have been on a cloudy day. She had no idea what the halos meant. Karl noticed them as well, but perhaps he understood them better.

"We're running out of time," he warned, pushing the gun harder into Cindy's head.

"Why are you doing this?" Cindy cried.

"Shut up and stay still!" he snapped.

"Our Karl is not who he appears to be," Ali said. "And you're wrong, Drugle, I don't need memory of times before this birth to know you're rotten. I only have to think back over the last few days. From the beginning, you were such a smooth talker. I should have seen it back then. You supported me when I talked about taking this adventure—without asking any questions—when even my best friends doubted me."

Karl continued to gloat. "I played you, it's true."

"You played us all. There were signs all along. The cabdriver called you by your first name when we got out of the cab. The way he said it, it was like he knew you, better than he knew us. That was because you had already been up the mountain with him that morning. You never went to Tracer, did you? You already had all our camping gear at home. Instead, you drove up the mountain early, with a can of gasoline, and lit the tree on fire. That's the real reason you were late joining us. Admit it."

"You saw all the signs, Geea. But you understand them too late."

A third and fourth halo appeared in the sky, each one bigger than the previous, making a gigantic bull's-eye out of the moon. She wondered if the rings were only visible from the mountaintop, or if they could be seen all over the country.

"Even when the dark fairies attacked, and you got burned," she said. "It looked serious but it wasn't as bad as it should have been considering where you'd been hit. If Cindy or Steve had been blasted in the stomach, it would have killed them. It was all a setup. You let the dark fairies hit you to draw suspicion away from yourself."

He was pleased at her insight. "You're right."

"Tell me, did you go talk to the dark fairies while we were asleep?"

"Sure. That's why I wanted to stand guard."

"Why did you tell them to attack?"

Karl shrugged. "I was getting tired of the big group. Figured it might simplify things to kill a few of the others before we got up here."

"The dark fairies never really tried to kill me that night?" she asked.

"No. I needed you, remember, for now."

"But you were the one who hit Steve on the head and then threw me in the river. I could have died then. Why did you do that if you needed me so badly?"

"You have to understand that you hadn't talked to the tree yet. You knew nothing about the Yanti. I didn't think you ever would. I didn't think there was a one in a million chance I could get you up here to help me. But I could see you were going to be trouble." He shrugged and added, "It seemed a good idea at the time to kill you."

"It was no big deal to you?" she asked.

He laughed. "I wouldn't say that. Killing the queen of the fairies is no small deal."

"Yeah, you knew who I was. You went way out of your way to keep Ali Warner from taking a hard look at Karl Tanner." She snorted in disgust. "Everything you've said in the last three days has been a lie!"

He continued to smile. "It worked, didn't it?"

Ali came closer, near to the line in the sand that separated them. "Did it? You got mad in the cave when I seemed to be going the wrong way. It was because you knew the way that led to the ridge. You had been up here before, probably many times over the last year, trying to get to the Yanti. You probably visited your old pal along the way—Radrine."

Karl snickered. "You don't have to tell me what I did. I remember."

"You don't remember everything. Not the first time we all hiked through the cave together. The time I took you guys the *wrong* way. It's true, Drugle, *I took the whole gang through the red door*, the one that leads straight to Radrine's hive."

Karl lost his grin. "Huh?"

"I think you're losing it, Ali," Cindy said, worried.

Two more halos appeared, huge sweeping circles, that stretched almost to the horizon. There was room for one more, maybe. Ali took another step forward. She put her foot on the line on the ground.

"It happened in a time out of time," Ali explained. "It was during that time that I passed the last of my tests. But along the way I ran into a little problem, we all did. We had to cross a deep gorge on a thin rope. Dwarves were chasing us and there was a panic. But everyone kept their cool, except you. You pushed Cindy out of the way to get to safety. Then you kicked her in the head. Really, you didn't care what you did as long as you saved your own skin. That surprised me then, but later, after being in Radrine's hive, it made perfect sense. My mother used to say that you never know a person until there is a crisis. Then you can see them for exactly who they are." Ali paused. "Down there, in that dark cave, I saw my old friend Drugle, the coward."

Karl was bitter. "What are you talking about? None of these things happened. You're just trying to pretend like you knew more than you did when you knew nothing. You were fooled in this world—the same way I fooled you in the other world." He lifted the hammer on the revolver and yanked Cindy's head back. "Give me the Yanti or I kill her. Now!"

A seventh halo appeared, so large it touched the horizon. Slowly, the lot of them began to turn, joining into a vast spiral with the moon at its center, and they began to take on color, with red at the edge. . . .

Ali smiled. "Poor frightened Drugle. Here you are a high fairy on the queen's council with all types of magical powers at your command and you bring a gun to this place. Fool! You are like one of those stupid kids who gets all worked up over nothing and grabs a gun and takes it to school. You are pathetic, really, I am disappointed in you. With your devious mind, I'd have thought you would have at least come up with a clever plan."

"Ali," Cindy gasped, her head held in a tight grip. "I don't think you want to make him angry right now."

Karl gloated. "If I'm such a fool then why are you standing there helpless while I am about to claim my prize?"

"Good question." Ali paused. "Shoot."

Karl blinked. "What?"

"Shoot her, I don't care."

"Huh?" Karl said.

"You can't shoot me," Ali said. "I'm on the other side of Lord Vak's invisible barrier. But you obviously want to shoot someone. So shoot Cindy."

"I am seriously not getting this joke," Cindy said.

Karl frowned. "You bluff. I know you. You would rather risk an entire world than give up on a friend."

"Okay, I'm bluffing. Shoot her."

"Enough! No more games! Give me the Yanti!"

"No," Ali said.

Karl shook Cindy hard. "I'll kill her, I swear!"

Ali mocked him. "You swear? Long ago you swore an oath of loyalty to me—your queen—but still you betrayed me. What good are the vows of Drugle the coward? Drugle the fool? Tell me, I want to know."

Karl was beside himself with anger. "I will kill her just to spite you!"

Ali spoke in a serious voice. "You underestimate me. I was not too late when it came to remembering what I needed to know. I knew everything when we came out of the cave, when I asked for your pack. True, it was clever of you to hide the revolver in that compartment at the base of the pack. I found it just the same, though, and took the bullets out of the gun." She paused. "Do you want to check?"

Karl froze, for a moment, then peered down the side of the gun at the six-bullet chamber. The empty chamber. Seeing his enormous mistake, he threw the gun aside and went to choke Cindy, possibly break her neck. Ali knew he had the strength to do it. Yet she had anticipated his move.

She was queen of the fairies, she had powers he could not even imagine. Leaping through the air, she pushed Cindy aside and grabbed Karl by the throat. She moved so fast neither of them were able to follow her. When she had him, however, trembling in her arms, she forced him to stare at her.

"I want to ask you a question," she said in a cold voice. "You want to answer it honestly. The night my mother died, the car was hit with red laser beams. Obviously the dark fairies attacked with their fire stones. I was carried to safety, away from the fire, before they could finish off the car. But before that, I saw a figure standing beside the car, a person who looked a lot like you." She paused. "Was it you?"

He shook his head anxiously. "No, Geea! I swear it!"

She heard the lie. "Wrong answer," she said.

Ignoring Cindy, ignoring even the cosmic spiral in the sky that had begun to pick up speed and color, Ali dragged Karl *past* Lord Vak's invisible barrier to the hole below the Yanti.

Yet the sight of the Yanti made her pause in wonder.

The medallion was no longer gold; it was moving with the same spiral that filled the sky: the outer edge glowing red, the second layer streaked with orange, then yellow, green, blue, violet, and finally white at the center, where the diamond was. The seven circles of light possessed all the colors of the spectrum. But the white light was the brightest; it quickly became blinding, as straight overhead the moon burst forth with a hundred times its normal light. Clearly, what was happening in the sky was happening to the Yanti, only she did not know which was causing which.

The top of the mountain was soaked in color. Shifting rainbows played over the snowy peak like buckets of watercolors dumped from the sky. A strong breeze rose around the mound; it too moved in a spiral, taking the shape of a tornado. Ali's hair lifted into the air; the strands sparkled in the colored beams. For a moment her anger faltered. So much was happening at once, and it was all extraordinary.

Then she thought of another night, one year ago, and her anger returned with a vengeance. Crouching beneath the Yanti, she held Karl's head above the hole that led to the center of the mound. She was not sure how far the fall to the bottom was, but figured it would be enough to kill him.

"You were there!" she said, as the wind howled in their ears. "You brought the dark fairies there!"

"No!" he cried.

"You killed my mother!"

"I didn't! Please!"

She shoved half his body over the edge. "I'm going to kill you!"

His face was a mask of terror. "No! I didn't kill her!"

She pushed him further. "Liar!"

"No, Geea! Your mother's not dead!"

Truth. She heard truth, finally. She pulled him back from the edge.

"What are you saying?" she demanded. "No lies."

He breathed heavily, the colors of the Yanti and the sky running over his twisted face like frightful emotions. "I got her out of the car. I took her away."

"But the burnt body? We buried her ashes."

"No. It was another body. The dark fairies brought it, I don't know from where."

More truth, she could hear it in his voice. Yet she could not accept what he said, could not let herself hope. The pain went too deep. Even so, she released him, let him stand away from the hole. The invisible barrier that guarded the Yanti no longer seemed to bind him. She supposed it had been enough that she had brought him across the barrier.

Across the top of the mound, the wind continued to spiral upward as the light poured down. Cindy stood thirty feet off to her right, and she seemed to be worried that Ali was listening to Karl.

"He's just telling you what you want to hear!" Cindy called.

"You know I'm telling the truth," Karl told her.

Ali considered. "Where is she?"

Karl shook his head. "Give me the Yanti and I'll give you her."

She snorted. "Don't give her to me and you'll die."

He was scared but he was still devious. "No. You won't kill me. I'm the only one who knows where she is. Even Radrine doesn't know. If you kill me there will be no one to rescue her."

"Rescue her from what?"

"From hunger. From thirst. I have been gone long enough as it is. She must be pretty hungry by now." He paused. "Do you still want to kill me?"

"He's lying!" Cindy shouted.

"Shh!" Ali snapped. The trouble was he was telling the truth. She had to move carefully. "How is she?"

"Fine, for now."

"Did she get burned in the attack?"

"Some, not much. I got her out quick." He paused. "Give me what I want and you can see her tomorrow."

"No. You cannot have the Yanti. You would use it to bring more elementals into this dimension, all over the place. You would destroy the world."

"That's my business."

"It's mine. You only care about yourself, your childish dreams of power. I have to worry about both dimensions. I won't give you the Yanti."

He was afraid but nevertheless acted cocky. "Then your mother will die. Slowly, alone."

She heard the lie. "No. My mother is the only lever you have left over me. You kill her and you have nothing." She pointed toward the rear of the mound. "Get out of here."

The order shocked him. "You will just let your mother go?"

"I'll save her later. Now that I know who you are, you have lost your advantage. It doesn't matter where you go, I'll catch up with you. And if I find you have harmed my mother in any way, you'll suffer." She turned back to the Yanti. "Now get out of my sight, you make me sick."

Karl crept away, but he called over his shoulder just before he climbed down the mound. "You'll never find her!" he shouted.

Then he was gone.

She would find her, she knew in her heart she would.

The light from the sky and from the Yanti were forming a bridge. Ali watched as a white beam pierced the collage of colors that rose between the two. She had to shield her eyes, it was so bright. Yet she saw a green sphere begin to form deep inside the mound, where the elven army would supposedly enter their world.

Ali could see no objects inside the sphere—no trees, fields or flowers—yet she knew she was glimpsing the border of the elemental kingdom. The sight filled her with longing; the green light was home. Her heart ached to step into it and leave the human dimension behind.

Perhaps the green sphere heard her wish. It began to expand, out of the cavity of the cave, until it surrounded the whole mound. Ali clapped her hands in delight. Yet still it grew, in brightness and wonder, until it encircled the peak. Standing in the center of it she felt as if she remembered an entire lifetime as Alosha. Only the memories came too quick and left too soon to make sense to her.

It did not matter. She felt happy, truly happy.

Until the white beam of light between the Yanti and the moon suddenly turned red and the green sphere was darkened by the ruby glow. She looked up to see giant flames leap from the edges of the moon. Like long arms of wrath striking at the space between two worlds, the burning moon signaled to Ali that the Yanti was finally opening.

CHAPTER TWENTY-ONE

She could stop it, she knew, by picking up the Yanti and disconnecting it from the light of the full moon. It was what she had come there to do, what Nemi had told her to do. To close the Yanti before it opened and the main army of the elementals came into their world.

Yet she chose to leave the Yanti in place.

A part of her wanted to talk to Lord Vak.

Another part told her that she was crazy.

The green sphere, although streaked red by the column that connected the moon to the Yanti, continued to expand, over the peak and down into the forest. In her mind, Ali had always thought the army of elves and dwarves would come thundering out of the cave at the top of the mountain. Indeed, she walked in that direction, to the edge of the mound, to see the elementals emerge. Yet the size of the sphere must have been the size of the opening. The cave was no longer necessary to bring in the enemy.

But were they really the enemy?

That's what she wanted to find out.

Then they appeared, in an instant, a thousand soldiers. No, a million, their legions spread over the entire mountain, row upon row, even down into the trees. Never in her wildest imagination had she thought there would be so many.

They were mostly elves, but there were plenty of dwarves, all clad in battle gear, with long spears and sharp swords, and steel armor that glistened in the burning moonlight like fires born of ancient grudges. Thousands were on horseback, more stood on foot, and they had brought bows and arrows and long iron ramming rods to take apart humanity's cities. They even carried canoes, she saw, to ride the river down to the base of the mountain and into the city and thus speed up their attack.

Yet Ali knew that these tools were the least of their weapons. These soldiers were elementals—each possessed some form of magic that could bewilder the bravest human solider. The army looked out of place and time, but it would take nuclear bombs to stop it.

Then what would be left of the world?

Ali had not realized it but Cindy had come up at her side. Both stared out at the vast army, and their hands reached out and their fingers clasped.

"Were we too late?" Cindy asked.

Ali sighed. "I let the army come through."

"Why?" Cindy withdrew her hand, an angry edge to her question. "Do you want them to win?"

"I want to talk to Lord Vak."

Cindy scanned the sea of soldiers. Several had begun to look toward the top of the mound, their expressions hard. "Where is he?" she asked.

Ali lifted her arm and pointed. "There."

Lord Vak was easy to spot. He stood near the base of the mound—two hundred feet below—and was the most striking of all the elementals. At least as tall as a man, he had broad shoulders and carried a black spear in his right hand that tapered into a silver blade. His gold crown was unusual. Lined on all sides with jewels, it rose to a sharp point that seemed to threaten the very sky. Ali had memories of that crown. She had told him once that he ruled with a weapon attached to his brain.

Like his soldiers, Lord Vak was arrayed in armor, yet his face was uncovered, and as she looked down their eyes met, and she felt as if an old stream of misunderstandings—it could have been an ocean—flowed between them. Once again she sensed her days as queen of the fairies, and she knew that as Alosha she had feared and often resented Lord Vak. Yet she had never hated him, and she had always respected him. The king of the elves was many things but he was not a coward, and he never lied.

He stared up at her and nodded in recognition. At least that was all she thought he was doing. But suddenly a swarm of arrows flew through the sky in their direction. She barely had time to raise a shield. The arrows hit the magical barrier and fell to the ground.

Lord Vak angrily raised his hand and the arrows stopped.

Ali called down to him. "Let's talk," she said.

"You wish for me to come up?" he asked. His voice was surprisingly soft, yet deep, and it carried with it the strength of countless years of life. She sounded like a chipmunk next to him.

"Yes," she said.

She was not sure how he would accomplish the task, but she should have known better. Stepping from his horse, he raised his hand and a series of pillow-shaped clouds appeared before him, leading up to the edge of the mound like a series of steps. He started up briskly.

Ali dropped her magical shield so he could get by. Then she groaned.

"Oh no," she said.

"What is it? Did you forget what you want to talk about?" Cindy asked.

"No. I remember talking to him before. He gets angry easily." She turned toward the center of the mound. "I need the Yanti!"

With Cindy at her side, Ali hurried back and grabbed it off the bamboo sticks and put the silk string around her neck. The moment she did so the sky stopped spiraling, and the columns of light and the green sphere vanished. They were left alone with the normal light of the moon. As she suspected, the three parts of the Yanti—the seven-sided outer band, the inverted triangle, and the diamond—although separate, stayed together.

The wind ceased blowing and the top of the mound went still.

Lord Vak reached the top and walked toward them. She couldn't help but notice he still had his black spear in his hand. He nodded out of respect as he approached. She worried she was going to have to do another one of those acts where she pretended to remember more than she actually did. Boy, she was getting tired of that.

He was handsome, seemingly youthful, his face much more human than she would have imagined, his long blond hair curled like an actor on TV. His blue eyes, especially, reminded her of her father's eyes. The elven king had ruled many, though, through hard times, and in his expression there was little joy, and no humor. He came straight to the point.

"You arrived here in time to stop my army from coming through," Lord Vak said. "Why didn't you, Geea?"

She tried to speak with authority, but it was not like when she had faced down Karl. Lord Vak was every bit as powerful as she, if not more so.

"I wanted to talk to you," she said. "This war is madness, you have to stop it."

Lord Vak sighed as if it were an old argument. "Thirteen years ago you threatened to take birth as a human to stop the war. I see you have carried out your threat. But tell me frankly, Geea, what have you accomplished with all your sacrifice?"

Ali hesitated. "I have learned what it means to be human."

"And?" he asked.

"Hey, I'm human and proud of it," Cindy interrupted.

Lord Vak glanced at her. He didn't say anything.

Cindy gamely offered her hand. "I'm Cindy Franken. You're Lord Wak?"

"Vak," Ali whispered. . . .

"That's what I said. How are things going, Vak?"

Lord Vak ignored Cindy's outstretched hand. "Who's this?" he asked Ali.

"A friend," she muttered. She added in a stronger voice, "She's a good friend, and that's one of the great things about being human. There's always plenty of love to share with your friends."

Lord Vak frowned. "Humans and love? Humans are the only species in the universe that kill each other. Even trolls do not do that. Do not lecture me on the heart of humanity."

Ali searched for an angle, knowing it was probably hopeless. He was not going to be persuaded by a speech, yet she felt she had to try. "I know they're not perfect. I know they can be stupid and mean. I've seen the way they treat each other, and the damage they've done to their world. But they learn quickly, and they try so hard. I've only got a chance to watch them for a few years, and all over the world things have changed for the better."

Lord Vak spoke seriously. "You see them through the eyes of your love for them. I see them as they are. Humanity is cruel and vicious. The more years they are given, the more pain they cause. No golden future awaits them, and there will be no future at all for us if we do not destroy them. I told you that the last time we spoke, and I tell you again tonight because I wish you would join us. Your powers are great. If you wanted, you could help us end this war in half the time." He paused. "Will you not join us, Geea?"

She paused. "No."

Lord Vak raised his spear. Ali immediately created a shield between them, made of earth, water, fire, air, and space. She simply had to will it into existence, without effort. It glittered between them like an energy field built of a million pulsating stars. The elf saw it and lowered his weapon.

"I do not want to harm you," he said.

"Could have fooled me," Cindy muttered.

"All I am asking is that you give humanity more time," Ali said.

"You know as well as I do that there is no more time," Lord Vak said gravely.

That was a huge remark. What did it mean? She desperately wanted to ask but she could not appear to be an ignorant thirteen-year-old girl. Then he would never talk to her.

"Can't we just talk about this?" she asked, feeling pain over the communication gap between them. But Lord Vak shook his head.

"There is nothing left to say," he said. "If you won't join us then you are against us. There can be no in-between in such matters. You must know it will only make the final battle that much bloodier."

Ali saw that pleading with him was useless. Sharpening her tone, she held up the gold medallion around her neck. "You forget I have the Yanti," she said.

He didn't look impressed, which did nothing for her confidence. "So? You did not use it in time. You cannot send us back, Geea."

Was that true, she wondered? He did not sound like he was lying but that did not mean what he said was true. According to Radrine, she had possessed the Yanti longer than Lord Vak, and she knew more about it than any elemental. Ali tried to remember her exact words.

"Lord Vak is ready to use the Yanti to bring his army into this world. No doubt he will succeed. But he cannot tap its full power. A code was placed upon it, I suspect, a mystical formula. The Yanti does not always obey his will, nor, I think, would it obey mine if I had it with me now. . . . What did you do to it, Geea?"

A code? What code?

That was the key, it had to be.

But what was the code?

Since she had met Nemi, there had been one thing she had hesitated to discuss with the others. That had been the name Nemi had called her by. He had never told her to keep it secret, and yet she had automatically known it was important. Many of the books on magic and fantasy she had read had spoken of the power of knowing a person's secret name. She remembered back to the instant when she had first heard the word *Alosha*, how it had sent shivers through her body. For that matter, she had never told anyone Nemi's name.

There had to be a reason. She did not consciously know what it was, but she was sure it existed. Radrine had spoken of a mystical formula. Was it possible she had tied the power of the Yanti to herself with her name? She did not remember doing it, but it *felt* like something she might have done.

There was only one way to find out.

Lord Vak looked at her strangely.

"Don't try to stop me, Geea," he warned. "It is too late for that. You would only anger me, and all the other elementals."

Ali backed up a step, taking a firm hold on the Yanti.

"What about angering me?" she asked. "Do you worry about that? You seem to forget that I am human now. I feel as they do, talk as they do, think as they do. Most of all I love like them, and I do love them. That's one thing I could never explain to you, or to any elemental."

He raised his spear again, stepped forward, bumped into the barrier. His face darkened; he saw she had something up her sleeve. "I know that tone of yours," he said. "There is to be no fairy magic used here tonight."

"Says who?" Cindy asked, glancing back and forth between them.

Ali smiled, suddenly feeling confident that her guess was right, that the Yanti would respond to her secret name. "But tonight is my night," she said. "And I am after all a queen."

Lord Vak raised the hand that had brought the magical steps to life, no doubt reaching for a spell that would counteract her barrier. But before he could succeed she held the Yanti close to her lips and whispered three times, "Alosha . . . Alosha . . . Alosha."

In an instant the mysterious power returned: the sky spiraled; the wind howled; the green sphere swelled; the red column that connected the moon and the Yanti burned, as flames leaped off the edges of the moon. Only now she stood in the center of the red beam and once more her hair was lifted from her head as a power unlike any she had ever imagined filled her body.

In that moment Ali felt deeply connected to all that surrounded her: the forest, the mountain, the elemental army, Cindy and Lord Vak, and even the stars in the sky. She felt they lived inside her and that she breathed through them, and because of that connection, she sensed that they were now under her command, at least for the moment.

Holding high the Yanti, that now shone with many colors, Ali spoke in a voice much greater than her own. "I command the elemental army and all their soldiers and leaders to depart from the human dimension!" she cried. "With the exception of Farble and Paddy, I want the elementals everywhere on this mountain to leave this world! Except for a single canoe, I ask that all their weapons be gone, and for their magic to return to their own world where it belongs!"

Lord Vak started to speak but froze, as if turned to stone.

His spear fell from his hand onto the ground.

All around the mountain top the elemental army went still.

The huge spiral in the sky halted. The light of the Yanti began to fade and the wind died down. Then slowly, as if evaporating in a sun that had yet to rise, the elementals started to disappear. One by one across the peak the army faded, dwarves and elves alike, like imaginary figures from the pages of fantasy books returning to places humans would call merely dreams. Last to fade was Lord Vak, and Ali caught his expression as he went to disappear.

He looked very angry.

"Goodbye," she said.

He suddenly pressed his palms together, in a prayerful gesture directed toward the moon, and he stopped fading. He chanted a word softly—Ali could not quite hear it. But she suspected it was his own secret name, for he said it three times, like an invocation of power.

When he was done he was as solid as before. The fact caught Ali off guard; she momentarily lost control of the magic shield that separated them. For an instant she even forgot about the Yanti, until Lord Vak took a bold step forward and grabbed the medallion with one hand, and put a knife to her neck with the other.

"You want to say goodbye? Forever?" he asked quietly.

Cindy jumped forward but Lord Vak kicked her in the chest—without losing an inch of balance—and sent her falling onto the ground, stunned. Ali did not move, merely stared into the deep blue eyes of the king of the elves. Finally, she realized, she was out of her depth. Her full powers had only begun to return, and this being that stood before her was centuries old, and no doubt knew every trick in the fairy book of magic. Her warm blood pounded beneath the knife, and the blade felt like ice against her skin.

Yet she knew she could not surrender.

"I cannot give you the Yanti," she said.

He pressed the blade deeper into her neck. "You will die, Geea."

"We all die," she whispered, and as the words came out of her mouth, she remembered that she had said them to him before. When his son Jira had died. Only then she had been trying to console him. Jira had been one of her best friends, and Ali recalled staying with Lord Vak through a long dark night as the elven king wept in agony over the loss of his only child. That is why Paddy had given her a strange look when she had asked about Jira. Even then, the leprechaun must have suspected who she really was.

She had worked no fairy magic that night, but Lord Vak had felt her love, for himself and Jira, and that had been magic enough. He had been grateful.

Perhaps he remembered that night now. His knife hand trembled.

"You have turned your back on all the elementals," he said, as if trying to convince himself. "It would be right to kill you."

"Humans and elementals are both dear to me. I turn my back on no one." Calling his bluff, she added, "If you're going to kill me, kill me now."

Angry, he let go of the Yanti and withdrew the knife.

"It is either us or them!" he shouted.

"Why?" she demanded. Yes, why, the one question that had never been answered, by Nemi, Paddy, or Radrine. Lord Vak was bitter.

"You know why! Because of the Shaktra! It drives us here!"

So the elementals had problems of their own, she thought.

"Then let us unite together, humans and elementals, and fight it!" she said, not even knowing what *it* was.

He looked at her like she was mad. "Geea, what is wrong with you? The Shaktra came from the human kingdom!"

Oh no, she thought.

"It did?" she gasped.

He shook his head and stepped away and picked up the spear he had dropped. With his back to her, he seemed to stare out at the mountain, the trees, and the town many miles below. Perhaps his gaze even reached as far as the sea, where the moon shone on the water as if it were a vast field of ice. For a long time he stood there, silent.

"You have taken my army from me," he said finally, his back still to her. "And I can take the Yanti from you and get it back. But I will not do that, not tonight. I will not kill you." Slowly he turned, looked at her, and sighed, as if saddened by the rift that had come between them. "I owe you, Geea, I have not forgotten the many kindnesses you did for my family over the long years. Nor have I forgotten the love you and Jira shared. But next time we meet there will be no debt between us—tonight settles all. I warn you, the next time the needs of the elementals will take precedence over the hopes of humanity. And if on that day you choose to stand against us, you will die."

"I understand," she said, and nodded.

Lord Vak also nodded, out of respect, and then turned and walked toward the center of the mound. Even before he reached the hole that led down into the cave, and the bamboo structure that had held the Yanti, he vanished. She could only assume he had his own secret way of traveling between dimensions.

For a long time Ali stood silent with the now still Yanti around her neck. She did not know what to say, how to feel. Cindy had recovered enough to stand, but she was not talking either. All around them the air was so calm the only thing left for them to hear was the beating of their hearts.

Her mother was alive. The thought was an echo inside her.

Her mother was not dead.

Cindy finally came over and gave her a hug and the tears Ali was close to crying turned to laughter and they giggled in each other's arms like thirteen-year-old girls, which was, after all, what they were.

Karl had left the rope for them to climb down—bless his hairy heart, Ali thought—and soon they were beside their friends, with Paddy and Farble all excited about what they had seen, and Steve just itching to yell at her. The first thing Ali did was take the tape off his mouth.

"How dare you accuse me of being . . ." he began.

"Steve," she interrupted.

"What?"

"I'm sorry." She would have to explain later how she'd had to use him to get Karl to drop his guard. Steve's muscles were in knots from being tied up, and he was shivering. She was sure he wouldn't understand right now.

He shook his head. "That's not good enough. You owe me . . ."

She grabbed his head. "Steve?"

"What?"

She gave him a quick kiss on the lips.

"I'm really sorry," she said.

He thought about that, then shrugged. "It's okay."

They had no supplies left, and no energy in their bodies to make the long journey home. On the hike to the top she had worried endlessly about such a situation, and she was glad she'd had the good sense to ask the Yanti to leave behind one of the elementals' canoes.

Unfortunately, her friends were not happy about the idea of riding the canoe back to Breakwater.

"Let me get this straight," Steve said as they hiked toward the front of the mound. "You want us to jump in this canoe and use it—first to snowboard down the top of the peak—and then to float back to town?"

Ali nodded. "We'll race off the snow and into the river near the tree line. The river will be strong enough by then to keep us moving. It'll be fun."

Steve frowned. "You can't use a canoe to ski down a mountain."

"Why not?" Ali asked.

"Because it wasn't designed for that," Steve said.

"Elves made the canoe. Who knows what they designed it for?"

"What about the falls?" Cindy asked. "What do we do when we come to them?"

Ali shrugged. "I'll use my powers. We'll fly over them. Trust me, there's nothing to worry about."

"You're sounding like a princess again," Cindy warned.

The remark would have hurt before. Now she only laughed.

"I am a queen," she said.

EPILOGUE

When they arrived back in Breakwater—after what could only be described as an unusual ride home—the gang was faced with the problems of Paddy and Farble. With enough makeup and ethics lessons, Ali could see the leprechaun functioning successfully in society. Indeed, now that he was the only leprechaun left in their dimension, she was sure he was going to strike it rich.

But the troll was going to be a problem. Especially since they had not fed Farble in two days. On the wild canoe ride home, he had begun to paw Paddy and Steve again, making them nervous. Ali was not sure where to put him.

They stood at the side of Mercer River, on the beach, where the river joined the sea. The elf canoe was pretty light, and Steve was going to carry it home and put it in the garage and save it to ride waves. He had changed his mind about what it could be used for.

It was five in the morning and the sun would be coming up soon. The ocean was oddly quiet—as was the rest of town—and the air chilly. Ali figured that the fireworks on the mountaintop had not been seen by anyone other than them. It was a shame in a way, it might have helped humanity understand that there was an elemental kingdom just around the corner.

"Why don't we have breakfast together at the all-night diner?" Steve suggested.

"Great idea," Cindy said. "I want bacon, eggs, toast, and coffee."

"Aye. Eggs and toast would be tasty," Paddy agreed.

"I can't, I need to check on Ted," Ali said. "But you guys go ahead without me. Get Farble some steaks to go, at least half a dozen. He can wait out back until you're done."

"That many steaks is going to cost money," Steve said.

Paddy cast an uneasy eye at the troll. "Laddie, it's money well spent. Aye, Paddy still has his bag of gold. It will be my treat."

"Cool," Cindy said. "I'll have a milk shake, too."

Ali spoke to the leprechaun. "Paddy, I want you to get some makeup at the drugstore, cover up your green skin. Where do you plan on sleeping tonight?"

"Don't worry about me, Missy. Paddy will get a motel room."

Cindy laughed. "Do you have a credit card?"

"Aye. Got one before we left."

They all assumed he was kidding, but maybe not.

Ali turned to Farble. "I'm going to leave you with my friends, but they're going to feed you soon. Just sit in the Dumpster at the back of the diner, out of sight, and they'll bring you some meat."

Farble nodded at the mention of food but looked sad that she was leaving. He stretched out a claw and patted her back. Incredibly, he still had her white sweater tied around his neck, if it could still be called white. It looked like it had been used to wipe down a gang of coal miners.

"Geea," Farble said with feeling.

Ali stroked his hairy hand. "It's okay, I'll see you later in the day."

"But where's he going to sleep?" Cindy said.

"The Barker house is empty," Steve suggested. "It sold last

week and no one is supposed to move in for a couple of months. I bet we could sneak in the back and fix up a room for him. We could make sure to cover all the windows so he doesn't get burned."

Ali felt relieved. "That's a great idea. Could you take care of it for me?"

"No problem," Steve said. "You could stay with him if you wanted, Paddy."

The leprechaun shook his head. "Paddy likes his privacy."

Ali gave them each a hug before saying goodbye. She wanted to thank them a million times over, but that was the great thing about having such great friends, she didn't have to. There was really nothing to say. They each knew they had helped save the world. At least for now, she thought.

The battle had been won but the war was not over.

Cindy pulled her aside for a second as the others headed for the diner. "Is your mother really alive?" she asked.

"Yes," Ali said.

"You're sure?"

"Yes."

Cindy scowled. "That dirty rat kidnapped her!"

"He's worse than a rat." Ali hugged her again. "Don't tell the others, not yet."

Cindy understood. Kissing her on the cheek, she chased after the others. Ali waved goodbye and headed for the hospital.

The clinic was silent, as would be expected at such an early hour. Ali didn't see a soul as she crept in the back door and walked toward intensive care.

It was just her luck to find the starch-faced nurse on duty again. Ali knew she could not get in to see Ted without being caught, so she walked straight up to the desk.

"How's Ted Wilson doing?" she asked politely.

The old nurse gave her one look and got to her feet. "I thought I told you never to come back! Why are you here at this hour? I'm going to call your parents!" She grabbed Ali's arm, twisting it back. It should have hurt, but it didn't. Her fairy powers continued to hum along at full strength. Ali merely looked up at her.

"Has there been any improvement?" she asked.

"No. The doctors say he's going to die. Are you happy?" The nurse began to drag her toward the door. "Now get out of here you little . . ."

Ali shook free. "I want to see him. And I don't want to be disturbed."

The nurse's face flushed an angry red. She looked like she was going to pop a blood vessel. Again, she tried to grab Ali's arm. "I'm going to call the police on you!"

Ali took a quick step back and smiled. "You don't want to do that. In fact, you don't want to mess with me at all."

The nurse went to shout some more but Ali had heard enough. In a blur too fast for normal eyes to follow, she grabbed the woman by the arms, put her out in the hallway, and locked the door behind her. The nurse almost fainted with the drastic maneuver, then went screaming down the hall. Ali figured she would have at least a few minutes alone with Ted. She hoped that would be enough.

Cubicle six, behind the green curtains. Ted looked awful when she entered. If anything his skin color was more lifeless than the other day, and the doctors had put a plastic tube into his throat to help him breathe. He was unconscious; it scared her that she could not *feel* him in the room anymore. Maybe she was too late. . . .

Quickly, she moved to his side and put her left hand on his bandaged forehead and her right hand over his heart. She closed her eyes, like before, but this time she did not concentrate on her power. She merely stood there silently and wished that he would get better.

The Yanti around her neck began to heat up. Because her eyes were closed, she didn't know if it also began to shine with spiraling colors, but she did feel a strange power enter the room and flood her body. The energy was different than before, much softer, and she was reminded of her mother for some reason. Perhaps there was a connection she was missing. The love that flowed through her right then could have been the love of a parent for a child.

The Yanti burned—it felt like a large coin that had been plucked from a fire and placed on her chest. The energy in her hands increased and she felt Ted begin to stir.

Ali opened her eyes; Ted did likewise a minute later. He looked at her, dazed. Using a technique she had learned watching TV, she quickly removed the tube from his throat. He coughed as he tried to speak.

"Ali. What am I doing here?" he asked.

"You had an accident, but now you're going to be better."

He frowned when he saw all the tubes and wires hooked to his body. "It must have been a bad one. Where's the doctor? What are you doing here?"

Tucking the Yanti beneath her shirt, she smiled and brushed a hair from his eyes. "Let's just say you helped me the other day when I was hurt, and I came to pay you back."

When she got home, the lights were on and her father was standing in the kitchen with the phone in his hand. His face was drawn and gray, but it broke with relief when he saw her come in. He practically dropped the phone on the floor.

"Ali! I've been looking all over for you! I called Cindy's house from the road and they said you were here but when I called here no one answered. I've been worried sick about you."

"How long have you been home?" she asked, thinking fast.

"Only a half hour. Where were you just now?"

"I went to see Ted Wilson, he had an accident. I wasn't at the hospital long." She added, "I'm sorry if I scared you. I didn't mean to."

He knelt and gave her a big hug. "That's okay, Hunny Bunny, as long as you're fine. Was Cindy with you? Her parents are looking for her."

"She's having breakfast with Steve and some other friends. She'll be home soon."

"How is Ted?"

"Much better. He said he feels like he's ready to leave the hospital."

"That's great news. Boy, I got so worried about you when I couldn't reach you. I didn't even make it to Florida, I just turned around and drove home."

"Oh no. I messed up your delivery."

He held her at arm's length. "You did, you naughty girl. I suppose I should be mad at you, but I'm too happy to see you right now."

"You can yell at me later."

He nodded. "Deal. Hey, what's this coat? I've never seen it before. And your face has dirt on it." He wiped the dirt off. "Were you and Cindy hiking in the woods tonight?"

She hesitated. "A little bit."

Her father paused and then frowned. Reaching out, he pulled off her hat. She had not taken it off since she had been at the top of the mountain.

Her father gasped. He wasn't the only one.

A wave of bright red hair tumbled down from her head.

"You dyed your hair!" he exclaimed. "Ali, it looks like your mother's hair!"

She studied the color in the kitchen light. She could only assume that when she had stood in the red beam that stretched between the Yanti and the moon, her hair had been affected. It was interesting how it sparkled exactly like her mother's used to.

"Do you like it?" she asked her father.

"It's beautiful."

"I like it," she said, thinking of all that had happened that night. It was true, the war between humanity and the elementals was far from over; there were many mysteries left to solve. All the doors in the mountain would have to be explored—as well as the caves—and she needed to learn exactly what the Shaktra was, how it had come into being, and how it could be stopped.

But first she had to rescue her mother.

She would do it. She was not afraid. She had power.

Ali reached out and gave her father a hug and stroked the back of his head as he buried his face in her red hair. He had been through a lot, they both had, but the time was changing.

"Everything's going to be all right now," she said.

**Ali's Story Will Continue in the Next Book in the Series,
*The Shaktra.***

ALOSHA

By Christopher Pike

ABOUT *ALOSHA*

Ali Warner is not an ordinary girl but, at the beginning of her thirteenth summer, she doesn't know this yet. Ali's affinity for the forest is another thing she doesn't quite understand. She turned to the trees for comfort in the wake of her mother's death, but is the wilderness much more than a simple place of solace? This question becomes crucial when Ali hikes into the woods to protest the actions of loggers and is pursued by mysterious, non-human creatures. Joined by her friends, Cindy, Steve and Karl, she returns to the woods to discover the identity of her attackers and is soon battling a wild array of trolls and dark fairies from another dimension. Guided by a mysterious being called Nemi, Ali learns that she must stop the entry of these elemental creatures into her world by climbing to the mountaintop to close an inter-dimensional portal called the Yanti. Buried deep within Ali's memories and dreams is the reason she is called to this mission, along with other important truths about her concern for the forest, about the people she calls friends, about her mother's death, about the powers she wields and, most importantly, about her real identity. If Ali does not realize this final truth in time, her beloved forest, and the rest of the earth, may never be the same.

ABOUT THIS GUIDE
The information, activities and discussion questions which follow are intended to enhance your reading of *Alosha*. Please feel free to adapt these materials to suit your needs and interests.

ABOUT THE AUTHOR
Christopher Pike is the author of numerous best-selling fantasy and horror novels. His critically-acclaimed books for young adults include *The Blind Mirror*, *The Season of Passage*, *Sati* and *The Cold One*. He lives in Santa Barbara, California.

WRITING AND RESEARCH ACTIVITIES

I. LEGENDARY CREATURES
A. The "elemental" characters in *Alosha* also exist in myths, folktales and legends. Go to the library or online to learn more about the concept of elementals. (Hint: Try researching Celtic folklore.) What are sprites? How do dwarves, trolls, fairies and leprechauns fit into the elemental lexicon? Based on your research, create a diagram defining these characters and showing their relationships to each other.

B. Paint or draw a mural featuring the elementals from *Alosha* on a large sheet of paper (at least 4' × 6'). Surround your images with definitions, descriptions, and the titles of folktales, myths, or contemporary stories about these creatures.

C. Find the definition of "leprechaun," which derives from the Gaelic word *luprachán*. How does this definition help you to understand Paddy? Using your research, clues from the novel, and your imagination, write a short biography-style story entitled, "Understanding Paddy" or "Paddy Revealed" in which you help to clarify his character.

D. Who, what or where is "Nemi"? Go to the library or online to research the answer to this question. Then write a short essay explaining why you think Christopher Pike chose this name for Ali's advisor and what you believe to be the true identity of this character.

E. Find examples of stories, poems or plays about mischievous fairies, such as William Shakespeare *A Midsummernight's Dream* and the fairy tale *Rumplestiltskin*. Make a recommended reading list of fairy stories. Or, write your own short story involving a mischievous fairy disrupting human lives.

II. TREES AND MOUNTAINS

A. Ali, who feels a special affinity for the forest near her home, objects to the actions of the local logging company. Learn more about the logging industry, techniques for forest preservation, and the environmental organizations for which this matter is of concern. Find a recent news article—from a local paper, if possible—describing a conflict between industrialists, such as loggers, and environmentalists over the treatment of a forest or other wildlife area. Divide a group of classmates or friends into two groups to debate the positions of the industrialists and environmentalists regarding the conflict. Write a newspaper-style article reporting the results of your debate.

B. The elemental characters in *Alosha* are not happy with the way humans have treated the earth. Write an additional chapter for the novel in which the elementals discuss their anger with the humans. Before beginning your chapter, decide which characters will be present, where the discussion will take place, and how they will come to the decision to enter Ali's dimension through the Yanti.

C. Farble calls Ali by another name, "Geea." Go to the library or online to learn more about the mythological Greek character Gaea and/or James Lovelock's Gaia theory of a living earth. Present your findings to friends or classmates. Although the spellings differ slightly, do you think Christopher Pike was thinking about mythology or Lovelock's Gaia theory when he wrote this novel? If yes, how does this information affect your interpretation of the story of *Alosha* and of the battle she fights? Discuss your research and analysis with classmates or friends.

D. Giant redwood trees, such as those found in California, have been suggested as models for the Gaia theory mentioned in exercise IIC, above, because they are mostly dead matter with a slender ring of living, growing bark at the outermost edges. Do you think that the tree in which Nemi first appeared was a giant redwood? Why might this make sense? Go to the library or online to learn more about this special tree. Then, create an informative poster about the giant redwood.

III. NAMES AND IDENTITIES

A. Are the names of things important? In the play *Romeo and Juliet*, William Shakespeare wrote, "A rose by any other name would smell as sweet." What does this statement mean to you? Do you think Ali would have been able to discover her special powers if she had not realized her secret names? In the character of Ali, write a paragraph in which you describe you frustration at not being able to realize your true identity, or a paragraph in which you explain the importance of your secret names.

B. Make a booklet or chart recording the human and/or elemental nature, personality traits and name(s) of the characters in *Alosha*. If desired, draw illustrations of the characters based on the descriptions found in the novel. Present your booklet or chart to classmates or friends.

C. Ali has more than one secret name. She also renames Farble and his friends. Look through the novel to find more examples of the importance of names and naming. Then, write a poem, song lyrics, or short essay in which you explore the relationship between names and identity.

D. Have you ever imagined that you were really someone else, perhaps a member of royalty or someone with some type of exceptional powers? Imagine you receive a mysterious letter from someone you have never met before explaining who you are, why you have your current identity, and what your future holds. Write that letter.

QUESTIONS FOR DISCUSSION

1. In the first chapter of *Alosha*, Ali wants to go to the logging site not merely to protest but also "to say goodbye to some of her favorite trees." What is unusual about Ali's feelings for the forest? In what other ways does Ali seem extraordinary?

2. What important elemental character does Ali meet in the novel's opening chapter?
What does he do? At the outset of the story, do you think he is a good or evil character?

3. How does Ali escape the misadventure that befalls her in Chapter 2? What dream does she have at the close of Chapter 3? How do these experiences foreshadow later events in the novel?

4. Describe Ali's relationships with her Dad and Cindy. How does she seem to have adjusted to the loss of her mother? Would you have adjusted similarly to such a loss? Explain your answer.

5. Who attacks Ali when she, Cindy and Steve return to the forest in search of a "bigfoot"? What powers does Ali realize within herself from this experience?

6. What is Nemi? Why do you think one meaning of its name is "No One"? After being called "Alosha," what does Ali mean when she tells Nemi, "I remember the name but don't really remember it"? Have you ever had such a feeling about a memory? Explain.

7. What is important about the attack on Ted? How does Ali's concern for Ted compare to her care for the forest?

8. What happens when Ali tells Karl about her experiences? How do Cindy and Steve react to Ali's tale? Compare and contrast these reactions.

9. How do the friends prepare to return to the forest? What strikes you as odd about their preparations? Does Ali truly know what she is supposed to do? Why is she so committed to climbing to the mountaintop?

10. Does Ali trust Paddy? What does he teach her about the other elementals in the forest? Why does Ali trust Farble? How do Paddy and Farble help Ali realize who she should trust? When does Ali truly understand their signals?

11. In the midst of chapter 10, Ali recalls the night her mother died. What important clues about Ali's true identity and current situation are revealed through this memory?

12. What new powers does Ali discover when the dark fairies attack? What happens to her friends during this attack?

13. Describe the seven tests Ali must endure. Why do you think she must face these tests?

14. What happens to time when Ali travels through the red door? What does she learn from her encounter with Radrine? What must Ali do to save her friends? Is the yellow door the "right" door?

15. As their adventure proceeds, Cindy and Steve object to Ali's bossiness. How does Ali feel about this? Have you ever felt that you ought to make important decisions for others in your group? Describe the situation and your actions.

16. As she travels forward again in time to save her friends, why does Ali call her "bad" self Alison? What does this reveal about the importance of names in the story? What is the significance and meaning of Ali's other name(s)?

17. What is Karl's true name and identity? Who is Lord Vak? What are Ali's relationships to these two characters? How are they the opposite of what they initially seemed?

18. What are the Yanti, the Shaktra and Nemi? How, if at all, are these forces related to each other?

19. Why doesn't Ali close the Yanti in time to stop Vak's army from coming through? Is this a good decision? Does Ali largely make good or bad decisions in the course of the story? Is the difference between a good and a bad decision always obvious? Why or why not?

20. Do you think human beings, in general, treat their natural surroundings well or poorly? Explain your answer.

21. Does Ali succeed in protecting earth's human dimension? Does she solve the problem of the elementals' anger about human treatment of the earth?

22. How has Ali changed at the end of the story? What has she learned? How do you think her life will be different now that she has realized she is a queen?

23. Do you have a nickname, middle name, or pet name that only some people know or by which only a few people call you? How does this name make you feel? What is your relationship to the people who know or call you this name? How does reflecting on your own special name affect your reading of Alosha?

24. Do you think another cast of characters, such as elementals, could inhabit earth in another dimension? In *Gaia* (Oxford: Oxford University Press 1979), James Lovelock writes, "Is it too much to suggest that we may recognize . . . the beauty and fittingness of an environment created by an assembly of creatures?" In the context of the world depicted by Christopher Pike in *Alosha*, answer Lovelock's question.

An exciting preview of the sequel to *Alosha*

THE SHAKTRA

Available October 2005
From Tor Books

A cruel voice spoke at Ali's back; it hissed like a reptile.
"Time to stop, Geea," Radrine said.

The queen of the dark fairies was a cross between a human, a lizard, and a bat. Coated with black scales, she had claws instead of fingers, and a long dark tongue that slithered in a nauseating motion as she stared at Ali. Her wings were rotting leather hides. The pulsating light of her eyes—buried deep in an egg-shaped skull—glowed a wicked red.

Radrine carried weapons, two exceptionally large and red fire stones, which she had pointed at Farble and Paddy. Radrine's tactic was now obvious. She had sent her minions to attack from the other side of the red door as a distraction; and, like a fool, Ali had fallen for the simple trick.

Radrine stood close behind the leprechaun and the troll. Ali could not get off a shot, not without hitting one of them.

Radrine smiled again. "Put down your fire stones. Or should I say my stones, since you stole them from me? The dark fairy nodded. "On the ground please."

Ali ignored her. Her force field—shimmering a faint blue in the cavern gloom—surrounded her, but did not extend to Farble and Paddy. Slowly, raising her right palm—the fire stones were in her left—she mentally stretched it out. But Radrine was not so easily fooled; she came up at Farble's neck.

"I think not!" Radrine snapped.

Ali drew back her field, but did not drop it.

"Your reason for being here?" Ali asked.

Radrine grinned. "I have come to congratulate you. Everyone is still talking about how you defeated Lord Vak on the mountaintop. Sent his army packing, I understand."

"There was no fight. We merely talked."

Radrine nodded. "Still, Lord Vak is not easy to talk to. And you took the Yanti from him. I see it hanging from your delicate neck. How lovely. May I have a look at it, please?"

"Really, Radrine, you have grown tiresome. I would just as soon hang it on the neck of a dragon as hand it over to you."

Radrine lost her smile. "But I think you will hand it over to me. And you will tell me about the mystical code you placed on it." She added, "If you don't, I will kill your two friends."

"Kill them. They are no friends of mine. I hardly know them." Ali added, "But when you are through killing them, I will kill you."

Paddy was anxious. "Missy, you said you were our friend. You said you would protect us . . . ."

"Stop," Ali snapped.

"But Missy . . . "

"Paddy! Shut up!"

The leprechaun closed his mouth and lowered his head, as if preparing to die. Farble stood frozen, his eyes fixed on her face. Ali felt him pleading for her to save them.

"They trust you, Geea," Radrine taunted.

"I'm not going to give you the Yanti," she said. "That will never happen, in this world or the next. But if you leave now, I'll let you and your servants live. That is my offer. Take it or die."

Radrine touched the back of Farble's neck with her fire stones; the troll flinched. "Geea, you forget how well I know you. How long I watched you rule Karolee from your beautiful palace at Uleestar. So wise, but so sensitive. Too sensitive to stand here and watch this troll and leprechaun be tortured to death. Yes, tortured. What a gruesome word. But you see, I would hate for them to leave this world and not hate you. And they will hate you, because as I peel off their skin, they will know that you could stop their agony, just by handing over a piece of jewelry."

"What will you do when they're dead?" Ali asked. "You'll have no one to stand behind."

Radrine smiled once more. "Oh, I don't think it will come to that."

The evil queen let her fire stones grow brighter, and a tiny line of red light poured out of them onto the top of Farble's back. There was dark smoke; Ali heard hair burning; smelled charred flesh. The troll shook and howled in pain. Without thinking, he dashed toward Ali, but immediately ran into her force field, which knocked him flat. Radrine crouched behind him—still using him as a shield—and returned to burning off his skin.

Radrine was right; Ali could not stand it. But she was nowhere near ready to surrender.

Raising her right palm, Ali dropped the field from around her body and rammed it into the floor. The volcanic sand exploded in a black wave, and the swell surged toward the others like a breaker thrown off by a deep space meteor crashing into a primordial sea.

The wave hit them hard, buried them in a gravel blanket, but Radrine's reflexes were equal to Ali's. Just before the sand hit, the evil queen fired. Because the bulk of her energy was bent toward the floor, Ali's body was exposed. Still, her field took something out of the blast. The shot hit her hand, and it did not take off the hand, or any fingers, but it burned her badly.

"Move!" she shouted to Farble and Paddy.